The Rewind

What Reviewers Say About Nicole Stiling's Work

Heart of the Storm

"Great addition to both f/f romance and romance mysteries. Great characterizations and dialogue."—Raychel Bennet, Librarian (Bullitt County Public Library)

"This is Stiling's third book, and I become a bigger fan with each one. Not only does she continuously improve as a writer, she shows her ability to grow by interweaving complex, contemporary themes along with her characters. Sienna and Juliet are wonderful to get to know as women, but even more so in a dynamic that is messy, chaotic, and loving all at once. If you're looking for a fun, mysterious, and passionate story with a blended family, definitely pick this one up today."—*Lesbian Review*

In the Shadow of Darkness

"I really liked this story because it concentrated on the relationship between two women. You get enough of the vampire lore to establish Angeline, and then you're thrust into this mysterious, intriguing and beautiful story of two people wanting love. This is a must read for anyone who's into supernatural romances and anyone looking for an unconventional love story between two lovely women." —*Lesbian Review*

"I enjoyed reading this book a whole lot. It's fun and clever, and well-written. When I reviewed Nicole Stiling's debut novel last year, I wrote that I was looking forward to her next book, and I'm happy to say she didn't disappoint."—*Jude in the Stars*

Secrets in a Small Town

"I really enjoyed this book. The chemistry between Savannah and Mickie is believable and the conclusion is sweet."—*poetryandreview*

"The romance was an enemies to lovers one, and I liked how the characters themselves were surprised by it, how fast and how easily it happened. I'm always amazed at the quality of some debut novels… and [I] look forward to the author's next one."—*Jude in the Stars*

"This was a good story. The mystery of who the stalker was along with the developing relationship between Savannah and Micki had me reading that I didn't realize the end was upon me until I saw 'Epilogue.' If you're looking for a good mystery with a heavy dose of sexual tension, then this one will definitely keep you on the edge of your seats in more ways than one."—*Lesbian Review*

Visit us at www.boldstrokesbooks.com

By the Author

Secrets in a Small Town

In the Shadow of Darkness

Heart of the Storm

The Rewind

The Rewind

by

Nicole Stiling

2024

THE REWIND

ISBN 13: 978-1-63679-572-0

This Trade Paperback Original Is Published By
Bold Strokes Books, Inc.
P.O. Box 249
Valley Falls, NY 12185

First Edition: February 2024

Credits
Editor: Barbara Ann Wright
Production Design: Susan Ramundo
Cover Design By Ink Spiral Design

Acknowledgments

To everyone behind the scenes at BSB, thank you. I'm so grateful to be a part of this wonderful and supportive family. Special shout-out to Sandy Lowe who is a master blurb crafter.

To my editor, Barbara Ann—my ultimate appreciation for your honing skills. I tend to get comma- and exclamation-happy and you whipped that right into submission from the get-go.

My wife, my kids, my parents—I truly couldn't do this without you. Donna, Mom, and Diana—thank you for reading and rereading my stories until you are utterly sick of them.

Dedication

For my dad, who taught me that the only limits
we have are the ones we set for ourselves.

Prologue

Camilla Lyons stayed on her knees, knowing how helpless and pathetic she must have looked. But she couldn't bring herself to stand. She watched Alicia shove shirt after shirt into the barely used mauve suitcase they'd bought together a few years ago for their trip to Cancun. The hangers fell carelessly to the floor.

"I'm sorry," Alicia repeated over and over. She swiped at her eyes every few seconds, as though the tears were just a minor annoyance. She seemed almost dazed. "It's not your fault. It's not mine, either. These things just happen. I'm so sorry."

Enough rage coursed through Cami's veins to propel her into the standing position. "*What* things just happen? A week ago, everything was fine, and now you're so unhappy you're leaving me? That's not something that just happens."

Alicia sighed heavily but still wouldn't meet Cami's eyes. She picked up the snow globe from her nightstand and gave it a quick shake. "I'm going to take this. Unless you want it?"

Cami turned toward the window, the tears that had been falling forever miraculously dried up. She wondered if she was in a state of shock. Below, Mike from 3C threw his trash into the dumpster, completely unaware that two floors up, Cami's life was falling to pieces.

"No, I don't fucking want it," she snapped, barely a whisper. She swallowed hard, trying to rationalize what was happening. It had been less than a week since they'd been leafing through brochures for a tropical getaway. Cami fought a sob. She'd said all she could say, but if she didn't try one more time, she didn't think she'd be able to forgive herself.

"Alicia, wait," Cami said. She took her by the wrists and forced her to look at her. "I love you. Whatever it is you're going through, I'll give you the time, space, anything you need. You are the great love of my life. The one. The only one. Please don't do this. Please." Cami knew she was begging, but she didn't care.

Alicia's eyes welled up again. "Cami, please stop. I just…I can't do this. I thought this was what I wanted, marriage, kids, the whole thing. But then I just kind of sit back and wonder if I'm doing it because it's what people are 'supposed' to do, and I don't want to imprison myself just so I can say I'm successful in life."

Cami took her point, but that didn't make it hurt any less. "So you think spending your life with me is a prison sentence. Got it."

"I didn't say that. You just deserve more than—"

"No." Cami held her hand up forcefully. "This is not about you being altruistic because you think I deserve someone better. Alicia, we've been together for six years. Six *fucking* years. We've had our ups and downs like anyone else, but you've never said you don't want to be with me, or you don't want a relationship or that you want to be alone. What changed? Is it because I've been too focused on my work? I know I've been focused on other things. We should have talked more. Is it because we started seriously talking about marriage? If it's the word that's freaking you out, then the hell with it! We won't get married. I don't need a wedding to know that I love you."

Alicia covered her face with her hands. "I love you, too. But that's not always enough."

The words Cami had been swallowing since Alicia had made her grand announcement had finally rose to the surface. "Is there someone else?"

Alicia hesitated.

Cami felt her stomach sink to the floor.

"No. There's no one else."

"Do you want there to be?" Cami asked.

"No. That has absolutely nothing to do with this. But I don't know what will happen in six months. A year? Five years?"

Cami shook her head. None of this made any sense. "You're breaking up with me because you might want to see someone else in five years? Alicia, that's insane. I might be *dead* in five years, does that mean I should leave you?"

Alicia took a step toward Cami, and for a fraction of a second, Cami's heart swelled with hope. Alicia danced her fingers along Cami's collarbone, and Cami shivered.

"I love you, Cam. I do, I honestly do. More than I've ever loved anyone. But I need to do this. I've been telling you that I'm in a rut. I just need something new, something different. There's more to life, there has to be. I'm a hostage in my own skin. I quit my job today."

Cami's eyes grew wide. "You did *what*?" Maybe Alicia was having some kind of breakdown, some kind of mental crisis. She'd been a headline reporter at the *Knox County Sun* for the last four years, and as far as Cami knew, she loved it. She'd had her days where she'd compared the politics of it all to a war zone, but for the most part, Cami was under the impression that Alicia was content and fulfilled. Maybe that was the problem. Maybe Cami didn't know her at all, even after six years together.

"Yeah, I did," Alicia said. She seemed defiant. "And I leave tomorrow for Perth. I'm going to be exploring western Australia for the next six months."

Cami's head swam. Alicia had to be dragged out of the house on the weekend to do just about anything, and now she was going to Australia? For six months? *Who is this person?* "Are you going alone?" Cami's voice sounded distant to her own ears.

"Yes. I'm staying at an Airbnb, and I set up a tour guide to help me get familiar with the area."

"How are you paying for this?" Cami sat on the edge of the bed, feeling a little woozy. "When did you make the plans?"

Alicia pursed her lips. "I made the plans over the last couple of days. I wasn't sure I was going to go through with it. I liquidated my 401K."

"Are you in some kind of trouble? I can help you," Cami said, reaching for her hand.

Alicia gave her hand a quick squeeze and dropped it. "No, Cami. I know you're trying to make sense of all this. So am I in a way. I wish I had answers for you. I wish I could tell you the whys, but I can't. It's just something I have to do. Something I want to do. For myself."

Cami squeezed the back of her neck. Nausea flooded her. "I think that maybe you should hold off on leaving for a few days. Talk to your parents. Your brother. Maybe call a therapist."

"I've talked to my parents. I've talked to Sean. I don't need a therapist. Well, maybe I do, but not about this."

"I don't know how to live without you, Alicia. I didn't think I'd have to try." Cami's chest heaved with sadness. Everything that had happened since that morning felt like a dream. A vivid, terrible dream.

"I don't know how to live without you, either. We'll figure it out. Trust me, I don't want to hurt you, Cami."

Maybe it was a midlife crisis. Alicia was a little young for that at thirty-four, but Cami had heard of it . What she would have given for Alicia to have gone out and bought a Corvette or for her to have gotten a gaudy tattoo across her back.

"Okay. I understand," Cami said, trying to rein herself in. She needed to be calm, pragmatic. "So take the six months. Enjoy yourself, live it up, figure out everything you need to figure out. When you come back, we'll talk, and maybe things will feel different for you. Maybe we can start over."

Alicia hesitated again. "I don't know what's going to happen, Cami. But I can't let you believe that in six months, everything will go back to the way it is now. That would just be cruel."

Cami breathed in deeply and craned her neck toward the ceiling. She was beginning to spiral, the perceived loss of control sending her into a mild panic attack. Her face flushed, and her heart fluttered.

"This is it? That's it, after six years together? We have a life, Alicia. Everything in this apartment is *ours*, we have friends and a checking account, and we spend the holidays with each other's families."

"You can have everything in the apartment."

Cami fought the urge to scream. "That's not what this is about. I don't give a shit about the apartment. What I'm saying is that this whole thing is just insane, and I don't understand what's happening. This isn't you. It isn't."

Alicia nodded. "It *wasn't*. But now it is. It has to be. I love you, I have to go."

In a daze, Cami watched as Alicia grabbed the suitcase from the bed and sprinted for the door. She wanted to follow. She wanted to yell for her not to go. When Cami tried to muster up something, anything, that might convince Alicia to stay, her voice failed her. Nothing came. Just the silence that blanketed her after the door closed behind Alicia.

Chapter One

Three Years Later

Cami sat back in her chair and rubbed her temples. Sunny April afternoons killed her. The tree pollen coated her windowsill like a fluorescent dust storm. But Cami hadn't taken a sick day since the New England Patriots had won their first Super Bowl, and she'd faked an ear infection so she could go to the Boston parade.

"Have you taken anything?" Kelsey Chandler asked, tossing a cough drop onto Cami's desk.

"Why, do I sound that bad? Yeah, I took some Claritin a little while ago. Didn't help," Cami said. She cleared her throat and popped the cough drop into her mouth.

"Yes, you do. You sound like shit. Why don't you just go home? Not like there's a whole lot you can do here," Kelsey said.

She wasn't wrong. Cami could feel her eyelids growing heavier by the second. But she just couldn't allow herself to leave. Their sleepy town had been a peaceful haven for as long as Cami had lived there, the entirety of her forty-two years. With the closest city about thirty-five miles to their east, Oakview was little more than a speck on the map.

They were known for one thing, and that one thing permeated just about every facet of Oakview's commercial viability: black pepper ice cream. No one could fully trace the ice cream's origin, but the first known recipe was found in Ginny Bower's basement back in 1947. The Bower family had sent it into an old magazine, and it had actually gained traction for a while. People from all over

New England came to Oakview to try Aunt Ginny's Black Pepper Ice Cream. Cami wouldn't say it out loud for fear of being blackballed, but she thought it tasted kind of like sugary seaweed.

The peace that their small town had come to take for granted was shattered a little less than a month ago. A jogger had placed a frantic 9-1-1 call to alert them to a seemingly unconscious woman lying facedown in the woods. The freak March nor'easter had left her covered in nearly a foot of snow.

Cami had been promoted to Detective II years earlier, and while that sounded like a prestigious promotion, she would quickly remind herself that there was a total of seventeen employees in the entire law enforcement agency. She had investigated many crimes over the years, the worst of them being a hit-and-run that had taken place on Main Street. When the call from the jogger had come in, Cami had an eerie premonition that this one might not have been as innocuous as the crimes she was used to investigating.

Sure enough, the woman that had appeared to be unconscious was dead. A single bullet hole in the back of her head had betrayed the notion that she was simply lying there, blissfully asleep. There was no evidence of robbery or sexual assault or anything else that led to a motive or a suspect. The town had grieved for her while promising to bring her killer to justice. Things like that just didn't happen in Oakview.

The only thing they had to go on was a wooden alphabet block that was found in her pocket. Sandy-colored wood with a bright green T on its front. It didn't appear to be from a collection in her house, she didn't have children or grandchildren, and she didn't teach, so it was just another dead end.

"I was just going over the cell phone reports again. All sorts of pings around town and then nothing after three o'clock that afternoon. Either she turned it off, which is unlikely since prior to that day, she never turned her phone off, or the killer made her turn it off. Which means she had to be in one of these places with him. Or her." Cami scrunched up her face, forcing herself to see something that wasn't there. A missing puzzle piece.

Kelsey sighed. "We've gone over those reports about a hundred times. Nothing new is going to suddenly appear. Go home, Cam."

Cami shook her head. "I know. Everyone in her orbit has a rock-solid alibi, and she didn't have any enemies that we know of. Did her mom call again today?"

"Every day. Nothing like telling an eighty-something-year-old that we're still coming up empty. Today, she asked me to reach out to the Los Angeles PD since she was sure they could help. It's so damn sad."

"I just need some coffee. I'll go home in a little bit, I promise," Cami said. She was probably lying, but if her head felt any fuller, she really might have to pack it up and head home.

Kelsey nodded, pursing her lips. Cami knew she didn't believe her, but she didn't care. Work was her refuge, and even when she wasn't feeling great, it was still better than sitting at home forcing herself to read a book or focusing on a movie that she had no interest in.

Cami shook the cobwebs from her head and plodded to the kitchen. She grabbed a pumpkin spice K-Cup from the cabinet and brewed herself a steaming hot cup in Kelsey's *Shh...there's wine in here* mug. Pumpkin spice never went out of season in New Hampshire.

Pulling her blazer a little tighter, Cami sat back down and yawned. She flipped through the notes on her desk, vowing to be more organized with administrative duties. She knew she had a few meetings coming up, but she couldn't remember when or why. She stacked the papers neatly and reread the one on top. Ugh. She had that meeting with some journalist the following day. She'd tried everything she could think of to get out of it, but the captain insisted that she take the meeting. The mayor wanted transparency, and a restless public wanted answers. Cami understood the motive behind the monthly reports that the mayor had requested, and she even agreed with it. She just didn't want to be the one to do it.

Public speaking and the press were the only drawbacks to becoming a detective. Cami knew it was all part of the job when she'd applied for it, but the kind of detective work that she was usually involved in didn't require much more than an email or a quick phone call to the paper. Kelsey was a Detective I—and a patrol officer since there was barely enough work for *one* detective on the Oakview force—why couldn't she do it?

"You're direct and to the point," Captain Brandt had told her. "You're the one with the experience here, not Kelsey. You've got, what, almost twenty years to her ten? The people want to hear from a face they know and trust."

"They know Kelsey, too," Cami had grumbled, petulant. But she had seen from the captain's face that the decision had been made.

Cami cracked her neck a few times before settling into the phone records again. Her head felt like a balloon about to detach from her body. The tiny numbers and locations began to blend together. She sighed dramatically and shoved them back in her drawer. Maybe it was time to call it a day.

She locked her office door and called out a couple of quick good-byes. Kelsey waved to her smugly.

Cami shoved another cough drop into her mouth to try to quell the scratchy throat that had been plaguing her since lunchtime. She checked her phone to see that she'd missed a call from her aunt, who was probably just checking to see how she was feeling. Earlier that day, one of the administrative assistants had told Cami that she'd seen her aunt at the Market Basket over by the bakery. They'd discussed the squelchy brakes in Cami's police cruiser as well as her red, puffy eyes.

Cami couldn't do much but smirk and shake her head. Privacy was all but nonexistent in Oakview.

As she pulled into her designated parking spot in the back of her brick apartment building, Cami could feel a sneeze coming on. She fumbled with her glove compartment and found an ancient pack of tissues shoved in the back. Stuck on the back of it was a small round sticker that read, *Sunkist Navel 3307*. Cami took out a tissue and threw the pack back into the glove box. No matter how certain she was that she'd purged Alicia from every facet of her life, every once in a while, something would pop up. Cami hated oranges.

Eh, just confirmation that it was probably time to get a new car. Not that she would ever do that. Her Jeep was her baby.

She unlocked the door to her apartment and tossed her keys on the kitchen table. It was quiet, and the sun was setting. She could see tiny dust motes swirling around the living room, mocking her. She quickly undressed and left her clothes in a pile on the floor. She crawled into her messy bed and was asleep within minutes.

CHAPTER TWO

A Knox County teen had his phone ripped from his hands by a thief on a bicycle, but it wasn't the easy getaway that the perpetrator had envisioned—the teen was livestreaming on TikTok when

Alicia Flynn jumped at the sound of the train whistle. She'd only been in her new place for a few weeks, but she thought she'd be used to it by now. Her home office was just about complete, in the small second bedroom that she'd painted gray with a brown accent wall to give the feeling of an old-timey private investigator's office. All that she was missing was a green-rimmed visor and a cigar.

Spring had been threatening to make an appearance for the last several weeks, but it seemed to have finally arrived. Her window was cracked open, even though it was after eight o'clock, and darkness blanketed her regular view of trees and train tracks. She pulled her ponytail out of its worn elastic and plucked a strand of hair from the shoulder of her T-shirt. Upon inspection, it was dark brown, not gray. Good.

Alicia swiveled back and forth in her chair to get back into the groove of her article. It would be her first byline with the *Knox County Sun* since she'd left nearly three years ago. They said you couldn't go home again, and Alicia wondered if there was more truth to that than she'd been willing to acknowledge.

It had been wonderful seeing her brother, sister-in-law, and nieces and nephew after being away for so long. She'd come back for holidays before, but that was pretty much it. Her parents had been overjoyed to have her back for good this time. Finding a place in Oakview had been fairly easy, even if it wasn't in the quietest of locations. But there was a black cloud that hung over her like an overfilled bubble of guilt, where the slightest provocation would cause it to burst and douse her in the regret she'd so deftly compartmentalized.

Cami.

Even thinking her name gave Alicia a pit in her stomach. When it had finally hit her, not long after landing in a strange place, and she had to think about—*feel*—how she had left things, she'd decided she would make things right. She had calmed her rising panic by talking herself into the notion that she could make up for the chaos she'd caused. She'd apologize to Cami for leaving the way she had, she'd call up her friends and family, and things could hopefully just go back to normal but with Alicia's newfound sense of appreciation for the world around her. Or something like that.

She still couldn't explain why she'd originally left, not really. She'd been spending so much time on social media and covering national politics and every other world crisis of the day that she'd just had enough. Facing her inevitable mortality, the state of humanity, and an overwhelming sense of unimportance had pushed her to the edge. It was vague and formulaic, but it was the only explanation she had. She wished she'd had something more concrete, something meatier to share with her family, and eventually, Cami, but the epiphany she'd been expecting while sitting alone on a secluded beach watching gentle waves lap at the sand had never come. She'd still felt the same, maybe just a little less…muddled. The profound insight she'd been seeking had eluded her.

Texting Cami had become a nightly ritual that she'd attempt but ultimately fail. *I'm sorry* sounded trite. *I didn't mean it* sounded empty. *I'll always love you* sounded vapid. She'd pulled up the message box and typed something, deleted it, and then continued that ad nauseam until she'd eventually tossed her phone onto her nightstand and fall into a fitful sleep. She'd left voice mail after voice mail, pouring her heart out, trying to get Cami to respond. Sometimes, they were sad and full of longing; other times, they were chipper, and she'd recounted happy memories. Cami had never called her back.

Not long before her journey was scheduled to end, she'd realized she hadn't planned for the *after*. Alicia wasn't the most organized and cautious person, but she wouldn't have called herself impetuous, either. Clearly, she was. She needed something solid to return to. She'd been too ashamed to ask for her job back, and she really didn't want to live with her parents. She certainly couldn't move back to her old apartment with Cami. She was pretty confident that Cami hated her, and she didn't have much justification for Cami to *not* hate her. She'd acted selfishly. Alicia knew that. All of her attempts to contact Cami had gone unanswered, so she'd known that she wouldn't be able to simply ease back into her old life as she'd imagined. She'd become adept at compartmentalizing her emotions so she didn't have to feel the full weight of her grief.

"Come stay with me," Alicia's cousin Leila had shouted when Alicia had told her the predicament she'd been in. "I'm only ten minutes from Boston. There are tons of journalist jobs around here."

"Tons" of jobs had been an exaggeration, but Alicia was still intrigued by the idea. It was the only option she felt she had. She'd worked for the local paper, *Knox County Sun*, but before that, she'd been mostly freelancing while working for a few different pop culture websites. The pay wasn't great, but the work was interesting. Reviewing movies and testing out video games had been like a dream come true.

She'd ended up taking a job with a Boston-based college in the external affairs department. Living with Leila had been a huge adjustment, but she was happy to have someone to talk to without the baggage of home. She'd kept Cami pinned to the top of her text message "favorites," even though the last thirty messages were all one-sided.

Renewing her friendships hadn't been as easy as she'd thought it would be either. Sure, her friends were Cami's friends, but she didn't think they'd hold her nihilistic crisis behavior against her until the end of time. She was wrong. Aside from a couple of cold texts, there wasn't much to go on. The phone calls hadn't been much better. Violet had made small talk with her, welcomed her back to New England. Said she'd be in touch so they could plan a dinner date. Never happened. Katie had cut right to the chase.

Alicia cringed as the conversation replayed in her head:

"Alicia? Wow, I'm surprised to hear from you," Katie had said.

"I know. It's good to be back, though. I've missed you guys so much," Alicia had told her, wondering why she'd thought calling Katie out of the blue had been a good idea. "How are things?"

"Fine. Does Cami know you're back?"

"I don't think so, I haven't talked to her—"

"What you did was really shitty. I didn't know if she was going to get through it. God, the crying, the wondering, the not *knowing*… it wasn't good."

Alicia had stood there with the phone up to her ear, stunned and silent. Was she really that out of touch? Obviously. "I…I know. I shouldn't have sprung it on her the way that I did. I never meant to hurt her. I was going through something that I didn't know how to deal with." Trying to explain it had made it seem even worse.

"Did you ever consider reaching out to me before you up and left the country? Or Taryn? Or Violet? We had no idea anything was wrong. No one did. I get that you were going through something, but you ghosted all of us. We had to pick up the pieces, comforting her and providing explanations that we basically had to make up. We were mourning the loss of you, too, for reasons none of us understood."

Alicia had opened her mouth to speak, but nothing had come out. She'd felt tears spring to her eyes but blinked them away. Katie, who was usually the pragmatic one, tackled issues logically and calmly, so her tone and palpable anger had surprised Alicia.

Katie wasn't finished. "And how long have you been back? Obviously, they don't have phones or internet in Australia. Otherwise, you could have called or texted, but it's been well over six months, and I'm just hearing from you now?"

Alicia had cleared her throat. "I wanted to settle back in before I reached out. To make sure I was in the right headspace before calling. I've left so many messages for Cami, but she hasn't returned my calls. I'm staying just outside of Boston and—"

"I didn't realize you needed to be in the 'right headspace' to have a conversation with me."

If she'd known how the phone call was going to go, Alicia probably would have put a little more thought into the whole headspace thing. "Katie, I really am sorry, but I had to make this about me. I felt suffocated by the open air, and I didn't know how to deal with it."

"Just don't, Alicia. You know I'm all about self-care and putting yourself first. It's the way you went about it. Just up and leaving like that without any notice or warning or anything. It was cold, and it was selfish. But like you said, you had to do what you had to do. Enjoy Boston."

The soft beeps following Katie's last word had confirmed that she'd hung up. Alicia had thrown her phone on the bed. She'd allowed herself to cry, the tears a mixture of anger and regret and a sprinkling of resentment, warranted or not. She'd done what she'd done. No second chance to do it the right way.

She'd wiped the moisture from her cheeks and picked her phone back up. She'd shot off another text to Cami this time, willing herself to just suck it up and contact her again, even though everything up to this point had gone unanswered. Let her rant and rave and yell at her, and maybe she could eventually forgive her. Just let her say *something.*

It's me. Can we talk? Please?

Simple, but to the point. She'd kept eyeing her phone while trying to occupy herself with other things, waiting for the unmistakable chime of a reply.

It had never come.

Sitting at the desk in her little room in Oakview now, watching the cursor flash in her unfinished article, Alicia forced herself out of her reverie. Maybe she shouldn't have come back here.

No, she told herself, everything will work out, one way or another. She wanted to be closer to her family, especially since her dad had been diagnosed with prostate cancer. He'd had the offending organ removed and was going to be okay, but it had made Alicia realize how precious and fleeting life could be. She wanted to be closer to her family and the town that she'd called home for so long. She didn't even necessarily have to interact with Cami or Katie or any of her old circle. The town was small, yes, but she was a grown-up and could nod curtly if she ran into any of them in the supermarket.

She hadn't seen Cami in the short time that she'd been back, but she felt like she would be able to handle it. Enough time had passed.

She missed her something fierce, and she'd played the night that she left over and over in her head. She'd gone on a few dates in the time since they'd split up, but since all she did was compare them to Cami, they were doomed from the start. That little jump in her stomach every time she'd see Cami walk into a room, even after being together for so long. That way Cami would gaze lovingly into her eyes while they whispered to each other in the soft darkness of their bedroom.

Why did I leave? Why did I leave her*?*

Alicia shook her head, forcing the thought away. Obviously, Cami had moved on, rightfully so, but Alicia did wish she'd had the chance to explain that her leaving truly wasn't about Cami or anything she had done. It might not have mattered, but she still wished Cami knew.

She looked at her calendar, the next day circled in bright red marker. Her stomach flip-flopped. Alicia might get her chance after all.

CHAPTER THREE

The screaming alarm caused Cami to bolt upright in panic. She didn't usually need an alarm; her body was so accustomed to waking up at seven thirty a.m., she awoke naturally. But since she had to meet that reporter at the diner for eight o'clock, she'd set her phone to blare some hard rock at seven. She fumbled for the stop button and flopped back on her pillow. Thirty minutes of sleep deprivation felt like a lifetime.

Sighing, Cami slid out of bed and turned on the shower. She let the hot water pulse over her shoulders while she longed for the days of catching kids carving their initials in trees and giving them lectures about the environment. Her town, and the memories she cherished, felt almost tainted now. She wasn't looking forward to providing what amounted to a thimbleful of information to the *crime reporter* that the *Knox County Sun* felt like they'd needed to hire. Times were changing.

By the time she arrived at the Crumbly Biscuit, the parking lot was full, and the tables were crowded. She could barely entertain the idea of a bagel, and these people were having three course meals. Cami scanned the restaurant, looking for someone sitting alone, but she didn't see anyone. Since she hadn't taken the call personally, she realized she probably should have asked for more info, specifically, a name. The captain had just told her it was the new crime reporter, and the *Sun* had said the optics would be better if they could meet at a neutral place.

Cami found an empty booth by a back window and sat. There were muffin crumbs on the table, so she used the side of her hand to swipe them into a napkin. Yuck. She fumbled with the napkin holder to pluck out another one, but they were packed in tight. She struggled to pull out a full one instead of the tiny pieces that kept breaking off.

"Detective Lyons."

Cami turned quickly and stood. "Yes, sorry—" She stood there, frozen to the spot next to the table. She couldn't quite bring herself to close her open mouth, though she was aware that no words were coming out.

Alicia was standing across from her wearing a gray suit and small gold hoops in her ears. Cami focused on her earrings. She didn't remember Alicia having pierced ears. She assumed that pierced ears were something she would have noticed in their six years together.

Alicia swallowed. "Cami, hi. Hi. I'm sure you're wondering what I'm doing here." She licked her lips and swallowed again. Her nervousness had always been pretty transparent.

"Are you the reporter they sent?" Cami asked. Her voice sounded like it was coming from someone else. From a tunnel far, far away.

"I am. I was afraid if they told you who you were meeting with, you would have said no, so I was purposely vague."

She could feel her blood returning to its normal state, and it flooded her face with vigor. "I would have."

Alicia seemed to falter. "I know, I'm sorry for the ambush. I shouldn't have…we can get right into it if you want and catch up later."

"I think I'm actually going to go." She pointed to the exit. "I'm sure Kelsey can meet with you at some point."

"Please don't go," Alicia said quickly. "We can do this quick. The town needs to know what's going on. Captain Brandt even said on the call that you would be the best person to interview. Please don't take whatever it is you feel toward me out on the people you serve."

Cami scoffed. Nice attempt at manipulating her sense of duty to the town. "Please. If it's really the story you're after, you can meet with a number of people who know what's going on. This is obviously not just about that."

Still awkwardly facing her, Alicia gestured to the booth. "Just sit with me for five minutes. Then you can go, and I won't try to stop you. I promise."

The desperation in her eyes was evident. Years of heartache and confusion and self-doubt came back in an instant. Cami wanted nothing more than to get out of there, but her curiosity was piqued, and her heart felt like it was frozen in her chest. She rubbed her cheek absentmindedly and sat. "You have five minutes. What do you want to know?"

Alicia sat, her relief visible. Cami stared while she pulled out a notebook. She knew her eyes were boring into Alicia, but she couldn't look away. She was seeing a ghost. Why was Alicia back in Oakview? Why now? She tried to assess her feelings, seeing the woman she'd loved for such a long time across from her now, a stranger. There were no feelings to assess. Cami was numb, and her chest felt tight, and her silky button-up blouse was choking her, even though the first two buttons were undone.

A server approached the table as Alicia clicked her ballpoint pen and tucked her hair behind her ear. Cami found herself staring again until the server interrupted. "Are you ready to order?"

"Can I just get an iced coffee, two creams, two sugars?" Alicia asked.

Cami could have mouthed the order along with her. Funny how certain things stuck.

"Well, the cream and sugar is on the table. For you?"

Silence ensued. It took Cami a few seconds to realize the server was speaking to her. "Uh, yeah, I'll have the same. Thanks."

"Again, cream and sugar is on the table. Two iced coffees," the server said. She sounded annoyed, but Cami was pretty sure that was just part of the job description.

"Still drinking iced coffee, huh?" Alicia asked, smiling.

Cami didn't smile back. She'd been a hot coffee purist before meeting Alicia, but Alicia had worn her down over the years. Against her better judgment, Cami had ended up ordering iced more often than not. It was pretty damn refreshing.

"What do you want to know?" she asked again.

"Right. Well, what can you tell me about the uptick of crime in town, as well as the murder? Can I record this?" Alicia positioned her phone in between them.

"No."

"Okay," Alicia whispered softly. She put the phone back in her bag.

"There hasn't been an 'uptick' in crime. Statistically, we're in about the same place as we were last year, and in some cases, lower than last year. There's just more awareness of what's happening in the community with the advent of that NeighborTakes app. Seems like the whole town is on it. We've deployed a few more police officers to patrol the neighborhoods, which has had a direct impact on property damage and vandalism. We're committed to putting the town's tax dollars to work in a meaningful way." Cami tried to make sure she regurgitated all the points the captain had wanted her to hit on. She'd felt good about her talking points before walking into the nightmare that sat before her. Now she couldn't even be sure what she'd said was accurate.

"And what about Beverly Lawson? Are you any closer to catching her killer than you were a week ago?"

Cami heard the words, but they were taking their time sinking in. The whole scene still felt surreal. "We haven't reached any definite conclusions. We are still combing through evidence, speaking with witnesses, and making sure we leave no stone unturned. It would be premature to discuss things like means or motive."

"Understood." Alicia wrote in the same flowery hand that Cami remembered. "Do you believe it was a targeted killing? Does the public have any reason to fear that an indiscriminate killer is on the loose?"

"As I said, answering those questions would be premature. But I can say that the Oakview Police Department is doing everything in our power to make sure the residents of this community are safe," Cami said.

"Got it. Did the killer leave behind any physical evidence? Have you checked to see if there have been any other murders in New Hampshire or anywhere, for that matter, that seem to have the same MO?"

"If you're asking about patterns or calling cards or anything like that, we have an active investigation going on, and there are details that I can't divulge." Cami focused on the iced coffee the server had dropped off. She was about four creamers in when Alicia spoke up.

"I didn't think you liked it that light," she said.

Cami didn't, but she'd been so focused on focusing that she'd lost track. "Yeah, well, things change." She took a long swallow that tasted a lot like iced half and half.

Alicia bristled. "Yes, they do. Sorry. Anyway. Is there anything else you want to say here? I don't want to make it seem like the Oakview PD is sidestepping."

"I've told you what I can tell you. Unless you'd like me to make something up, I think we're done here." Cami took out a few dollars to pay for her coffee. If Alicia thought she was going to cover the bill, she was mistaken. She'd be damned if she was indebted to Alicia for a sip of rainwater, never mind a coffee.

"Listen, Cami. I know this is weird, but I just want to tell you how sorry I am. I've tried to reach out to you so many times. I've been waiting for this moment for years. Can we just have a conversation?" Alicia asked, reaching out to place her hand on top of Cami's.

Cami snatched her hand back. "Nope. I don't know why you're back, and frankly, I don't care. I'm not going to be a stop on your rehabilitation tour, so you can scratch me right off that list. It's been three years, Alicia. Let it go. I have." She grabbed her keys from the table and walked toward the exit door that had a little bell above it that tinkled sweetly when anyone walked in or out. Cami contemplated shooting it with her service weapon but decided that would probably be seen unfavorably by the other diners.

Fuck Alicia and whatever amends she was seeking. Fuck her for dropping back in after all this time and thinking Cami was just going to welcome her with open arms to have a drippy conversation about the way things had ended or the way things should have been. Fuck Alicia for going halfway around the world and leaving Cami behind like a lost sock. Fuck her and fuck *it*.

She slid behind the wheel of her Jeep and closed her eyes. She took a few deep breaths, trying to ground herself. She was parked next to a shiny blue Prius, and she just fucking knew that it was Alicia's.

Cami had been driving the same military-green Jeep Wrangler for nearly a decade, so Alicia had parked next to her on purpose. Of course she did.

Alicia exited the restaurant and headed in her general direction. At one time, Alicia's predictability had been one of Cami's favorite things about her. But then she'd upended everything and thrown all dependability out the window. Cami started her ignition and nearly peeled out of the parking lot. *Fuck her.*

Chapter Four

Maybe she didn't have a right to be pissed off in the grand scheme of things, but Alicia was. Watching Cami fly out of the parking lot like she was fleeing from some kind of criminal exacerbated it. In hindsight, springing herself on Cami the way that she had might not have been the best idea, but it was her only one. She knew Cami wouldn't talk to her willingly, but she'd thought that if they were in the same space at the same time, maybe Cami would realize that she *did* want an explanation or closure or *something*. Apparently not.

Alicia stormed into the small office of the *Knox County Sun*, which had basically downsized into a one-room bullpen. At one time, the Sun had occupied three full floors, but with the downturn of print media and employees working from home, that kind of space had turned into an unnecessary expense.

"Didn't go well?" Jade Conley asked, peeking up over the frame of her dark-rimmed glasses. "Told you it wouldn't. What are you doing here anyway?"

Alicia sighed in exasperation. She considered Jade a friend as well as a boss, and she knew she had her to thank for welcoming her back to the Sun in spite of her hasty exit. Anyone else would probably have been a lot more reluctant to let her back in. "No, it didn't go well."

"Did she give you anything?"

"Not much. But I don't think she would've given anyone much, not just me. She was cordial when we were speaking professionally. Cordial-*ish*."

Jade nodded. "More than I expected, to be honest. Did you get anything out of her that we can use?"

"They don't seem to have much, to tell you the truth. She may have been holding back a little, but I don't think they have a whole lot to go on." Alicia handed Jade her notebook, even though she hadn't been able to fill it with anything significant.

Jade pursed her lips. "What's your plan? Any particular angle?" she asked while skimming Alicia's notes.

"I know the mayor's whole deal is transparency, so that's what I plan on giving her. The PD won't be happy with it, but I think there's only one way to approach this." Alicia chewed her lip thoughtfully.

"Thankfully, making the police department happy is not one of our objectives."

Alicia smiled, feeling a tiny swell of excitement that she'd been missing. The thrill of a good story—as bare-bones as it might have been at the moment—was inexplicable. "Even though overall crime may be down, this homicide has the police department scratching their heads. They don't know what they don't know, and since we don't normally have this type of crime in our community, I wonder if they're in over their heads."

Jade leaned back in her chair. "The small-town police, perfectly adept at breaking up neighborhood squabbles and citing bikers for riding without helmets, don't have what it takes to solve a real crime. Kind of a Barney Fife meets the Zodiac Killer case. Inept police department."

Alicia shook her head. "I didn't say inept—"

"No, I like it. Run with it. I thought you were working from home? Or now that the cat's out of the bag, is that not a thing anymore? There's a desk over by the trash can."

"Tempting. But, no, I am working from home. I think. I just wanted to stop in for a minute. I thought you'd be good for moral support."

Jade scoffed. "You know I love you, Alicia, but at this point, I'm too cynical to provide much beyond a shoulder pat and a 'there, there.' You had to know that ambushing her wasn't going to work."

"I guess." Alicia had to force herself not to pout. "I think I was just desperate. I'm back home, and nothing is the same, even though everything is the same. It's just that nothing is the same for *me*. And believe me, I know, consequences of my actions, etc., etc., but it still hurts. I just want my old life back. I miss her, Jade."

"They say that home only exists in the mothballs of your memory, or something like that, for a reason. Your expectations will never match what you actually find. But look, you're here, you have people who love you and care about you, so don't try to escape what happened. Embrace the changes and accept that things are different. Not bad, just different."

Alicia nodded. Too much time had passed. She should have come back immediately. Maybe if she'd flown directly back from Australia to Oakview and apologized for leaving everyone in a haze of confusion, they'd have been a little more open to welcoming her back into their circle. Into their lives. She could show herself a thousand different ways that things might have been altered for the better, but the truth was, she would have found a way to sabotage it.

Because she wasn't ready to come back to a settled life that she'd felt a fervent compulsion to flee. She'd just gone about everything—*everything*—the wrong way.

The three years since she'd gone hadn't been bad, per se. She'd made a few friends in Somerville, the city she'd stayed in with Leila; she'd gone on a few dates; and she'd enjoyed working at the college for the most part. She hadn't loved it, and it wasn't her dream job, but it was fine. She didn't feel tied to it. She didn't feel tied to anything, and maybe that was what she truly needed at that time.

Looking back, she really *hadn't* been tied to anything. She still talked to her cousin, of course, but the friendships she'd made had just sort of faded away, and after a few emails and texts, her coworkers had moved on as well. She'd get the random group text with a funny education-related meme time and again, but it was probably someone who'd forgotten to use the updated group text that didn't include former employees.

So this was it. Here she was, right back where she'd started. Except now she was thirty-seven, single, friendless, last-in in a dying industry, living on top of rickety train tracks.

Alicia sighed again before she left the office.

❖

Alicia pulled her Prius into the parking lot of a tiny convenience store not too far from where Beverly Lawson's body had been found. It was one of the more rural parts of town, on the outskirts near Copper Lake. The sun sank into the water surrounded by dazzling rings of mauve and gold that flowed across the horizon. Alicia just sat there for a few minutes, allowing the majesty of the view to erase some of the constant turmoil she was mired in.

She got out and walked to the edge of the woods where a chilling breeze blew through her. The snow cover had all but melted in the waning days of the cold, and little green sprouts were taking hold against their better judgment. There was a well-worn path that led deeper into the perennially thick tree cover, but Alicia stayed on the rocky edge at the entrance. It would be dark soon, and she didn't want to find herself wandering in the dark woods alone. Last year's pine needles crunched beneath her feet. She cast one last glance down the path and headed toward the small store. Most of the sign's lights were out, so it read MAR E' C VENIEN E ST RE.

"Can I help you?" the woman behind the counter asked when Alicia walked through the glass door. It was more of a statement than a question.

Odd. That was something that employees of clothing stores and car dealerships did, not convenience store clerks. "No, I'm all set, thanks. Just passing through."

"Nobody passes through West Oakview. We've got trees and fields and the side of the lake that's got nothing but rocks and weeds in it. The only people who come around here are people who live here, work here, or are looking for something. Which one are you?" The silver-haired woman narrowed her eyes.

Alicia was pretty certain the woman already knew the answer to that question. She wondered if she was in a horror movie. "Uh, I was actually just coming in to grab a lemonade," she said, heading toward the refrigerator in the back. She could feel the clerk's eyes on her.

"If you're here looking for 'clues' or whatever in that Lawson woman's murder, you're not the first. We've had lots of amateur sleuths combing through these woods, trying to be heroes. Nobody's found nothing yet. A dollar ninety-five." She rang up Alicia's lemonade without making eye contact.

Alicia nodded awkwardly. She pulled out her debit card but quickly slid it back into her wallet at the woman's deep, put out sigh. She found two crumpled dollar bills and flipped them onto the counter. Alicia waited for a second before realizing that no change was coming and turned to leave.

"Should be careful out here. Once I close up shop in about an hour, there's no one around for miles. Just me and ol' Rusty." The clerk nodded to the corner behind the candy case where an 80's era shotgun was leaning haphazardly.

"I will do that," Alicia said. She walked out backward and fought the urge to salute the woman in some sort of clumsy acknowledgment. "Have a good night."

Once inside her Prius, Alicia clicked the lock button and felt a surge of relief when all the locks engaged. She'd lived in Oakview for close to a decade, and it was true, she couldn't remember a time when she'd ever been to this part of town except to cut through to Chester Bluffs. There were a few houses scattered around, but overall, it was pretty barren.

"Nice place," she muttered to herself before heading toward home. That investigative spirit she'd felt when she'd first arrived had dissipated and been replaced with a general sense of uneasiness.

CHAPTER FIVE

Did you know about this?" Cami asked, throwing her keys onto the kitchen table. She switched the phone to speaker and tossed that on the table next to them while she grabbed a beer from the fridge.

"Of course not," Katie said. "I just asked Taryn, and she hasn't heard anything from her, either. It's been like two years since I talked to her. Something like that. You know I would have told you."

Cami took a long swig of Coors Light. "I know. I was just completely blindsided, and I'm furious. I wasn't expecting to see her. Ever again."

"Are you okay?"

"Yeah, I'm fine. I think. I just can't fathom in what world Alicia would think I'd be up for sitting down to breakfast and rehashing our breakup over a fucking blueberry muffin. Why would the *Sun* even rehire her? She left them high and dry when she left." Cami sank into her plush gray sofa.

"Jade is still there. She always had a soft spot for Alicia. Have you talked to Violet? Maybe she knew something."

Cami, Katie, and Violet had grown up together, all residents of Sherman Street during their formative years. Cami was grateful that they'd been able to maintain such a close bond after all these years. They'd all welcomed Alicia in with open arms and treated her as though she'd always been one of the gang. Until she'd proven that she hadn't been.

"Not yet. I'll call her later. I just wasn't prepared to have all these feelings bubbling to the surface, you know? It's not like I'm not over her. I am, totally, but it was still a shock to the system. Just to see her.

Standing in my space. It was surreal." Cami finished off the last of her beer.

"I don't know why she's even back. Why didn't she just move to Newport where her brother lives? Maybe she came home to taunt you because she's a sociopath. Or maybe she wants you back. Either way, bad news," Katie said.

Cami scoffed. "Please. I don't know why she's back, and I don't care. I'll talk to her if and when I have to for this stupid newspaper deal the captain is making me do, but otherwise, nothing has changed. She doesn't exist in my world anymore." Cami sounded more confident than she felt. Truth was, she was angry and confused all over again. It seemed that all Alicia brought to the table was chaos.

"Good. That's how it should be. To hell with her. Moving on. Anything new on the case? We're still getting all sorts of tips in Chester Bluffs, but the chief said that so far, they've all turned out to be dead ends." Katie was the administrative assistant to the chief of police at the Chester Bluffs Police Department, so she was usually up to speed with whatever law enforcement in the area was up to.

"He's right. Nothing has panned out. I feel so bad for her mother. She calls every day asking for an update. Three weeks is a long time to make up excuses."

"I know. Something will break. Either the killer will do something stupid or some other type of evidence will show up eventually. It usually does."

Cami could always count on Katie to be a cheerleader.

"Taryn just got home. I should get going. Not to bring her up again, but be careful with what you tell Alicia. I know this isn't your first rodeo, but reporters can be sneaky. I can't tell you how many times the chief's words have been twisted or taken out of context, and then we get blamed when the piece is proven wrong. And you know this one. I just don't want her to find you at a weak moment and make you say something you're not ready to say," Katie said.

Cami sighed. "I handled it. She wasn't too pushy, but I wasn't exactly friendly either, so that may have had something to do with it. I wasn't specific at all, and I gave her the standard lines. Hopefully, she'll put out a puff piece, and that'll be the end of it until we have something firmer."

"Okay. Let me know what Violet says," Katie said.

"Will do."

Cami thought about waiting until the following morning to call Violet, since she'd probably be getting the kids ready for bed, but curiosity was getting the best of her. She was positive that Violet would have said something, unless, in her own sweet Violet-ish way, she thought it might be better if Cami didn't know Alicia was back in town.

"Vi, it's me."

"I had no idea."

"No idea about what? How did you even know what I was going to say?" Cami asked.

"Oh, Katie texted me while she was on the phone with you. Filled me in on everything. I can't believe she's back. Maybe she's only here to work on the murder story. 'Murder in a small town' and all that. It does have that certain can't-look-away flair that people love to read about."

Nice, Katie. Couldn't even wait until we hung up. "I have no idea. I had no intention of sitting down with her and catching up on what she's been up to the last three years."

"Oh, come on, you have to be at least a little curious."

Cami thought about it. Sure, she was curious in the abstract way of why Alicia was suddenly back in Oakview but not because she *cared.* "Not really. I just feel weird about it. All these ugly feelings came charging back, and I wasn't ready for it. That part of my life is a closed book. Opening it again, even unintentionally, was never the plan."

Violet hummed her agreement. "I know. Maybe it's a good thing. You never really got closure with the way she left."

"Fuck closure."

"All right, then," Violet said with a chuckle. "What does Maya think about it?"

"I haven't even talked to her today. Violet, she's not my girlfriend. We've gone on a couple of dates. I told you, it's very casual. Which is how I like it."

"I know that's what you told me, but it doesn't mean I believe it. I've known you for a hundred years, and you've never been 'casual' about anything."

"People change, my friend. I'm no longer the uptight, rigid, controlled girl you used to know. I'm a freewheeling, go-with-the-flow, spontaneous woman of the world. I might start dating a couple more women right now just to mix things up."

Violet belly laughed on the other end of the line. Cami wasn't sure whether to be pissed at her or laugh along. She could be all of those things if she wanted to. Keeping it relaxed with Maya felt right. She didn't feel any type of urge to solidify things or move any faster.

After deciding on a Pepsi instead of another beer, Cami put her feet up on the coffee table and turned on the TV. She wanted to focus on something mind-numbingly stupid so she didn't have to replay the events of the day or the stagnant case through her head again. She was just about to nod off during a rerun of an old sitcom when her phone vibrated to life next her.

"Lyons," she answered, rubbing her eye.

"Lyons, it's Brandt. I need you down here at the corner of Chestnut and Brewster. We've got another one."

❖

It was nearly eleven p.m. when Cami pulled up to the glut of police cars with their lights flashing. She parked in the middle of the road, effectively blocking traffic. The area seemed to be deserted aside from law enforcement, but they couldn't take any chances. She zipped up her windbreaker against the chill and wondered why she hadn't grabbed a heavier jacket. True spring was still elusive.

One of the third-shift police officers that Cami didn't know very well approached her. She nodded. "Detective Lyons, we've got officers out patrolling the area but nothing to report yet. Our only witness was driving home and saw the body leaned up against the telephone pole. He called it in right away. He didn't see or hear anything else."

"Thanks, Pratt," Cami said, seeing the name pinned to his lapel. She inched toward the body, careful not to disrupt anything in the surrounding area.

She squatted to get a better look. A young woman in her late twenties or early thirties was propped up against the pole. She was wearing a gray sweater with a long skirt and white Crocs. She had a messenger bag lying beside her with the heel of a dress shoe poking out of it. Cami stood slightly and saw it. A gunshot wound in the back of her neck. Her strawberry blond hair was matted and darkened by blood.

Cami stood and exhaled deeply. *What. The. Fuck.* Another one. No way could it have been a coincidence.

Kelsey arrived and stood next to her, surveying the scene with wide eyes. Cami leaned in and whispered, "You good?"

Kelsey nodded. "So much for sussing out burglars and doing paperwork."

Cami scoffed in agreement. "Our jobs have certainly evolved."

"She was moved," Kelsey said.

Cami nodded. She turned to the officer waiting nearby for instructions. "This homicide didn't take place here, obviously. Please make sure a full sweep of the area is completed. No stone unturned. It's too early to make any connections, but I seriously doubt this and Beverly Lawson are unrelated."

She paused and turned back toward the victim. The woman had a small yellow stain on her sweater. Looked like mustard. Cami couldn't help but wonder if the woman had known she'd be eating her last meal if she would've picked something different. Somehow, a bologna and cheese on wheat didn't seem like a fitting way to send someone into the great beyond.

"Once her bag's been labeled and dusted for prints, please have it sent to my office. Is the coroner on the way?" Cami asked.

The officer nodded.

"Okay, let's get this whole area cordoned off. It's easier to condense it later than try to enlarge it. Once again, we don't have much to go on here. We have no on-scene witnesses, at least not yet, so we need to make sure anything that even *might* be useful is bagged and tagged. Kelsey, you start over there, and I'll start here. We need to be completely thorough, follow every protocol. When we're done, we'll do our second walkthrough, and then we can head back to the station. Do we have coffee? We need coffee." Cami ran her hand across her forehead and pulled a notebook out of her back pocket. It was going to be a long night.

CHAPTER SIX

Rather than sit alone at home, Alicia decided to go into the office the morning after her weird encounter at the convenience store. Maybe being in close proximity to other writers would help stimulate her brain. She'd turned in the article on the Oakview PD and the mysterious circumstances surrounding the murder of Beverly Lawson. She felt a sweep of apprehension flow through her at the thought of Cami and the others at the PD reading it. She doubted it would go over well, but it was a damn good article. Hopefully, they would see that in the interest of transparency, she'd done what the mayor had asked them to do. She didn't want Cami to be angry with her, but she just kept telling herself she was doing her job. She tried to ignore the pit in her stomach.

Sitting alone at home wouldn't have been much different since she was also sitting alone in the office. She had her laptop hooked up to a docking station with a giant monitor so that was a perk. The blinking cursor was mocking her, daring her to write something. She'd felt the creative juices really flowing on her last article, and now, nothing. She needed to paraphrase a few AP articles for the national section of the paper, normally a pretty easy task. Maybe she was just distracted.

Alicia couldn't help but feel that she'd made a giant mistake coming back to Oakview. It wasn't like she'd thought she'd be able to just slip back into her old life again; she wasn't *that* naive, but she didn't think she'd feel like such a pariah.

"Hey, Felicia," a voice said from behind her.

Alicia jumped.

"We've met before, but I'm not sure if you remember me. It was when you worked here last time. Not for long, though, I think you left a few weeks later. I was an intern at the time. Now I'm the human-interest slash classifieds lackey. Samantha. Sam," the woman said. She held out a hand.

"It's Alicia," she said, shaking Sam's hand. "I'm not sure I remember you. I apologize, but that last year was a bit of blur. Nice to meet you. Again."

"Sorry, I could've sworn I heard Jade call you Felicia. That's embarrassing. Sorry."

Alicia waved her off. "No, it's fine, honestly. Do you come into the office a lot?"

Sam shook her head, her wavy auburn hair gliding easily over her shoulders. "Nah. Once in a while, usually to steal supplies. How about you? Do you like working from home, or would you prefer to be a cube dweller?"

"Home, definitely. But I thought being around people, you know, the whole hustle and bustle of a newsroom, might spark some inspiration. Clearly, I was imagining the newsroom of the *Washington Post*, circa 1980, and not the *Knox County Sun* in the two-thousand-twenties. I suppose this is what it's always like? A few stragglers using the docking stations and a couple others stealing supplies?"

Sam laughed. "Pretty much. It's really changed over the last few years. There used to be a lot more people around, but it's basically a wasteland most days. I doubt you'll find much inspiration here." She leaned against the desk Alicia was working at. "I took a stab at an editorial about those corrupt district court judges and the whole broadband monopoly. Jade usually likes me to keep things light, but I wanted to try something different. It might be shit. It's so hard to honestly critique your own writing."

"You want me to take a look?" Alicia asked. "I can give you some feedback, as limited as my knowledge of the local justice system might be."

Sam smiled warmly. "That would be awesome. Thank you." She handed Alicia the pages that were curled from Sam forming them into a cylinder.

"Anytime. I can't keep staring at this gigantic monitor anyway. I think it's bigger than my TV. It's giving me a headache."

"That's why I stick with my fourteen-inch laptop screen. It doesn't magnify my lost dreams and failures," Sam said with a smirk. She shrugged.

"I feel that in my soul," Alicia said, chuckling. "Okay, now go away so I can read this."

Sam nodded and looked around the office. "I guess I'll…go raid the K-Cup closet to see if I can find any more of that chocolate glazed doughnut coffee."

Alicia watched her go, acknowledging how nice it felt to have a pleasant interaction with someone who didn't know who she was or who she had been. She wouldn't be opposed to making a new friend.

Since it was just the two of them in the office, Alicia kicked her feet up and leaned back in her chair. Sam's article wasn't particularly long, but it had a lot of cross-outs and handwritten notes in the margins. She had a few punctuation issues, but Alicia wasn't sure that was the type of feedback Sam was looking for.

She was a good writer; that much was evident. But Alicia was nervous that her content might have gone a little off the rails. The article started off innocently enough, with the facts and the players, but then Sam went off on a tangent of conspiracies and incompetence and involvement by local law enforcement. There didn't seem to be much evidence to back up her claims. It was mostly hearsay from parties who had a clear conflict of interest.

"You done?" Sam poked her head around the corner, a hesitant smile on her face.

"I am, come back in," Alicia said. She took a breath. She wasn't sure how honest she should be. She didn't know her at all, and critiquing someone's work always had the possibility of ending badly. *Usually* ended badly. But she didn't want to mislead her, either.

Sam sat across from Alicia in one of the empty office chairs and raised her eyebrows expectantly. "Well? What do you think? Am I ready to branch out a little?"

Alicia giggled nervously. "Yeah, I think so. Your editorial writing has a comfortable flow to it, and you present the data points with conviction. Are you sure you don't want to present this as an opinion piece instead of an editorial?"

Sam's smile faltered slightly. "I mean, I guess I could, but it's more than just my opinion. It's kind of well-known in intellectual circles that these were bad guys, aided at every turn by the supposed good guys. Don't you think we should get that kind of thing out in the mainstream? It's important."

"Sure, I just think there needs to be a little more hard evidence, you know, maybe fewer anonymous sources for such weighty accusations. Your writing is really good. I'm sure Jade will be thrilled that you're looking to expand into different areas." Alicia handed the papers back. "Did you find that doughnut coffee you were looking for?"

"Uh, no. Actually, the bin was almost all decaf or that peppermint mocha shit. We definitely need a supply order ASAP."

Alicia smiled. She pronounced it a-sap. She seemed distracted but not upset.

"I'll do a little more work on this before I submit it to Jade. I appreciate you reading it for me. Means a lot."

Alicia was positive Jade wouldn't publish Sam's article as an editorial. But she couldn't tell Sam that. "Yeah, I think that's a good idea. With a little polish and some more concrete accounts, you might really have something there."

Sam nodded and smiled. "I'm glad I made the trip into the office today, *Alicia*," she said, emphasizing the correct name. "I hope to see you again soon."

Whether it was the thought of going home to an empty house or a vibe she thought she picked up on, Alicia stepped out of her comfort zone. "Do you play pool?"

Stopping in the open doorway, Sam turned, seemingly pleasantly surprised. "I'm not great at it, but I do enjoy it now and again. Why, you up for a game?"

Relief coursed through Alicia's bloodstream. The thought of more rejection—even one as innocuous as that would have been—made her want to crawl into a hole. "Sure, whenever you have some time. Let me know?"

"How about later tonight? We can meet at Birdie's if that works? Maybe around eight?" Sam cocked her head to the side.

"Yes," Alicia said, maybe a little too quickly. She cleared her throat. "Yes. That sounds good. I'll see you tonight."

"Okay, then."

They exchanged numbers, and Sam sent Alicia a text that contained a smiley face. She smiled broadly and walked out, letting the door close loudly behind her.

Alicia just sat there in the same spot, staring after Sam with the same frozen wide-eyed smile that seemed to now be a permanent fixture of her face. Was it a date? Did she *want* it to be a date? She didn't even know if Sam was into women. Maybe she'd get there, and Sam would introduce her to her longtime boyfriend Brad, who wore a puka shell necklace and Ray-Ban aviators pushed on top of his head.

That image actually made her chuckle, which freed her from her insane perma-smile. She tried to think back to the last time she'd been to Birdie's. Jeez, probably almost ten years ago. She'd gone with Cami and the rest of the gang for Violet's thirtyish birthday party.

The laughter and alcohol had been flowing easily that night. By her third or fourth glass of wine, Alicia had given up trying to call shots in the game of pool she had been playing with Cami. She was just hoping to get a ball in a pocket, *any* pocket. Cami had laughed as she'd continued to scratch on nearly every shot. She'd sidled up behind her like an 80's movie sleazy bad boy and firmly grasped her hips. Alicia could remember laughing as Cami had leaned into her, her lips tickling the back of Alicia's ear as Cami made some suggestive joke about pulling off a combo.

But it was later that night that Alicia remembered most. They'd just moved in together, their things scattered around the floor, boxes still stacked against the walls. The effects of the alcohol had mostly worn off, except for that soft glow of sleepiness that had blanketed her. She'd dropped her keys on the table and started to head to the bedroom, but Cami had grabbed her wrist and spun her around. Cami had smiled at her, that tender, understated smile that melted Alicia's whole insides. Cami had clasped her hand and pulled her tightly against her own body. She'd swayed back and forth, a relaxed slow dance that was more about their proximity to one another than rhythm. Alicia had leaned in and kissed her, slowly at first, sweetly, until she couldn't hold back any longer.

The backfire of a garbage truck nearly made Alicia jump out of her skin. She checked her phone and realized she'd been sitting there, still looking toward the door that Sam had left through, for almost fifteen minutes. She swallowed hard, pushing down any of those feelings that threatened to poke through here and there, and grabbed her laptop off the docking station. She wondered why she'd suggested

Birdie's in the first place. It wasn't like there were tons of choices for casual pubs with pool tables in Oakview, but there *was* more than that particular one. *Oh well. Too late for a change of venue now. I'm not going to think about what it means. I have a non-date to get ready for.*

❖

Jeans, slacks, and even a few dresses were strewn around Alicia's floor. She couldn't even remember the last time she'd gone out with someone in a non-platonic way. If that even was what this was. She'd dipped her toe in the online dating pool about a year ago, just to see if she was ready to move on. After three chemistry-less dates, she'd decided the problem was her, not the women she was meeting, and had taken down her profile.

She didn't want to appear overeager and wear something too dressy, but she didn't want to be rude and show up in a hoodie if Sam was going to wear something chic and stylish. Alicia caught a glimpse of herself in the mirror and laughed. She was standing there in a sports bra and bikini briefs, the light giving her dark blond hair those goldish highlights that she wished she could replicate with hair color. When she was younger, she hadn't imagined her life would be like this at thirty-seven. She figured by now she'd be down at the state capital, covering breaking news for the *New York Times* or the *Washington Post*, someone waiting for her at home to fill in on all the scoop she'd found out and what famous people she'd met that day.

Whenever she ran that scenario through her head, even though she knew it was just a pipe dream, the petite blonde with the haunting blue eyes never changed. She really had to find a way to replace Cami as the dream woman in her head canon. The yearning was starting to get old.

Alicia settled on a pair of black jeans and a short white sweater. She hadn't had the length taken off her hair in a long time, so it was all the way to the middle of her back. She put it up in a loose ponytail and then let it fall back down. No reason to invite a headache in.

She parked her Prius in an open spot near the front door. Birdie's was always pretty busy on Thursday nights, so Alicia wasn't surprised to hear the drumbeat of the band from outside. She had a fleeting urge to just get back in her car and go home, text Sam that she didn't feel well, and maybe they could reschedule for another time. She rolled her neck back and forth and sighed. *Just go in and get it over with.*

Alicia plastered a smile on her face and made her way through a small crowd of people gathered near the bar who were downing shots of something that was pale yellow. Lemon drops, probably.

On the other side of the group, the three pool tables had a few people gathered around them. She caught sight of an auburn-haired woman chalking a pool cue and wondered for the second time if she should just leave. *Knock it off.*

"Sam?" Alicia called, depriving herself of any further hesitation.

The auburn-haired woman turned, and Alicia was right. Sam's face brightened at the sight of her. She felt bad that she had so desperately wanted to bag out of their meetup.

"Hey, so good to see you." Sam leaned in and gave Alicia an awkward half hug.

Alicia turned her head as Sam came in, so she got a face full of hair. She patted Sam on the shoulder blade and immediately regretted it. *I'm officially my nana.*

"I got here a little early, so this couple let me crash their game to get a little practice in. I wasn't sure if you were some kind of pool shark, so I didn't want to embarrass myself. They're super nice. They went to get drinks."

"I'm definitely not a pool shark." Alicia hurriedly pushed the memory of playing pool with Cami out of her head before it could break through. "I'm a pool…tuna."

Sam laughed. "That's perfect. We're probably about the same skill level then." She looked up at the couple walking toward them. "Hey, guys. This is—"

"Alicia," Violet said. She looked like she'd seen a ghost.

Alicia could relate. Part of her wanted to run, and the other part of her wanted to throw up. Of course she'd see someone she knew. She was convinced that some part of her subconscious knew it, and even though she wasn't ready to have a face-to-face confrontation with her old friends, at some point, she'd have to see them.

Violet looked the same. The same stylish stacked bob, dangly earrings, lipstick that was just a bit too light for her complexion.

Jack, her husband, hadn't changed much either, except for a well-maintained goatee that was now more gray than brown.

"Violet, Jack, hi," Alicia said. "How've you been?"

Jack moved first. He leaned forward, supplying Alicia with her second awkward hug of the night. "It's been a long time. You're back from Australia for good now?"

Violet scoffed. "I told you she wasn't staying in Australia permanently. Remember when I told you she called from Boston?"

"Yeah, Australia was just an extended…trip. But I'm back now. I missed home too much. How are the kids?" Alicia changed the subject as quickly as possible. She didn't want to talk about Australia or Boston or anything else that could make the encounter any more uncomfortable than it already was.

"Good. Madison just turned fourteen, and Gavin is eleven. Time flies, huh?" Jack crossed his arms and shot a glance at Violet.

Alicia wondered how much she had told him. Jack was a nice guy, and he was always good for a laugh, but he tended to stay away from the more scandalous aspects of their conversations. It was very possible he didn't know much at all.

"It sure does," Alicia agreed. "I remember Gavin's kindergarten graduation like it was yesterday."

"So how do you all know each other?" Sam asked. She took a sip of whatever Jack had handed her.

Alicia had forgotten she was there. "Oh, sorry about that. I've known Violet for years, we're old friends." She nodded as if confirming the information.

Sam must have sensed something was off, with the way Violet was sort of frozen, and Jack was still wearing that uncomfortably large smile.

"How nice. Small world," Sam said. "Alicia, grab a cue."

"How do you two know each other?" Violet asked, finally moving from the spot she'd been stationary in.

"We work together," Alicia said. She cut Sam off, but she wanted to make it clear that it was just a friendly, platonic game of pool between coworkers. Not that Violet cared, of course. But she didn't want the phone tree lit up once the night was over. She wasn't even sure she rated enough to be a topic of the phone tree at this point, but better safe than sorry. She certainly didn't want Cami to think she was on a date.

"Right, I did hear you were back at the *Knox County Sun*. Katie told me you were doing a piece on the murder of that poor woman. Cami's been straight out since that happened," Violet missed the cue ball when she went to take her shot and stood up straight, as though she realized she'd brought up a taboo subject.

So they had been talking about her. "Yeah, the article will be in tomorrow's paper. Online first thing in the morning."

Sam kept looking back and forth between them. Jack was sitting on a barstool in the corner looking at something on his phone. Violet kept picking at an imaginary imperfection in the hem of her shirt. Alicia prayed that a meteor would end the misery.

They were able to evolve into something resembling small talk, thanks mostly to Sam and Jack and New England sports, but Alicia was grateful for it just the same.

"Well, we should probably get going. We only have the babysitter until eleven," Violet said.

Alicia glanced at her watch but didn't mention that it was only ten past ten. "It was so nice to see you two. It really has been such a long time. Give the kids a hug for me." It was sad that she felt so uncomfortable around someone she had considered a good friend for such a long time.

"We will," Jack said as Violet was putting on her coat. "Hey, we're having a little spring barbecue on the twenty-fifth—if the weather cooperates—and you should come by. You like those vegetable skewer things Violet makes me cook, right?"

Violet whipped around in slow motion, a tight-lipped smile and raised eyebrows turning her pretty face into a caricature. "Yes, that *would* be nice. So nice."

"Great, I will definitely try to make it. I do love those marinated veggies, yes. Thanks so much. I look forward to it." Alicia had less than zero intention of going, but she appreciated that Jack invited her.

"You should come, too," Jack said to Sam. "Hopefully, your cornhole skills are better than your pool skills."

Sam laughed as they said their good-byes and turned to Alicia once Jack and Violet were out of earshot. "What's *that* all about?"

"What?" Alicia asked, knowing full well what. For the first half of the night and the final few minutes, the tension in the air could have been cut with a butter knife. She aimed for the orange striped ball and smacked it unceremoniously against the green felt.

"Oh, come on. It was like a blanket dropped from the sky when the two of you saw each other. Did you used to date Jack or something? Or Violet?"

"No," Alicia yelled. She brought her voice down a few octaves when a couple next to them turned in her direction. "No, of course not. My ex is a good friend of Violet's. We had a weird breakup that made everything else weird. It's sad, really. I used to go out with Violet every Sunday morning. We'd meet at the Crumbly Biscuit, have coffee and bagels, and then go next door to do our weekly grocery shopping together. It seems like such a little old lady thing to do, but I loved it, and I looked forward to it. And then it just ended."

Sam gave her a half-smile. "Wasn't mutual, I take it?"

Alicia didn't know how to answer that. It certainly wasn't, but probably not in the way that Sam was assuming. Rather than get into a drawn out explanation of all the ways she'd fucked her life over, Alicia just shook her head. "No."

Thankfully, Sam seemed to be able to sense that she didn't want to expand any further on the conversation. "Another drink?" she asked.

"Is this a date?" Alicia asked. Might as well stop pussyfooting around and just ask the damn question. Alicia felt as though she'd been fast-forwarded into letting Sam in on a little more than she'd planned.

Sam coughed into her rum and Coke. "Ah, well, I don't know. Do you want it to be?"

"I don't know."

"That's a hit to the ego. But seriously, I think you're attractive, and from what I can tell, you're funny and definitely a little quirky. I guess we can call this 'getting to know each other,' if that works for you?" Sam asked. For the first time, she didn't seem to be able to maintain eye contact and looked at the ground.

Alicia breathed a sigh of relief. "That's perfect, actually. No pressure, just getting to know each other. I like it."

"Good." She rubbed Alicia's shoulder. "Now let me kick your ass one more time before we wrap it up. Rack 'em up."

Chapter Seven

A copy of the *Knox County Sun* dropped onto Cami's desk with a soft thud. She looked up to see Kelsey standing over her, her gaze pointed. Kelsey's face softened when Cami only stared at her.

"I take it you haven't read it yet," Kelsey said.

Cami glanced down, and the headline screamed at her:

"Is the Oakview Police Department in Over its Head? Troubling Signs Point to Yes."

"What the fuck is this?" Cami yelled, scanning the article and turning to page two to see the rest. "I didn't say that. Oh, and *that's* bullshit!"

Captain Brandt walked into her office, shaking his phone angrily. "Was I unclear when I said the public wanted to be put at ease? What part of 'trust and transparency' didn't you understand?"

Cami stood instinctively. "She took everything I said and made it sound like we're bumbling fools from Mayberry. I specifically told her I couldn't share facts about the ongoing investigation, and it looks like she took that to mean we didn't *know* any facts about the ongoing investigation."

"The mayor is pissed. And I'm pissed, too. Maybe you were right, maybe Kelsey would have been the smarter choice," Brandt said, shaking his head at his phone again.

Kelsey took that as her opportunity to leave Cami's office. *Coward.*

"I intentionally told her that crime in nearly every other area was at the same level or lower, and I was vague about the Lawson murder because we really *don't* know much. I'm going to demand a retraction." Cami could feel rage bubbling inside her. It was a hit piece by Alicia because she was mad Cami wasn't more open to her forgiveness tour. There was no other pretext that would have made the department seem so incompetent and out of touch.

"That makes it look like we have something to hide. As it is, you were apparently *so* vague that we look like we are deliberately keeping the town in the dark. Why did you tell her we found a calling card on the victim? We have no idea what that block is or means. That was irresponsible."

"I didn't. She asked a few hypothetical questions, and I told her that it was an active investigation and that I couldn't comment. And I left it at that." Cami skimmed the article until she found the section where Alicia wrote, *Detective Lyons hinted at something more sinister than a random shooting when she refused to invalidate the presence of a calling card, an object intentionally left at the scene of a crime to lure law enforcement into a deadly game of cat and mouse.*

Cami's rage was now at a boil.

"Well, she printed it, and now it's gospel. The town thinks we have a serial killer in our midst, and we're too inept to handle it. The worst part is that they may not be wrong. Word about the second victim wasn't even out at print time. We're going to have to schedule a press conference to address all these questions. Have you gone through the bag yet?" Captain Brandt nodded to the second victim's things that were bagged and in a box on Cami's credenza.

"Not yet, the tech dropped it off just before you came in. Listen, Cap, I really am sorry about the article. I should have been more cautious with…that reporter. I tried to keep it as light as possible given the circumstances, and that was obviously the wrong move." She racked her brain to come up with the things she actually said. It wasn't like that was Cami's first interview with local media. Alicia had knocked her off her game, and that was her own fault. *I should know better.*

"Well, you have a chance to redeem yourself. Meet with her again for the follow-up edition on transparent policing."

"Me? Don't you think it might be better to send Kelsey at this point? Maybe I just didn't gel with that reporter. If it has to be me, see if they can send someone else." Cami didn't care if she sounded like a coward. She had no interest in Alicia manipulating her words again and playing her for a fool in front of the captain, the department, and the entire town.

"No can do. Any deviating from the first interview looks like weakness on our part. You just need to brush up on your bullshitting skills. If you tank another one, the mayor is going to want me to make sure you're pulling your weight in other areas."

Cami nodded reluctantly. The implied warning didn't slip past her. She had to make it work with Alicia, or else she'd be branded as a "problem."

Brandt's admin poked her head in to let the captain know he had an urgent phone call on line two. He stuck his phone with the offending article in his back pocket and pointed to the box on the credenza. Cami nodded.

She snapped on a pair of gloves and refocused her attention. Alicia should not be taking up so much headspace, especially with everything else going on. Couldn't she have just stayed away and let Cami keep pretending that she didn't exist?

The woman, who'd been identified as Laurie Garrett, was a twenty-seven-year-old retail manager at the Pottery Charm. She had a boyfriend they were looking into, but he seemed to have a solid alibi. She had no children and no other family in the area. She was originally from Greensboro, North Carolina and had moved to Oakview a few years earlier when she'd transferred to take the management position. She had very little in common with Beverly Lawson, and at first check, they didn't know each other.

Cami looked through the contents of the messenger bag carefully. Lip gloss, a pair of black pumps, two tampons, a pair of sunglasses in a soft case, a hairbrush, and a wooden building block with the letter C on it. Goose bumps broke out on Cami's forearms.

She took the block to the captain's office where he was still on the phone. He waved her in while he wrapped up his call.

She held the block up for him to see.

His eyes widened. "You're shitting me. So we really do have a calling card type of situation here. Anything the techs can get from it?"

She shook her head. "No prints. Looks like it came from the same set as the last one, but nothing is certain yet. Obviously, they mean something. We have a C and a T. Not a lot to go on."

"My fear is that if someone is trying to send a message, these might only be pieces of a larger puzzle. Which means they're not finished." He called Kelsey in.

Kelsey seemed just as surprised and disheartened to see the small wooden block in Cami's hand. "We have a serial killer? In Oakview? How is that even possible? I mean, I feel like I know just about everyone."

Cami shook her head. "It feels that way sometimes, but the truth is, there are lots of people we don't know. It would be a hell of a lot easier if we could pin this on Rob the angry drunk or Pat the shoplifter, our usual suspects. But I'm pretty sure we can rule them out in about five minutes flat."

"Did you get the word out to the local channels? The Garrett family members have been notified." Brandt flipped through the pile of notes on his desk.

Kelsey nodded. "They're going to run with the bare minimum for the time being. People will obviously draw their own conclusions, but we don't want to start an unnecessary panic."

Cami wondered just how unnecessary the panic would have been.

"Tip line up and running?" Brandt asked.

"Yeah, and we have a few already. Nothing too exciting, but maybe there's something there." Kelsey handed Cami a few Post-its she'd been hanging on to.

Cami scanned them. Wild animal near victim's location about an hour earlier, likely fox or coyote. Nope. Greyhound bus driving senior citizens home from one of the Connecticut casinos' tourist trips; one senior thought they saw the victim walking down the street. Probably not. Early indications were that the body was moved to that location postmortem. A nearby resident recalled a black van driving slowly down the street with an advertisement for Hargrove's on the side panel: *Hauling Your Junk for 30 Years!* Again, probably nothing, but worth a look.

Cami handed the notes back to Kelsey. "Follow up on the van first, the bus tour second. We know a coyote didn't do this so that one isn't worth much, but maybe the guy saw something else, too." She turned to Brandt. "I need to run out for a little bit, but I'll be back shortly to follow up with Kelsey on any additional tips that come in. Hopefully, we'll have the ME reports soon."

He nodded. "You believe this, Lyons? In my forty years on this police force, I've never seen anything like it. Not one but *two* murders in less than thirty days. What's the world coming to?"

"I don't know, Cap. We're out of our comfort zone here, for sure. Working the Acorn Festival traffic stops and dealing with those unruly parade participants was the highlight of last year. I'll be back soon."

❖

The tires of her Jeep actually squelched when she pulled into the parking spot. She got out and slammed the door, a copy of the morning's *Sun* tucked under her arm. She could almost hear "The Imperial March" playing as she stormed toward the building.

Cami found Jade Conley sitting at the heavy oak desk in her office, ensconced in glass-block walls with beige wingback chairs for guest seating. The 80's decor of the *Knox County Sun* office would probably outlive them all.

Jade looked up in surprise at Cami's forceful entrance. "Detective Lyons. Been a while. How are you?"

"Why did you let her print this? It's a complete fabrication of our interview," Cami said, doing away with any niceties. She'd always had an open and honest relationship with local media, so the betrayal cut deep.

Jade sat back and crossed her arms. "Was it? Alicia may be a lot of things, but I've never known her to be a liar. Her professional ethics have always been one of her greatest strengths."

"Yes. She made it sound like we're a group of blundering fools who don't know our asses from our elbows. That's not what I conveyed to her *at all*."

Holding up a hand, Jade leaned forward. "I read the article. I approved the article. I can assure you that the police department is not portrayed as 'bumbling idiots' but as a group of law enforcement officials who don't often deal with the type of violent crime that happened here. Or more accurately now, *crimes*. You're taking the criticism to heart when it's really just an observation."

"That's bullshit, Jade. And you know it. We may not deal with these types of crimes all the time, but we're trained, we're professionals, and we'll find out who did this. To demean us the way Alicia did was totally uncalled for and unnecessary. It's not the paper's job to belittle us to our community." Cami slapped the paper in her hand to emphasize the point.

"It's not the paper's job to paint you out to be heroes, either."

Cami whipped around to find Alicia standing in the doorway. Red hot anger crept up the sides of her neck. Seeing Alicia standing there, indignant, made it so much worse.

Also…had Alicia changed her hair? It was always fluffy and flowy—one of Cami's favorite things about her—but at that moment, it seemed even fluffier and flowier. She forced herself to focus on the issue at hand. "I never said it was. But what you printed is blatantly untrue."

Alicia faltered but regained herself quickly. "I wouldn't print one word that could be proven false. You should know that about me."

"See?" Cami asked, pointing at her. "You're doing that thing, you're phrasing things in such a way that makes it seem like *I'm* being misleading, but it's really you. Yes, I know your vagaries can't be proven false, but you also made it appear that we have no idea how to investigate a homicide. And that's not true."

"I didn't say that. You're assuming my intent because you're defensive. I've always been very pro-police, and my reporting reflects that. I said that the department may be out of their depth since these types of crimes don't usually happen around here. Is that untrue?" Alicia accentuated her question by raising an eyebrow.

Jade stepped in. "Okay. Detective, if that was all, I do have other things I need to get to. I'm sure the two of you can hash this out." She looked back and forth between them. "I will say that I stand by Alicia's article. It wasn't entirely flattering, but I know you'd never ask us to compromise our integrity to put out a fluff piece."

Cami looked at Jade, incredulous. "This is not about me 'asking' for anything. I just want our department to be portrayed *accurately*. Because this isn't it." She held the paper in the air again. Shaking her head, she decided that it was a wasted trip, and she should have just let it go. Obviously, Jade sided with Alicia, and there would be no changing her mind.

"Cami, wait."

Against her better judgment, Cami sighed and turned as she seethed. "What?"

"Before I gave it to Jade, I knew this article wouldn't be well-received, but I guess I had hoped that you'd see that there wasn't any malicious intent. I have all the faith in the world in you. It's just that this is totally outside what you're used to."

"No malicious intent?" Cami asked. "What was that line again…oh right…'Detective Lyons was at times both ambiguous and evasive.' What kind of intent was behind that particular line?"

For her part, Alicia seemed to withdraw the condescension a little. "Well…you were? I tried to get a full statement out of you, and it was like pulling teeth. You just kept feeding me the company lines. This was my first important assignment as the new crime reporter. I couldn't treat it like a throwaway article. I really am sorry if I upset you."

"I don't know why Brandt thinks I'm the right choice for this assignment, but he does. So I think it would be best if you passed this monthly task to someone else. Someone a little less biased, maybe." Cami looked Alicia directly in the eye, bracing for her response. Either she'd agree, which would make life easier for both of them, or deny, enflaming an already volatile situation.

Alicia widened her eyes and smiled, tight-lipped. "I can't. I've been back with the *Sun* for a few weeks, and I'm going to pass a huge assignment on to someone else? I know you're angry at me personally, and you have every right to be, but we can keep things professional if you outright refuse to talk to me in any other way. We're both adults."

And there it was again. The spine-tingling fury that she couldn't remember feeling until Alicia's unexpected re-invasion into her life. "Fine. So all of that bullshit you spewed at me at the diner about being sorry and the pleading voice mails you say you've left over the years meant nothing, as is usually the case with you. Why did you even come back? Ruining my life once wasn't enough for you? You thought you'd like to give it another go?" Cami said, swallowing a huge lump that had formed in her throat. She was surprised by its appearance, and she decided she'd rather choke on her own tongue than let Alicia see one solitary tear slip out of her eye.

That little outburst seemed to surprise Alicia just as much as it had surprised Cami. She opened her mouth to speak and then abruptly closed it. Her eyes were shiny. "I came back here," she finally said, clearing her throat. "Because I missed my home. I missed *you.* I missed my family, my friends, my job, my *life*. I am certainly not here to ruin your life, Cami. I guess I hoped, naively, that you and I could be friends again someday. We shared such intimate parts of ourselves with each other, and I was closer to you than anyone I've ever known."

The lump was back. Cami swallowed hard and steeled herself. "Why did you leave, Alicia? Why did you leave the way you did?"

"I wish I could give you the concrete answer you deserve. I felt suffocated by everything I've come to miss so much. My family, my job, my path in life, and I suppose even you to some degree, though it really had nothing to do with you. I should have told you how I'd been feeling, but I thought if I ignored it long enough, it would go away. It didn't, and then everything just exploded. I really am so, so, sorry." Alicia wiped at her eyes before anything could fall.

Cami nodded, resigned. She hardened herself from any emotions. It wasn't the right time. "I need you to back off this story, Alicia. I can't do my job to its fullest with a hostile press. I'm sure Jade can give it to the guy we usually deal with, Brett Something. Having one-on-ones together isn't going to work."

Alicia straightened, seeming to regain some of her early resolve. "No, Cami, I can't do that. I won't. This is my assignment, and I have to stick with it. I think we can do this together, but maybe you can ask Brandt to reassign it to Kelsey again. I don't want you to."

"A selfish leopard can't change its spots." Cami scoffed and shook her head. "You want it to get ugly between us? Let's do it. We can have a publicly contentious relationship, and the town will have to choose who they believe. Sounds like it'll be good for morale, huh?"

She didn't wait for a response. She marched out of the newspaper office and entered the comfort of her Jeep. She slammed the back of her fist into the passenger side headrest and sobbed.

Chapter Eight

Alicia sat at the desk with two giant monitors, questioning every life decision she'd made in the last few years. She was furious at Cami for making her question her own journalistic integrity. Would that story have come out differently if she had interviewed Captain Brandt or Detective Chandler? She had assured Jade—and herself—that there was no conflict of interest. Her past relationship with Detective Lyons had no bearing whatsoever on her ability to write an article about the work the police department was doing. She could pine for the old days with Cami until she was blue in the face, but it wouldn't reflect in her writing. She wasn't using her voice as a way to compensate for the fact that Cami wouldn't talk to her.

And damn it, she stood by that. Convinced that she was on the right side of the argument, Alicia resolved to write her next article for the monthly series with the same balanced and equitable mindset she was certain she'd had for the last one. Screw Cami's accusations. If anyone was being subjective about it, it was *her*. Yeah.

"I assume you worked it out with Lyons?" Jade asked, a look on her face that Alicia could only define as judgment.

"It's fine. Everything is fine. We'll meet again, and she can clear up any misconceptions. I don't believe anything was misrepresented."

Jade nodded. "Okay." She paused. "Alicia, when I hired you back, it was because I knew your previous work, and I admired it. You were a straight shooter who got the job done with little direction and a flair for a catchy headline that drew readers in. I still believe you are that reporter. But whatever might be going on between you and Cami, you need to quash it. I won't have drama or animosity in my newsroom. As it is, we're barely keeping our heads afloat, so any type of scandal—even for a press as small as we are—could spell the end for us. I don't want to see this type of thing again."

"I understand." Alicia felt about two inches high. If she could have crawled under the desk for the rest of the day, she would have. "It won't happen again. I'll make sure that everything is strictly professional and nothing of a personal nature gets in the way."

"Am I interrupting something?" Jade's husband Evan spoke up from the doorway of the office.

Alicia hadn't noticed him, and it appeared that Jade hadn't either.

"Sorry, honey, just finishing up here. I'll get my things." Jade pursed her lips one last time at Alicia and breathed in deeply.

Her reaction didn't give Alicia the warm fuzzies, but she appreciated the sentiment behind it. Alicia had another chance to make sure everything was on the level but one chance only. If Cami came into the office to chew Jade out for Alicia's work again, she was history. She had to make it work with Cami one way or another.

"We're heading out to dinner. With an old colleague of mine," Evan said.

Alicia nodded, trying to think of something to say. She'd met Evan a few times over the years, but they'd always had Jade around as a buffer. He usually just bragged about the extravagant trips he got to take as the CEO of Oakview Savings. She'd never say anything to Jade in case she was misinterpreting, but Alicia sometimes felt that Evan gave her the once-over just a little too long. "Nice. Anywhere good?"

"Of course. We're heading to Boston. I got us a table at this exclusive new Indian place right on the water. Pays to know the right people," he said, raising his eyebrows.

Gross.

Alicia smiled and nodded. She turned back to her monitor and prayed for Jade to come rescue her.

❖

Once word got out about the second murder, Oakview was clearly on edge. There was a muted tittering among the people that gathered outside the mayor's press conference, both media and citizens alike.

The fact that there was no clear link between the two victims put everyone in the killer's crosshairs.

Alicia stood below the mayor's podium, her lanyard credentials poking into her sternum. There was a tripod set up with a crude poster of the two victims, the words, "Special Bulletin," and, "Information Needed," in large letters above the two photos. Below the photographs was the number of the tip line and in smaller print, the number to the Oakview Police Department.

The mayor, Captain Brandt, Cami, and Kelsey were all standing on the podium. Alicia couldn't help but notice Cami fidgeting with her belt loop. She'd never been a huge fan of the public aspects of her job.

Mayor Donna Stevens, an attractive fifty-something with a stylish blunt cut, adjusted the microphone toward her. The crowd quieted. "First, I wish to share my heartfelt condolences with the families of Beverly Lawson and Laurie Garrett for their terrible losses. Our community has been devastated by these tragedies, and we are doing everything in our power to bring the perpetrator to justice. I encourage anyone who knows anything or has any information that could help with our investigation to come forward. The suspect is still at large, and while we don't want you to be fearful, the community should remain vigilant. Nothing is certain at this time, but there could be a danger to the public. The people of this town are kindhearted, helpful, and honest, and that has not changed. Remember, if you see something, say something. Captain," Mayor Stevens finished, turning over the microphone to Brandt.

Alicia scribbled furiously in her notebook, even though she was recording the conference. Brandt was trying desperately to dodge the "calling card" reference that Alicia had alluded to in her article. He looked at her pointedly while trying to downplay the significance of that detail. Cami stared straight ahead with her hands clasped behind her back.

Once the captain had wrapped up the question and answer period, there was a mad dash toward the podium for photographs and interviews with some of Laurie Garrett's family and friends. A reporter from Channel 32 bumped Alicia's arm, causing her phone to fly out of her hand.

"Really?" she asked angrily. The reporter didn't turn back.

From seemingly out of nowhere, Cami handed Alicia her phone.

She took it, surprised. "Thanks. It's a stampede. You'd think half of these people have never covered a crime before," Alicia said, half smiling.

Cami didn't return the smile. "Half of them probably haven't, at least not of this magnitude. Obviously, the Boston and Manchester reps have but probably not many of the locals."

"I suppose that's true."

"I talked to Violet this morning. She told me about Jack's little barbecue slip of the tongue the other night. I told her that I'm sure you wouldn't be going, but I think she's still under the impression that you might show up. You may want to decline the invite formally." Cami adjusted her sunglasses.

Alicia couldn't hide her smirk. Was Cami really that disgusted by her that she wanted assurance that Alicia wouldn't be within a fifty-mile radius of the cookout? Alicia had no plans to attend the nightmare of a barbecue with all of her old friends and Cami, but Cami's insistence made her question the decision.

"I actually haven't decided yet," she said. "I thought it might be nice to hang out with the old gang for the night. Like a little rewind, even if it's fleeting. I don't want to feel like I have to avoid all of you for the next twenty years."

Cami's face clouded over. "You're not serious."

Alicia shrugged. "Why not, Cami? I'm obviously persona non grata with everyone in your orbit, so I can either meekly accept that and hide away, or I can try to rebuild some of the goodwill I used to have with these people. They were my friends, too. I know they were your friends first, and closer to you, but that doesn't mean that I can just walk away unscathed."

"Didn't you?"

"Absolutely not—"

Cami shook her head and interrupted. "It doesn't matter."

Alicia scoffed as Cami walked away. She was right, it didn't matter. Alicia knew what she'd felt and how it had affected her, and Cami's dismissal didn't make it any less true. She angrily shot off a text to Sam to ask if she was free for Jack and Violet's cookout. She didn't want to raise eyebrows, but she also didn't want to be standing by herself in a corner nursing a frozen mudslide while everyone else happily played cornhole. She winced at herself for dragging Sam into the whole mess, but she'd been invited at the same time. It would be fine. Maybe the only way to really put her past behind her would be to confront it head-on.

There was no point in dwelling on it. Cami had no interest in speaking with her or rekindling *anything*, so Alicia had no choice but to move forward. It wasn't like she could just slink back to Somerville and live with her cousin again or find a new place with no ties. All of that took money and passion for the project. Alicia had neither.

She took a deep breath and headed toward the podium where the family members were giving interviews. Laurie Garrett's sister was there, eyes red and puffy. She had two blown up pictures of Laurie, one where she was in line at Six Flags with giant red sunglasses on, flashing the peace sign to the camera, and in the other, she was holding a newborn. In both photos, Laurie was smiling and happy. *Smart. Humanize her as much as possible. If anyone is hesitant to come forward, this could certainly help.*

Beverly Lawson didn't seem to have the same crowd rallied for her. Beverly's mother, a frail, sad-looking woman, sat in a folding chair next to the podium. Her legs didn't touch the ground. She mostly looked straight ahead, but every once in a while, she'd shield her eyes and look to the sky. The other reporters were gathered around the Garretts, so Alicia walked over to Mrs. Lawsons's chair.

"Hi, Mrs. Lawson. I'm Alicia with the *Knox County Sun*. Do you mind if I ask you a couple questions?" Alicia didn't use her phone to record. She pulled out her notebook and pen instead.

Mrs. Lawson shrugged. "I guess so. I don't have much to tell you. When it was just an old spinster like my Beverly who turned up dead, there didn't seem to be as much of a hullabaloo as there is now that a young career type met the same fate. I'm not saying it's the police's fault, but I do think they could have done more."

"How?" Alicia asked. She wasn't sure if Mrs. Lawson was talking in the abstract or if she actually knew something that wasn't acted upon.

"I don't know, exactly. But you see on those television shows. They have all kinds of technology now that can solve murders. DNA and blood splatter and those mass spectrometer things. Something should have been brought in to find out what happened to Beverly. She was a good woman, you know."

Alicia nodded. "I believe you."

"She stayed out of everyone's business. Did the crossword puzzle in your paper. Every day. Fed the pigeons that gathered on our lawn. Some neighbors thought they were a nuisance, but Bev didn't care." Mrs. Lawson's rheumy eyes watered. "She always said, 'I can only take care of my little corner of the world, and dammit, I'm going to do the best I can.' I took to feeding them when she was no longer around, but I won't be here forever. What will happen to the pigeons?"

Alicia found herself speechless, with a golf-ball sized lump in her throat. With everything going on around her, Mrs. Lawson clung to the well-being of the pigeons. Something she could control in her own little corner of the world.

"I don't know," Alicia said quietly. "But I promise you that as long as I live in this town, I'll fill the bird feeder every time I pass your house. Beverly's legacy doesn't have to die out. I'm sure when I can no longer do it, someone else will step up and take the reins."

She had no idea if that was true, but the despondency in Mrs. Lawson's eyes was too much to bear. Adding some seeds to a feeder seemed like the least Alicia could do.

"You're a good woman, too." Mrs. Lawson said. She patted Alicia's hand. "I don't know who did this to Beverly, but I can tell you that they didn't have a reason. This wasn't a revenge killing or anything like that. Beverly didn't have many friends, but she didn't have any enemies, either. She just was. This is something more sinister than an old boyfriend coming to get his retribution or someone looking for a big payout. Beverly only had a small life insurance policy, enough to cover her services. Whoever did this did it because they have the devil inside."

Alicia wrote down the bulk of what Mrs. Lawson said, but she didn't think she'd need to refer to her notebook much. A chill ran down her spine. Maybe for her next meeting with Cami, she'd focus on the connection between the two women. There had to be *something*.

Chapter Nine

"You do know that detectives don't usually attend these events, right?" Katie asked. She smirked at Cami as she was organizing the applesauce cups and canned beef stew.

"Yes, I am aware of that," Cami answered sarcastically. "But we're also having the Paint Oakview anti-graffiti thing in town today, so most of the department is tied up in that. Once we get a name or address for that junk van, I'm out of here. Here, do the oatmeal."

Katie handed the box of instant oatmeal cups to Taryn. They'd been married for nearly fifteen years, so words weren't necessary. Taryn nodded and went to work sorting the brown sugar cinnamon from the peaches 'n cream.

"Cram-a-Cruiser is one of our most popular food drives of the year. We're doing fairly well, but I feel like people just aren't coming out as much these last few weeks. Everyone's afraid we have a serial killer hiding in plain sight, and no one wants to be around for the next unprovoked attack." Katie stood and brushed her long dark hair away from her face. "Just feels like we're waiting for the other shoe to drop."

"I feel the same way," Cami told her. It was true. Even the air felt different. As though it were thick with secrets and tainted with invisible darkness. There were jolts of laughter and a sense of community, doing a good deed for the less fortunate, but the mood would quickly turn somber and sullen in the heavy silence.

Taryn seemed to realize a need for a mood lightener. She pushed aside the oatmeal and reached for the mac and cheese. "Violet told me about their little run-in with Alicia at Birdie's the other night."

Cami dramatically rolled her eyes and groaned. "Why does everyone think I need every detail about Alicia's life? I have enough to deal with right now without worrying about what she's doing. She obviously came back to make my life hell, but I can honestly say I have no idea why."

Taryn made eyes at Katie, who shrugged. "Please don't kill me for saying this. You know I am one hundred percent on your side. Of everything."

Cami braced herself.

"I just wonder if maybe, possibly, she came back because she truly did realize she made a mistake," Taryn continued. "And I'm not minimizing it in any way, I promise you. It wasn't just a mistake. It was a colossal, poorly handled, life-altering, terrible judgment mistake. And I know how much you suffered."

She clasped Cami's hand.

The physical contact made Cami's eyes well up, so she looked at the ground. Dammit, when had she gotten so *emotional* about every little thing?

"But maybe she suffered, too. Maybe after all this time, she found the courage to try to right her wrongs or at least show you—and us—that she realizes her disappearing act was unfair and did a remarkable amount of damage. She reached out to us. All of us. Too late, of course, the damage had been done, but I do wonder what she would have told me if I'd picked up her call instead of letting it go to voice mail."

Katie grumbled something about "Oh, poor Alicia," but Cami didn't join in. She didn't have the heart for it right then, not with everything else going on. As much as her anger toward Alicia hadn't dissipated—and never, ever would—and even though Alicia's reemergence was proving to be a giant thorn in her side, maybe there was a *tiny* nugget of truth in what Taryn was saying.

"I don't know." Taryn refocused her attention on the bright blue boxes of macaroni. "I'm not saying you should forgive her or anything, but maybe ruining your life isn't actually her priority."

"Then why did she write that article the way that she did? She really made us look bad. I didn't get from Brandt that the point of these monthly articles was to undermine our police work."

Katie pointed at Taryn indignantly. "Exactly. There was no reason for her to do that."

Taryn just rolled her eyes and ignored Katie completely. "I urge you to reread the article. Yes, there were definitely some parts of it that painted the Oakview PD as out of their league on this. But she actually did a nice write up on *you*. Aside from the 'evasive' line or whatever it was, she basically referenced you as a local hero. She mentioned the time you saved those two fawns from Copper Lake, when you handed out quarts of Aunt Ginny's Black Pepper Ice Cream to the construction workers on Route 202, and the time you helped raise all that money for those people facing eviction. She threw in a couple things about Brandt and some of the other officers, but there was a heavy focus on you."

"I don't remember reading that." Cami had read the article when the paper was dropped on her desk, but she'd skimmed the background piece to focus on their handling of the murder case that was on the forefront of everyone's mind. "And even still, I may be a local-yokel hero, but when it comes to real investigating, I'm a chump? That doesn't exactly make it better."

Katie opened her mouth to agree, but Cami shot her a look. She appreciated the commiseration, but it wasn't helping. Katie went back to her checklists without further comment.

"All I'm saying is that you should reread it now that the initial shock has worn off. It wasn't a glowing recommendation, but it also wasn't a hatchet job."

She nodded but didn't want to talk about it anymore. There were so many feelings stirred up since that day in the diner, Cami didn't want them to overwhelm her. She just needed to focus on the things she could control instead of the things she couldn't. And right then, fitting about twelve boxes of food into a four-door sedan was the one thing she had complete control over.

❖

The call about the black van came a short while after Cami had finished packing up the cruiser. She met Kelsey at the car rental service located in the end unit of a run-down strip mall a few towns over. Through the six-foot fence, Cami looked at the fleet of vehicles that ranged from old vans and out-of-commission tow trucks to a sleek little Ferrari parked all by itself in the far corner.

Cami followed Kelsey through the glass door into a small lobby. Like every small automotive shop she'd ever seen, there was a slight sheen of grease on everything. She could see a man working on the underside of an SUV through the glass wall to the shop area.

A young woman working at the counter greeted them warmly. "I think I spoke to you on the phone earlier?" she asked.

Kelsey nodded. "Yes, that was me. Good to meet you, Elaine."

"You too. Rod will be with you in just a moment." Elaine disappeared into a back office while Cami and Kelsey looked around.

Cami knew it was a long shot, since driving around at night wasn't illegal, and there was a good chance the van had nothing to do with Laurie Garrett's murder, but grasping at straws was all they had.

Kelsey sat on the velvet-covered bench near the entrance, her gray slacks covered in a fine mist of dirt from the unpaved parking lot. Cami was too uptight to sit and walked around the lobby looking at the plethora of business cards they'd taped to the bulletin board.

The office door opened a few minutes later. A balding man in his early sixties emerged with his hand extended. Kelsey and Cami showed him their badges and shook his hand. "Rod Bingham, manager here. What can I do for you today?" he asked, leading them into the office. He shut the door behind them, rattling the decades-old paneling. There were about five different calendars hung on the wall, most of them flipped to the wrong month.

"We need to know who rented one of your vans the other night. The black one that has a Hargrove's decal on the side. Here's the information," Cami said, sliding over a slip of paper containing the pertinent details.

Bingham adjusted his glasses while squinting at the note. "Yes, I should have that. Give me just a minute." He brushed some dust off his keyboard and clicked a few times on the mouse. "Well, that's strange."

Cami perked up. "What?"

"The van was rented out that evening at around seven o'clock. By a man named John Smith. Address listed as 1 Main Street here in Oakview. Phone number is 603-555-1212. He paid cash."

Cami shot Kelsey a look. Main Street was entirely commercial, and Cami didn't even think the buildings started with one. The lowest number she could recall was a hundred. And 555-1212 was the number for Directory Assistance. Maybe there *was* more to this van than they had suspected.

"Do you have a camera in the lobby?" Kelsey asked.

Bingham shook his head. "We had one of those Ring cameras for a while, but the subscription expired. I didn't bother to renew it. We never had a need for it." He looked at the ground in what seemed to be shame.

"Do you have any memory of what the customer looked like?" Cami pulled a small notebook out of the inner pocket of her jacket.

Bingham shook his head again. "I don't handle the intake portion, just the back end. Elaine might remember something. Elaine?"

She poked her head into the office a few seconds later. "Yes?"

Cami turned to her, waving her in. "Do you happen to remember John Smith from Oakview who rented a van here the other night? He was given the black Hargrove's van. Wednesday around seven p.m."

Elaine was visibly uncomfortable. "Not really. Why?"

"We have some questions relating to an investigation. Can you tell us what protocols you have in place? Do you take a copy of the renter's license, anything like that?" Kelsey stood from the chair in front of Bingham's desk.

He did, too. "Yes, the employees are advised to take copies of licenses and confirm all information that's provided on our rental forms." He swiped his forehead with the heel of his hand.

"Advised?" Cami raised her eyebrow. "Is it a requirement? How is it enforced?"

Bingham looked at Elaine and then back to Cami. "Yes, it should be done on every transaction."

"Do you have a copy of Mr. Smith's license for the Wednesday rental?" Cami already knew the answer.

"I didn't see one." Bingham cleared his throat. "Elaine, do you have a physical copy that wasn't scanned into the system?"

Elaine pursed her lips. "I don't think so," she whispered.

"What was that?" Kelsey crossed her arms and tilted her head.

"No," Elaine said, louder this time. "I don't have a copy of the license."

"We'll need to see a copy of his contract, please." Cami was beginning to lose patience with both of them.

Elaine nodded and scuttled into the lobby. She flicked through the contents of a manila folder and came up with a filled-in white form. "This is it. We only had a few rentals on Wednesday."

Cami quickly scanned it. John Smith, 1 Main Street, all the same information that Bingham had read off the computer. Under license number, it read NHL87654321.

"None of this stood out to you?" Cami pointed to the license number. "Do you read these forms before you hand over the keys?"

"Normally, I do. But he said he was in a hurry because he had an appointment, and he left his license at home. So I rang him up and got him out of here quickly. I'm really sorry, I didn't know he was doing anything weird. Rod always says to treat the customer like family, so I made sure—"

"That's not true, Elaine," Bingham interrupted. "Well, it is, but I never said to cut corners."

"When anyone from Jake's Towing or that bar downtown comes in, you always say to get them in and out without a hassle."

Bingham smiled much too widely. His nerves were apparent. "Again, I didn't mean—"

Kelsey interrupted this time. "Mr. Bingham, we're not here to discuss your business practices, as lacking as they might be. We need to focus on *this* transaction. We can dig a little deeper once we have this particular situation worked out."

He swallowed. "That's fine, we'll obviously have to have a refresher on our protocols and record keeping," he said. He looked pointedly at Elaine, who had the proverbial deer-in-the-headlights look on her face.

"Elaine," Cami said, bringing the focus back to the rental customer. "Is there any particular reason you let this customer get away with giving false information? Why didn't you demand a copy of his license?"

"I didn't actually review the form until he left. By then it was too late. I figured I could update the system when he returned the car. But he just left the keys in the drop box." She blew out a deep breath. "I didn't think much of it because I recognized him from TV."

Cami snapped her head up from the form she was still reading. "From TV?"

"Yeah. He's in those commercials they play during Sox games. You know, the one for the bank where he's standing in front of a building shaking hands and waving to little kids." Elaine deepened her voice to mimic the line from the commercial. "'Evan Conley, CEO, Partner, and Friend.'"

Chapter Ten

"You're here again?" Jade asked, smiling.

"I know, I know," Alicia said. "My internet's been spotty, so I came in. It's probably fixed by now, but I hate to leave these beautiful screens."

"You're here again?"

Alicia turned to see Sam walking through the kitchen door, a steaming cup of coffee in her hand. "*Yes*. Jeez, I didn't realize coming into the office a couple times a week made me a fixture."

"At least you're a nice fixture. You class the place up." Sam winked before taking a seat at a nearby desk.

Alicia smiled and booted up her laptop. She wasn't sure how she felt about Sam's flirting. It felt good to be noticed and appreciated, that was for sure. She liked Sam, and they had a nice time when they went out, but Alicia kept waiting for a spark or the inexplicable tickle in her stomach, and it wasn't happening. At least, not yet.

Or maybe Alicia was just at a point in her life where that sort of thing didn't happen anymore. There was no reason *not* to feel it with Sam; she was pretty, good sense of humor, driven, seemed to be very interested in pursuing something with Alicia. She'd had that *zhuzh* she craved with Cami, there was no question about it. But she'd also been younger and more willing to let herself become enveloped by whatever felt right. Maybe that ship had sailed.

"Have you finished that piece on the DUI boaters on Copper Lake? Seems to be happening more and more. Harbor patrol has been on high alert since that Jet Ski crash last summer. I'd like to get it out before the late spring tourists start showing up." Jade inspected the nail on her index finger while Alicia pulled up the article.

"Almost. I wanted to talk to you about the layout. Are we thinking—"

Their conversation was interrupted by a blast of cool air as the outside door opened. Alicia's heart sank when Cami walked in.

Cami glanced at Alicia but focused on Jade. She leaned in. "Can I talk to you in your office for a second?"

Jade crossed her arms defiantly. "You can say whatever you need to say right here, Detective Lyons. We don't want any ethical misunderstandings, do we?"

Cami bit her lip and looked at the wall. Alicia had seen that look many times before. She was contemplating something. "Okay," Cami said, sighing. "Would you mind coming down to the station with me to answer a few questions?"

The crossed arms of defiance slowly broke apart. Jade's demeanor went from condescension to concern. "Why? Have I done something illegal?"

"No. Your husband is at the station now. We need to corroborate some facts about Wednesday evening."

Alicia's head was swimming. What had Evan done? Why did Cami need Jade? Alicia instinctively put a hand on her arm.

Jade squeezed her hand and took a step toward Cami but faltered. Cami and Alicia both jumped to steady her.

"She's okay," Cami said, nodding to Alicia. "Just a little shocked, I'm sure."

"I'm fine," Jade said. "I'd like Alicia to come with me if that's okay."

Alicia's eyes widened. Of course she'd go with her, but she was surprised that Jade had even requested it. She exuded more independence and confidence than anyone Alicia had ever known.

"Yes, that's okay," Cami confirmed after a brief hesitation. "Do you want to ride with me, or would you prefer to have Alicia drive?"

"We can ride with you," Jade said.

Another surprise. So Alicia's car would be left at the office, and she'd be at Cami's mercy for a ride home? *Enough.* Obviously, Jade needed her, which was unexpected anyway, so Alicia needed to focus on her and not herself.

Cami looked at Alicia apprehensively. She appreciated the sentiment because she felt the same way. Jade took a deep breath and led the way to Cami's Jeep, keeping her head high. Sam stood in the corner of the office, her untouched coffee probably cold by now. Her expression was something between concern and shock. She couldn't have heard the conversation, but she clearly knew something was wrong. Alicia gave her a small wave on their way out.

The green Jeep looked the same. Still had the Lake Winnisquam sticker on the back window, the tiny dent near the taillight that Cami had freaked out over when they came out of HomeGoods. There had been a shopping cart nearby, so Cami had assumed that some "lazy-ass degenerate" had just pushed it into her car instead of taking the time to put it into one of the cart corrals. Alicia couldn't help but smile at the memory. Cami didn't get angry over much, but certain things set her off. Her Jeep and shoppers leaving carts everywhere were two of them.

Alicia's stomach dropped when Cami clicked the unlock button on her keychain. She hesitated at the door to the back seat. She could see inside where the gray cloth still appeared to be in excellent shape. Even with her farfetched hope of a someday friendship with Cami, she'd never honestly believed she'd ever sit in that Jeep again. The SUV they'd taken on so many road trips, held hands in while watching movies at one of the last remaining drive-ins in the state, loaded up with groceries and small children when Alicia had her brother's kids for the weekend.

When she realized she'd been standing there for a beat too long, she opened the door, and the scent that wafted up almost made her pass out right then and there. It was just so fucking familiar. The smell of Cami's favorite Little Tree air freshener, coconut, always coconut, mixed with the leathery smell of her messenger bag, and just a hint of Cami's perfume. It was almost too much.

"You okay?" Cami asked, adjusting her rearview mirror.

Alicia nodded, not realizing that her eyes had filled. She couldn't manage to get out any words, so she just nodded again. She clicked her seat belt, and they rode in relative silence to the police station. It was easier to just look out the window.

❖

"Are we going into an interrogation room?" Jade clutched her purse as though it would be taken away from her at any moment.

The police station wasn't bustling the way Alicia had pictured it. On a regular day, it wasn't busy at all, and there were usually a few officers standing around yukking it up about the Patriots or the snowfall. But Alicia had assumed that with the current state of their town, there would be hot and cold running police, medical examiners, forensic experts, and just about anyone else she'd expect to see after two murders. Small town journalism had obscured a few truths.

"No," Cami said quickly. "We're just having a conversation. You're not in any trouble at all. The only reason we're here is so we can get your statement on the record. We'll sit in my office."

"Can Alicia sit with us? For moral support. I'm nervous."

Alicia bit her bottom lip. Was that how things worked? Were people allowed to have someone in with them while they were being questioned by the police? And why did Jade want her in there in the first place?

"Well, it's not generally how it's done, but since this isn't an interrogation, I suppose it should be okay. You don't have to be nervous, Jade, I promise." Cami gestured to the two open chairs in front of her desk.

Alicia looked around Cami's office. Not much had changed, though the framed picture of the two of them in Disney World she'd had sitting on her filing cabinet had been replaced with an inspirational canvas that read, *Believe There Is Good In The World.*

"Now, what's going on?" Jade asked.

Cami folded her hands in front of her and quickly unfolded them. Another habit of hers that Alicia remembered. She usually did that when she was trying to figure out how to act in any given situation, usually in a professional setting. Funny how things stayed the same no matter how much they appeared to change.

"We need to know what was going on last Wednesday night. The eighteenth. Do you remember if you were at home?" Cami asked.

Alicia appreciated the gentle way Cami asked questions. She had no idea why this information was necessary, but she wasn't entirely surprised that Evan was suspected of doing something shady. He had that air about him. Alicia always wondered how someone as down to earth as Jade had ended up with someone so dodgy. Looks only went so far.

"Can I see your calendar?" Jade licked her lips and studied the desk blotter Cami turned toward her. "I was, uh, at the office until about seven, I think. I picked up pad thai on my way home." She hesitated, thinking. "Yes, that was last Wednesday. I remember preparing for my Thursday interviews while I was eating. They didn't add enough peanuts."

"Excellent, thank you. That's a perfect detail. Now, do you remember where Evan was that night?" Cami asked.

Jade looked at Alicia. Alicia didn't know what she wanted; confirmation that it was okay to give Cami that information? There were many things that Alicia didn't know, but she *did* know that Cami wasn't trying to trap Jade into something that would hurt her. She nodded her affirmation.

"Well, I don't think he came home until late that night. I went to bed around midnight, and he wasn't back yet. I think he had a work dinner or something with one of the bank's investors. I might be wrong on the times, so please don't hold me to that. I didn't keep track or anything."

"Estimates are fine. This is really helpful. Did Evan say anything about his dinner the next morning? Did he give any details?"

Seeing Jade near tears broke Alicia's heart. But she held herself together. "No, I don't remember any. I only spoke to him briefly in the morning. Probably about breakfast or something. I left before he had even showered."

Cami nodded. "Understood. For this next part, I do need to speak with you alone, if that's okay. Alicia, would you mind stepping out for a few minutes?"

Alicia turned to Jade, who just stared straight ahead. Cami gave Alicia a tight-lipped smile that she interpreted as a sign that Jade really wouldn't like what she was about to hear. Alicia stood and squeezed Jade's shoulder. "I'll be right outside if you need me."

Jade patted her hand lightly.

When Alicia exited Cami's office, Kelsey was standing by the front desk. She'd come a long way from the young officer that Alicia had met so many years ago.

"Hi, Alicia, how are you?" Kelsey asked.

"I'm okay. Things are weird," Alicia said, nodding toward Cami's office.

"Very."

Behind Kelsey, a poster of Barbara Lawson and Laurie Garrett was on a metal stand with an array of phone numbers beneath the pictures. Cami couldn't want to speak to Jade about Evan in regard to *that*, right?

Right?

CHAPTER ELEVEN

Cami sat across from Evan Conley, who had positioned himself defiantly in his seat. Forensics had gone over the interior and exterior of the van, although it had appeared to have been cleaned recently. For a rental, it was in remarkably good shape.

The report had come in quicker than they'd expected. While they didn't find blood or a building block or anything as outwardly incriminating, they did find some trace evidence: a couple of gray fibers on the back of the passenger seat. They didn't have the results as to whether it was a match with Laurie Garrett's sweater yet, but it was more than enough to bring Conley in for questioning.

Kelsey stood in the corner of the small conference room, her hands in her blazer pockets. She was always more comfortable standing, so Cami usually had to convince her to sit to make whoever they were questioning more at ease. This time, she let her stand without saying anything.

"What do you want from me now? I have a business to run, you know. I didn't want to get a lawyer since we're just a couple of townies have a conversation, but it looks like I may need to?" Conley asked, thrumming his fingers on the table. "I already told you about Wednesday, I was home watching TV. A rerun of *Friends*, I think."

"Yes, you did. But there are a few things that aren't adding up, so we need you to fill in the blanks. That's all," Cami said with a wave. They could both play the game.

"Can't help you with any gaps. I was home in bed." Conley shrugged.

"At seven p.m.?" Kelsey asked.

"No, but I was probably up in my office at that time. Paying bills, who knows? But I went to bed early, watched some TV, and fell asleep. So whatever it is you think that I'm involved in, you're wrong."

Cami tilted her head toward Kelsey. She nodded and slipped a photograph of Laurie Garrett in front of Conley. He rolled his eyes and put on his reading glasses. He froze when he saw the photo, stared at it for a second, and then removed his glasses. Cami shot a look at Kelsey. She'd noticed it, too.

"Do you know who this is?" Cami asked.

"I don't believe so."

"Mm-hmm. We spoke with your wife, Evan. You weren't home on Wednesday night. At least not until after midnight. So where were you?" Cami asked, leaning back in her chair.

Some mix of anger and worry clouded Conley's face. "Why do you immediately assume *I'm* the one with the bad info? Jade probably just mixed up her nights. And why are you talking to my wife?"

She ignored his question. "She gave verifiable details about that night. And we received word from another source that you were at Bingham's Auto on Wednesday evening. You rented a large van using an alias. Wednesday happened to be the night that Laurie Garrett was killed, and the van you were driving was spotted near the scene. Maybe you mixed up *your* nights, Evan. If you can confirm why you were near the scene of the crime in a rented van, we can clear your name and move on with our investigation. Does any of this jog your memory?" Cami tapped her finger on the picture of Laure Garrett.

Conley opened his mouth to speak and then quickly closed it. He looked at the table and took a deep breath, seemingly gathering his courage. After a long moment, he met Cami's eyes. "I need to speak to my lawyer."

❖

On her drive home, Cami was having a hard time shaking the frustration of the interview with Evan Conley. She had a feeling he'd lawyer up, but she'd hoped for *something* they could run with. He gave them nothing, except for the fact that he was willing to throw his wife under the bus if it'd save his ass. Other than that, nothing.

Still, it was the closest they'd come to an actual suspect. There wasn't much of a motive, or anything tying Conley to Laurie Garrett—or Barbara Lawson, for that matter—but there was enough there to draw some lines, wavy as they might have been.

The barbecue at Violet and Jack's was probably in full swing by that point. Cami checked the clock again to see if she could just bag out of it. The thought of going to Violet's and being around all kinds of people sounded pretty terrible. But it was their first of the year, and Violet had practically begged her to go after the whole inviting Alicia debacle, so Cami felt like a heel not showing up. She supposed she could go, have a quick burger, and blame work on a hasty exit.

By the time she got home, she felt like going out again even less. She sucked it up and changed into jeans and a light sweatshirt. An evening in late April that topped out in the sixties in New England was a gift. She was positive the kids would be in shorts and T-shirts. She tried twisting her long curls into a messy ponytail, but it looked more messy than chic. For her whole life, people had complimented her on her natural curly hair, but Cami found its unruliness more of a nuisance than a blessing. *Grass is always greener and all that.* She decided to just leave it down.

Her phone chimed with a text message, Violet asking her where the hell she was. Cami rolled her eyes and texted back, *OMW*. That seemed to satisfy Violet since she didn't feel the need to respond. Another pop-up chimed on her phone, that one from a ticket reseller she'd used in the past to buy Red Sox tickets. She clicked on it to delete it, but the full message popped up before she had a chance.

Hey Alicia! It's been a while since we've heard from you...

Cami deleted the message and closed her eyes. Apparently, they'd used Alicia's name to purchase the tickets the last time she'd gone to a game, probably five or six years ago. The more she tried to distance herself from all things Alicia, the faster they seemed to come at her.

It had been a warm, sunny, August afternoon in Boston. The Sox were in the hunt for the wildcard, so the tickets were outrageously expensive, but Cami had insisted that they go. Alicia had never been to Fenway Park, so Cami was dead set on making sure she had the full experience. They'd gotten there early, walked around the park drinking ten-dollar beers in clear Solo cups. They'd each had a Fenway Frank in their lower grandstand seats, had even waved the Cracker Jack vendor over so they could share a bag. Cami had looked at Alicia cheering and screaming for the team, her beer sloshing over the side of her cup, her baseball cap backward on her sea of dark hair, and realized just how deeply she'd loved the woman sitting beside her. She'd been about to take Alicia's hand to profess how she'd been feeling when a pop-up baseball had headed straight for them.

Someone behind them had yelled "Heads," but it was too late. Cami had tried to deflect the ball with her hand, but she'd missed. Alicia had covered her head with her hands, thankfully, because the ball had landed right on her left pinky finger. She'd yelled out in pain, and the ball had bounced into the aisle and under one of the rows in front of them. A beefy guy with the sleeves cut off his T-shirt had held up the ball triumphantly.

Alicia had held out her finger to Cami, who'd swallowed hard. The finger was bent at an angle no finger should ever bend. An older man a few rows back had yelled at the guy to give Alicia the ball. The guy had shaken his head and told the man to mind his own business, which had prompted others around them to get in on the action. Soon after, a rousing chorus of "Give the lady the ball" was being chanted by their entire section. Shamed into it, the guy had handed over the baseball.

When they were sitting in the stadium infirmary getting a splint, Alicia had turned to Cami, her face streaked with dried tears, and tossed the ball to her with her good hand. "I want you to have it," she'd said. "Because you're quite the catch, baby."

Cami had groaned but wrapped Alicia up in her arms. She'd pulled away slightly and kissed her; Alicia's lips had still hinted at the spearmint flavor from the lip gloss she'd applied earlier. Cami had been so thankful Alicia hadn't taken a direct hit to the head. They'd gone home content that night, with a goody bag from the Fenway customer relations team and two ticket vouchers to see a game at a later date. Alicia's finger had hurt, but it would go on to heal as though it had never happened. Cami was satisfied that Alicia had received the *full* Red Sox game experience.

Out of habit, Cami looked at the shelf below the TV where that baseball had sat encased in plastic for a few years. Now, it was stashed in a box in the back of her closet along with some old gloves and a CD player-alarm clock.

Cami locked the door behind her and headed over to Violet's barbecue, even though she really didn't want to. She would have preferred to just stay home and flip on the Major League Baseball channel.

Chapter Twelve

It had been a long time since Alicia had been to one of Violet and Jack's parties. Whenever they did anything, they did it big. She pulled up to their house where a long parade of cars already lined the street. Her stomach fluttered at the thought of seeing so many people that she hadn't seen since she'd left. Even people who didn't have an effect on her life, like Jack's cousins, must have known what had happened, even if only on the surface. She and Cami had been joined at the hip for all parties and get-togethers, so seeing Cami on her own must have been telling.

Alicia sighed at the thought.

"Nice house," Sam said, looking up at the meticulous colonial. It was technically still too early in the season for flowers, but that hadn't stopped Violet. She had oak buckets filled with lilies and greens and solar lights lining the front walkway.

"They do a beautiful job on their landscape," Alicia said absentmindedly. She'd picked up Sam at her apartment, and they'd made small talk on the way to the barbecue, but her heart wasn't in it. Alicia was having big-time second thoughts about attending. What if everyone was rude to her because they didn't really want her there? What if Cami didn't show up as a protest to Alicia's appearance? What if…

She didn't have time to think too much more about it since Sam was already on her way to the backyard. Alicia hurried to catch up. Walking in alone sounded like the worst possible scenario.

Jack met them at the gate. He was already a few drinks in by the glassiness of his eyes. "You made it," he yelled and gave Sam a quick hug. Alicia deeply appreciated his easygoing and friendly nature at that moment.

"Alicia, good to see you." He hugged her and opened the gate wider to allow them entrance.

The backyard was decorated just as she remembered. String lights hanging everywhere, the huge bar with a beach umbrella covering it, stations set up for the kids like horseshoes and Nerf guns, and a buffet table that stretched for a mile. She felt both at home and like a total outsider. It was hard to reconcile.

Violet caught sight of them and came right over. As a hostess, her guests' feeling welcome had always been her number one priority, and Alicia was relieved to see that that hadn't changed. Violet took her hands and smiled. "I'm glad you could make it. Please, grab a drink and something to eat. Sam, nice to see you again. We have a pool table in the basement. I think we need a rematch."

Alicia scanned the crowd. She recognized Violet's family and some of Jack's. Her stomach dropped a little when she saw Katie and Taryn sitting at a small patio table having cocktails and chicken wings.

"She's not here yet," Violet whispered.

Alicia startled. "Oh, yeah, I wasn't—" She didn't finish her sentence since she was pretty sure she wouldn't be able to come up with something convincing anyway.

"Those watermelon champagne coolers look delicious." Sam grabbed Alicia's arm and led her to the bar.

Jack's brother was playing bartender. "Here you go, ladies." He handed them two fizzy pink drinks with watermelon slices hanging over the side as garnish. They really had gone all out.

"Sam," a voice called from the patio area. Alicia turned to see a group of women she didn't know waving her over.

"Oh, it's the girls I played softball with last year. Come join us," Sam said.

Alicia shook her head. "You go ahead. I want to say hello to Violet's family."

Sam nodded and ran to her friends. The last thing Alicia felt like doing was meeting new people. She wondered if she could just fake a headache and leave. Sam wouldn't have a problem finding a ride home. It had been a mistake going there at all.

"Well, hello, stranger."

Alicia turned and came face-to-face with Taryn. Three years was a blink of time and also an eternity. Taryn's dark brown hair had a streak of gray that Alicia didn't remember being there before. Contact lenses had replaced her signature wireless frames. She was still thin, but her face was fuller than it had been the last time Alicia had seen her.

"Taryn, hi," Alicia said. She was trying not to gush. She wanted to bear-hug Taryn for being friendly, but that seemed inappropriate at the moment. "You look so good."

Taryn smiled. "So do you. You haven't changed a bit. I didn't know if you'd all of a sudden sound like an Aussie."

"I don't think it happens that quickly," Alicia said, chuckling. "Although I did feel the urge to ask what concoction Jack was whipping up on the barbie."

"Seems like everyone was surprised you came back to Oakview." Taryn nodded to a group of people talking. They were looking over at them, and one person, Alicia thought maybe one of Violet's friends from college, pointed. They quickly turned when they realized Alicia and Taryn were looking at them. "I'm not surprised at all. Just surprised it took you so long."

"Yeah?" Alicia was genuinely curious how Taryn was seemingly so comfortable with her. "I was kind of surprised by it myself, to be quite honest. With the way things went down and the…unpleasant reactions to my reaching out to those I was close to, I didn't think I'd ever come back. But the pull was too great, I guess. I sometimes wonder if I made the right decision."

Taryn nodded. "I understand that. I mean, I won't sugarcoat it. The way you left sucked. Truly, truly sucked."

Thanks for that.

"But I do think there is a distinct possibility that you've realized that, and that your need to right wrongs may have pushed you back here. If that's the case, I say good." Taryn raised her cocktail and drank to Alicia.

Don't cry, don't cry, don't cry.

"I appreciate that." Alicia's voice cracked a little, but she didn't think Taryn heard it. "I really am sorry. I feel like I say that so often that the word has become meaningless. But believe me, if I had a do-over, I'd take it. I wish I could rewind the clock to the day before I bought that plane ticket and smack myself. Hard."

"You know that Katie is fiercely loyal to Cami, and it'll take her a while to come around. But I'm sure she will eventually. Even if you two can't be friends again, she'll at least be civil. Is that what you want? To be friends again? Like it was?" Taryn cocked her head.

Alicia sighed. "I'm not under any illusions that it'll be like it was. Looking back, that was the best time of my life. I had a six-month aberration and fucked everything up beyond repair. I think I just missed my old life, and I wanted to be part of it again. Even if I have to stay on the outskirts."

Taryn pursed her lips. "Took a lot of nerve for you to show up here tonight, I'll give you that. That girl you brought with you, is she your date?"

"No," Alicia answered quickly. "Work friend."

"Taryn!"

They turned. Katie was standing with one hand on the table and one hand on her hip. "Yeah?"

Katie held her hand out, clearly asking if Taryn was coming.

She laughed. "Her highness is calling. I'll talk to her. You know, if you can somehow make up with the head of the snake, the body will follow. Food for thought."

"Thanks, Taryn. It was really good to see you. I missed you."

"I missed you, too."

Taryn went back to the table. Katie made a few frantic hand gestures and said something Alicia couldn't make out. Taryn rolled her eyes and stuck a plate of cheese and crackers in front of her.

It hurt to know how much Katie was against her general existence anywhere the friend group would be, but Alicia also knew it wasn't unwarranted. She hoped Taryn was right, and that Katie would eventually forgive her and welcome her back in whatever manner that might be. The conversation had filled Alicia's heart with optimism.

Sam was still talking with her softball friends, and Violet and Jack were playing some game that looked like musical chairs with the kids. Alicia took the opportunity to check out the buffet. She filled her plate with a variety of salads and some extra-gooey mac and cheese. She was reaching for a napkin when she heard the gate open, so she looked up to see who had arrived.

Her heart stopped.

Cami walked in, her long hair falling in soft waves over her shoulders. She had on snug-fitting black jeans and a cropped, long-sleeved, red T-shirt that said Portsmouth across the front in faded white letters. She wore her black-and-white Chuck Taylors that she'd owned for a decade yet somehow managed to keep looking new. Her face lit up as Violet's son Gavin ran up and threw his arms around her waist. She put an arm around his shoulders and allowed herself to be led to the game stations.

Alicia just stood there with her plate in her hand, watching Cami laugh and play with the kids. She threw a horseshoe, and it hit perfectly, so she raised her arms in the air and cheered. Alicia couldn't help but smile.

"She won't stay mad forever."

Alicia jumped out of her Cami-induced trance, and her plate nearly toppled to the ground. Thankfully, she only lost a few chunks of potato salad. "You always catch me in compromising positions that aren't actually what they seem. I was trying to decide if I wanted a cheeseburger to go along with my smorgasbord," Alicia lied.

Violet wasn't buying it. "Sure. Well, if you decide you want one, make sure you ask Danny for his teriyaki burger special. It's out of this world. I'll let you go back to your super-serious decision making."

Alicia shook her head as Violet walked away. Was she some sort of masochist but just didn't realize it? It wasn't like she'd show up to the party and Cami would just give her a hug and ask if she wanted to play lawn darts.

She thought about leaving again when Cami looked in her direction and caught her eye. Her smile faded. *Fuck.* Alicia's stomach turned over. Rather than prolong the inevitable, Alicia broke eye contact first and sat at a nearby picnic table to pick at her food since her appetite had all but vanished.

Sam slid onto the bench at the other side of the table. "They really know how to throw a party, huh? The girls are getting a beer pong table together. I haven't played since I was about twenty. Have you tried these little banh mi baguette things? To die for." Sam stuffed a big bite into her mouth. "When you're finished, you wanna play? We could make it interesting if you're up for it." Sam wiggled her eyebrows.

"I actually have a little bit of a headache. I think I might head home after this. But please, stay and have fun. Do you think one of your friends could give you a ride home?"

Sam's face fell. "No, it's fine if you don't feel good. I'll leave with you. I don't mind."

"No, honestly. Stay. You're having a good time, and you should. Violet does throw a great party."

"Well, only if you're sure. I don't want you to leave by yourself if you're sick."

"Just a small headache, I promise."

"Okay. I'll give you a call or shoot you a text to check in." Sam leaned over the table and kissed her on the cheek.

"Thank you." Alicia smiled.

As soon as Sam was back with her friends, Alicia couldn't stop her gaze from drifting to find Cami. She wasn't with the group of kids anymore, and she wasn't with Katie and Taryn. Maybe she was so pissed off that Alicia had shown up that she'd left. Alicia sighed again and grabbed her phone and her keys. She should have stuck with the original plan to skip the barbecue.

"Don't leave on my account." Cami stood behind the picnic table with a bottle of Sam Adams in hand.

Alicia straightened, surprised and also nervous. This was the first time Cami had initiated contact, which could have meant she was ready to have it out with Alicia for coming back. Alicia wasn't sure she was up for a fight at that moment. She was exhausted, though she couldn't pinpoint exactly why. "I have a bit of a headache. I was going to go home and lie down." She flipped the carabiner key ring over her index finger. "I know you asked me not to come. I should have respected your wishes, so I'm sorry about that."

Cami shrugged. "I probably didn't have the right to ask you not to come in the first place. I just didn't want to be uncomfortable in my friend's home. But as it turns out, I'm not all that uncomfortable. It's weird to see you here, for sure, but I get the feeling you're a lot more uncomfortable than I am."

Alicia couldn't help but be skeptical. What was Cami's angle? Why was she speaking to her so freely when she'd been so closed off and determined to ignore Alicia in their previous meetups?

Oh, fuck it. "Yes, I probably am," Alicia said with a tight-lipped smile. "Feeling uncomfortable is something I'm getting pretty used to. Were you able to make any headway with Evan Conley?"

"None that I can speak about."

"Jade is convinced that there's been some colossal misunderstanding, but I'm not so sure. I never trusted that guy." Alicia wasn't sure if she should be making small talk or throwing herself at Cami and begging for forgiveness for the fiftieth time.

"I can see why."

There was an awkward pause. Cami continued to stand there, sipping her beer but not saying anything. Alicia was hesitant to give up the only nonbusiness mutual contact she'd had with Cami since she'd been back, but Cami seemed off somehow.

"Okay, well, I'm going to go. Enjoy the party. Food's amazing, as usual," Alicia said. "Have a good night."

"Why? Violet has Advil in the bathroom. I thought you wanted to talk. That's what you've been saying for the last month or however long it's been. I'm here. So talk to me."

Alicia didn't know what to say. Cami took another long swallow of beer and raised her eyebrows, almost a challenge. Alicia supposed she had a point. She'd been desperate to talk to her for the last three-plus years, and apparently, this was her chance, as odd as it might have been.

"Um, okay. Yes, let's talk. You want to go over to those lawn chairs in the corner?" Alicia pointed to a private corner of the yard where two flowery chairs and a small table in the middle sat.

"Lead the way."

Alicia nodded. She stopped by the bar on the way and grabbed another one of the pink drinks that sat on the edge. The ice had melted a little, and the watermelon on the side was kind of wilted, but Alicia didn't care. She took a gulp before heading to the chairs. She tried to ignore Katie's and Taryn's eyes following them. Violet was probably staring from wherever she was, too.

Cami sat and crossed her legs. She gestured to the open seat next to her that Alicia took cautiously. The whole thing felt so fucking weird. She was waiting for someone to jump out of the woods behind them and throw a burlap sack over her head.

Cami spoke first. "Well, Alicia, it's been what? Four years? No, three. I was under the incorrect assumption that I would never see nor speak to you ever again. I can't say I've never thought about this moment and what I would say to you if I ever ran into you, but that day at the diner robbed me of all of my prepared speeches. So now it's your turn. Take your shot. What, after all this time, after all the pain and heartache, after all the confusion and turmoil, after turning my life inside out, do you want to say to me?"

Her head swimming, Alicia was left speechless.

CHAPTER THIRTEEN

Cami's heart was racing, even though she was clearly the one in control. Alicia seemed flustered and nervous, which hadn't been Cami's intent, but she couldn't bring herself to put an end to it. It almost felt justified.

She wasn't surprised to see Alicia; Violet had said she'd be coming, but it still hit like a ton of bricks. Cami had just assumed that Alicia wouldn't show up or that she wouldn't stay long after being ostracized by everyone. Cami had been late, so she didn't know how many people Alicia had interacted with before she arrived, but when she'd seen Alicia sitting at the picnic table by herself, she hadn't been as gleeful as she should have been. She'd actually felt a twinge in her heart that had startled her. She didn't feel *bad* for her, did she? Whatever Alicia faced, it was self-inflicted.

The whole thing happened in some strange fog. Cami felt like she was watching the scene play out in front of her instead of being part of it. She didn't want to hear what Alicia had to say. It didn't matter. She didn't care what Alicia was feeling or what she felt guilty about. It was all in the past, and that was where it needed to stay. *Say it enough, and it'll be true.*

Cami was really trying to fight against the notion that maybe she *did* care a little, and maybe this *wasn't* all a ruse to tell Alicia off once and for all and just be done with her. Forever. She needed to stick to the plan. *Alicia, whatever we had once is gone. There is nothing left between us, friendship or otherwise, so I'd appreciate it if you would extract yourself from my life, and I can just go back to pretending you don't exist.* Maybe not quite so harsh, but that was what needed to be said.

Steeling herself to say those things, Cami took another sip of beer that was now lukewarm. She choked down another swallow while Alicia fiddled with the hem of her shirt. Cami remembered that shirt. Alicia had bought it off Amazon and wanted to return it because she'd said it was too pastel-y and too tight. Cami had told her not to return it, *please*, because it fit her perfectly in all the right places, and the color brought out the blue in her eyes, making them even more striking than usual. Alicia had rolled her eyes and scoffed, but she hadn't returned the shirt.

Funny that she wore it to Violet's barbecue. Much to Cami's chagrin, it still fit snugly and hugged her in places Cami shouldn't have noticed. She looked to the side and noticed a giant ant crawling up the side of Violet's shed. Good distraction.

Alicia breathed deeply. "Now that I have you here, I'm struggling with what to say. I genuinely didn't think it was going to happen." She laughed humorlessly. "I'm honestly and truly sorry for leaving you in the lurch the way that I did."

Cami sighed. "Alicia, if this is just about more apologies, I get it. You're sorry. Thanks. But what's done is done, so saying sorry a thousand times doesn't erase anything."

"I know, I know," Alicia said, shaking her head. She seemed almost frantic to speak before Cami decided to end the conversation and walk away.

A part of Cami wished she could do that, but a bigger part of her didn't want to. Not yet anyway.

"It's not about that because I can't possibly convey with words the deep, all-encompassing regret that I have about that night. And what followed. I guess I just wanted you to know that I knew almost immediately that I had made a mistake. A colossal, life-altering mistake. But it was too late. Or so I thought, anyway. I was on an airplane in a complete daze, assuming that once I arrived in Perth that I would be overcome with clarity, and everything would make sense since these types of spiritual journeys transform people. I'd read so much about how life-changing walkabouts could be, so I just waited for the change to fall into my lap. It never came because it turns out that it wasn't what I needed."

Cami leaned forward. Her lukewarm beer sloshed in her stomach.

"I was naive," Alicia continued. "That's not an excuse, it's just the truth. I was so wrapped up in the idea that the only way out of my existential crisis was to leave everything I loved behind in order to find this magical lucidity that I soon realized didn't exist. At least, not in the way that I was searching for it. But you know me, Cam." Alicia took a drink and stared at the stars. "Stubborn as a bull. I kept telling myself I just needed more time. Even though every day I spent away from you, from my family, from my *home*, was just driving the wedge deeper and deeper. And I knew it. But when I finally summoned the courage to call you, to see if I was too late, I had my answer. I became very well acquainted with your voice mail over those few months."

Cami shifted in her seat. She knew Alicia was telling the truth, at least in theory. She still had twelve, maybe thirteen voice mails saved on her phone from that spring. She'd never listened to any of them. She couldn't. There was no good that could come of anything Alicia had to say, so Cami had convinced herself that the torture of Alicia's voice wouldn't be worth it. But she never had deleted them. She couldn't seem to do that, either.

"What did you expect, Alicia?" Cami was hoarse and scratchy sounding. "That I'd answer your call, and all would be forgiven? You were right. It was too late. Why didn't you talk to me before everything came crashing down? I didn't even know you were unhappy."

Alicia dropped her head. "And that is truly my biggest regret. I didn't talk to you about it because I didn't know how. I couldn't put a fine point on exactly what was going on with me, so I just said nothing. Trust me, I replay it over and over in my head. Things could have turned out so differently if I'd just been open with you. You were my best friend and my great love, and I lit it all on fire because I was so sure that my existence was meaningless and that if I didn't 'find myself,' I'd shrivel up and die. And I am so fucking sorry."

Tears fell freely down her cheeks. She looked at Cami as though she was trying to gauge her reaction, to feel her out. Cami thought about staying stone-faced because she'd been taught that vulnerability equaled pain but quickly realized she didn't have the energy to do that. "Why did you come back to Oakview? Why now?"

"I couldn't stay away any longer. I don't know how much you know, but I stayed just outside of Boston with my cousin Leila when I got back from Australia. I kept trying to call and text, but I still didn't hear back. I was so afraid you were going to change your number. I thought about just showing up on your doorstep, but I couldn't bring myself to do it. I was too scared. I assumed you'd see me and tell me to fuck off, and then I'd know for sure that that part of my life was truly over."

"That's a good assumption. I probably would have done that." Cami relaxed back into the chair and crossed her arms. She couldn't fight off the chill that had invaded, even though the outside temperature hadn't changed much at all.

"I guess…I don't know. I just needed to be back in your orbit. Even if it's just on the outside looking in. When I say it out loud, it sounds pretty stupid." Alicia chuckled. "But it's the truth. And if that's unfair to you, once again, I'm sorry."

Cami didn't know how to respond. Yeah, it was pretty unfair all around since Alicia had just kind of swooped in and inserted herself into Cami's life again. Cami didn't own Oakview, so it wasn't like she had any right to tell Alicia that she had to leave, but there were still so many question marks. And feelings that Cami just didn't want to deal with.

"Okay." Cami sighed again, deeply. "I will never understand what happened to make you leave, and I don't think there's anything that *could* make me understand. But I believe you. You were going through something you didn't know how to talk about, and you did what you felt you had to do. You hurt me, Alicia. In a way I've never been hurt in my entire life. When you left, it crushed me and upended everything I thought I knew. You were my rock, and you grounded me. And then you were just gone."

Alicia shook her head and smiled sadly, a tiny sob escaping her lips. "I know. With everything that happened, I don't know how I can make you believe me, but I need you to know how much I loved you. You had my whole heart in a way I can't explain, and I don't think I'll ever be able to replace that piece that disappeared when we split up. You haunt me every day. I fucked up the absolute best part of my life, and I will have to live with that until the end of time. And I am so, so sorry."

"I can't guarantee that we'll be friends or that I'll ever be able to *not* be bitter toward you. But if we're going to live and work in each other's 'orbit,' as you call it, I will be civil. That's all I can promise."

Alicia looked as though she'd been flooded with relief. She even smiled, genuinely this time. "I'll take it. I'll take it."

Dry mouth had set in, and Cami desperately needed a drink. The idea of piss-warm beer made her stomach turn, but she also didn't want to leave. There was something in the air that might evaporate the second she stood, and for some reason, she couldn't bear the thought of that.

She didn't need to wonder much longer. A woman she recognized from Alicia's office was walking over to them as though she had a purpose. Alicia's eyebrows raised.

"Hey," the woman said, looking at Alicia. "I thought you had a headache, and you were leaving, like, an hour ago?"

Alicia swallowed. "I was. I did. I do. I was just catching up with…an old friend."

Cami stood. She wasn't sure if they had come together or what, but the woman seemed put out that Alicia was there talking to her. "Cami," she said, extending her hand.

"I know who you are, Detective Lyons. I'm Sam from the *Knox County Sun*. Samantha Lewis. I've run searches for you in the past."

"Ah, okay. Nice to formally meet you. I'll leave you to it." Cami cast one last look at Alicia, whose tearstained face and tired eyes gave her away.

Sam seemed upset, but maybe it was because she thought Alicia should have gone home to lie down. Alicia did say she had a headache when she and Cami had first started talking. The niggling thought that maybe they were dating was pushed right out of frame. It wasn't any of her business.

Katie nearly tackled her when Cami walked by the table. Violet and Taryn leaned forward. "What was that about?" Katie shout-whispered.

Even though Cami was thoroughly exhausted and just wanted to go home and cry into her pillow like she was thirteen again, she couldn't help but smirk. Her friends were so transparent. "She told me—and all of you—that she's been trying to talk to me for the last three years, so I gave her a chance. That was it." Cami shrugged. She knew they were frothing for more information, but she wasn't really in the mood to rehash the whole thing. "I told her I'd be civil since we apparently have to work together for the next couple of months. And since Violet is intent on playing happy hostess and inviting her to things."

Violet rolled her eyes. "I told you I was sorry."

"Maybe it was a good thing," Taryn said. "You guys were talking forever. Obviously, something must have come from it. Do you feel any better?"

"I don't know how I feel, if I'm being honest. I'm sad. I'm tangled up. That's really the best way I can describe it."

"I don't feel any better. I don't know why you even bothered." Katie waved like she was swatting a fly.

Taryn and Violet both shot her a nasty look. Katie tutted and sat back down.

"We'll talk later, I promise. I'm parched." Cami leaned over and took a sip of Violet's colorful concoction and winced. "That tastes like candy corn."

"I know, isn't it delicious?"

Cami turned to look over her shoulder. Alicia and Sam were heading in their general direction, and Cami wanted no part of it. She thanked Violet, called a quick good-bye, and bolted to her Jeep.

Cami woke up later than usual the following morning. By the time she'd gotten home, she'd just wanted to forget about her conversation with Alicia, or at least table it in her mind until she was in the right headspace to process it. She didn't know if she could just speak to her in passing as somebody that she used to know. Cami was hesitant to admit it, but knowing that Alicia felt as badly about the way things had unfolded as she did actually make the tiniest bit of difference.

She'd gone right to bed and thrown the TV on and watched some mindless game show while she'd drifted off into a fitful sleep.

As she was heading into the shower the next morning, focused on the day ahead and absolutely nothing else, her cell phone rang. Kelsey's number popped up on the caller ID.

"I hope you're up and dressed."

"Why, what's up?" Cami was decidedly *not* dressed. She looked at her polka-dotted shorts and pink tank top.

"We need to request a warrant to search Evan Conley's house."

Cami shook her head. "What did I miss? Did he confess or something? I know he's being shady as hell, but I don't think we have enough to arrest him on."

"Probable cause. He has no alibi, his wife disputes his whereabouts on the night of the murder, and a witness placed him in the van. Forensics just came back. Those gray fibers they found in the front seat match the sample from Laurie Garrett's sweater."

"Well, fuckin' A. Let me get some pants on, and we'll go get him."

Chapter Fourteen

"It's so nice being able to have you just pop in."

Her mom added a splash of milk to Alicia's cup of hot tea. She grasped it with both hands and let the cup warm her. It reminded her of her childhood, when her mother had Alicia and her brother sit at the kitchen table after school to recount their days. Alicia would have tea, and Sean would have milk unless it was a special day, and then they'd both have Mountain Dew.

"You're right, it is nice." Alicia blew the steam away. "Do you think I made the right choice coming home? I was doing fine in Somerville with Leila. I mean, I was happy. Ish. Happy *enough*, I guess. Not exactly happy, but I was fine. I talked to Cami last night."

Her mom's eyes widened. She sat across from Alicia and propped her chin on one hand. "And? Come on, spill. Don't leave anything out."

Alicia threw her head back. She wasn't in the mood to regale anyone with the whole saga, but once she started, she couldn't stop. The floodgates opened. Her mother alternated between patting Alicia's hand, shaking her head, and using a napkin to wipe invisible crumbs from the place mat in front of her. She'd done that as far back as Alicia could remember.

"And then, she said she'd be civil, and I was so grateful that I wanted to just burst into tears and throw my arms around her and thank her like she'd offered me a kidney instead of offering to be 'civil.' Ugh." Alicia wiped her eyes again in disgust. She was sick of the constant watery eyes she'd been living with for the last month.

"Well, it's a start. You know I love you, and I'll always be on your side no matter what, but you hurt her, Lee-see. I'll never forget when I ran into her at JB's Farmers' Market. She looked like she'd seen a ghost. I gave her a hug because I didn't know what else to do. She hugged me like I was a long-lost soldier returned from war. I could feel her trying not to cry, and I told her that she could come and see me and your father anytime she wanted. She thanked me and speed-walked out of that market. She left her basket of peppers and bananas right there on the ground in front of me."

Lee-see. Her mother only pulled out the old nickname—Sean couldn't pronounce "Alicia" until he was about three—when she was trying to make a point or attempting to instill a life lesson. Dammit, it usually worked.

"I *know*, Mom. I am fully aware of how much pain I caused her. And everyone else in my life, too. I should have the words 'I'm sorry' tattooed on my forehead." Alicia fiddled with the label on her tea bag.

"Oh, don't be a martyr," her mother said, waving her off. "I'm not saying you committed an unforgivable sin or anything like that. Your dad and I were upset, too. You called us at seven o'clock at night the day before you left on a flight to the other side of the world. It wasn't like you to be so impetuous, and we were really afraid that something was wrong. But once we talked to you, we felt better about the whole thing, even though it didn't make much sense. Cami didn't have that luxury."

"I tried to call her. A hundred times."

"How long did you wait to call?"

Alicia sank back into her chair. "I don't know. It wasn't long after. I knew I'd made a mistake, but I obviously couldn't just turn around and go home. I put everything I had into that trip. Including my sanity. I figured if I just gave up, I'd be admitting defeat. Without notching any wins at all since it seemed likely she'd never talk to me again."

"Did you?"

"Did I what?"

"End up notching any wins at all? By the time you left Australia?"

Alicia looked at the ceiling and heaved out a huge sigh. She really hadn't, had she? Perth was beautiful and magical, and everything she'd read about it was true for the most part. But she'd left feeling as empty as she had when she'd arrived. Different maybe. New perspective. Because by then, she'd been filled with regret. "No."

"You just need to look at it as an impromptu decision you made in a haste of uncertainty. You can't beat yourself up for it for the rest of your life. Either Cami will forgive you or she won't. But you've made amends. Done all you can do. The rest is up to her. But you've got to let it go and move on, Alicia. If you moved back here as a way to get back into Cami's good graces, you might be in for a hell of a disappointment. She doesn't have to accept your apologies. Nevertheless, I'm glad you're home. I missed the shit out of you," her mom said and walked around the table to put her arms around her.

Alicia hugged her back tightly. The smell of her mother's Chanel No. 5 and the taste of tea on her tongue brought her back to a time when she was ecstatic to have her very own phone line—that she'd had to pay fifteen dollars per month for—and "Livin' la Vida Loca" was all the rage. She let herself lull into it for a few moments before her mom stood and started cleaning off the table.

Her jaunty ringtone startled her. She saw Jade's name on the caller ID and frowned. Jade was a serial texter. She never called anyone unless absolutely necessary. Her voice mail even said, "Why are you calling me? Unless you're a time traveler, send me a text."

Alicia answered the call cautiously. "Jade? You okay?"

"Can you come to my house right away?" She sounded frantic and chaotic.

"Sure." But before Alicia could ask what was wrong, Jade hung up. It must have had something to do with Evan.

Alicia kissed her mother good-bye and ran out to her car.

When Alicia pulled up to Jade's contemporary two-story, she saw two cars parked in her driveway, and one of them was an olive-green Jeep. Cami.

Jade was sitting on her stairs, her head in her hands. Alicia ran to her, a bitter breeze reminding her that it was only fool's spring, and that the real thing was still a few weeks away. Jade didn't seem to notice.

"What's happening?" Alicia asked, touching Jade's arm.

Jade dabbed at her eyes with a tissue. "Evan and his lawyers are inside. Apparently, they found something that tied him to one of the dead women. None of it makes any sense. The two detectives and a few guys in black jackets showed up here. Detective Lyons had a warrant to search the house. She was sympathetic, I guess, but I can't wrap my head around this. He wouldn't even look at me! Am I married to a murderer? Really?"

Alicia was stunned. Of all the things she'd imagined the police were investigating Evan for, murder hadn't even crossed her mind. She'd assumed it was some white-collar thing, like insider trading or embezzlement. Maybe he just had information, or maybe he was hiding something to cover up his actual crimes, and it made him look guilty for the murder. Either way, she could understand why Jade was so confused. She didn't quite understand why Jade was calling *her* instead of a close friend or family member. Maybe Alicia's natural distance from the situation was what Jade needed.

"We have a good marriage, Alicia," Jade nearly yelled. Her cheeks were wet, and her nose was dripping. Alicia didn't think she even noticed. "At least, I thought we did. There has to be some massive mistake here. A misunderstanding like you read about in *People*. Happens all the time, right?"

Jade looked up at her with such hopefulness that Alicia didn't have the heart to tell her the truth. Sure, those things *did* happen, but as a reporter, Alicia knew that for the most part, Occam's Razor was usually the right application.

"Of course. It could be something like that." Alicia sat next to Jade on the doorstep, feeling helpless. She didn't know what to do or say.

Thankfully, she didn't have to wait too long for something to break the silence. The front door opened, and Cami stepped out.

Alicia jumped up and brushed the dirt from the back of her jeans. "Hey."

Cami seemed surprised to see her, but she regained her composure quickly. "Hi, Alicia." She was probably wondering when Jade and Alicia had become so close. Alicia was wondering the same thing. *Nothing like a tragedy to bring people closer.* "Jade, I just wanted to let you know that they're almost done in there. I've asked them to be as respectful as possible, put everything back where they found it, leave things alone that can be left alone. They assured me they would," Cami said. She was looking at the ground, almost as if she was ashamed.

Jade and Cami had exchanged words on more than one occasion, but Alicia also knew that Cami respected Jade immensely. Jade insisted on calling Cami "Detective Lyons," even though they had known each other for years. She felt it would be inappropriate to address her any other way, which Cami found amusing. This must have been uncomfortable for her, too.

"They were going through our cabinets and our closets and our desks, Detective. I watched as some guy was rifling my personal medical files. I had vaginal polyps removed last year. Do you think that will help with your investigation?"

Cami winced. "I'm sorry about that. I know this is a violation of your personal belongings and your privacy, but they have to be thorough."

"Do you want to get out of here for a bit? We can go get a cup of coffee or something until they're done?" Alicia asked. She felt powerless and frankly, a little out of place. She still wasn't entirely certain what Jade wanted from her. Moral support, she supposed.

"No, I have to stay here. Like a captain going down with the ship," Jade muttered. She laughed bitterly. "You're probably wondering why I asked you to come over."

Now that you mention it…

"You're the only one who knows what's going on, Alicia. Well, now there will obviously be a whole lot more who know." Jade motioned to the neighbors walking slowly by the house, trying to appear as though they weren't being nosy or attempting to eavesdrop. "But as I'm sure you know, I'm a proud woman. You were with me when the shit hit the fan, and you didn't judge me. I won't forget that. I needed someone, but I needed someone that I didn't have to spin some elaborate tale to. I didn't trust myself to be honest. Thank you for being here."

Alicia nodded and rubbed her shoulder. "Of course. I'm here for whatever you need."

Kelsey poked her head out the door. She saw Alicia and scrunched up her face. Why was everyone so astonished by her presence? Jeez. "Conley's ready to talk. He's going to meet us at the station with his lawyers."

"Ready to talk?" Jade asked, jumping up. "About what? Is he saying he killed that woman?" She was nearing hysterics. Alicia took a step closer, but Jade put her hand up.

Cami shook her head. "Not necessarily. He may just want to clear up some confusion about the night that it happened or speak to us about something he might know. We'll just have a conversation. Go have that coffee with Alicia. She can bore you with her stories about being a forest activist in her college days. Unless you've already heard all of those by now."

Alicia knew that Cami wasn't being malicious. There was something almost gentle about the way she recalled Alicia's retellings, reflective maybe. Alicia's stomach fluttered the tiniest bit. Not now, she scolded.

"I have," Jade wailed.

As Cami was walking back into the house, Alicia noticed the upturned corners of her lips. Maybe she really had told everyone in the universe about her tree-sitting days.

"Come on." Alicia held out her hand to Jade. She had no idea what they would talk about or how awkward it would be, but she had to get Jade out of there. "I'll even order your ridiculous vanilla, soy, Stevia, frothy milk latte thing for you. I know how much you love to see me stumble over that."

Jade crossed her arms and looked at nothing in particular out in the distance. "Yeah. I really do," she whispered.

CHAPTER FIFTEEN

Cami wasn't sure why Conley had reconsidered, but he was obviously afraid of something they'd find, whether in the physical forensic investigation or the digital one that was about to take place on his laptop and other electronic devices. When she walked into the small interrogation room, Conley and his lawyers were already sitting at the table. He had a sour expression on his face.

"Hello again, Mr. Conley. I hear you're ready to talk about that night. Are you sticking with the story that you were home all night, even though your wife wasn't able to corroborate that?" Cami smiled tightly as she clicked her pen and readied her notebook. She knew she was being confrontational, but Conley had shown himself to be such a prick, she couldn't help it.

"Mr. Conley may have mixed up his dates," the lawyer in the expensive gray suit offered. "He remembers things a bit more clearly now."

"Excellent." Cami turned to the door as Kelsey walked in.

Conley rubbed at his lips with his knuckles. "I actually did take that van out for a spin on that Wednesday night. I didn't lie about it for the reason you think though. I was, uh…" He looked at the table. He was rapidly shaking his right leg, as though he'd leaned on a nerve. "I was looking for company."

"Company?"

"Yes." He was exasperated. "Of a woman."

What a sleaze. Poor Jade.

"Why did you rent a van to do that?" Kelsey's brows were furrowed.

"I didn't want to be seen in my car, okay? I've rented vehicles in the area a few times in the past. There are a few places around that take cash and don't ask any questions, and it's a lot safer to leave my car in a lot somewhere than parked at a place I…probably shouldn't be. Vans and SUVs are obviously preferable for…reasons. I didn't want it to get back to Jade. I'm human, okay? I made a mistake, but I'm not a killer!"

"A few times? How many is a few?" Cami asked.

"I don't know. Two, three."

Cami just stared at him.

"For the last two years. Once a month or so. You wouldn't believe how many girls from here to Concord are looking for a good time. I don't usually do anything so close to home. Now I remember why."

Cami swallowed. *Of course that's what he's upset about. Not that he's a cheating scumbag, that he got caught.*

"Let's talk about Laurie Garrett. Why was she in the van with you? Was she your 'good time' for the evening?" Cami asked.

"That was the plan. I was at Marge's Convenience Store by Copper Lake, picking up a few scratch tickets. Laurie was outside on her phone. When I went in, she kind of gave me a 'look,' so I smiled at her. When I came out, she was still there, and we got to talking. She was taking the bus because her car was in the shop, so I offered her a ride. She hesitated a little bit but not much. Then she told me she recognized me from TV. That set off a few red flags because I was close to home, but I was already…interested. I put my hand on her leg and I guess, made my intentions known. She freaked out. She said she was going to ask me if I could get her boyfriend a spot in one of my commercials. I was pissed off, so I pulled over. She called me an asshole, got out of the van, and I drove off. That was it." He shrugged.

And now we have a motive. Cami shook her head. "So you were afraid that this woman you hit on would tell your wife, or whoever, that you were out looking to score, so you dropped her off in the middle of nowhere, and she was murdered no more than an hour later?" Cami leaned back in her chair and raised her eyebrows.

"Yeah. That's what happened. It wasn't in the middle of nowhere. It was right outside a Dunkin' Donuts. She had a phone. She could have called someone or found another bus or something. That's not on me."

"Maybe. But why should we assume that you didn't make *sure* this one wasn't going to be a problem for you? In a permanent way?" Kelsey asked.

"I have an alibi." Conley sighed.

Cami looked over at Kelsey. She tilted her head and narrowed her eyes. "An alibi? That couldn't verify your whereabouts last time we asked?"

"That was by choice, obviously a mistake." He slid a folded piece of paper to Cami. "Name and address of the woman I spent the night with. She has one of those Ring doorbell things, so I'm sure you can get the old footage from that thing if she deleted it."

Actually, they couldn't; once video clips from motion detection cameras were deleted, they were gone forever. But Cami didn't want to confirm or deny anything yet. She unfolded the sticky note. *Tracy Shaw, 214 Broadway St, Manchester*.

"Don't you usually remain anonymous?" Cami asked. "Isn't that the whole idea?"

He cleared his throat. "Yeah. But Tracy is, uh, someone I've seen more than once," he mumbled, looking at the table again. Cami wasn't sure if it was shame or exhaustion.

"And this woman will confirm that you were with her the night of the murder. But how do we know you didn't just kill Laurie and then head up to Tracy's house to finish the evening you'd planned for yourself?"

"Look, I know I wasn't honest about all this up front, but give me a break here. I didn't want to blow up my marriage or my image, for that matter. I'm the head of Oakview Bank, the people in this town know me and love me. They trust me. I can't let them down."

Cami had to restrain herself from rolling her eyes in the most epic way possible. He was in charge of a bank; he wasn't a benevolent minister who'd solved the housing crisis. He made a lot of money and attended a lot of parties. And he had a commercial that played during baseball games.

It wasn't like they had much of a choice at that point but to take his word for it and attempt to corroborate his story. Without a murder weapon or anything else that tied him to Laurie Garrett or Barbara Lawson, they didn't have anything that would stick.

She held up the paper he'd given her. "We'll talk to Tracy Shaw and see what she has to say. I'll also need the name of every rental service you've visited in the last twelve months. Stick around in case we have more questions."

"Can I have my laptop and the files you took? I told you everything you need to know."

"We'll be finished with everything shortly, and we'll get it back to you ASAP."

He stood and adjusted the cuffs of his dress shirt. "Are you going to tell my wife? I know she has that friend from work who's always around now. You're involved with her, yeah?"

Her first instinct was to tell him to mind his own fucking business, but Cami reined that in. "It's not our place to tell your wife. But these things have a way of being found out. Maybe *you* should tell your wife."

He scoffed. "Jade's the best thing that ever happened to me. I didn't mean for her to get hurt in all this, but these things just happen sometimes. It wasn't anybody's fault."

"These things 'just happen sometimes'? Once a month for a year?" Cami asked. His insolence was truly astonishing.

"Okay, we'll be in touch," Kelsey said, herding them out of the interrogation room.

His lawyers hadn't said much, but whenever Conley started going off on a tangent, one of them would either touch his arm or cough. But Cami didn't have the appetite to go after him for solicitation, and she knew Kelsey wouldn't either. Once Jade found out about his behavior—and Cami was certain she would—she was pretty sure his perfect little life would face a complete upheaval without any help from them.

❖

By the time Cami got home after updating Captain Brandt on the situation and coming to the realization that they were probably still at square one with the investigation, she was exhausted. Kelsey was working on corroborating Conley's story with the woman he'd said he was with, but the car rental places had checked out. He'd had to use his real info at a few places, but none of them were particularly close to Oakview. Conley had clearly put a lot of thought and effort into his adultery.

Cami stuck a frozen pizza in the oven and glanced at the copy of *Food Network Magazine* that had been dropped at her apartment door and addressed to "current resident." The recipe for stir-fried chicken with rice and asparagus made her oven-ready, almost-like-real pizza pale in comparison. She chucked the magazine into her recycling bin and munched on a few dried apple chips so she could tell herself she was eating healthy.

While waiting for the ding of the oven, Cami was startled by a knock on her door. She wasn't expecting anyone, and thankfully, her friends weren't the drop-in type. She opened the door and was even more surprised to see Maya standing there.

She'd been seeing Maya for a few months, but it wasn't unusual for them to go a week or two without seeing each other or even speaking, for that matter. They'd both said from the beginning that neither of them was looking for anything serious, and they would just take it as it came.

It was a foreign concept for Cami, who'd been in semiserious relationships until she'd met Alicia, who she'd fallen in love with at warp speed. Cami had tried to play it cool in the beginning. She didn't want to come on too strong or make Alicia think she was trying to rush things. The mask had melted pretty quickly, and Alicia had been the one to drop the "I think I'm in love with you" bomb after a month or so. Cami remembered feeling like she'd been attached to a hot air balloon that was carrying her through the heavens. She longed for that sensation of weightlessness.

"Hey, sexy," Maya said, cocking her head to the side. "Where ya been?"

Cami had to collect herself. With everything that had been going on, she hadn't thought much about Maya or the state of her romantic life. Well, not her current romantic life anyway.

"I've been here. I'm sorry, things have been so hectic. Do you want to come in?" Cami motioned to the living room.

"I figured as much. I'm sure you have your hands full. Are you making dinner?" Maya threw her jacket on the back of Cami's couch and followed her nose to the kitchen.

"Yeah. Nothing fancy, just a frozen pizza. And some apple chips," Cami said, holding out the bag.

Maya declined. "You should have called me. I could have made you dinner." She smiled seductively. "But since you've already got that going, the least I could do is offer you dessert."

Cami chuckled nervously. She didn't know why she felt so out of sorts around Maya. They'd done this dance plenty of times. Have dinner, flirt, sometimes sleep together, sometimes not, discuss the state of the world, and then go their separate ways until the next time. It was a routine that had worked for them for quite a while, and Maya was obviously interested in continuing it. Cami was too…or so she'd thought. Something felt different. It was probably the investigation. She'd been so mired in it that she hadn't paid attention to much else.

"I did text you, you know." Maya pointed at Cami's phone. "A few times. I wondered if you were intentionally blowing me off, but then I said, 'nah, she likes me too much.'"

"No, I wasn't blowing you off, sorry about that." Cami picked up her phone. Maya wasn't lying. Cami had an ungodly amount of text messages that she never got around to reading since most of them were restaurant coupons and political solicitations, but she tried to be good about getting back to real people. She must have just missed them. "I really have been consumed by these cases. I think it's doing a number on my psyche."

"I'm sure." Maya tucked a piece of straight brown hair behind her ear. Cami wondered if she'd had it straightened. But just in case she hadn't, better not bring it up.

The oven dinged. Cami slid the pizza onto a cooling rack and placed it on the stove. Maya came up behind her, sliding her arms around Cami's waist. "I missed you," she murmured. She moved Cami's hair to the side and kissed the back of her neck. "I think I can change your mind for a little bit."

Cami closed her eyes and put her hand on Maya's that was still around her waist. She patted it. "I'm sure you can, but I am honestly starving," Cami said with a light laugh. "The last thing I ate was a stale granola bar at about six this morning."

Maya backed up. "Okay. We can eat first. Only if you have extra." She sat at one of the counter stools and crossed her legs.

"Of course. I'm hungry, but I don't think I can put away a whole pizza. Here." Cami slid two slices onto a paper plate. "Can I get you something to drink? Water? Pepsi?"

"Do you have any wine?"

"I don't think so." Cami checked the cabinet above her stove where she'd keep it if she had any. "I don't. I have a couple of beers in the fridge?"

"Sure."

Cami took out two beers and popped the top off each. She handed one to Maya, who promptly downed half of it.

They talked about work and Maya's employees at *Cannabusiness*, a pot shop just over the border in Massachusetts. Their antics always provided a few laughs. Maybe Maya was right; Cami did need this. Just an easygoing night off from the stress around her. No murders, no sleazy cheaters, no meddling friends, and no Alicia.

Her heart skipped a beat. She quickly shook it off. Alicia shouldn't have any effect on her life at this point. Just because she was close didn't mean that she had to take up space in Cami's head. Civil. That was all she had to give, and Alicia had accepted it.

Eleven thirteen. Cami kept glancing at the clock on her wall, trying not to make it obvious. She would have been in bed at least an hour ago if Maya hadn't been there, but she didn't want to come right out and say that. She tried to stifle a yawn, but it didn't work.

"Sorry," she said, covering her lips with two fingers. "Been a long day. Week."

Maya snickered. "That's okay, I won't take it personally." She leaned toward Cami and started massaging her shoulders.

Cami's head dropped as she allowed Maya's fingers to grind into her muscles. It hurt but not enough that she wanted it to stop. She hadn't realized how tight everything was. She was about to shift lower on the couch so Maya could reach the area just below her collarbone when she felt a hand caress her cheek. Her face was pulled slowly toward Maya's where their lips met in a light embrace. Cami was mildly taken aback, even though she'd known it was coming. She closed her eyes and leaned in, sliding an arm around her waist. Maya put her other hand on Cami's neck and pulled her in closer.

This is nice. Enjoy it. Her lips are soft. She tastes like pizza. Ouch, something is digging into me. It's probably that pen I dropped earlier. Dammit, Cami, concentrate. *Her hand just dropped. Even lower. Okay, this is good. I need this. Yes, I want this. This is what I want. This is what—*

"Wait," Cami said, pulling back a little.

Maya jumped back. "What's wrong?"

"Nothing," Cami said. A little too quickly. "Nothing. I'm really tired. I have a lot on my mind. Just in kind of a weird space at the moment."

"Okay, I understand that. But you've been acting strange all night. Are you sure nothing else is going on?"

"No." Cami thought for a second. Was there something else? She really was tired, and she'd been working eighty-hour weeks since the body of Beverly Lawson had been found. The whole thing with Alicia had been on her mind, too, but that had nothing to do with Maya. "I mean, nothing that I can pinpoint. I just feel off, you know? I'm sure it's just everything going on."

"Why don't we just sleep together, then?"

Cami's eyes widened, but Maya shook her head.

"Sleep, actually sleep. I'll stay the night. Cook you breakfast before you have to work in the morning." Maya rested her hand on Cami's leg.

Unusual. That had never been their MO. Their connection had never been about cuddling or chaste sleepovers or domestic bliss. It wasn't that Cami was opposed to those things, but she hadn't really explored the possibility of doing them with Maya. She'd assumed that if that type of relationship was going to develop between them, it would happen organically. *Maybe this* is *it happening organically.* Her first reaction wasn't a good one. She probably just needed more time.

"Don't be mad, but I really just need a good night's sleep, and if you're here, it probably won't happen. Not because of you, just because I'm so set in my ways." Cami felt like she was in a no-win situation. She felt like shit asking Maya to leave, but she didn't want her to stay, either. She hoped Maya wouldn't take it to heart.

That hope was futile.

"Really? Is that the way it is between us? I'm only good enough to have around when you're in the mood?" Maya stood and angrily threw her jacket around her shoulders.

"I didn't say that, Maya," Cami said, also standing. She adjusted her shirt. "I just kind of thought we had an understanding, where, you know, we could be honest about how we felt, and neither of us would get upset." She didn't mean to turn it around on Maya, but she wasn't wrong. They'd had that discussion many times when they'd first started seeing each other.

"And we do have that understanding. Now I *understand* that we're fuck buddies. I knew we were taking things slow and enjoying each other's company, but I guess I didn't know that we could only 'hang out' when there was going to be sex involved."

"Didn't we just 'hang out' for, like, three hours? The only thing I said was that I wanted to go to bed, and I wanted to sleep alone. I don't know where you're getting this whole fuck buddy thing from. I didn't mean to hurt your feelings, I'm really fucking exhausted." Cami could almost feel tears forming in the deep recesses of her eyes, but she kept them at bay.

Maya sighed. "Fine. I just missed you and wanted to see you, and I guess I'm not feeling that reciprocated. So, yeah, that hurts. But it's my problem, not yours."

"Oh, Maya, come on," Cami said with a groan. "Of course it's my problem, I don't want your feelings hurt. Like I said, I've got a lot going on."

"Well, I'll give you your space, then. I'll see you when I see you." She shrugged nonchalantly and closed the door loudly behind her.

Cami closed her eyes and rubbed her eyebrow. She'd been looking forward to a relaxing night with frozen pizza and mindless television, followed up by a sound sleep.

Beer bottles clanged together as she cleaned up before going to bed. She had been honest with Maya. She truly didn't mean to hurt her, but she didn't want to completely compromise herself either. She couldn't isolate what was bothering her, not really, but she knew she didn't want to fake it with Maya. It wouldn't have been fair to either of them.

Cami threw on an old tank top and a pair of shorts and snuggled under her covers. She turned on her ancient clock radio to find calming music to hopefully lull her to sleep. "Set Fire to the Rain" by Adele was in full swing, and Cami used her palm to slap the "off" button. On their road trip to Washington, DC, Cami and Alicia had laughed at the number of times they'd heard that song on the seven-hour road trip. She could remember Alicia hanging out the window of her Jeep, singing at the top of her lungs as they flew down the New Jersey Turnpike. And when they were in the hotel room that night, Alicia had sung as many words as she could remember into the pen she'd found in the desk drawer.

Cami smiled and shook her head before dropping down on her pillow. *Fuck you, Alicia.*

CHAPTER SIXTEEN

Evan Conley was putting cardboard boxes into the back of his SUV. Alicia walked by and tried to avoid eye contact, but he called out to her anyway.

"She call you over here?" He nodded toward his front door.

"No. We were talking earlier, and I thought I'd come check on her. Why?" Alicia remained as aloof as always, but at this point, she couldn't even stand to look at him. All those times she'd wondered if he'd been giving her the eye, chances were, he had been. Ew.

"Your buddy in the detective's office has it in for me, you know. You can't believe everything you hear. Two sides to every story."

"I didn't hear anything from her. Not sure what you're talking about."

He started to say something else, but Alicia ignored him and walked up the front pathway to the door. She hoped it was unlocked so she wouldn't have to stand there and wait awkwardly for Jade to open the door. She was in luck. The knob turned easily.

"Jade?" she called as she stepped into the foyer.

Alicia heard footsteps coming down the rounded staircase. Jade certainly looked put together for someone whose life was coming apart at the seams. She had on a cream-colored pantsuit with wide legs that swished as she walked. The pearls around her neck complemented her smooth skin.

"Alicia. What are you doing here?"

"Just came to check on you. After our conversation this morning, I thought you might be in the mood for some company. If not, I can take off. I totally understand if you'd rather be alone."

Jade shook her head. "No, I'm glad you're here. Come on up."

Alicia followed her up the stairs, impressed by how impeccably clean Jade's house was. The carpets in the bedrooms were still impossibly white. Alicia thought about the dark spot on her tan carpet where she'd spilled an entire cup of coffee. She missed the hardwood floors she'd had when she and Cami had lived together.

The bedroom was a bit more unkempt. There were men's suits strewn on the bed, shoeboxes on the floor, containers of cords and computer accessories on the dresser.

"What are you doing?" Alicia asked.

"Packing up all his shit. I suppose I should be grateful that I've been married to a serial cheater instead of a serial killer, but it doesn't feel that way right now. I want the son of a bitch out of here." She continued to throw stuff into cardboard boxes with vigor.

"I'm honestly surprised he even told you," Alicia said. "Was he at least apologetic?"

Jade scoffed. "Please. He started out apologetic and sincere but very quickly spiraled into it being my fault for being so 'unavailable.' I let him finish his rant, but when he started saying we could figure things out, I shut him down so hard, I think his future-self winced. No fuckin' way is he going to make a fool out of me twice."

"Are you going to stay here?"

"That's the plan. I already called a divorce lawyer. I meet with her tomorrow. You know, I'm sure it will hit me sooner or later, but for right now, I'm strangely okay with the idea of being alone. After our conversation, I didn't see him as my husband anymore. I saw him as a pathetic old man who didn't know how lucky he was. And I'm not saying that because I'm full of myself. I mean it in all ways. He had it all, as the saying goes. And he threw it away." She shrugged and stuffed a plastic display case holding a signed baseball into a duffel bag.

"You're right," Alicia said, removing the hangers from the polo shirts Jade had on the bed. "And you're being very pragmatic about the whole thing. That's impressive."

Jade waved her off. "That's today. Talk to me in a week and see where I am. But I can tell you one thing, I'll never let him back into my life or into my heart. He set that ship on fire and sunk it to oblivion."

Jade picked up speed and packed Evan's things feverishly. While Alicia was glad that Jade seemed to have a plan and wanted to cut all ties, she feared that the apparent lack of processing was going to catch up with Jade and slap her across the face. She knew all too well how that felt.

By the time she left, Evan's car was no longer in the driveway. The days were getting longer and longer, but it was full dark, even though it was just after seven. Alicia pulled the Prius into the small parking lot behind her apartment and looked on as the train sped by. It must have been fairly new since the shiny red metal was nearly free from graffiti.

She fished her keys out of her bag and walked up the two cement steps toward the door but backtracked to get a better look at the bench on the sidewalk. There was a man sitting there, his chin resting against his chest. He was balding on top and had a full grayish beard.

Alicia's heart began to beat faster. He was probably just asleep, but it was a little too chilly to be sleeping on a bench in just a short-sleeve shirt and a pair of jeans.

"Sir?" She crept closer to the bench, but she was afraid to get too close. What if it was a trap? Maybe he was waiting for an unsuspecting tenant to show up so he could grab them and do who knew what. Alicia scanned the area for an unfamiliar vehicle but didn't see anything out of the ordinary. "Sir?" she said again, a little louder.

No response.

She swallowed. Her mouth was dry, and she felt like her lips were sticking together. Her instinct was to call 9-1-1, but she hated to do that if it was just a guy sleeping on a bench. Maybe he'd been drunk and was trying to sleep it off before returning home. She inched forward, expecting him to jump up at her any minute. Maybe it was a prank for one of those stupid YouTube channels.

But he didn't move. At all. Alicia got as close as she was willing to go and noticed a dark spot beneath the bench. She leaned down to see if it was actually what it looked like, then turned and ran at full speed toward her apartment door.

It was blood.

Once inside the small vestibule, Alicia fumbled her phone out of her back pocket and called 9-1-1. She gave them her address and a quick description of what she'd found. She ended the call and without thinking, dialed Cami. *Come on, come on, pick up.*

After the third ring, Cami answered, sounding weary. "Hello?"

"Cami, hi, it's Alicia. I'm sorry to call you, but can you come to my apartment? It's the little brick building on Crescent. There's a guy here sitting on a bench, and I think he's dead." Alicia's hand was trembling so violently that she could feel the phone repeatedly thumping her ear.

Cami's voice changed into one of concern. "Where are you now?"

"I'm standing in the vestibule. It's glass. I can see the corner of the bench from here. I don't think he's moved or anyone else has come."

"Did you call the police?"

"Yes."

"Is the door locked?"

"No, it's always unlocked."

"Lock it."

Alicia nodded, even though Cami couldn't see her, and flipped the dead bolt on the metal door. The rest of it was made of glass, but it was still a solid barrier between her and whatever had happened to the man.

"Can you come?" Alicia asked again. Her voice was breaking.

"I'm already on my way. Has anyone else arrived yet?"

Relief washed over her. "Not yet. I hear a siren in the distance. Hopefully, it's them."

"I'll be there in four minutes. Stay on with me. Do you know who he is?"

"I didn't get close enough to see. His head is hanging down. He doesn't look familiar, but that doesn't mean much. There are three apartment buildings here, and I've met, like, two people." Alicia kept her eyes trained on the bench and rubbed the back of her neck.

Finally, an Oakview PD SUV and an ambulance whipped into the area in front of the bench. A fire truck was close behind. The lone streetlight cast a shadowy spotlight on the man, who still hadn't moved a muscle. Alicia didn't hold out much hope.

"They're there?" Cami asked. "Okay, good. I'll be there in about ten seconds. Stay in the lobby."

"I will. Thank you." Alicia ended the call, and hot tears sprang to her eyes. She was overwhelmed by what she was witnessing and grateful Cami had come without hesitation. Some things didn't change, even though they had every right to.

A policeman came to the doorway with a pad and pen, and Alicia unlocked it for him. She gave him her statement, how she'd found the man on the bench, where she'd been, and what else she'd seen, which was very little. She could see the medical team looking him over out of the corner of her eye. The policeman didn't say whether the man was alive or dead, but Alicia didn't think she needed him to tell her. She looked over his shoulder and saw Cami jogging toward the door.

The same relief flooded her again. The tousled curly blond hair and oversized sweatshirt over a pair of leggings alluded to the fact that Cami had been comfortably at home. Alicia's tears that had been dormant began to erupt. Her chest heaved, and she nearly pushed the officer out of the way to get to Cami.

She ran down the steps, crashed into Cami, and threw her arms around her, not even contemplating the idea that Cami might push her away or tell her she was completely out of line.

Thankfully, she didn't need to worry. Cami embraced her fully and even had her hand around the back of Alicia's neck, pulling her closer in. "You're okay," she whispered. "I'm here now. Everything's okay."

For a brief second, Alicia forgot that there was a dead man on a bench less than a hundred feet away. Her senses were overtaken by the coconut shampoo Cami was obviously still using and the comfort her strong arms provided. She felt like she was home.

"Cam," a voice called.

Reluctantly, Alicia let go of Cami, who stiffened. Kelsey was standing with her hands in her pockets. Alicia wondered how long they'd been there. It could have been twenty seconds or twenty minutes; either way, it wasn't long enough.

"Is he?" Cami asked.

Kelsey nodded.

Dammit. It wasn't a surprise, but a small part of Alicia wanted to believe he was just in a coma or something, and he could come out of it. Hurt but alive.

"I need you to see something."

Cami nodded and followed her. Alicia stayed a pace behind. She wasn't about to be left alone near the train tracks with a possible psychopath on the loose.

"Look at his pocket."

His left jeans pocket was pulled taut against his skin, and there was a definitive shape sticking out of the denim. A square.

"Oh shit," Cami said under her breath, just loud enough for Alicia to hear.

"I assume that's what I think it is?" Kelsey asked.

"Certainly looks like it."

Well, what is it? It didn't look like anything too exciting. It couldn't have been a weapon, not at that size. Alicia wanted to hurry the conversation along but was afraid they'd clam up if they knew she was listening.

"Same MO, too. Gunshot to the back. I can't be one hundred percent sure, but it looks like he was killed here." Kelsey nodded to the area behind the bench.

Cami walked over and leaned down. Alicia tried not to think about what it had felt like to be in her arms, even in such an awful circumstance. Cami had held her out of the kindness of her heart; that was all. And there was a dead man in front of them.

She averted her eyes and turned away. *Have some respect.* A crowd had started to form outside the apartment building, a mix of residents and people in cars. The area was being taped off by the techs before anyone could get too close.

Alicia heard Cami coming toward her again. "Are you okay?" she asked quietly.

Alicia nodded. "Yeah, I'm okay. I'm sorry I called you in such a panic. I just didn't know what to do. Thank you for coming. I can't tell you how much that means to me."

Alicia thought she saw Cami's eyes soften a little before hardening back up. "Don't even worry about it. It's all part of the job.

There will be all kinds of people here throughout the night, so you can feel safe to get some sleep. We might have more questions tomorrow, but I think we have everything we need."

"Thank you again." Alicia felt completely deflated by Cami's brush-off, that her racing over was anything other than "part of the job," but she tried to keep perspective. Cami was in for a long night again, and Alicia's feelings were probably not top of her mind. Before the night had turned to shit, Alicia had been alternately fretting and looking forward to their next meetup that was supposed to take place within the next few days. They'd have plenty to talk about.

Cami's eyes lingered on her for a moment, or at least Alicia imagined they did, before she nodded and headed back toward Kelsey. The noise around Alicia faded into a muffled din, and she trudged up the stairs to her apartment. She looked back one more time and saw Cami speaking animatedly to the medical examiner before she closed the door behind her.

Alicia could confirm two things after the events of the evening: her heart was still broken, even after all this time.

And there was most likely a serial killer loose in Oakview.

Chapter Seventeen

Dressed much more suitably than the night before, Cami sat at her desk and combed through the evidence they had on the latest victim. Patrick McCallum, aged 39, divorced with no children. He lived in the apartment building two doors down from Alicia's. He was still friendly with his ex-wife, who'd sobbed the entire way through her interview with the police. She'd answered all the questions they'd asked, and none of the answers stood out as alarming or even interesting.

Patrick was a customer service representative for a local cable company, he played Dungeons & Dragons with a couple of his buddies on the weekends, and had divorced because they'd come to the conclusion they'd be better off as friends. No enemies to speak of and no connection to Evan Conley.

Their instincts had been correct: the bulge in his pocket was a small wooden block with the letter T on it. Another T. There was no other physical evidence at the scene except for a shoe print in the area where the gunshot had most likely originated. Shoe prints didn't usually hold a lot of weight, but Cami was grasping at straws.

Kelsey poked her head into the office. Her eyes were heavy, and she looked much paler than usual.

"You okay?" Cami asked.

"I'm fine. Tired. Frustrated."

"Same here. I really don't want to prove Alicia right with her whole 'out of their league' column, but do you think we need to bring in the big guns? None of this fits together. We have three victims. A sixty-four-year-old retired woman, a twenty-seven-year-old retail-working woman, a thirty-nine-year-old customer service representative, male. The only thing they have in common is that they're single. But that's a stretch. We have three calling cards, wooden blocks with the letters T, C, and T on them. I've looked up all acronyms that use those letters, and I've come up with a whole lot of nothing. We need to issue a mandatory curfew until we nail this son of a bitch." Cami threw her pencil on her desk and rubbed her face. "What the hell is going on in this town?"

Kelsey sat back in her chair and crossed her arms. "Brandt told me the mayor is 'this close' to calling in state investigators," she said, making a pinching motion with her thumb and forefinger. "She doesn't want to make us seem like we can't handle it, so she's giving us a little more time, but if we don't figure something out soon, it's over."

"Where was Evan Conley last night, just for shits and giggles?"

"Some bank function in Manchester. First thing I checked, even though everything he's told us since we searched his house has panned out. I can't believe he hasn't been fired yet."

Cami scoffed. "Rich white guys have a different set of rules to play by, you know that. He probably gave the board a sob story about sex addiction or something and told them he'll be on his best behavior if they just give him a chance. Happens every day." Cami looked at the report in front of her and flipped a page. "Same gun used as the last two. Forensics will need to confirm, but we've definitely got a serial killer on our hands."

"Serial killer is four, I think," Kelsey said, shrugging.

Cami rolled her eyes. "Really, you're going to bring semantics into it? Someone has killed three people in two months in a town that hasn't seen anything like this. Ever. Remember when the black pepper ice cream recipe was taken hostage and whoever had it was waiting to sell to the highest bidder? It was utter chaos around here for weeks."

"It ended up being a photocopy of some other recipe. Good times," Kelsey said wistfully.

"No kidding. I'm heading over to Patrick McCallum's office in a few minutes. He was apparently working late with a few other people.

I'll see if they know anything or can think of anyone that might have a vendetta against him. Not too hopeful, but it's worth a shot. You coming?"

Kelsey pursed her lips and gestured to the door. They walked through the mostly silent police department with heavy shoulders.

"When are you meeting with Alicia again?" Kelsey asked as they pulled into the cable company's parking lot where Patrick McCallum worked.

"What do you mean?" Cami snapped.

Kelsey raised her eyebrows. "Don't you have that monthly meeting with the *Knox County Sun*? Was that a one-shot deal?"

"Oh." Cami laughed insincerely. "That. Yes, I actually have that tomorrow I think. I don't know what the mayor expects, honestly. I have no new information to give her that won't make us look worse than we already do. I'll have to try to schmooze my way through the usual talking points."

Kelsey nodded with a smirk.

The office was solemn, and only a few employees sat in their cubicles. There appeared to be a company meeting taking place in the conference room, and Cami could see people dabbing their eyes. A man in a suit approached them from the conference room.

"Detectives?" he asked.

"Yes, Mr. Cote?"

He nodded. "The two employees Patrick was working with last night are right over there. Josh Grayson and Mike Heinz. We've been expecting you."

Cami and Kelsey followed him to a set of cubicles. They thanked him, and he went back into the conference room. "Divide and conquer?" Kelsey asked.

"Sure. I'll take Josh. We can compare notes after."

Josh's cube was messy, but he seemed to have an organized mess that he could interpret. He pushed up his glasses and offered Cami a seat, a folding chair near his set of metal drawers.

"Did you know Patrick well?" Cami asked, sitting.

"Yeah, pretty well. We've worked together for almost three years. He was a good guy. I'm still in shock."

"I'm very sorry for your loss. I just need to ask you a couple of questions, and then I'll let you get back to your day. We're going to find whoever did this to Patrick."

Josh nodded. "I hope so."

"Who else was working late last night?"

"Just me and Mike and Pat."

"Do you know if there was anyone Pat didn't get along with? Someone who might have wanted him dead?"

Josh had a Godzilla calendar hanging up on his cube wall along with some patches tacked around it. Most of it was foreign to Cami, but she noticed one that was a red die with a "20" on the front of it. She didn't know much about Dungeons & Dragons but was pretty sure it was played with twenty-sided dice.

"No, no one that I can think of."

Cami nodded. Josh seemed to be on edge, which wasn't out of the ordinary. Most people were a little nervous when being questioned by a detective, even if they had nothing to do with the crime. "Do the two of you play Dungeons & Dragons together?"

Josh coughed. "Um, yeah. Sometimes."

Huh. He didn't mention that when Cami asked how well Josh knew Patrick. "Is there anyone at your games who had a problem with Patrick?"

"Not that I know of."

"Was Patrick the last person to leave the office last night?"

"No, I was still here when he left. Mike left before him."

Cami made a note. "And there was no one else in the building? When Patrick left, was he alone?"

"How would I know that?" Josh asked, nearly shouting.

"Why did that question upset you, Josh?" Cami kept an even keel to her tone and cocked her head.

"I'm upset because my friend is dead. And you're making it seem like I had something to do with it."

"I'm not sure how you made that connection, Josh. You're not a suspect in Patrick's murder. I'm trying to figure out who he was with and who might know something. If there's something that you need to tell me in a more private area, by all means, let me know."

Kelsey poked her head around the corner from where she was speaking to Mike. "Everything good here?"

"Yes, we're fine." Cami smiled.

Kelsey nodded and turned back around the corner.

"No, I don't have anything else to tell you. Sorry," Josh muttered. He pushed his glasses up on his nose again and sighed.

Cami asked a few more inane questions and got the same quick, one-word answers that Josh seemed disposed to give her. She thanked him for his time and met up with Kelsey outside the office building.

"What was up with your guy?" Kelsey asked.

"Something. I don't know yet. How about you, anything interesting?"

Kelsey nodded. "Yes, actually. Mike left before Patrick McCallum but forgot his cup of coffee on the picnic table over there. He was barely out of the parking lot when he realized it, so he turned around to come get it. He said he saw Patrick walking home. When he drove by after he had gotten his coffee, Patrick was walking with a woman."

"Really. Did he know who she was?" Cami asked.

"No. He didn't remember much about her. Only that she had dark hair with colored streaks in it. Maybe blue or green, he thought. Shouldn't be too hard to track down."

Cami smiled tightly. "I bet someone in there knows who she is."

"You think Josh knows?"

"I'd bet on it. He was cagey about Patrick leaving with someone. I'd like to find out why he was withholding her identity, if he does know who she is. I'll be back in a minute."

Cami jogged back toward the building and walked toward the cubicles in the back of the room. Mike was at the copier. "Forget something, Detective?" he asked.

"I had one more question for Josh. Do you know if he's at lunch?" Cami asked, seeing the empty cube.

"Actually, he wasn't feeling well. He left for the day. Our manager figured it was just a physical reaction to everything that's going on. It's still so surreal."

"Probably. Thanks, Mike."

The front door of the office was an old school revolving door. Cami hadn't been in one in about ten years, so she'd forgotten how slow they could be. She tried pushing the bar in front of her, but it didn't help. By the time she got outside, she didn't see anyone leaving or any cars pulling out. Josh must have left in a hurry.

Cami decided she'd pay him a visit the following day, since he was apparently too sick to continue working. She'd run a quick scan on him when she got back to the station, although with the way things had been going, she wasn't expecting much.

As she made her way through the office toward the back lot where she and Kelsey had parked, Cami's phone vibrated in her pocket, a text from Alicia. Her stomach fluttered a little, but it was just because she hadn't eaten yet.

Hey there. We're supposed to meet tomorrow for our monthly thing. Can you make the diner at 9 tomorrow morning? If not, just let me know when you're free, and I'll make it work. She ended with a smiley face.

Cami looked at Kelsey, who was leaning against her Jeep with her face buried in her phone. She looked up when she heard Cami coming and waved at her to hurry. Patience wasn't her strong suit.

That frantic phone call from Alicia the night before had rekindled something Cami had assumed long dead: an intrinsic urge to protect her. She'd told Alicia she'd just been doing her job by being there, and while that was true, the drive that had propelled her to the scene so quickly had nothing to do with the job. The overwhelming need to get to her; the huge exhalation of held breath when she'd seen her standing safely in the vestibule. *Old feelings kicked up by freakish circumstances. It happens.* With the intensity of the situation, it was no wonder that familiar and uninvited emotions had wormed their way in. Alicia had been a big part of her life. Besides, she'd hugged many people who were upset or scared while she'd been on duty. The encounter with her was no different.

Cami nodded and shot off a quick response: *See you then.*

Chapter Eighteen

Alicia sat at the giant monitor in the newsroom, scrolling through old lawsuits to find precedents for her latest article. She had a pretty interesting lead on retaliatory actions from a statewide clothing store against a couple of local union organizers. She knew she had to meet with the legal team before publishing, but she wanted to get as much research out of the way as possible.

Jade's office was empty, as it had been for the last week. Her white pleather jacket still hugged her office chair as though she had just stepped out for a bit, but Alicia knew she'd been avoiding the office to sidestep any questions. Jade was a private person, and the whole thing was an embarrassment to her, even though Alicia had assured her a thousand times that she had nothing to be ashamed of. It didn't seem to work.

"Is she okay?"

Alicia looked up from the article she'd been reading and was surprised to see Sam standing by her desk. She didn't usually come into the office so early. Sam nodded into Jade's office. "She will be. I think she's trying to sort through it all right now, but you know Jade. She's tough, and she doesn't take shit from anyone, never mind someone who's been betraying her for the last however-many years. She deserves a good breakdown, and then I'm sure she'll be back at it." The basics were out in the open, but Alicia didn't know how much Sam knew or how much Jade wanted her to know. Anyone, for that matter.

"I'm sure she's looking at everything through a different lens now." Sam hesitated. "Do you ever just wish you could press the rewind button and do a bunch of things differently?"

"More than you know."

"Yeah. Me too. I'm sure Jade will be fine. And if she wanted to date again, there'd be no shortage of suitors. She turns heads everywhere she goes. Speaking of dating." Sam curled a piece of thread from her sleeve around her finger.

Alicia braced herself. After the barbecue, Sam had tried to conceal the fact that she wasn't happy that Alicia had said she was going home and then stayed for a conversation with Cami. She hadn't done a great job of it. Alicia knew she was upset, and she understood why to a point. She hadn't been lying about leaving; she really did plan on going. But Cami had showed up and wanted to talk to her, so what was she supposed to do?

But she also couldn't tell Sam the millions of reasons she couldn't have just left. Alicia didn't know her well enough to divulge that kind of information, and even if she did, some things were just private. They'd talked here and there since the barbecue, but Alicia had felt a little awkward around her.

Sam seemed to sense her change in demeanor. "I wanted to know if you wanted to grab dinner a night this week. Just friends. I'm getting the impression that maybe you're not in the market for a relationship."

Alicia breathed out. "I'd like that. I'm sorry, Sam. I'm sure I've been sending mixed signals, and that's not fair to you. I like you, I really do, but you're right. I'm just not in a place where I can start something new. I could certainly use a friend, though. Thank you."

"Good. Then we'll set it up."

Alicia got the sense that Sam wasn't thrilled with her response based on her body language, but she was gracious enough. Alicia checked her watch and detached her laptop from the dock. "I have a meeting I need to get to," Alicia said.

"Oh, okay. The monthly one with Lyons?"

"Yes," Alicia said, surprised. "I can't even remember what happened yesterday. You're good."

Sam shrugged, smiling. "That's why they pay me the big bucks."

"Text me when you want to go out. Have a good day if I don't see you again," Alicia said. She headed out to her car with her mind refocused on Cami and their meeting. She wondered if it would be more comfortable than last time since they'd had that conversation. Civil, Cami had said. Alicia had no choice but to embrace the civility.

❖

The Crumbly Biscuit was more crowded than usual. But the atmosphere felt off. Instead of the usual loud banter of political arguments and Boston sports talk and upcoming summer plans, the conversations were muted and serious.

Alicia made her way toward the back booth where she and Cami had sat last time, and sure enough, Cami was there drinking an iced coffee and munching on a cinnamon roll. At least she seemed more relaxed.

A man in his mid-forties or so was leaned over the back of his booth, gesturing to Cami. "But how long are we supposed to live like this? A curfew is something you see in a friggin' police state."

Cami sighed. Alicia wasn't sure how long this conversation had been going back and forth, but it seemed like maybe it had been a while. "We're just trying to keep everyone safe. We all need to be diligent…oh, hi," Cami said as if noticing Alicia for the first time. She smiled.

The fact that Cami appeared to be reasonably pleased to see her, even as simply an escape from the guy in the booth, caused a tiny shiver to run up Alicia's spine. "Hey. Have you been here long?" Alicia slid into the booth and took out her notebook and pen. She assumed that Cami might be more open to a recorded conversation this time around, but she didn't want to chance it.

"Long enough. I got here early. Not your fault. People act like I'm the final word on the matter. I can give my input, but ultimately, the decision to implement a curfew or any other measure is up to the captain. And even then, it can be upheld or overturned by the town council." Cami took a bite of her cinnamon roll and shrugged.

Alicia wrote down the gist of what she had said. Might be a good idea for a quick refresher on who did what at the town level. She could incorporate that into the beginning of her article. "I have to address the elephant in the room before I ask any other questions," Alicia said.

Cami stiffened, and Alicia realized it was the second time that day she'd caused someone to brace for what she'd been about to say. Seemed to say more about her than them.

"The thing in the victim's pocket that you and Kelsey noticed. You didn't seem surprised by it and appeared to know what it was before looking at it. Can you tell me what it was?"

Cami relaxed. "I can't. But I will tell you that your 'calling card' theory wasn't completely unfounded. We've found similar items at all three crime scenes."

Alicia sucked in a breath. *Holy shit.*

Cami had obviously noticed her reaction. "I know. I have to ask you to keep this between us for now. If the killer thinks we're asking the public for help with that particular piece, it could hamper the investigation. Can you agree to that?"

"Yes. You have my word."

"Thank you." Cami lowered her voice to a barely audible whisper. "We've found these little blocks, like toy building blocks, on each of the victims. They aren't remarkable except for a single letter on each of them. T, C, and T."

"Is the killer spelling something? Or do you think it's a red herring?" Her whole ordeal just got a lot more real and a lot more terrifying. If these weren't targeted killings—and it didn't seem like it based on basic victim profiles—Alicia could have been the one who'd ended up dead in front of her apartment building.

"We don't know. There aren't any three-letter words you can make with those letters, which means that either the killer has more murders planned, or he's not trying to spell a word. The only four-letter word we've come up with is 'tact,' which doesn't mean a whole lot. None of the victims were particularly foulmouthed or known for being vulgar based on interviews with their family members and coworkers. We're working every angle with these things, but nothing has made a lot of sense so far."

Alicia could feel her frustration. "Attic?"

"Maybe. But that's a really broad and common word. Just about every house in Knox County has an attic, so that doesn't narrow it down much."

"True." Alicia sighed. "So do you have *any* leads?"

"A few. You can put that on the record. We are diligently chasing down every viable tip, examining every piece of evidence, and following every lead that crosses our path. We are confident that we will catch and apprehend the person responsible for these heinous acts very soon." Cami punctuated herself by tapping Alicia's notebook with her index finger.

"Very good, Detective. I will make sure the public knows we're in good hands." Alicia couldn't help but smile as she transcribed the rehearsed statement. "I take it you've had some time to hone your interview skills?"

"It's the truth." Cami finished the last of her cinnamon roll and rubbed her hands free of crumbs. "I just made sure to tie it in a neat little bow so, um, *liberties* couldn't be taken. I know everyone is only interested in the murders and the curfew, but we do have a couple of non-murder related crime initiatives coming up. We're partnering with the Neighborhood Watch committee in Chester Bluffs. Katie set up the whole thing. I think it'll be good for everyone to feel like they have some control. And we're also implementing a new nine p.m. lock up reminder for people to lock their car doors. Prevent some unnecessary heartache when hooligans break into cars for cash or electronics."

Alicia looked up. "Wait. Hold on. Did you really just say *hooligans*?"

"Oh, shut up." Cami rolled her eyes. "You know what I mean."

"I do. I for one am sick of all the hooligans around here, with their tomfoolery and podsnappery." Alicia wrote hooligans in big black letters across the top of the page and circled it.

"What the hell is podsnappery?"

Alicia laughed. "I forget. I think it means 'smug' or something like that."

"Well *anyway*, as I was saying, we have a lot of safety stuff planned for the community. I think it will help, even if it's just to create an illusion of control until we catch the fucker. Don't write that down."

"I won't. Jade is going to be pissed if I make it too touchy-feely, all is well, so I have to include something at least a little controversial."

Cami sighed. "I guess you can include something—very little—about the fact that we don't have a definite link between the victims yet. That'll play into your whole 'the police are inept' storyline from the last article."

"Stop, there was no storyline. There may have been a few sentences that *alluded* to the fact that our fearless local PD was dealing with something unprecedented for our area, but that was it."

"Yeah, okay. If that's what makes you feel better."

"Do you remember when you first made detective?" Alicia rested her chin on her hand. "You were so proud. We both were. We'd stay up late at night watching reruns of CSI and NCIS, even though you loved to remind me how unrealistic they were. You wanted to give back, to make the bad guys pay for taking advantage of the good guys. You've always had a profound sense of justice. It was one of the many things I loved about you."

Cami seemed, for a second, to be lost in the moment. Alicia's heart ached at the wistfulness in her eyes. She coughed suddenly and straightened. "But do you remember my first case? The one Brandt assigned to me with all the seriousness of a major felony?"

"Of course I remember. You were in your brand-new suit, black slacks and jacket with a gray shirt so you'd look super professional, those uncomfortable leather shoes my mom bought you, your hair up in that twist so the criminal couldn't grab it. I remember it like it was yesterday." Alicia paused. She reached across the table and lightly tugged on one of Cami's curls that hung well beneath her shoulder. "Is that no longer a threat?"

"Having your hair pulled in the wild isn't as big of a problem as I'd assumed. Kind of like quicksand and erupting volcanoes. Much less of a hazard than some would believe," Cami said, smiling. "I'll never forget knocking on that guy's door. It was this little dilapidated bungalow, and the chief had briefed me on his suspected history of organized retail crime. He'd been out stealing goods and reselling them for a profit. I was nervous as hell, too." She shook her head.

Alicia chuckled. "You must have been terrified when he ran."

"Yeah! He opened the door, took one look at me, and dashed off through the house. I didn't get a good look at him at all. He had this giant sword lying on his coffee table. I thought for sure I was toast. First assignment. I called for backup, drew my gun, and went to find him. Totally by the book. I felt like Clarice in *Silence of the Lambs*. The main floor was clear, so I had no choice but to go down to the basement that was more of a stone cellar type of thing. Out of nowhere, I started to hear it."

Alicia laughed. Cami could tell a story like no one else. The restaurant had faded into a colorless backdrop against Cami, who had leaned in for effect.

"*Hic. Hic.* Then nothing. Total silence. I moved along the wall with my back against it in case he jumped out at me. Then again. *Hic. Hic.* I kicked in the wooden door to this small room, I think it was used for canning or something at one time. And there he was. A twenty-two-year-old kid with braces and a bad case of the hiccups, surrounded by hundreds of Thin Mints, Tagalongs, Do-Si-Dos, Samoas…you name it. Girl Scout Cookie crime ring."

"You were *so* pissed," Alicia said, laughing harder than she had in a long time. "Brandt really made you think you were infiltrating the mob."

Cami was laughing, too. "He could have sent anyone. I still think he was trying to teach me a lesson about humility."

"I forget, what was the deal with the sword?"

"Oh, he was part of a medieval cosplay group on the weekends. It was made of really shiny plastic."

Alicia wiped tears from her eyes. It was a good thing no one around them was paying much attention, or it might have seemed inappropriate for the county crime reporter and the detective of Oakview to be yukking it up during a serious interview.

Cami checked her phone. "I have to go. Duty calls. Do you have enough for your article?"

"I should. If I have any gaps to fill in, I'll just make something up." Alicia shrugged.

Cami shot her a look.

"Kidding. I'll call you if I need anything else?"

"Okay. Have a good day."

Alicia watched as Cami walked through the restaurant, her phone to her ear, a mission on her mind, and the quiet confidence that Alicia had always found so attractive.

She gathered up her things and sighed heavily. "Regret the past and mourn the future," Alicia muttered. Her heart was an oxymoron, full but empty at the same time. She sighed again before sliding out of the booth and heading for the exit.

Chapter Nineteen

"Who was she, Josh?"

Cami sat on the corner of the desk in the conference room. Kelsey had spoken with Patrick's ex-wife, who didn't know of any woman in Patrick's life with blue or green streaks in her hair. She'd also spoken to his father and sister, who lived in Rhode Island and hadn't seen him since Easter. Neither of them could place her, either.

"Why do you think I know?"

"Do you?" He was clearly nervous and jittery, so Cami kept it calm and cool. Her persistent eye contact seemed to make him dart his around the room.

"Lots of women have funky hair. It's not like it's a rare thing."

"Certainly not rare. But not common to the point of say, blue eyes. If you mention a person with green hair, chances are that someone who knows them would be able to identify them."

He didn't say anything.

"Okay." Cami nodded at nothing in particular and paced the room. "You don't have to tell me anything. My partner spoke with other members of your D&D group. They didn't have a name for us, but they did mention that they'd seen you a time or two with a woman who fits our description. They said you looked 'close' when they saw you walking with her last year at King Arthur's Faire. I haven't followed up yet. Elise probably knows her?"

Josh's head whipped around. "Elise doesn't know her. What does my girlfriend have to do with any of this?"

Cami held her hands up. "Nothing. But we need to talk to the last person Patrick was seen with. Since you won't tell us, we thought Elise could help. If you're 'close' to the green-haired girl, and Elise is your girlfriend, it only makes sense that she would know her."

Anger, and maybe a touch of fear, clouded over Josh's face. "Isn't this blackmail?"

"How? By asking your girlfriend if she can identify a woman that was seen with a man not long before he was murdered? How is that blackmailing *you*?"

"I know who she is. It's not what you think. I didn't cheat on my girlfriend, but she's not a fan of hers, so I don't want to get her mixed up in anything, okay? So if I tell you what you want to know, you won't talk to her?" He stared straight ahead.

"As long as the information you give me doesn't facilitate a need to talk to her, no, I won't. Tell me, Josh, who is she, and why were you so hesitant to tell me?"

"Patrick knew her from some medieval reenactment thing he was involved in. Her name is Crystal…Caruso, I think, and she lives in Chester Bluffs. She's big into mycology. If I tell you this stuff, I can't incriminate myself, right?" He scratched his fingernail along an imperfection of the wooden table.

"Well, that depends on exactly what you'd be incriminated *of*. If it's something minor, I'll make sure to put in a good word for you since you're helping us with the investigation." She wanted to make sure Josh felt like he was doing the right thing for morality's sake and not being strong-armed. Which, Cami knew, he sort of was. But it *was* the right thing to do if it would help them catch Patrick's killer. "Mycology, you said?"

"Yeah. Fungi. You know, mushrooms. She grows psilocybin mushrooms. The trippy kind. She kind of mastered the art of growing them in her basement, and it turned out to be, um, lucrative. Her entire basement is a complete fungus factory. So me and Patrick got in on the action, and we all made a little money. I stopped a while ago. Months. I mean, I still buy from her, but I don't sell anymore. I don't want to go to jail. Am I fucked now that I've told you this?" He chewed the side of his thumbnail down to the quick.

Cami sighed. Not at all what she'd been expecting. "Selling drugs is a serious criminal offense, which you're obviously aware of. But in the spirit of 'doing the right thing,' I'll speak to the local DEA in Chester Bluffs. We'll work something out, okay?"

"Don't tell Crystal you heard any of this from me. I don't know who else she sells to. Maybe she works with mafia guys who'll snuff me out like a mosquito."

"We'll make sure you're safe."

He nodded. "Okay. My girlfriend doesn't have to know about any of this, does she? There are some things I keep to myself. That whole ordeal was one of them."

"No, she doesn't, not from me anyway. But you may want to be more open with her. Silence can be a killer. Trust me."

Cami told him that the Chester Bluffs Police Department would be in touch, but she had to reassure him one more time that he wouldn't go to prison for the rest of his life. But if what he had said turned out to be true, Crystal Caruso was in a lot of trouble.

Cami sat outside the Chester Bluffs Police Department at a picnic table underneath one of the oak trees that lined the back of the station. They were sending units out to Crystal Caruso's house, and as long as Josh had told her the truth—which Cami was confident that he had—they'd be bringing her in for a whole lot more than being the last person seen with Patrick McCallum. A few states had adopted leaner penalties for drug offenses, but New Hampshire was not one of them.

Katie brought out a plastic container full of salad and a wrapped sandwich. She tossed the sandwich to Cami.

"Egg salad?" Cami asked, inspecting the soft white bread with the pale-yellow substance poking out of it.

"Yeah, that was all they had left. It was either that or congealed seafood chowder."

"Egg salad is good." Cami smiled and happily unwrapped the sandwich after knowing her other option. "I love a warm mushy sandwich on a hot day."

"You're lucky there was anything in the caff. Everyone grabbed lunch and hightailed it out of here as soon as they could. Eighty-seven degrees in early June doesn't happen very often."

Cami closed her eyes and let the sun warm her face. "This case is going to be the death of me."

"I know. There's like this unspoken thing around town, 'am I next'? Nobody will come right out and say it, but everyone's thinking it."

"That's why we're trying to be proactive. The curfew, asking people to travel in pairs, etc. I know it's not always possible, but at least until we have some sort of profile or a connection between the victims. Better safe than sorry." Cami took a huge bite and instantly regretted it as a swath of cracked pepper hit the back of her throat. She coughed harshly. "They couldn't even mix it?"

"Oh, stop complaining. Taryn and I are going to see *Chicago* next week at the Belmont. We were supposed to go with her brother and his wife, but she has to go out of town for work. I think she just doesn't want to go, but Taryn said I'm being cynical. As usual." Katie pushed her salad to the side. "I should have brought my own dressing. That one leaves an aftertaste. Anyway. Do you want to come with us? I know you loved the movie. Maybe you can take Maya?"

Cami sighed. "I don't think so. Last time I saw her, things didn't go so well."

"What happened?" Katie asked, leaning forward. "And why didn't you tell me?"

"I don't really know what happened. It was weird. She showed up at my house, we had pizza, watched a little TV, and then she wanted to…you know…and I wasn't up for it."

Katie rolled her eyes. "Are we twelve? Why weren't you up for it? What did you say to her?"

Cami ignored the first question. "I just wasn't in the mood. So I told her that. And she said she would stay over anyway, and we could just, I don't know, cuddle or something. And I told her that I really just wanted to be alone and maybe next time. Or something like that."

"You said…" Katie dropped her head dramatically onto the table. "You said *that*? I thought you liked Maya. Why didn't you want her to spend the night?"

"I just didn't." Cami was exasperated with the questioning, although this wasn't anything out of the ordinary. Katie's badgering was usually part of her charm. "With everything going on, I just wasn't in the mood to be 'on,' you know? I wanted to just relax and sleep and not worry about someone lying next to me."

Katie narrowed her eyes. "When you're with her, you feel like you have to be 'on'? It's not just a natural thing to spend time together?"

"I hadn't really thought about it. I like her, I do. There just isn't that comfort level yet. Like where I can do my own thing while she's in my space. I feel like I have to entertain her, or she'll get bored. And then I'll be edgy trying to figure out if she's bored. It's a whole thing." Cami balled up the plastic wrap and tossed it into the garbage can from her seat.

"Have you called her to talk about it?"

Cami looked at a knot in the wood. "Not yet."

"Cami! What's wrong with you? She's going to think you don't care and that you're just not interested." Katie lowered her voice when a couple of people walking by slowed to get an earful.

"I know. Honestly, I've just been avoiding it because I'm still not in the right frame of mind to make it up to her. Everything feels off lately. It's work."

"It's not just work."

"What does that mean?"

Katie scoffed. "Please. Everything was going fine with you and Maya, and all of a sudden, *she* swoops back into town, and here you are, ending it with Maya because you need 'space' or whatever. I knew this was going to happen."

Cami held up a hand. "Whoa. What are you even talking about? Alicia? She has nothing to do with this."

"She has everything to do with this. Cam, you've been my best friend for as long as I can remember, and I know you. You may think that you're all shrouded in mystery, but you're as transparent as a ghost. From the second she showed back up here, you've been different. You're distant and moody, and you tend to space out and daydream in the middle of a conversation. She's bad news. You gave her every chance to make it up to you, to choose a different path, and she didn't. She chose not to. She chose herself over the two of you. The sooner you remember that, the better off you'll be." Katie shook her head and finished off her lemonade.

Cami didn't even know how to respond. Half of her was pissed at Katie's callousness; the other half was in shock. Was any of what she'd said true? *Had* she been acting differently since Alicia had walked back into her life? Cami prided herself on her keen sense of self-awareness, but maybe she really did have a blind spot when it came to Alicia. She'd been through so many sets of emotions: anger, sadness, resentment, nostalgia. Ad nauseam.

"So am I supposed to just hate her and ignore her until the end of time? That was a lot easier when she was across the globe, or even when she was fifty miles away. When she's here, in our town, and I have to *work* with her, it's not so easy. What would you like me to do, Katie? Am I supposed to feel enraged every time I see her?"

"No. You're not supposed to be enraged, and you're not supposed to hate her. You're supposed to be indifferent, Cami. You're supposed to not care where she is or who she's with or what she's doing. You're supposed to look at her like she's in the rearview, someone you used to know, someone you used to care about, but that was a long time ago. You're supposed to remember how deeply she hurt you. How upside down your life was until somewhat recently. How many nights you cried in my arms because you didn't understand why she left the way that she did. And then you toughened up. You steeled yourself and said no more. When those calls and texts started trickling in, you knew that no matter what she said on the other end of the line, nothing was going to make it okay. Apologies and declarations of friendship or anything else she might come up with were shallow and irrelevant. What was done was done. You're supposed to feel *nothing*, Cami. Nothing."

Katie's eyes were glassy, and her lips were pursed tightly. Cami swallowed hard. She hadn't seen Katie this emotional about something in a long time. What she'd said made sense. All the sense in the world. But it wasn't real. Cami didn't feel nothing. She didn't feel indifferent. She felt a lot of things, but indifference didn't seem to be one of them.

"I tried to keep it. Those feelings." Cami traced the mountain on her water bottle with her index finger. "When I first saw her, after the shock wore off, I was furious. I was so pissed off at her for just waltzing back to Oakview like everything was fine, and the world just kept on spinning after she'd left. Mine didn't, as *you* know by having a front row seat. Everything she did just made me angrier and angrier. And then she wrote that article, and I thought that was it. That was the straw that would break the camel's back. She and I would have it out, I'd tell her to fuck off once and for all, she'd move away, and we'd never have to see each other again. But it didn't happen that way. She just kept, I don't know, *being* there and saying the right things, and I could feel my fury dissipating. I didn't want it to."

"Why did you let it?"

Cami scoffed. "Let it? I held on to it with everything I had. Every time I'd feel the slightest little hint of *not* hating her, I'd pull it back. I'd go through that night again in my head. I'd remember sitting alone at the events she and I were supposed to attend together. I'd remember how distraught I'd felt in the aftermath. But then something happened. I couldn't do it anymore. I just couldn't generate enough of the anger to sustain the *loathing* that I thought would be my faithful companion till the end of time. I saw her that night at Violet's barbecue, and instead of the recoil I was expecting to feel, I…smiled. I actually fucking smiled because she looked good, and she was clearly watching for me, and I noticed the second she saw me that she looked away, I assume because of nerves, and then she was about to leave. I was so angry at myself for smiling—even though it was just a fraction of a second before I realized what I was doing and turned my face back to stone—that I wondered if maybe I was on the wrong side of this. Maybe I should let it go, just a little bit. And before I knew it, I was walking up to her and telling her to go ahead, say what she needed to say."

Katie looked toward the parking lot and blinked a few times. Cami thought about getting up and storming off, but she knew Katie's heart was in the right place. She was her friend, she'd seen her at her lowest, and Katie didn't want her to forgive the person who had put her there. Cami didn't know if she'd ever forgive Alicia, but she also knew she couldn't keep feeding the fury. She didn't have it in her anymore.

"So that's it?" Katie said, her voice barely above a whisper. "She gets to leave, destroy everything, have a wonderful time for herself, and just come back into the fold? Like nothing ever happened? Are you two getting back together?"

"No! That's not even in the realm of possibility. I've moved on. She's moved on. I'm just not going to hate her anymore. I don't want to feel guilty for saying hello when I see her or worrying that I might smile if she's in the same room. It's stupid. Life's too short, Katie. She said she regrets what she did more than anything she's ever done. We all have our demons. She just decided to look hers in the face every day."

"I get where you're coming from. I do. But I feel like all you're doing is making it easy for her. It's a lot easier to live with those demons when they've rolled out the red carpet of forgiveness."

Three uniformed police officers came through the back door. Cami and Katie both stood when one of the officers approached. Cami was thankful for the interruption.

"Detective Lyons?"

"Yes."

"The chief wanted us to let you know we're heading over to Crystal Caruso's house. Everything is in order, and we have what we need," he said, and tapped on the manila folder he was holding.

"Perfect. I'll follow you in my Jeep."

He nodded and went to his cruiser.

Cami turned to Katie before going. "I love you, K. I promise you, I'm not acting like some naive fool. I'm just trying to, I don't know, lighten my load, as the saying goes. I can't carry all that shit around all the time. I'm too tired."

Katie nodded. "You better get going. This killer isn't going to catch himself." She turned and walked back into the building, the door closing tightly behind her. Cami thought about stopping her, to tell her she'd stay away from Alicia, to say that she'd keep Alicia in the past where she belonged. Instead, she followed the flashing blues of the car in front of her in silence.

CHAPTER TWENTY

Detective Camilla Lyons wants you to feel safe. While the unfolding situation in Oakview is alarming, Detective Lyons, or "Cami" as those around town know her, wants the community to know that precautions are being taken, and police presence has increased dramatically. Safety alerts via email, text messages, and mobile apps are front and center for both prevention and engagement. While standard practices, such as tip lines are still in effect, the new technology allows tipsters to create a two-way conversation using the new tools, all while remaining anonymous. Det. Lyons believes that community engagement is the fastest way to apprehend the Small-Town Slayer, as many have been referring to the seemingly indiscriminate shooter.

Alicia leaned back in her chair and rubbed the back of her neck. She had her hair thrown up in a messy ponytail, and one of the fine hairs at the back of her neck was caught in her necklace.

"Ouch," she said as she unclasped her necklace and tugged on her hair. She'd been distracted all evening. One thing or another had kept her from writing the article, from the mundane of turning the fan off and on to the nonexistent sounds outside her window.

She'd put on the Tiffany bracelet Cami had given her a long time ago. It had been stashed in her jewelry box, but she thought it might finally be okay to put it back on. Her wrist felt complete. The infinity loop caught the light a few times and created shiny spots on the wall. Her apartment was hot, but she refused to turn the air-conditioning on yet. It was barely June, and her electric bill was already through the roof.

It wasn't that she didn't want to write, she did, but she knew that Jade wanted her to keep on the same course as the last article. Since no suspect was in custody yet, the piece nearly wrote itself. But knowing what Cami had told her, and what she'd seen with her own eyes the night in front of her apartment building, it didn't feel right to come up with a derisive take on the police department's investigation. Was she being biased?

She tried to get herself in check. "Fair and neutral. Impartial. Balanced. Cami is just some police detective who hasn't dealt with this kind of crime before because she's from a hokey-poke town where these things don't happen. Kelsey is a dedicated but inexperienced sidekick, and Captain Brandt is trying to keep everything else afloat while this dominates the news cycles and everyone's psyche. Of course the department is stretched thin. The public should know that."

Even saying it out loud felt disingenuous. It felt like kicking them while they were down, which wasn't what she had planned on doing. Maybe instead of focusing on the shortcomings of the Oakview PD, Alicia could write about her personal experience with the killer. What it had felt like when she saw Patrick McCallum sitting lifelessly on the bench, what she'd been thinking when the sirens had broken the silence of the night, and the comfort of—*Cami's arms around her*—knowing that the police were on the scene and piecing together the evidence needed to catch the psychopath responsible for all of this. She hoped Jade would go for it.

After having a quick snack, checking her phone a few times, doing a quick vacuum of the hallway, applying a cucumber melon face mask, and some other general procrastinating, Alicia sat back down to her laptop and finished the rest of the article. Writing two thousand words had never seemed so daunting. It ended up, she thought, a very good article. She could only skim the surface on what she'd seen, but she felt that it tied in nicely with the mayor's column request. She finally met the required word count and shot it off to the *Sun's* editor mailbox.

Alicia looked out her bedroom window before getting into bed. She could make out a small portion of the bench she'd found Patrick

McCallum on. She wanted to get the image of him sitting there out of her head, but she found that easier said than done.

She'd never seen a dead body before. Not like that, anyway. She'd been to many funerals and had even covered a few for stories she'd written in the past, but she'd never been up close to a dead person before. She hadn't been *that* close, not really, but close enough to see his limp arms and sagging head. She tried to shake the thought away before it took hold and kept her up all night again.

Big Business was playing on cable, which was exactly the kind of lighthearted comedy Alicia needed to focus on. She brought a bowl of popcorn and a bottle of water from the kitchen and snuggled into her bed to think about nothing but Bette Midler and Lily Tomlin trying to save their town.

❖

Alicia's fears had not been unfounded.

"This reads like propaganda for the Oakview Police Department. Do you need me to pull you off this? I can ask Sam or that new guy Jared that the higher-ups made me hire to take over the meetings with Lyons. I thought we were going with the 'out of their league' storyline?" Jade crossed her arms and looked at Alicia over the rim of her glasses.

Alicia felt like she was being reprimanded by a high school teacher. "Jade, come on. It does *not* read like propaganda. This isn't an easy case, and there aren't any clear-cut theories or models that make sense. I just didn't think it was the right time to hammer them on it, especially when tensions are so high right now."

"I don't remember asking you to take the town's temperature before turning in your piece. Since when do we base our reporting on peoples' feelings?"

Yikes. She was really pissed. "I'm not saying that. I just…what about backlash? Everyone is sort of rallying together right now. Trying to find comfort in that community-family vibe. If you want me to rewrite it with a harsher perspective, I can try to do that, but I still don't think it's the right move. Not right now."

Jade pursed her lips and pushed her glasses back up on her nose. She skimmed the article again and highlighted a few things. She typed some notes in the margins, something she hadn't done to Alicia's work since Alicia had started at the paper all those years ago. She usually just gave her suggestions verbally or through email if there were any.

"I'll let it go this time because you may be right. Unity could be the smart angle to take. But I still feel like this is subjective, and that's because you're looking at Lyons through rose-colored lenses. You can try to tell me that you're not, but I won't believe you. If I think it's becoming too much of a problem, I'll have to replace you on the monthly column."

Rather than protesting in vain, which Alicia was sure she'd be doing, she just nodded and left Jade's office. Something, aside from the obvious, had to be going on with Jade for her to lash out like that. Even if what she'd been saying was truly how she'd felt—and it certainly might have been—Jade wasn't usually so harsh. Alicia had seen her snap at and condescend to writers in the past, but it was normally after she'd spoken to them numerous times about the same issue. Alicia thought about asking her what was wrong, but that might have sent her even further down the angry hole. She didn't want to question Jade's judgment or chalk it up to her having a bad day.

Alicia sighed heavily and waited for the return email with Jade's notes on her article. After about fifteen minutes of refreshing her inbox and scoping out local police logs, she gave up and went into the kitchen. Sam was sitting at one of the small round tables on her laptop.

"Hey," Alicia said. She took her small bowl of fruit out of the fridge and opened up her container of caramel dip to go with it. "You working in the kitchen today?"

Sam looked up at her and nodded. "Yeah. Bad vibes in the office today. Jade was on a tear this morning with Linda. She told her the obits needed to be condensed to fit on half a page, even though Linda told her there were more than usual this week, *and* a few memorials. For the victims, well, you know. Anyway. Nothing good was coming out of that office, so I'm steering clear."

"I was going to pack up and go home, but I didn't want her to think I was running away because she yelled at me," Alicia said, popping a caramel-covered apple into her mouth.

"Oh, she got you too?"

"Yup."

"Ouch. I'd go home, too, but I have to wait until the cable company turns my internet back on. They said it could take a few hours."

"Was there an outage?" Alicia asked.

"No, it was my fault. I forgot to pay the bill. I'm not a legacy opinion columnist or a fancy crime reporter, so I have to stretch my pennies." Sam smiled. She turned back to her laptop and pointed at the screen. "Hey, did you see all the restaurant thefts that have been taking place around Copper Lake? Large quantities of rock bass have been going missing from a bunch of local eateries. I think there might be more to the story than the police are letting on."

"I did hear about that, yeah." Alicia chomped on another apple slice. "It seems pretty cut-and-dried. They caught a vendor who'd sold napkins and other paper products to the restaurants packing a cooler."

"Yes, but who is he selling the fish to? I wonder if it's a statewide crime ring. Or something like that. I haven't figured it out yet. Have you thought about reporting on it?" Sam asked.

Alicia shook her head. "I did a small write-up for tomorrow's release. But it's just a quick recap."

"I really think we're sitting on something big here."

"I honestly don't think so. The city papers have been doing a deep dive on this for a few weeks now. They've done thorough coverage of it, and it looks like it was just a rinky-dink con job between a couple of down-on-their-luck guys. Doesn't seem like a sophisticated setup." Alicia threw the empty bowl and container in the trash and washed her hands. "I did mean to tell you, though, for one of your human-interest stories: there's a little girl on Magnolia Lane filling her front yard with mini flags for the fourth of July. She's coloring them all, I think. Her grandfather is a veteran."

"Cute." Sam looked at her laptop again and began typing.

Did I offend her? Alicia thought they were volleying ideas back and forth, but Sam seemed to shut down after Alicia didn't run with the stolen fish idea. Truth was, Alicia *had* looked into the story when word had gotten out about it a week or so earlier. There really was nothing there.

"Okay, well, I guess I'll head home after all," Alicia said. The air in the room had changed.

Sam looked up. "Sorry, I was distracted. We still have to grab dinner soon. I know it's been crazy with everything going on."

"Definitely. See you later."

Alicia turned and left the kitchen. She wasn't sure if Sam was upset with her, but she really had no reason to be. Ideas went unrealized all the time; it was the nature of the business.

Jade was still in her office, now with the door closed. She was on the phone with someone, flailing her arms and slapping her desk. Alicia quickly remembered why the idea of working from home had been so appealing.

Chapter Twenty-One

Crystal Caruso's basement looked like a farming experiment gone wrong. Very wrong. There were clear totes covering nearly every available inch of floor space, and the ventilation was nonexistent. Every tote contained piles of dirt, some with mold spreading around the bottom, some sitting in shallow water puddles, and there were mushrooms everywhere. Skinny ones, bulbous ones, brown ones, beige ones, and a few red ones. They'd evidently been experimenting with different strains.

When the Chester Bluffs drug unit had shown up to Crystal's door with the warrant in hand, her wide-eyed panic had given her away. She'd fumbled at first, trying to blame a non-existent roommate for the state of her house.

"I don't know what you heard about the basement, but it's not me. It was Paul. He stayed here for a while when he didn't have any money, and he turned this place into a drug lab. I've been trying to figure out how to get rid of it all without just throwing it into the trash. I wouldn't want kids to get ahold of it, you know?" Crystal had asked, flipping her hair over her shoulder. The streak was decidedly green.

Not wanting to interfere in another department's investigation, Cami had nudged one of the officers next to her and nodded to the coffee table. There were a few magazines splayed out, each with the title *Fungilove* plastered on the cover. They all had mushrooms on the covers, in every shape and size. One magazine was open with a highlighter lying in the crease. The page's header read *TIPS ON GROWING YOUR OWN PSYCHEDELIC TRANCE!* in big block letters.

The officer had smirked. "Is Paul here now?"

"No, he left…a few days ago."

The officer had pointed at the table. Crystal had winced. "I haven't had a chance to clean up," she said weakly.

"Okay, come on. Lead us to it."

Cami had followed at the back of the group. The house had seen better days, with its peeling wallpaper and worn carpets. But the smell that had hit them in the face when the basement door had been opened was enough to nearly knock Cami on her ass.

The wooden stairs had creaked as they'd made their way down. The stone walls kept the basement pretty dark, and the fact that Crystal had boarded up all the windows didn't help. It was pitch black until she'd grabbed a chain attached to a single lightbulb.

"Listen, it's not my fault. I hurt my back, and I couldn't get a job, so I had no choice but to do something so I wouldn't be homeless and starving. It was all Paul's idea!"

"I thought mushrooms didn't have a strong smell?" Cami asked now, covering her face with her hand.

The officer in front of her grimaced. "They're not supposed to. I think she must have a good number of rotten ones down here, too."

Once she tired of making excuses and blaming Paul, Crystal admitted that she'd had a *little* something to do with the mushroom harvesting. It turned out she had over fifty thousand dollars stashed away in a savings account in Vermont. Josh Grayson hadn't been lying. It *was* a lucrative arrangement.

After they put Crystal in the police car, she started to freak out again. Yelling about her parents and society and how if it hadn't been for Paul, she'd probably be an insurance salesman in New York City, her arms waving over her head like she was pretending to be a gorilla.

Thankfully, once they had her in the interrogation room, Crystal calmed down. The investigators were nice enough to let Cami have the first crack at her so she could straighten out what happened that night with Patrick McCallum.

"I didn't kill him. You can't frame me for that just because I sold some mushrooms!"

Cami rested her hand on her hip. "No one is framing you for anything, Crystal. Why don't you just walk me through the events of that evening? Did you have a destination in mind when the two of you were walking?"

"Look, I was friends with Pat, and that's it. We were in business for a while, too. He still bought from me sometimes, and that's what we were doing. He always said he felt the most at peace after he'd eaten a few. I met him after work, and we were walking to his apartment. It was kind of nice out, so we sat on a bench near his building. Next thing I know, I hear a loud bang, and Pat just sort of slumps forward. I jumped up and ran. They could have been trying to kill me." Crystal twirled a green strand of hair around her index finger feverishly.

"Why didn't you come forward? You just left your friend there to bleed out on a sidewalk bench and never said anything to anyone?" Cami tried to keep her voice even, but she struggled. That was a shitty thing to do, even if Crystal *was* mixed up in something illegal and trying to save her own ass.

"It's not like it happened in some remote part of the woods like it did to that Beverly Lawson lady. It was right near a building. It wasn't like nobody would ever find him. I panicked, okay? Either I had to run or I was going to get shot or go to jail. I chose to run."

Cami sat across from her and leaned forward in the uncomfortable folding chair. "What did you see?"

"Nothing. Whoever did it shot him from behind. I looked back while I was running, but I couldn't make anything out. There was a row of bushes behind where we were sitting, so he must have been hiding in there. Is this another one of those serial killer murders? I thought it was an old client that I pissed off or something. I've been staying home since it happened."

Cami ignored the question. They'd been heavily advised by the mayor's office to refrain from saying serial killer at all costs. It wasn't as though everyone in town didn't already think it, but police confirming it made it much more real. "Do you have any clients that you think would target you like this?"

Crystal shook her head. "No. I've always been real open and honest with the people I do business with. I've had a couple of tussles over cost, but nothing we didn't work out. I've been racking my brain to think of someone who'd want me dead, but I can't come up with anyone or anything."

"Where's Paul?"

"Clarksville, I think. Somewhere up there. He's a piece of shit anyway. It wasn't him, he doesn't have the motivation to follow through with something like that. He's a lazy ass who just wants to watch YouTube and smoke pot and eat Doritos all day. He went up there because he's got a buddy who rents a cheap apartment. So he took off and left me holding the bag." She seemed to be relaxing.

"Can you think of any reason someone would want to hurt Patrick? Is there anything we should know about him?"

Crystal shook her head. "No, he was the nicest guy. Kind of a loner, pretty quiet. He loved his role-playing games, and he missed his wife a lot. We kept it surface for the most part. Even when Pat and Josh were helping me with the harvesting and bagging and all that, we usually talked about work and music and stuff like that."

Cami wasn't sure if Crystal had realized she'd brought up Josh, but it did corroborate his story that he and Patrick had worked with her for a short time. Cami let it go.

"Have you seen anything suspicious since? Anyone lurking around your property, packages you didn't order, that type of thing?" Cami asked. An officer had handed her a note that confirmed they didn't find any weapons in Crystal's house. They'd have to do a more thorough investigation into her connection with Patrick McCallum and see if there were ties to any of the other victims, but Cami was under no illusion that she was the killer.

"No, nothing like that," Crystal said, shaking her head. "And I've been watching for it, believe me. Even if they weren't after me, they could have thought I saw something and wanted to kill me for being a witness or whatever. I've been on pins and needles since it happened."

"You know you could have taken some of that anxiety away by alerting the police, right? Sometimes, we really are the good guys," Cami said.

"Are you saying you would have let my little 'arrangement' go if I had just called the cops that night?"

"I didn't say that."

"Well, there you go." Crystal folded her arms indignantly. "My freedom isn't worth a little peace of mind."

Cami sighed and gathered her notes. She called the Chester Bluffs investigators back in and gave them the rundown. She was tired of dead end after dead end. Someone, somewhere must have seen something. She just had to find that person before it was too late.

❖

They'd been going to the Book Cabin for as long as Cami could remember and really only went at this point for nostalgia's sake. Only Violet still read paperbacks, so she was the anchor that kept them there. Their comfort food wasn't all bad either.

Cami sat next to Katie and eyed her grilled cheese. She wished she'd gotten one of those instead of the veggie and egg white omelet she'd opted for. Even Violet's low-rent charcuterie board was calling out to her.

"Hands off," Katie said, slapping Cami's hand away as she reached for a chip. "Why did you get that anyway? Are you starting some sort of health regimen we need to know about?"

"I had bacon and doughnuts for breakfast and a hot dog with tater tots for lunch. I felt like I needed to balance out the day, or I'd end up with a huge case of indigestion," Cami said. She took a bite of her omelet and winced. "It's fine. Delicious."

"That kale poking out the side looks amazing." Violet popped a Ritz cracker with a cheddar cheese wedge into her mouth.

"I hate you both." Cami forked another bite. Some of it fell off.

"What is that, a mushroom?" Katie asked.

"Ugh." Cami grimaced at the plate. "I should have asked her to hold those. I am mushroomed out."

"Guys," Violet shout-whispered. "Is that who I think it is?"

Cami and Katie turned toward the register where a small line had formed. Just behind the first customer was a tall brunette reading the back of a paperback. She had on a scoop-necked gray sweatshirt that read *Knox County Sun – Your Source for the Truth.*

"Alicia?" Violet called.

"What are you doing?" Katie glared at Violet.

Cami just stared in Alicia's direction, unsure if she wanted to smack Violet or thank her. She wouldn't have wanted to call her over herself because that seemed too…forward. Or something. Cami was afraid that if she initiated contact, it would leave her too vulnerable. It was stupid, and she knew it, but she wasn't about to challenge it. Maybe Alicia would wave and go on about her business anyway, rendering all of Cami's hand-wringing moot.

Alicia spotted them at their table and appeared to be taken by surprise. She held her hand up and waved almost cautiously, as though maybe they weren't actually talking to her. Cami felt a small pang of regret that they had made her feel so unwelcome, as justified as it might have been.

"Should I invite her over?" Violet asked through clenched teeth like a ventriloquist.

"No," Katie said. "That would be awkward."

"Katie, come on." Cami raised her eyebrows.

Katie just shrugged and rolled her eyes.

Violet waved Alicia over. Again, she looked surprised. She held up a finger to signal one minute and completed her purchase. She walked over to the table with the plastic bag swinging in her hand.

"Hey." She smiled directly at Cami and then at Violet. She looked at Katie but quickly looked away.

Cami's stomach jumped. She chided herself for being so on edge. It had been a while, a little while, and they'd had enough encounters that Cami shouldn't have been so flummoxed every time she saw her face.

"Here, sit." Violet pulled a chair from an empty table nearby and squished it between her and Cami.

"Oh, uh, yeah. Sure. This feels…strangely familiar," she said with a light laugh.

Katie scoffed. Cami shot her a dirty look.

"It does," Violet agreed. "It's been a long time, but it sure doesn't feel like it. What did you buy?"

Alicia pulled out the paperback. "It's dumb," she said, turning it over. "It's called *Murder in Tinytown, USA*. It's basically about small-town killings and how they affect the community differently than murders in big cities. I was thinking about doing a piece on it, you know, *after*. Once we go back to normal."

"It's not as though our police aren't trying to get us there. Between Cami and her people and everyone at my PD, nothing is being swept under the rug. It's not like this is *CSI* where every crime is solved in sixty minutes minus commercials." Katie bit off a big chunk of grilled cheese.

"No, of course not. I know how hard everyone is working. I've discussed it with Cami more than once." Alicia ran her hand through her hair, something she usually only did when she was uncomfortable.

Cami cleared her throat. "Alicia is fully aware of how tirelessly we're working to catch this guy. Since her up-close-and-personal brush with his handiwork especially," Cami said. "I think that'll be a good piece to write. Once justice is done, we'll have to work on healing."

The gratefulness in Alicia's eyes made Cami almost uneasy. She couldn't lie to herself; she was glad that Alicia regretted the past, but she also didn't want Alicia to continuously flagellate herself every time she was in Cami's presence. The thought actually surprised her. She'd just assumed that she'd *always* want to be surrounded by Alicia's guilt and remorse, but in reality, she could stand a bit more of the unbridled Alicia she used to know.

"Do you girls want a trivia slip?"

The owner of the bookstore was walking around with slips of paper and pencils, handing them out to each table. There were only about four tables that had customers, but the Book Cabin never had been known as a hot spot.

"Sure," Cami said. "We'll play."

"I hate trivia," Violet whined. "You always make fun of me for not knowing the stupid pop culture questions."

"And we always make fun of Taryn for her shitty geography skills. It's what we do," Katie said. "Hopefully, there aren't too many old movie questions. Those are usually Taryn's forte."

"We should be fine." Cami nodded to Alicia. "I swear, she has an eidetic memory for movies. I'll go grab us a bowl of the free popcorn Shelly gives out to the sad people who play."

There were a few brown salad bowls lined up on the counter with fluorescent yellow popcorn in them. Shelly's carnival popcorn machine was unplugged in the corner, so the odds of it being fresh were pretty slim. She looked back at the table and saw an animated Violet telling Alicia something and Alicia laughing heartily. The wide neck of her sweatshirt had slipped down one of her shoulders, revealing the purple strap of her bra. Cami cleared her throat and ignored the twinge in her chest.

"Thank you," Alicia said as Cami placed the bowl on the table. She smiled warmly at her, that unnecessary appreciative look present again. Cami smiled back.

"Question one," Shelly yelled into a needless megaphone. Just her voice would have carried through the entire shop. "Which chess piece is able to move the most spaces in any direction on the chess board? Remember, keep your discussions quiet so other tables can't hear you. No phones."

Cami leaned in. "Queen," she whispered. They all agreed, and Katie wrote the answer down.

"Question two. What food item never expires and never spoils?"

Katie pursed her lips. "Vinegar?"

"Oh, good answer," Violet said.

Alicia leaned in. "I think some types of vinegar have a shelf life. I could be wrong. But I think the answer might be honey?"

"Ah, I think she's right," Cami said.

"Of course you do," Katie muttered.

Cami heard her, but she didn't think Alicia or Violet did. She frowned. "I remember seeing something about it on Food Network," Cami said.

Violet nodded. "Actually, that does sound right. Go with that one, Katie."

Katie sighed loudly and wrote "honey" on line two.

"Question three. Which scientist suggested that the sun was the center of the universe?"

"I've got this one," Violet yelled. They all shushed her. "Sorry. Copernicus."

"Question four. What Disney movie had main characters named Lightning McQueen, Sally, and Mater?"

"Cars," Cami and Alicia both said the answer at the exact same time. They'd watched that one numerous times with Alicia's nephew.

"And finally, Question five. What is the most populous city in the entire world?"

Katie wrote down Tokyo without even waiting for confirmation.

"That does it, folks," Shelly shouted through the megaphone. The distortion turned it into "folksh." "Let's see what lucky team won a ten-dollar gift card to the Book Cabin. New releases excluded." She collected all of the slips and started marking them with a red Sharpie.

"We got this," Violet said, cramming a handful of popcorn into her mouth.

"The only one I'm not sure about is the second one. If it was vinegar, I'll be pissed," Katie said.

"Oh, knock it off, it's just a game," Violet whacked Katie lightly on the arm.

"If it was vinegar, I'll buy you a ten-dollar gift card as penance." Alicia chuckled and grabbed some more popcorn.

"No, I'm good." Katie smiled even though it was clear she was being serious.

Cami was officially annoyed. Yes, Katie still had every right to be angry at Alicia, but she did not have the right to treat her like shit. Alicia looked at the table, ignoring Katie, but Cami still caught the second of hurt in her eyes.

"Okay, everyone, we officially have a winner. It was a close game, but one table answered all five questions correctly. That was… table four."

Everyone looked around the room since the tables weren't clearly marked. Cami looked at Violet and shrugged.

Shelly rolled her eyes and sighed. "On the side of the table, people."

Katie leaned over and checked, then pumped her fist in the air. "We won."

"Yay," Violet yelled.

Without any thought, Cami raised her hand to Alicia in a high five motion. Alicia slapped her hand, smiling broadly.

"Team one was so close, but they answered 'vinegar' for question two. You'll get 'em next time, team one."

Cami had to hide her smirk. Katie was clearly fuming, even though she kept the toothy smile plastered on her face. Alicia said nothing.

Shelly dropped their ten-dollar gift card on the table and went back to her perch behind the register. Violet scooped it up. "Now that we each have two dollars and fifty cents to spend, what should we do? Go a little wild?"

Cami laughed. "I'm willing to donate my share. Buy Gavin a book from us."

"Me too," Alicia agreed.

"Well, if I don't agree, I look like an asshole, so, yes, take my share, too," Katie said.

Cami knew she was kidding, but because she was moody after the vinegar debacle, it didn't necessarily come across that way.

"Since we're on such a roll, maybe we should go over to Birdie's and challenge the regulars to a game of pool," Alicia offered. Cami could feel the vulnerability oozing off her, and it sort of broke her heart. These people had been her closest friends at one point. "Anybody in?"

Chapter Twenty-two

As soon as the words were out of her mouth, Alicia wished she could have taken them back. The jubilance they'd experienced—over something as benign as a bookstore trivia win—had dissipated.

"I can't. Taryn is waiting for me." Katie crumpled her napkin and tossed it onto her empty plate. "It's pretty late."

Alicia stole a glance at the giant wooden clock on the far wall. Seven forty-two p.m. They weren't exactly burning the midnight oil. But she honestly hadn't expected Katie to accept the invitation anyway. After how cold she'd been, Alicia was surprised Katie didn't just get up and leave.

"Rain check for me, too. Gavin needs to shower and brush his teeth before bed, and Jack is so lackadaisical about it. He'd let him rinse with mouthwash and call it a night," Violet said. "At least Maddie is up on her hygiene. Maybe we can do it some night soon. Cam, you coming?"

Alicia grabbed the plastic bag off her chair and stood. Violet and Katie were already heading toward the door. She started to follow.

"Actually, I think I'll go with Alicia."

Alicia whipped her head back toward the table. Had she heard that right? She wasn't the only one who was surprised. Katie and Violet stopped dead in their tracks and turned back toward them.

"What do you mean?" Katie asked.

Cami raised her eyebrows. "What do you mean what do I mean? It's quarter of eight, it's been an epically shitty week, and a game of pool sounds pretty good. That's it."

Alicia clamped her mouth shut. Did Cami actually just agree to go to Birdie's with her? She hadn't *really* been expecting anyone to say yes, though she'd hoped that Violet would agree. And then maybe Cami would too if there was going to be a threesome. She didn't think Cami would go alone with her in a million years.

"I'll meet you there?" Cami asked, swinging her keys around her index finger. She pushed her chair in and walked by Katie and Violet.

Alicia followed slowly, giving them a chance to congregate. She knew they must have questions, especially since Cami had only agreed to be civil, *not* to go out and play pool with the enemy. At least, that was how Alicia assumed Katie saw her, anyway. Violet was more of a question mark, but she probably had reservations as well.

On cue, they caught up to Cami and whispered something furiously. Alicia saw her shrug and shake her head, then walk toward her Jeep. Whatever they'd said hadn't deterred her. Alicia's throat tightened. This was really happening. After all the years that had passed, after all the daydreams she'd processed, after all the fantasies she'd chalked up to longing delusions, it was really happening. She was going to be in the same space with Cami, not as adversaries or fragmented acquaintances, but as…friends. Or something like it.

Alicia scurried out of the Book Cabin and found Katie's sedan parked next to her Prius. She waved, but Katie didn't wave back. She lowered her window a few inches and crooked her index finger to call Alicia over. Alicia threw her bag on the front seat and walked over. She didn't know what to expect, but she was pretty sure it wasn't anything good.

"Alicia. Listen. I know you're not a bad person or specifically out to hurt anyone. I don't really know what your angle is."

"Katie, I don't have an angle, I promise—"

"I just need you to leave Cami alone. Please. Let her live her life. She was doing okay before you came back, for whatever reason you say you did, but now she's all mixed up. Again. After a really fucking bad time, she made it through the devastation you left behind. She might not make it through again. I wouldn't be a good friend if I just let you waltz back in and pretend like nothing ever happened. Please. Let her be."

She shut her window and drove off, leaving Alicia standing alone in the shadowy parking lot. Her taillights faded into the oncoming darkness after a few moments, and Alicia watched until they disappeared completely. She sighed deeply, her excitement muted by the reality of how she was seen by her old friends. A problem that had to be dealt with. A distraction that needed to be tiptoed around.

"Fuck it," she said aloud. She started her engine and peeled out of the parking lot, although doing it in a Prius lacked the punch she'd hoped for it. Birdie's was only a few miles away, so Cami would start to wonder where she was if she didn't show up soon.

Music wafted out into the parking lot. Birdie's was moderately busy, as usual for a Thursday, so the parking lot didn't have a whole lot of open spots. She didn't see the Jeep. For a horrifying second, Alicia wondered if Cami had decided against meeting her and had gone home instead. Realized that it was more trouble than it was worth.

But, no, the Jeep was parked on the side of the building next to a massive SUV that obscured the top of it. Alicia breathed out a quick sigh of relief.

The band was playing a Maroon 5 cover, and a few people were up dancing. Alicia spotted Cami in the corner chalking up a pool cue. It was familiar; it was new. Affection washed over her like a warm wave.

"Hey." She set her light jacket on the barstool beside Cami. She probably didn't need it, but she couldn't seem to shake the chill.

"Hey. I wondered if you'd changed your mind."

Alicia quickly shook her head. She thought about telling Cami what Katie had said but pushed it aside. She understood where Katie was coming from, but she knew her own intentions. She wasn't out to hurt Cami, that much was guaranteed. "Of course not. I was fumbling around in my car. Sorry it took me so long."

"Want me to break?"

"Please."

Alicia grabbed a cue off the stand and watched as Cami assumed the position. Her hair was down, falling around her shoulders and into her face as she concentrated. She tucked a piece behind her ear before taking her shot.

"Your turn?" Cami said with a smile.

Alicia realized she'd been staring, lost in a reverie. She cleared her throat. "Oops. I was too busy watching you. You don't even have to try." She made a shot that sent the seven ball careening into the side of the table.

"I don't play as much as I used to. I'm a little rusty." Cami banked the nine ball into the corner pocket off the ball Alicia had been aiming for. She shrugged. "Just luck."

Alicia laughed and continued to suck as they played. They mostly talked about pool and the trivia game and Katie's competitiveness, but the conversation was easy and flowed as though they didn't have a giant wedge between them, the dark cloud that Alicia wanted so desperately to dissipate.

"See? Totally out of shape," Cami said, flexing her fingers. They'd just finished their second game, and Cami put the cue back on the wall rack.

"Aw, that's it?" Alicia tried to hide the disappointment, but she didn't think it was possible. She didn't want the night to end.

Cami smiled again. "I'm old now. Nine o'clock is basically my bedtime." She paused. "Do you want to have one more drink before we call it a night?"

"Yes," Alicia answered way too quickly, but Cami didn't seem to notice. "Grab us a table. I'll go to the bar."

Why am I doing this to myself? She hadn't had any preconceived notions about how her relationship with Cami would evolve once she came back. When she'd first arrived, she was all but certain that any chance of *anything* between them ever again was wildly impossible. But this. This was torture. Sweet, unrelenting, heartbreaking torture.

She took Cami's beer and her glass of wine to the small round table where Cami was sitting. She was texting with someone and had a hint of a smirk playing on her lips. Alicia fought the urge to ask who she was talking to.

"Ah, thank you," Cami said. She took a long swallow. "Nice and cold."

Alicia nodded and sipped her wine. She murmured appreciatively. It slid down her throat like velvet, dangerous if she let it. "I'm surprised you're not home in bed curled up in the fetal position after the last few weeks. Have you slept much?"

Cami gave her the so-so hand gesture. “Some nights, I hit the pillow and fall right into a deep sleep, and others, I stare at the ceiling and wonder where the hell we’re going wrong. Three people have died on my watch. I’m tired of waiting for the other shoe to drop instead of being proactive. We’re going to meet with the state department next. Brandt wants me to get everything together in a neat little binder for their review. I’m not opposed to a fresh set of eyes, I just wish it hadn’t gotten to this point.”

“I know. Don’t get down on yourself, though. You’re a *good* detective, Cami. I’ve seen it firsthand.”

Cami looked at the ceiling and scoffed. “Yeah. When it comes to things that don’t matter. Throw me into a murder investigation and I’m floundering like a fish on a dock. Just makes you reevaluate things, I guess.”

Alicia furrowed her brow. The Cami she knew wasn’t downtrodden like this. She always kept a positive attitude toward work. Obviously, this was different than her usual cases, but Alicia stood by what she’d said. Cami was nothing if not dedicated.

“You’ll catch this guy. I have no doubt about that. He’ll slip up somehow, he’ll seek more attention, he’ll do something that will lead you right to him. You were born for this. It’s in your veins.”

Cami put a hand over Alicia’s briefly. She put it back in her lap once she’d realized what she’d done, Alicia assumed. Still, it had taken everything in her not to turn her hand and clasp Cami’s with all her might. Her hands still looked the same. Short, squared nails, a silver ring on the index finger of her right hand and the pink and blue friendship bracelet Violet’s son had made for her years ago on her left wrist. The only thing missing was the white gold ring with amethysts and diamonds encircling the band that Alicia had bought her for her thirty-seventh birthday. She’d worn it on her ring finger like an engagement ring.

Alicia had to fight against asking her where it was. Had she thrown it in Copper Lake? Was it sitting at home in a drawer collecting dust? Had she given it to another woman out of spite?

“Thank you. I appreciate it. Hard not to question things when you’re failing miserably at your job.” Cami laughed bitterly.

“What made you agree to come with me tonight?” Alicia asked and regretted it instantly. She seemed to be making a habit of that tonight. *Well, if that doesn't ruin it, nothing will. So much for comfortable conversation.*

Cami did look taken aback, but she recovered quickly. She fiddled with an imperfection in the table and pursed her lips. "I don't really know. It was an impulse decision, I guess."

Alicia chuckled. "You're about the least impulsive person I know."

"Maybe I've changed," Cami said, smiling. "I don't know. I just…didn't want you to feel like you were some sort of pariah."

"Even though I kind of am?"

Cami laughed. "Yeah, even though you kind of are. Listen, I do have to get going. But not because you're a pariah," she said quickly.

"Sure, sure. Okay. I'll go settle up our tab." Alicia grabbed her bag from the chair and dug for her wallet.

"No, it's all set. The bartender ran my card earlier. I'll just let her know we're finished for the night." Cami slid her phone into her back pocket and walked to the bar.

Alicia felt like she was in a haze of unreality. It all felt a little surreal. Almost like it was four years ago before everything exploded but with an infuriating asterisk next to it. She thought of the day she'd left, the planning and secrecy, and felt her stomach flip. Why hadn't she just fucking *talked* to her?

"All set?" Cami asked.

Alicia tried to push the thought as far away as possible. She swallowed the lump in her throat and nodded. "Yeah, all set." She led the way out, the band still playing covers of pop hits. It had somehow faded into the background while she'd been sitting with Cami.

There was a group of people gathered near the exit door, so Alicia had to shimmy her way through. She felt a hand lightly touch the small of her back and nearly gasped. Thankfully, she was able to keep it in so she didn't make it weird. Though that ship had probably sailed a long time ago.

"I'm over here." Cami pointed to the side of the lot where her Jeep was parked. Alicia knew it but certainly wasn't going to tell Cami that she'd scoped it out before entering Birdie's.

"I'm right here." Alicia gestured to a spot a few paces away in the opposite direction. "I'll walk you to your car, can't be too careful these days."

"Very chivalrous of you." Cami smiled again. "Although if the killer is nearby, we're probably better off walking back-to-back."

"Well, that's terrifying." Alicia looked behind her as she walked next to Cami. "Wouldn't even see it coming."

Cami opened the door to her Jeep and leaned in to start the engine. She stood upright again and came face-to-face with Alicia. "This was nice. Thanks."

"No, thank you. Really. I know it sounds corny, but I can't tell you how much this meant to me. If you ever want to get together again, just let me know, and I'll drop everything." Alicia briefly wondered if she sounded too eager, then decided she didn't care. "Have a good night, Cam." She stuffed her hands in her pockets, the chill of the night settling into her bones. She headed toward her car when she heard Cami behind her.

"Alicia?"

"Yeah?" Alicia responded, walking back toward her. Maybe she'd forgotten something inside or wanted to schedule their next community update meeting.

"Did you think about me?"

"What?"

"During that time that you were…gone. And then after. You know what? Forget it, I don't even know why I asked that." Cami opened her Jeep door again.

"No, Cami wait." Alicia touched her shoulder to turn her back around. "Did I think about you? Every second of every day. You were *all* I could think about. I replayed that night—and the days leading up to it—over and over again. I realized pretty quickly that I'd made the biggest mistake of my life. I made myself push on, keep searching for what I thought I might find, and then magically, it would all make sense. It never made sense, and all that came of it was a soul-crushing realization that I'd lost you. I tried to call and message you to tell you that I realized how stupid I'd been. But you didn't answer. I think it was then that I knew. I'd really, truly, broken everything. The spiritual guide I was working with told me I had to focus or else I'd get nothing out of the journey, so I tried. But I couldn't focus on anything but you."

Cami took a deep breath. Her eyes had glassed over. Alicia could feel tears forming in the back of her own. It was too late to stop now.

"Why didn't you come home then? I didn't answer you because I didn't want to hear that you were sorry or feel your pity or have you ask me to ship you a T-shirt you'd left behind." Cami tried to subtly run the back of her hand along her cheek.

"Didn't you listen to the voice mails? Or read the texts?"

Cami took out her phone and swiped up. She held it out to Alicia, showing her the voice mail tab on her phone. There were nine from Alicia, all with red dots next to them signifying that they hadn't been accessed.

"I didn't want to hear your voice. I couldn't."

"But you didn't delete them?"

"I couldn't do that either. Had quite a few conversations about *that* with my therapist at the time."

Alicia swallowed. "Did you read the messages?"

"In the beginning. You were mostly sending 'hey' and 'how are you,' which I honestly didn't want to deal with. I thought you were trying to reach out to smooth things over or relieve your own guilt, and I wanted no part of it. I was so angry at you. I didn't even want to hear your name. Anytime anyone brought you up, I'd either leave the room or change the subject. I know it wasn't healthy, but I didn't have any other choice. I was wrecked." Cami looked at the ground, but Alicia could hear the break in her voice.

"I know, and I'm so sorry, like, so *fucking* sorry—"

"You don't have to keep apologizing. I know you're sorry."

"I don't know what else to say! Or do." Her voice had raised a few octaves in pure desperation. She needed Cami to know how truly sorry, every single day since the night she'd left, she really was. And there was no way to properly convey that. "I feel like the only thing I can do is tell you constantly how much I regret everything that happened, how absolutely ridiculous I was, how deeply I loved you."

"But if you loved me so much, then why did you leave?" Cami asked, nearly shouting. She couldn't seem to hide how red her eyes had become.

"I wish I had an answer for you. I know it's frustrating, and believe me, I want to just lay it all out there with a concise explanation, but I don't have one. Because one doesn't exist. I was just floating in this space where nothing made sense, and I felt like I had to get away from it. Away from everything. And yes, that included you, but not because I didn't love you or want to be with you, but because I needed something else, something different. At least, I thought I did. I should have talked to you about it instead of keeping it bottled up. I tried a few times, but I felt like you weren't getting it, so I just stopped and internalized it instead of being open with you. I should have done more." Alicia wiped her eyes and ran her fingers through her hair. Her chest felt so full, she wondered if her heart was just going to stop beating. Right there at the side of Cami's Jeep.

"Yeah. I wish you had, too. I'm lucky that I had Katie and Violet to help me through it. I thought I'd never be able to get past it, to move on. The world was a much darker place without you in it. But they helped me see that there were still bright spots. I just had to reach for them."

Hearing Cami say she'd moved on hurt, however irrationally. But she *was* lucky that she'd had a support system in place to deal with Alicia's sudden disappearance. If she'd been alone, who knew how she would have dealt with it.

Alicia breathed deeply, her exhalation ragged from holding in the tears. "I'm glad they were there for you in a situation you never should have been in. I'm happy you found peace."

Cami nodded but didn't say anything. After a prolonged moment of silence, Alicia got the feeling that she'd had enough conversation for the evening.

"Thank you for coming with me." Alicia turned toward her car, trying to hold in the sobs that threatened to break free until she reached safety.

She'd only gotten a few steps away before she felt a hand on her wrist tugging her backward. She turned, startled.

Before she could process what was happening, Cami's lips pressed against hers. Soft at first, then gradually more intense as Alicia wrapped her arms around Cami's waist, pulling her as close as she possibly could. A million different emotions flowed easily through her veins. Elation took the top spot, and Alicia turned her head to allow Cami better access.

Cami cupped the back of her head, bringing her even closer, which Alicia thought impossible. The tiny moan that escaped Cami's lips brought on another feeling, this one carnal in nature.

It was a dream. It had to be. Alicia had been picturing this moment, fantasizing about it, playing it over and over in her head like an old record. It was the stuff of movies: long-lost lovers reunited under a streetlight in the rain. Unrequited love realized after years of longing and veiled flirtation. Or maybe this time, an early summer night outside of an old bar with muffled notes of "Somewhere Only We Know" drifting into the parking lot. It was real.

Alicia tried to make sure she was fully present, photographing every second with her mind so the moment would be etched forever, but the pounding of her heart and the weakness in her legs kept her drifting. She ran her hands up the length of Cami's back, fisting a handful of her hair. She tasted like Coors Light and Big Red chewing gum, and it was probably the best taste Alicia had ever experienced.

She parted her lips a tiny bit more, encouraging. If nothing else, she needed Cami to know that yes, *God yes*, this was what she wanted, and she didn't ever want it to stop. Cami deepened the kiss, the tip of her tongue playing softly on Alicia's bottom lip. Alicia's stomach dropped at the contact, and she wondered if she was going to make it through this alive. The fire between them was as bright as she remembered. The eternal flame that she'd craved for so long would apparently spark forever.

"Stop." Cami pulled forcefully away and backed into the Jeep. She was breathless. "I'm sorry, I shouldn't have done that. I'm sorry."

"Cami, no. I wanted you to, I—"

Alicia took a step toward her, but Cami held her hand up. "No, I can't do this. I can't. I promised myself never again, I'd never put myself in this position again. I'm sorry, I have to go."

Cami slid behind the wheel of the Jeep, her hands shaking a little. Alicia wanted to say something, to tell her not to go, but she didn't think she could. She didn't have the right to ask her to stay, not after everything.

Cami didn't look back. She just stared out through her windshield, turned to back up, and drove out of the parking lot, going a little faster than she probably should have. Alicia just stood there in silence, watching the steam from her tailpipe dissipate into the air.

CHAPTER TWENTY-THREE

The road ahead was blurry. The streetlights had a halo around them as though it had rained. But the only real moisture was the tears spilling down Cami's cheeks. She hit her steering wheel with the side of her fist.

"*Fuck!* What am I doing?"

Of course, there was no one to respond, and no answers were coming through her speakers, only an acoustic version of some old rock song, so she used the heel of her palm to smash the button to the off position. The only sounds breaking the silence were her sobs, and somehow, she found that comforting.

She didn't know what to do. She wanted to go home, yet she wanted to talk to someone. Katie was probably not the best option. Violet was putting her kid to bed, so she most likely wasn't available. She could talk to Kelsey, but with everything they'd been dealing with at work, Cami didn't want to burden Kelsey with her shit, too. She took three deep breaths to get her emotions in check and the crying under control, and then she headed home.

The apartment was dark as usual, but it seemed even darker. Colder, maybe. After Alicia had left, Cami had rearranged everything, painted a few walls, tried to make it as "new" as possible without actually having to move. She'd thought about it many times, but the rent was good, and she was a creature of habit. The thought of packing everything up and moving to a new address gave her hives. She did ditch the bedroom set after a few months and ordered a plain wooden one with matching nightstands. It was a stark difference from the black and white marble set Alicia had picked out all those years earlier.

Cami thought about having another beer, but the thought turned her stomach. She sat on the couch in the dark and threw her head back against the cushion. She could still feel the tingle of Alicia's lips on hers. She could still smell the flowery scent of her hair and feel the softness of her body. She needed to view it as a one-off, an aberration, nothing more. There were no circumstances where she could be with Alicia again. Too many promises made, too many nights steeling herself against the heartbreak, and too many walls in between them. That Cami had enjoyed it—an understatement—made no difference. She would always feel *something* toward Alicia, that much she'd accepted. The indifference thing hadn't worked out. The anger and bitterness had lasted a little while but not nearly as long as she'd expected. She didn't think those feelings would ever dissipate. And yet.

The fact that she was sitting there, on her couch, yearning for Alicia in ways she hadn't for a very long time? That juiced up some of the anger again. *How dare she put me in this position? Again.* But then she remembered that she'd been the one to kiss Alicia, not the other way around, dammit. Alicia had been ready to leave, to go home and just be happy that Cami had given her the time of day. That didn't make Cami feel any better.

She didn't want to put the TV on. She didn't want to check her phone that had dinged a few times since she'd been home. She didn't want to go to bed. She didn't want to move. After slouching back in the same position for an indefinable amount of time, she finally fell into a restless sleep.

The police department was on edge. Far too much time had passed since Beverly Lawson's murder without having a suspect in custody. Thankfully, the town had cooperated with the curfew for the most part, and most people were uneasy as it was, so even the nuisance crimes the PD usually had to deal with were at an all-time low. There was nothing happening, but they were all waiting for the shoe to drop. Without any solid leads to follow up, it was only a matter of time before someone else turned up dead.

And for Cami, that was nearly too much to bear.

She was tired, and her neck was killing her. Sleeping on the couch like that had caused cramps in places she didn't even know existed. The hot morning shower had done nothing to relieve them. And all they were doing was serving as a reminder of what had happened the previous night.

The texts that had come through had been from Katie asking how it was going and from Pizza Shack letting her know that her ten percent off coupon was about to expire. Cami ignored Katie's message, even though she must be frothing at the bit for a recap of their evening. Judging, Cami was sure. She'd have to tell her eventually, but she wasn't up for it just yet.

Alicia's article calling out the killer as the Small-Town Slayer had added fuel to the publicity fire. Their phones were ringing off the hook with tips and theories from armchair sleuths. Beverly Lawson's poor mother was still calling nearly every day looking for an update or to offer her own hypotheses.

Kelsey waltzed through Cami's door and dropped a file on her desk. "Forensics came back with the shoe print analysis from behind the bench McCallum was found on."

"And?" Cami opened the folder and leafed through the paper-clipped reports.

"Nike Air Force 1, one of the most popular shoes in America because why wouldn't it be? Size seven and a half, which is fairly small but still popular. There are a couple of interesting variations in the mold, so if we actually had a suspect, this might actually be helpful."

Cami sighed in disgust. "Couldn't have been like a 1970's one-of-a-kind platform boot or something? No, we get a Nike sneaker. We can't catch a goddamn break."

There was a small commotion at the entrance. Cami stood to get a better view and saw Jade Conley waving her hands at one of the front desk officers. Cami furrowed her brow and went out with Kelsey to see what was going on.

"Detective Lyons," Jade yelled, pointing at Cami. "I told you she'd know me. I was just trying to get in to see you, but Biffy over here is too busy playing tough guy."

Officer Michaels—who Cami feared would always be Biffy to her from that point forward—didn't seem to appreciate the slight. He stood, but Cami placed a hand on his shoulder. "Mrs. Conley is correct, I do know her. Thank you for looking out. She can come back to my office."

Michaels gave Jade a dirty look but buzzed her in. Jade raised her eyebrows and smirked as if to put a punctuation mark on how right she was.

"Sorry." Cami shrugged, and Michaels shook his head in disgust.

"What was that all about?" Cami gestured to the empty chair across from her, and Jade took a seat. "Why didn't you just call me?"

"I haven't severed my cell phone from my joint account with Evan's yet. For all I know, he's bugged my phone and put a tail on me."

"Why would he do that?" Cami knew they weren't going to have an amicable split, but she didn't think it would turn *that* ugly.

Jade waved her off as though she was being ridiculous. "Money, Detective. Everything comes down to money. You know that as well as I do. I told him I'd take him for everything he's worth, and he knows I mean it."

"Has he given you any indication that he's setting you up?" Cami asked.

"Well," Jade began, inspecting her fingernails. "He showed up at the house last night. Asked me for copies of our tax returns and bank statements. He also wanted to take an autographed baseball card he got when we were first married that I *know* is worth a lot of money."

"What did you tell him?"

"I told him to fuck off and leave my property, or I'd take out a restraining order."

Cami sighed. She wasn't a divorce attorney or a property specialist, but she was pretty sure he had certain rights to their joint documentation. "I understand that you don't want to see him—after what he did, who would—but I'm not sure that qualifies as 'setting you up.' Maybe he's getting his affairs in order for an attorney?"

"What if he's the killer?" Jade dropped her voice. "I'd be the perfect mark to make all his troubles go away."

Cami shrugged. "His alibis check out. We don't have any further reason to suspect him at this point."

"He has a gun."

"What?" Cami asked, leaning forward. "We checked local firearm sales and background checks, and his name wasn't found anywhere. E-trace came back with nothing. You both said you didn't own any guns."

"We got one for protection a while back since we're both in public positions with great exposure, not always positive, and we have a lot of assets worth protecting. Going through the proper channels turned out to be a hassle, so we found another way. Craigslist, if you can believe it. But that was a long time ago. I don't know where it is now." Jade sat back and pursed her lips nonchalantly.

"Jade," Cami cried. "Why didn't you tell us this when we were investigating Evan? This is obstruction of justice. You could be charged, both of you."

"You don't need to be so dramatic! I wasn't concealing anything. It just wasn't pertinent because it was so long ago, and we decided having it in the house was more of a headache than it was worth. So we got rid of it. Well, we planned to. I told him I was going to dump it in Copper Lake, but I was afraid if someone found it, it would be traced back to us. So I buried it in my flower garden."

Cami rubbed her face and tried to make sense of what Jade was telling her. "How long ago was this?"

Jade looked at the ceiling. "Ten years ago?"

"You've had a gun buried in your garden for ten years?" Cami closed her eyes.

"Something like that. Evan didn't know about it. Or so I thought. I dug it up last night in case he came back, and the shoebox was empty."

"So you know that we have a killer in town, a killer *shooting* his victims, in which your husband was a prime suspect, and you didn't think it was pertinent to tell us this?" Cami had to restrain herself from shouting.

Jade was starting to get agitated. "The garden was untouched. It had a row cover on it that the landscaper set up before winter, and he ties that off with stakes. No way is that coming up after a freeze. Once the weather started getting warmer, he did his usual shtick with fresh soil over the old, and it looked completely undisturbed. So as far as I was concerned, neither of us had any guns."

"Okay. We're going to need to see where it was buried. But now that you *have* disturbed it, that creates a whole new issue for the forensics team. And you're telling me you haven't seen this gun in ten years?" Cami was angry but kept an even keel.

"Or so."

"If we go search your house right now, we won't find it there?"

"No, you will not. I'm not the killer, Detective Lyons. But I think the killer might have his sights set on me."

Jade was a smart woman. Why she thought concealing the possession of a gun was a good idea was beyond Cami. Even if they hadn't obtained it legally, finding out after the fact did a lot more harm to her credibility. If she had just been straightforward about the whole thing, they could have dug it up before someone else did.

"Are you all going to come to my house now? To see if you can figure out when that cheating bastard found out I didn't dump that thing in Copper Lake?" Jade stood and pulled her purse up over her shoulder.

"Yes, we'll come check it out. Don't touch anything, and don't move anything."

"I don't love the way you're speaking to me, Detective."

Cami shot her a look that Jade seemed to understand. She backed off and exited Cami's office, waiting outside the door. Cami called Kelsey in and filled her in on Jade's latest revelation. The whole investigation had turned into an absolute clusterfuck.

As they were getting ready to head over to Jade's house, where an empty shoebox would hopefully provide them with *something*, Jade walked in lockstep with Cami. "I'm sure by now you've read Alicia's latest article about the state of the Oakview PD. I assume it's more to your liking?"

"I don't have an opinion either way," Cami stared straight ahead as they walked briskly through the parking lot.

"Have you talked to her?" Jade appeared to be searching Cami's face for a reaction.

Cami wasn't having it, especially not today. "That's none of your business, Mrs. Conley. I'll follow behind you."

Chapter Twenty-four

Friday afternoons were a good time to grocery shop. The aisles were mostly empty except for a few shoppers gearing up for the weekend, mostly inhabiting the chips and soda aisles.

"I feel like I'm having a clandestine affair," Taryn said, plucking a box of pancake mix off the shelf. She smiled and raised her eyebrows at Alicia.

Alicia laughed. "Honestly, you didn't have to come. I don't want you to keep things from Katie on my account. She hates me enough as it is."

"Oh, stop," Taryn said. "She's being ridiculous about the whole thing. I know she holds a grudge, but come on, you didn't stab anyone."

"No, but I don't want to minimize it, either."

"Haven't you inflicted enough self-flagellation over this? How long are you going to beat yourself up over something you can't change? You apologized, you meant it, and you're trying to make things right. I don't know what else you can do."

Alicia sighed. "I never feel like it's enough, to be honest. It's like if I apologize just *one more time*, maybe it'll be the right amount. The one that makes it all okay. I have to tell you something. But you absolutely cannot tell Katie. So if you can't do that, I totally understand, and we can pretend like I never said anything."

Taryn stopped in the middle of the aisle, her eyes wide. "Now you have to tell me. What is it? Are you seeing someone?"

"No. Nothing like that. It was a onetime thing, and I'm sure there is deep regret swirling around today. But, uh, I kissed Cami last night."

Taryn looked like her head was about to explode. "*What?*" she asked, much louder than she probably meant to. "You kissed Cami? How the hell did that happen? What did she say? What did you say? How was it? Was it a peck? Are you getting back together? Does anyone else know about this?"

Alicia couldn't help but laugh. It was nice, genuinely nice, to have a friend to talk to about what had happened. She hoped that Taryn wouldn't tell Katie. She assumed Cami would eventually, so it wasn't like Taryn would never have found out at all. Just a little sooner than she was probably supposed to.

"We came out of Birdie's, and we were talking at her Jeep, and it just sort of happened. She asked me if I'd thought about her much over the years, and I told her the truth. I thought about her every fucking day. I apologized again, as usual, and then I was about to leave. Next thing I know, she pulled me back and kissed me."

"*Cami* initiated it? Holy shit, that adds a whole other level to this."

"Don't get the wrong idea. She regretted it pretty quickly. She pulled away and took off before I even realized what was happening. I wanted to call her or just show up at her house so badly, but I doubt that would have ended well. So I went home and just pined away for her like a teenager. I didn't even know how to feel." Alicia turned the corner and grabbed a box of Cheerios off the bottom shelf. She turned back to see Taryn standing there staring at her still, her mouth in an open half-smile.

"I'm in complete and utter shock. How did it feel? Did you still have the spark that you guys had? That was one of the reasons I was so surprised that things happened the way they did. I used to always give Katie shit, asking her why she didn't look at me the way you two looked at each other. Then when you left, her I-told-you-so was epic. Oh. Sorry." Taryn pushed her shopping cart slowly up the aisle.

Well, that hurts. "Yes. The spark was immediate. It just made me realize that it's never gone away. After all this time, there's like this current that still exists. It's just dormant. But ready to be resurrected at any moment. It's actually sort of depressing."

"Yeah, I can see that. But who knows, maybe this is the start of something. Are you going to call her?" Taryn asked.

"I don't know what to do. I don't want to push her away, but I don't want her to think I don't care or that I don't want her. I've never wanted anything more. Coming back here was either the exact thing I had to do or the second worst mistake I've ever made." Alicia tried to temper the sliver of hope that rose in her chest. The possibility of Cami ever forgiving her enough to consider being with her again was minute. Miniscule. She had to keep that at the forefront of any fantasy she might allow herself to slip into.

"I'll have to feel Katie out when she gets home later. See if Cami said anything to her. Although I don't know if Cami would even want to. I told Katie she needs to work on how judgmental she is, but she doesn't see it. She honestly thinks she's easygoing. I know it comes from a good place, but she's judgmental as hell."

"But remember, you *can't* say anything to her. I don't want it getting back to Cami that I'm flaunting her business all around town. That would piss her off and probably make her trust me less than she already does. So please don't."

Taryn shook her head. "I won't. I promised you I wouldn't say anything first, and I won't. But I hope Cami told her and Katie fills me in herself. Then, all bets are off."

Alicia checked her watch. "I should really get to the office. I have to do some research on gang violence in neighboring states trickling into New Hampshire, and I'd much rather do it on the theater-sized monitor than on my laptop screen."

"I'm just about finished anyway. You have to tell me if there are any updates to the saga. My life is so boring at this point, I get excited when my brand of dryer sheets comes out with a new scent. This is the most excitement I've had in months." She elbowed Alicia gently and winked at her.

Alicia smiled. "What I wouldn't give for boring. I remember we used to have spaghetti night every Wednesday, and our biggest concern was whether to have garlic bread or cheese sticks."

"Well, you can't go backward. So stop trying to. Maybe it will work out, maybe it won't. But you can't go on living in that sea of regret you've become so accustomed to. It's not healthy."

Taryn had a point. But it wasn't as easy as just sitting back and letting fate take its course. If she'd been able to do that, her life would have probably turned out very differently.

Out in the parking lot, Alicia and Taryn said their good-byes. Alicia slid behind the steering wheel both heartened that she'd been able to reconnect meaningfully with at least one of her old friends but still dismayed at the way things had ended with Cami the night before. She checked her phone just to make sure she hadn't missed anything. Voice mail, text, even an email for God's sake. She hadn't.

❖

Her aspirations of entering an empty office to get her work done in relative silence were shot pretty quickly. Jade's car, Sam's car, and the new guy Jared's car were all lined up in a neat little row in the parking lot outside the entrance.

Alicia walked in and dropped her bag off at her usual workstation. Jade exited her office with an empty coffee cup.

"You know, for people who chose a home office as their primary method of working, you all are here a *lot*." She shook her head in disgust before disappearing through the kitchen door.

Alicia nodded in question to Sam, who shrugged in response.

As Alicia was plugging her laptop into the docking station, Sam rolled her chair over. "I've only been here for a little while, but she's clearly on edge. She's been biting everyone's head off. I've never seen her like this. You've known her longer, even with your time away. Have you?"

"No. I mean, she has a lot going on with her upcoming divorce and all that, so I can only imagine it's taking a toll. But, no, she's usually so composed. Seeing her like this is unsettling," Alicia said.

Jade came out of the kitchen in grand fashion and set her eyes on Alicia. "I need to see you in my office in about ten minutes." Without waiting for a response, she retreated to her office and closed the door tightly.

"Great," Alicia muttered.

"When I first walked in, she was here by herself on all fours under her desk. Like she was looking for something. I asked if I could help her, but I guess she didn't hear me come in. She jumped up so fast, she slammed her head on the desk and called me an asshole for scaring her. Then, she told me she needed that story on the Oakview

High lacrosse player that met the president tomorrow instead of next week. I was about to ask why since it's not slated until Thursday's issue, but I was afraid I'd get fired. Is this officially a hostile work environment?" Sam asked.

Alicia sighed. "Pretty much. But I think we should give her a little breathing room before we call human resources on her. She's honestly never been like this before. If she's at some sort of breaking point, piling on will make it even worse. I know it's a lot to ask, especially for Jared the new guy, but maybe we can just try to ride it out for a little while longer?" Alicia hated to put Sam in that position, but she also didn't want to see Jade completely implode.

"Yeah, that's fine with me. I'm not especially bothered by it, I just think it's strange. She's on this roller coaster spiral right in front of our eyes."

"I wish we could help. But she definitely doesn't seem open to it, at least not now."

Sam nodded. "I've actually been reading a lot of material that the writer who was here before you turned me on to. It's all by this sage—don't judge—who has really done a lot for people. His concepts would probably help Jade, too. I thought about bringing it up with her, but I highly doubt she'd want to hear it. I'll save that for another day. I can show you some of the stuff I have if you're interested?"

After the experience she'd had surrounding her own spiritual guide, through no fault of his, Alicia bristled at the thought. "Not sure if it's my thing, but maybe someday."

"Alicia?" Jade asked, poking her head out of her door. She raised her eyebrows impatiently.

"Has it been ten minutes?" Alicia asked quietly.

"Not even close."

Alicia grabbed a notebook and a pen from her bag and steeled herself for Jade's inexplicable wrath. Sam whispered a quick "good luck" before rolling back to her own desk.

The office looked even less inviting than usual. Jade's chair was facing the window so only the top of her head could be seen from the doorway. One of the guest chairs had a pile of papers on it; the other was open but askew. Alicia cautiously sat. When Jade didn't turn right away, Alicia cleared her throat.

"Oh, Alicia. Right." Jade spun and dropped her phone on her desk.

"What's up? Everything okay?"

Jade laughed bitterly. "Not exactly. I do want to apologize to you, specifically. I know my behavior recently has been…unbecoming. And you were there for me through a lot of difficult revelations."

"Of course. First and foremost, we're friends. I wish you hadn't been subjected to all of that. Not that it helps, but Evan was crazy to do what he did. You're amazing, Jade," Alicia gave Jade a tight-lipped smile. "This too shall pass."

"I hope you're right. But if I don't make it, I want to be sure you know where to look and what to tell them."

Alicia frowned. "Don't make it where? What do you mean?"

Jade sighed impatiently. "Don't make it, make it. You know, dead."

"What? Why would you even say that?"

"Because, Alicia! The killer is still out there. It could very well be Evan, and what better way to make all his problems go away than to make me the next victim? He's basically been written off by the cops, so he has carte blanche to do whatever he wants. I think I'm being followed. Watched. This office is bugged for all I know." Jade looked toward the ceiling with wild eyes.

Alicia followed her line of vision. There was nothing out of the ordinary. "Are you sure you're being followed? Have you talked to the police?"

"I tried. But your girlfriend Lyons just waved me away like *I'm* the criminal."

"She's not my—"

"I told them something isn't right, and I need a police detail, but they weren't listening. They're going to send a car by my house a few times during the night. Big deal. He could get in and shoot me dead in the span of five minutes. While Princess Policewoman is out having a jelly doughnut on the taxpayer's dime."

That wasn't fair, and Alicia knew it, but Jade didn't seem to be in a reasoning kind of mood. The officer assigned to that detail most certainly wouldn't have been Cami; Jade, with her wealth of knowledge and law enforcement exposure, would have ordinarily known. Something had her distracted and paranoid.

"When was the last time you saw Evan? Did he threaten you?"

Jade scoffed. "He showed up at my house demanding financial records. He didn't threaten me because I didn't give him the chance. But I've seen little black Audis show up just about everywhere I've been. Coincidence? I highly doubt it."

Alicia hated that she had doubts about Jade's story. But just the way she was acting, almost out of control and feral in her mannerisms, caused Alicia to question whether or not it had all been too much, and Jade was in the midst of a very understandable breakdown.

"Are you afraid to be alone?" Alicia asked. "If you want, I can stay with you tonight. If he shows up, we can tell him to get lost together."

Jade seemed to soften at the suggestion. Alicia didn't really believe that Evan was trying to kill her, but maybe he *was* doing something to intimidate her. He did have a lot to lose in the dissolution of their life together. Not more than Jade had already lost, but Evan didn't seem like one to care about that.

"That might work. He'd be less likely to cause a scene if someone else is there. If he's trying to stay hidden in order to kill me, I don't want you becoming collateral damage. It would probably be better for him if he takes out the two of us. Then it would look like an unhinged psychopath instead of a carefully crafted homicide. It's too dangerous." Jade shook her head to put a period on it.

"I'm not worried about it. If he tries anything, we'll be ready for him. Besides, you said the police were going to send a car by during the night. We'll have backup if we need it." Alicia wasn't sure playing into Jade's fears was the right avenue to take, but she didn't think telling her she was being paranoid was the proper road to take either. Maybe if she saw that the night was uneventful and safe, it would go a long way toward assuaging her suspicions.

"You know what? I'll take you up on it then. Again, I'm sorry I was being so rude. Sometimes my anxieties get the best of me, and I react poorly."

Alicia nodded. "Understood. I'll come over tonight after dinner, and we can shore up the house. Sound good?"

"It does."

The bullpen was empty by the time Alicia went back to her laptop. The new guy Jared's desk had been cleared of his stuff, but Sam's bag was still slung over her chair. She came out of the kitchen with a gigantic mug of coffee. "Everything okay?" she asked.

"Yeah. Just a lot going on. I think everything happening with her husband and the Small-Town Slayer wreaking havoc on Oakview has muddled itself into a toxic mess. I do think she'll be okay, though."

"Wait a minute." Sam rolled over to Alicia's desk again. "Does Jade think Evan is the Small-Town Slayer?"

Did I allude to that? Oops. "Not necessarily, she's just being cautious. All around."

"Man, if the police had him and let him go, that would be the scandal of the century around here. Heads would roll." Sam looked almost gleeful at the thought. The human-interest stories of the victims' families would be highly sought after and right in Sam's wheelhouse.

"No, they cleared him. He's an asshole, but he's not a killer. Have you finished the piece on black pepper saltwater taffy yet? I can't imagine there's a huge call for it, but Aunt Ginny has proven us wrong before."

Sam lit up and pulled a wrapper out of her desk drawer. "They have the marketing done, but there weren't any available for sale yet. I did get some samples, though."

Alicia listened half-heartedly as Sam gave her all the details about the new candy, nodding in hopefully the right places. Was it possible Cami and Kelsey and the rest of the Oakview PD had made a horrible mistake by letting Evan Conley go? Alicia shifted uncomfortably in her seat and tried to focus on the comfort of Aunt Ginny.

Chapter Twenty-five

The garden area in Jade's backyard was bigger than Cami expected. There were rows of purple flowers bookended by rows of yellow and white. She could pick out the hydrangeas, but that was where her knowledge of local flower growing ended. Living in an apartment building had taken away the ability to plant a garden, although Cami wouldn't have planted one even if she'd lived on acres of land. There were just too many worms roaming in dirt.

"I can't believe Jade went to work while we were digging through her garden and rifling through her things," Kesley said.

"She was adamant," Cami said. "She said she had nothing to hide, and there were more pressing things happening at work. Said she was tired of feeling like her house was a crime scene."

"Well, her and her husband have done a damn good job of making it one."

Cami nodded. "Very true."

"The forensic soil scientist is collecting samples now." Kelsey nodded toward the area Jade had dug up.

"I'm embarrassed to say that I didn't know soil had its very own dedicated forensic scientist. I don't know if we're just sheltered here, or if it's like this in most towns in the US. We're on a pretty steep learning curve." Cami shook her head as the analyst carefully added soil to the collection bags.

"You're not alone, I didn't either. Brandt called her up from somewhere. I don't understand a word of what she's saying, but it's pretty impressive."

The scientist was speaking into an old-school mini tape recorder. Cami hadn't seen one of those in years. "Sample number 110.6.2, dark brown moist, brown dry, common textures, sand, silt, clay, digital photo number d2366…"

"Yeah, it really is. I can't imagine having a passion for something like that. It must be nice to be consumed by something that never lets you down. Science doesn't disappoint," Cami said.

Kelsey looked at her and cocked an eyebrow. "You okay?"

"I'm fine."

Cami wasn't sure if she was lying. She was fine, by all measurable standards, but she also felt like she was drowning in turmoil. This fucking case was dragging on and on with no end in sight, she was pissed at her best friend for being so stoic and cold, and the whole Alicia thing was spinning her into a chaotic web of confusion. She just wanted to go home and bury herself under the covers, but the idea of being alone with her thoughts for an entire day sounded like its own version of hell. Nothing sounded appealing. She felt like she had nothing to look forward to. The only sliver of anticipation she could muster involved something, *someone*, that she swore she'd never do.

She had no choice but to press on and hope she'd fall into evidence that would break the case wide open. That was the best option to break out of the cage she'd locked herself inside.

Kelsey obviously didn't believe her, but she didn't push. "We don't have anything concrete yet, too early, but Dr. Morrison doesn't believe that there was any type of soil disturbance other than the shoebox coming up. Which leads us to believe that whoever dug it up knew exactly where it was buried."

"Jade."

"Right. There was no wild-goose chase of digging up the garden to find something and putting it back together after the fact. She said that under the topsoil the gardener had used to freshen up the flower beds, the soil was still intact from the winter."

Cami sighed. "So either Jade is telling the truth and the gun mysteriously disappeared, Jade has the gun, Evan Conley knew exactly where the gun was buried and was able to put the box back without leaving any evidence, or there was never any gun to begin with. Doesn't she have any security cameras?"

"She does, but they're all out front and on the side. Near the doors. Nothing back here."

"Of course not. What kind of shoebox is it?" Cami asked.

"Brown and orange. Nike."

"Air Force 1, by chance?"

Kelsey nodded at Cami's line of thinking. "Maybe. Most of the writing is worn off. Let's go check some closets and get some shoe sizes."

Cami had known Jade for years and couldn't come up with a single reason that Jade would go on a killing spree. They hadn't been close, but through Alicia and the newspaper, they had spent some time together over the years. She'd never thought of Jade as anything other than a dedicated journalist and a decent, if a little snooty, person.

The upstairs closet was massive. There were rods full of suits, dresses, sweaters, slacks, even silk pajamas were hung with care on wooden hangers. Rows of shoes, mostly heels and boots, lined the back wall. There was a small section of running shoes and sneakers off to the side.

Cami snapped on a pair of gloves to be on the safe side. A pink pair of Michael Kors trainers. Dolce Vita gold mesh running shoes. And a single pair of blue Nikes.

She turned the sneaker over and over in her hand. They were very clean, with almost no wear on the soles. She lifted the tongue to see the small white tag sewn in. Women's size 7. The shoe print they'd found at the scene of Patrick McCallum's murder was a men's 7.5, or if converted to women's sizes, a 9.

Too big.

It was possible that Jade had worn shoes larger than she normally did in order to throw law enforcement off the trail, but the sneaker Cami held in her hand was certainly not the one they'd been looking for.

"Any idea what kind of Nike this is?" Cami asked, holding the shoe out.

Kelsey leaned in. "Definitely not Air Force 1. Maybe a Revolution."

"Okay. This is all she has for Nikes. Did you find anything in Evan's old closet?"

"No. The few things he left are mostly track suits and random ties. They really played their parts, huh?"

Cami nodded. "No kidding. We need to get in touch with him, yet again, to find out what he knows about this gun."

"At some point, he's going to nail us for harassment," Kelsey said.

"Trust me, I've thought of that, too. But we don't have much of a choice. If there's a gun floating around out there and it matches the type of gun used in the murders, we're that much closer to an arrest."

Kelsey sighed. "You're right. Let's go back to the station and file *another* report, this time on the soil and the shoe. If this whole detective thing doesn't work out, I think I could be a pretty good technical writer. Or whoever else writes company documents. I'm a pro."

Cami chuckled. "You are getting pretty good at it. Somehow, I envisioned that if we ever worked on an important case like this, writing reports wouldn't be the primary skill we came away with. Clearly, I was wrong."

"I'll meet you in your office. Everything needs to be locked up before we go."

❖

Violet's name popped up on Cami's screen. She pressed the accept button on her steering wheel.

"You busy?"

"Just on my way back to work. What's up?" Cami asked, setting her phone in the holder attached to the vent.

"Nothing important. I was trying to book that band everyone loved last year for the Fourth of July party, and then I started thinking about the guest list. I'm sure you can guess what I'm thinking."

Of course. Cami sighed. "Alicia?"

Violet stayed silent for a beat. "Yeah. Sorry. I know it's awkward, I just wanted to make sure it was okay. I assume it's fine since the two of you went to Birdie's the other night, but I still wanted to make sure you'd be fine with it."

"Yes, Vi, it's fine. You can invite her." She still hadn't really dealt with what had happened in the Birdie's parking lot. It was easier to try to push it out of her mind. Every time it tried to creep back in, whether it was because of the feelings it brought up or the thought of Alicia's lips against hers, Cami blanked it immediately.

She brought her fingers to her mouth without even recognizing she had done it. She quickly put her hand back on the wheel once she realized.

"Good. I'm glad you two are getting along again. So…do you want to talk about it?" Violet asked with a lilt in her voice.

Cami smirked. Violet tried so hard to be less transparent and continually failed. "Talk about what?"

"Just, you know. Like, how was it?"

"It was good." Cami could almost feel Violet's frustration. She smiled to herself.

"What time did you leave?"

"Um…nine, maybe? Somewhere around there."

"What did you guys do?"

"We played pool, talked, had a few drinks. I made a great shot. The four ball, I think, was positioned near the corner pocket but off to the side. I had to aim the cue ball at a specific position on the felt to make sure the angle was right. Sure enough, it was, and the ball sank like a stone. It was a thing of beauty." Cami wanted to laugh but kept it in. Violet didn't give two shits about Cami's pool shots, and she knew it.

"Nice. Cool. Cool." Violet's enthusiasm was comical. "What did you two talk about?"

"Lots of things, actually. Mostly work, family, stuff like that. Alicia told me that her apartment has a really nice reading nook built into the living room. She put a bench in there for now while she figures out what she wants to go there. Maybe a small chaise or something—"

"Cami, come on. You're doing it on purpose. Did you talk about the past? Did you argue? Are you going to be *friends*? Do you still have any feelings for her? Does she still have feelings for you? Come on!"

Cami laughed out loud. She couldn't help herself. "I can read you like a book. We had a nice time. There was no arguing or anything like that. It felt weird to be around her without that pit in my stomach I've grown so used to. My feelings for her are inconsequential. I've said it a million times, I wouldn't put myself in any position for anything like what happened before to happen again. So really, it doesn't matter."

"Are you trying to convince me or yourself?"

"Knock it off, Vi. We've both moved on."

"Did she say that?"

"In those words? No, but based on our conversation…I don't know. Again, it doesn't matter. You can invite her to the Fourth of July party, and I am fine with it. Wasn't that the original question?"

Before Violet could answer, the sharp squeal of brakes pierced the air. Cami turned to her right just in time to see the grill of a red sedan hurtling toward her passenger door at an ungodly pace.

It was mostly just noise. Screeching tires. An explosive bang. Shattering glass. Metal crunching. Cami watched the door of her Jeep implode inward, but she wasn't really seeing it. She was more of a spectator, watching the events unfold from the outside.

Was it really happening? Maybe. Maybe it was a dream.

Her head snapped back against the headrest as her seat belt locked against her chest. She closed her eyes and waited for something to happen. She might wake up, she might never open her eyes again and just slip away peacefully, or she might have to spring into action.

As the acrid odor of burning rubber mixed with the sweet, syrupy smell of coolant, Cami opened her eyes and quickly checked herself. Still intact. She didn't feel any specific pain, just an overall surge of adrenaline.

Something had to be done, and the nagging sense of dread bubbling in her chest had to be ignored. Cami tried to recall the continuing ed training she'd had to go through a few months earlier. *Guardian, not warrior. Not everything has to be a battle. Someone might need help. Focus.*

She unbuckled her seat belt and jumped out of the Jeep. Cars were already starting to stop along the side of the road. Cell phones were out and pointed toward them. Cami could hear someone talking to what sounded like an emergency operator.

She ran to the driver side of the red car that had hit her. The driver was still in there, leaned over the steering wheel with his head turned to the side. Cami opened the door and felt his neck for a pulse.

"Sir, can you hear me?" she asked.

The pulse was strong. He lifted his head up and tried to speak but couldn't seem to get the words out. He sat up slightly and turned his head toward Cami.

Josh Grayson. "Oh, shit. Really? *You?*"

"Nice to see you, too, Josh. What the hell happened? Stop moving." Sirens rang out in the not-too-far distance.

"I don't know. You came out of nowhere," Josh said.

Cami pointed to the stop sign that he had blown through. "Did you miss the giant red stop sign cemented into the ground?"

"I stopped," he said weakly.

"You know that they can tell those things, right? By tire marks and vehicle damage and all that?"

"Is it your mission on earth to make my life a living hell? Ouch." He cringed as he touched his lip that was covered in blood. "I think my tooth poked through my lip."

An ambulance screeched to a halt across the street. Three paramedics leapt out and rushed toward them.

"You ruined my Jeep, asshole."

"Are you allowed to say that to me?" Josh asked, still touching his lip.

Cami held out her badge to the paramedics. "Detective Cami Lyons. This is my Jeep. It's in a lot worse shape than I am."

"I'd still really like to check you out, Detective. Lots of hidden injuries can happen in car accidents. Broken bones, neck injuries, back issues. Even if you feel okay, you might not be."

Cami nodded. She knew the drill. "Of course. Just a second, I want to take a look at the car." The urge to scream was almost too great to ignore. Cami ran her hand along the front wheel well where the metal turned inward, the green paint ripped off like a sheet and the silver underneath it exposed. The grill of Josh's red Elantra was firmly embedded between the passenger door and the back seat. The back door was pushed in so far, it was hanging from its hinges.

They were loading Josh onto a stretcher even though he kept trying to sit up. Cami could hear him complaining about the neck collar they had on him. "Do you think I'm going to get a surcharge on my insurance for this?" he asked one of the paramedics.

A surprise to even her, Cami laughed. A big, hearty, from-the-depths-of-her-stomach laugh. She was starting to feel a few twinges in her back and legs, but it wasn't enough to keep her from laughing. She held on to the mangled window frame of the passenger door and just laughed and laughed and laughed.

Chapter Twenty-six

Alicia laid out a pair of flannel pants, a T-shirt, undies and socks, toothbrush and toothpaste, and her face wash. She hadn't packed for a sleepover in a long time. She figured she'd just come home early to get ready for the day, so she wasn't concerned about the following morning. Besides, she was sure Jade would have just about anything she could have forgotten.

She stuffed everything into an old blue duffel bag she had under her bed. Alicia truly hoped spending the night with Jade would calm her fears and get her out of the paranoia fueled spiral she seemed to be in. Alicia was nervous about the killer, too, but Jade seemed to be taking it to a whole new level.

As she was deciding which pair of flip-flops to wear over, Alicia's phone rang. She brightened a little at seeing Violet's name on the screen. "Hey," she answered. She tucked her phone between her chin and her shoulder as she zipped up the duffel bag.

"Alicia, it's Violet."

"I know." Alicia chuckled. Did Violet forget caller ID was a thing? "You okay?"

"Cami's been in an accident."

"What?" Alicia felt the blood drain from her face. "What kind of accident?"

"A car accident. I was on the phone with her when it happened. She's okay."

Relief washed over Alicia like a warm wave. "What happened?"

"I still don't really know. We were talking, and then the next thing I knew, I heard a crash, and the phone went silent. I talked to her on her way to the hospital, though she didn't want to go. She said she was fine, but the paramedics insisted."

"Thank God." Alicia exhaled. "Where is she now?"

Violet sighed. "Well, that's the thing. I've been calling to check on her, but there's no answer. I'm at Madison's parent-teacher conference, or I'd go over there. Katie and Taryn are in Vermont visiting Taryn's dad. I guess I could call Kelsey, but I don't know if she's on duty. I'm sorry, I probably shouldn't have called you. I made it awkward, just forget it. So sorry."

"No, no. It's not awkward at all. I'll call her. If she doesn't answer, I'll go over. I'm really glad you called, actually. She never admits when something is wrong, so it's not like this is out of character. Did you try her at work?"

"I did. Voice mail."

"Okay. I'll let you know what I find out. Thanks, Violet. I mean it. Thank you."

"Don't thank me, you're doing me a favor. Keep me posted. Thanks, Alicia."

Alicia ended the call and immediately dialed Cami. She could feel her pulse quicken a little as the line just rang and rang. She couldn't even leave a message since Cami's voice mailbox appeared to be full. It felt like it had all those times in and after Australia when she'd prayed for Cami to answer the phone. She never did then, and she didn't now.

Be there shortly. Have to make a stop first.

She texted Jade and threw her bag into the car. The drive to Cami's was bizarre. Alicia didn't know what to expect when she arrived. Was Cami even home? Maybe after her wreck of a day, she'd decided to go out for a drink to calm her nerves. Maybe she was called into work and out questioning someone.

Walking up the front stairs and beneath the forest green awning that announced building six was like walking through a time capsule. Alicia was overcome with memories of carrying too many groceries and dropping half in the hallway, the upstairs neighbors decorating the mailbox area with their holiday crafts, seeing Cami waiting for her in the doorway at the end of the hall with that goofy "come hither" look she'd perfected. Alicia smiled at the thought of it.

Not much had changed in the last few years. The same mirror was hanging in the hallway above the skinny black table with the fake lilies on it. The wooden bench next to the stairs still had a faded "Go Pats" decal on one of the legs. The sticker on Cami's mailbox had been cut in half. It only read Lyons where it used to read Lyons/Flynn. The backslash was still partially visible.

Alicia's heartbeat quickened as she walked the length of the hallway toward their old end unit. It was quiet, as it always had been. The soft squish of the navy blue carpet beneath her feet was familiar and intimidating at the same time.

She knocked lightly on Cami's door. No answer. She knocked a little harder, but there was still no response. She pressed her ear to the cool wooden door and listened for signs of movement. Maybe she just wasn't home.

There was a faint hum in the background. Alicia leaned up to look through the peephole and didn't see much, but she did see a light coming from the kitchen or possibly the bathroom. It was hard to tell.

If Cami had remained true to form over the years, she would *never* forget to turn a light off before leaving the apartment. She used to follow behind Alicia before they went anywhere to shut everything off in her wake. It was one of those things Alicia had just come to accept over time.

She took a deep breath and dug in her pocket for the small silver key Cami had painstakingly painted an A on with red nail polish. It was highly likely that she had changed the locks soon after Alicia left. Maybe even installed a security latch to be sure Alicia couldn't find a way in.

To her immense surprise, the key slid into the doorknob with no resistance. Alicia knew opening Cami's door was morally ambiguous at best, but she was genuinely worried. She would just poke her head in. If Cami wasn't home, she'd quickly lock back up, send her a message admitting what she'd done, and leave the key on the table near the door. Assuming it was still there.

Still unsure if she was doing the right thing and realizing she probably wasn't, Alicia inserted her key into the dead bolt. Like butter. She turned the lock before she could change her mind and opened the door.

The light was coming from the bathroom. There was also a steady flow of steam floating into the entryway. To Alicia's horror, she realized Cami must be in the shower.

Oh God. She's going to kill me. Talk about a violation of privacy. I'll go. I'll just go.

A small whimper emanated from the open door. Alicia froze, wondering if she'd imagined it. And then, it happened again.

Fuck it. She can't possibly be any angrier at me than she was before.

"Cami?" Alicia called. "Are you okay?"

She mustn't have heard her. Alicia tiptoed toward the bathroom door and cracked it open a little farther.

"It's me, Alicia, Cami. Are you okay?" she asked again, louder this time.

The crying stopped. "Alicia? What are you doing here?" Her voice was ragged and hoarse.

Alicia opened the door wider and kept her eyes on the floor. "Violet called me. She's been trying to get you for a while, and you weren't answering. Are you okay?"

"I'm fine." Cami's voice broke. "I'm fine. You didn't have to come here, I'm sorry. I'll call Violet when I get out."

She didn't sound fine. Alicia opened the door wide enough to see. Cami was sitting on the floor of the shower, hugging her knees and letting the hot water run over her. Her hair was hanging in wet strands around her face. She had her chin resting on one knee, and her eyes were closed.

"You are *not* fine, Cami." Alicia grabbed one of the green fuzzy towels from the same spot they'd always been. She reached in and turned the water off. Cami trembled. "Come on." Alicia slid the shower door to the side and wrapped the towel around Cami's back. She slung her arm around Cami's shoulder and under her arm to coax her up.

"Ugh, this is so embarrassing. Alicia, please, you don't have to do this. What little dignity I have left is quickly slipping away."

"Oh, stop." Alicia turned her head while Cami wrapped the towel fully around herself and stepped out of the shower. "Now what's wrong? Really?"

Cami opened her mouth to say something and then closed it. Her eyes filled up, and she cleared her throat. "Everything," she whispered. She didn't bother to wipe the tears away.

Alicia's heart cracked inside her chest. She opened her arms and pulled Cami close. Cami kept her hands balled around her towel so it didn't fall, but she leaned in and rested her forehead on Alicia's shoulder. She kept it steady for a second and then just let go. She cried openly as Alicia rubbed her back in small circles. The weight of Cami against her, even in her current state, felt like…home. For the first time in a long time, Alicia sensed that she was finally home. Where she was meant to be. But she couldn't shake the notion that her homecoming was only adding to Cami's misery.

"What do you need?" Alicia asked quietly. "Is there anything I can do for you?"

Cami shook her head. She pushed her hair out of her face and took a deep breath. Her face was red and splotchy and streaked with tearstains. "I'm sorry. This really is humiliating. I could kill Violet for sending you here."

"There is nothing embarrassing about this at all, trust me. Remember the time you and I were at Six Flags, and that woman asked if anyone wanted cookies? And I saw those people line up, and I got in line too? I mean, who doesn't want cookies? And then you came up to me and grabbed my hand and told me that it was actually a family picnic, and she was asking her *family* if they wanted cookies?"

Cami erupted in laughter. In spite of herself, Alicia thought. She laughed, too. She pushed Cami's hair off one shoulder so the water would stop running onto the front of the towel and soaking it.

"See? Now *that's* embarrassing. This? This is nothing. Just a blip on the radar. Are you hungry? I can make you something real quick. I don't mind."

"No, I'm okay. I just…I just need this investigation to turn something up. We need a breakthrough soon, or I'm afraid he'll just get away with it, and those three people will never have justice. And I'm in a weird place because of what happened the other night at

Birdie's. I shouldn't have done that. I'm sorry for putting you in that position. And now my Jeep is all mangled. And I'm really fucking sore." Cami craned her neck back and forth, and there were all sorts of cracking noises. "Wait. How did you get in? Did I leave the door unlocked?"

Alicia cringed. "I still have a key. I know it's super inappropriate, and I should have sent it back or thrown it out a long time ago but I… didn't. I just assumed you'd changed the locks. I didn't think it would even work. Don't be mad."

Cami just kind of stared at her with a hint of a smile. Alicia couldn't tell if she was amused or furious. "I kept meaning to change the locks. I just never got around to it. I'm not mad." Cami looked at her towel. "I should probably get dressed."

"Right. If you're sure you're okay, I'll head out. Again, sorry about the whole key thing. It's weird. I get it." Alicia really wished she would shut up, but her mouth just kept going. "I'll leave it on the table."

"I'm actually sort of glad you came by. I *was* fine—technically, anyway—but I guess I was just really fucking sad. And I appreciate you pulling me out of it with your stupid Six Flags story," Cami said with a quick roll of her eyes.

Alicia couldn't help but smile. Seeing Cami at her most vulnerable was not what she'd expected that evening, but she was glad she was the one to be there for her. She sighed deeply. "Hey," she said, mostly unsure of where she was going. "Honestly, Cami. I didn't come back here to be a thorn in your side. I didn't want to mess with your head or anything like that. When my lease on the apartment is up, maybe I'll just go. I have no interest in making your life any more complicated than it is. I don't want to hurt you again."

Cami looked down, one hand still gripping the knot of the towel. "Alicia. I think I'm past that. I complicated things the other night, but other than that, we've been coexisting just fine. Don't do anything dramatic."

Alicia laughed. "Isn't that kind of my thing? Dramatic and over-the-top?"

"Yeah, it kind of is. It's cold in here." Cami held out her arm to show Alicia the goose bumps that had popped up.

"It's because you're wet. Go get dressed. I'll talk to you soon, okay?"

"Yeah. Thanks again."

Alicia nodded. She wanted to hug her again, but Cami was still in a towel, and she didn't want to seem presumptuous. But, ugh, she wanted to.

Instead, she turned toward the door. She slid the key out of her pocket. The little red A was still bright and obvious. She squeezed it in her hand one last time before leaving it on Cami's kitchen table.

Chapter Twenty-seven

Popcorn ceilings were the bane of every home renovator on HGTV. Cami stared at hers, the pointy white peaks mimicking a blanket of snow. She'd scooped her hair into a high ponytail so the damp ends wouldn't rest on her T-shirt and soak through. She couldn't seem to shake the chill in her bones. Everything was quiet and still.

She'd been trying to sort through her feelings, *again*, after Alicia left the apartment. Cami was tired, achingly tired, but her mind was racing. She closed her eyes and tried to will herself to sleep even though it was barely eight o'clock. At some point, her body needed to just shut down and recharge.

It was pointless. She tossed and turned for as long as she could bear it. Angrily, she threw the covers off and sat up too quickly. She rubbed her face vigorously and checked her phone. Eight nineteen.

Cami threw on a pair of capris and a faded U2 T-shirt she'd had since her twenties. It was old and worn, but it was comfortable. She wanted something old and worn and comfortable. *Might as well stick with what works.*

Every muscle and bone in her body shouted at her to turn around and go back to bed. She thought about it for a fraction of a second and decided she'd just have to plow through the pain. The thought of lying in bed for another minute while her mind was on a delirious fast-forward setting was revolting. She walked through the kitchen with a hand on her lower back and saw Alicia's key sitting in the center of the table. She remembered sitting on the floor between Alicia's legs and using her nail polish to painstakingly paint a perfect A on it. It had been worth the effort since the A was still as clear and bright as it had been the night she'd done it.

Cami picked up the key and turned it over and over in her hand. Maybe it would be best if Alicia moved away. Not that Cami had the authority or the wherewithal to ask her to do so, but it would probably make her life a whole lot easier.

Was that what she wanted? Really? Cami exhaled and tossed the key back onto the table.

Downstairs, she eased into the driver seat of the small rental car and instinctively tried to turn on the radio. This car had a giant LCD screen with all sorts of different options. AM, FM, Satellite, Bluetooth, USB, Auxiliary. She pressed the FM button, and some adult contemporary blasted into the car. Cami cringed and tried to find the volume button. Christopher Cross was great and all, but not at an earsplitting decibel. She managed to find the arrows and turned the volume down to three.

She didn't know for certain where she was going, but she did find herself hungry all of a sudden. Maybe some greasy fast food would do the trick. Or maybe a strawberry salad was what she needed. Neither sounded all that appealing.

As she pulled out onto the dark road adjacent to her apartment building, she kept turning to check the cars behind her. She wasn't used to being so low to the ground. The headlights of the SUVs and trucks trailing her were blinding in the rearview mirror. Cami flipped it to the night vision mode and tried to shake off her general sense of unease.

She settled on a bagel and cream cheese. Not exactly health food but not a burger and fries, either. She thought about going into the small coffee shop and eating at one of the empty tables that lined the windows but decided she'd rather just drive. It wasn't the same in this tiny car instead of her Jeep, but it was fine.

Katie's number appeared on Cami's phone screen as the phone vibrated back and forth in the cup holder. Cami took a deep breath and pressed the speaker button. "Hello?" she answered around a mouthful of bagel.

"Hey." Katie sounded surprised. "I just got off the phone with Violet. You okay?"

Cami threw her head back and focused on the beige ceiling of the car. Violet really wasn't wasting any time looping everyone in. She knew that Violet's intentions were good, but man, a little discretion about her breakdown would have been appreciated.

"Yes, I'm okay. Just had a lot hit me at once. I'll be fine."

Katie was silent for a moment. "Are you avoiding me? I've texted you a hundred times and left you a message at work. Is it because of the other night? At the Book Cabin?"

"I'm not avoiding you, K. I mean, maybe I am a little. I just didn't feel like getting into it with you again about Alicia. I know how you feel about her and the situation, and I understand it. But I don't want to feel like every time I'm polite to her or not actively being an asshole that you're judging me for it. It's not fair." Cami balled up the rest of her bagel in the wrapper and stuffed it into the bag.

"You sound like Taryn," Katie scoffed. "I'm sorry. I just have a hard time trusting that anything she says or does is genuine. I feel like the only reason she came back was to relieve her own guilt or something, and you're just playing right into her hands."

"See?" Cami should have sent the call to voice mail. "This is exactly what I'm saying. You're treating me like a victim who's so naive and foolish that I'm just letting Alicia breeze back into my life with no regard for what happened in the past. I haven't forgotten, Katie. I'll *never* forget. But I believe her when she says she's sorry, and I believe her when she says she knows it was a mistake. She offered to leave town once the lease is up on her new place. Not because she wants to leave but because she thinks her presence is making my life more difficult."

"I'm trying, Cam. Really. My first instinct when you tell me that is that she's bluffing. If you actually called her on it and told her that it would be best if she packed up and left, she'd be blindsided and find a way to prove that she *couldn't* leave. When did she say this?"

Huh. *Was* Cami as naive as Katie had painted her? Because that thought hadn't even crossed her mind. Maybe her judgment was just too clouded to see Alicia for the diabolical conspirator that Katie believed her to be. Or maybe Alicia was just trying to make things right in the only way she knew how.

"Earlier tonight," Cami answered. "She came over when Violet told her she couldn't get in touch with me. We talked a little, she made me feel better, and then she left. That was it."

"Well, I'm glad you feel better. Listen, you're my best friend in the world. I don't want this to come between us. I just remember how it was. How you were. I don't ever want you to go through that again."

Cami sighed. "I know. I just need you to back off a little bit. I promise you that I'm protecting myself. I spent the first year after she left grieving her, the second year hating her, the third year trying to forget her, and now, here we are. I can't say that I miss the massive amount of energy expelled on someone who wasn't even a part of my life anymore. I just need you to trust me."

"Okay." Katie exhaled loudly. "I'll stay out of it. Since Taryn and Violet and even Jack seems to have just accepted her into the fold again, I suppose I'll try to as well."

"If being around her makes you uncomfortable, I understand that. I'll keep it separate if that works better for you."

"No, I don't want that. Then there would just be this big chasm between us, and that's not how we roll. We tell each other everything, and I don't want that to change."

"Me either. Hey, Kelsey is beeping in. I'll call you later?"

"Definitely. Love you, Cam."

"Love you, too."

In spite of herself, Cami felt a weight lift off her like a dissipating cloud. She hadn't even realized how much the unacknowledged rift with Katie had been bothering her. Maybe now they could just go back to normal.

"Hey, Kels. What's up?"

"We just got a 9-1-1 call from the Conley house. They called about an intruder. A unit's on their way now."

Cami squinted. "Jade's place? I wonder if she's being paranoid or if Evan showed up. She did seem pretty freaked out the last time I talked to her. Are you heading over?"

"I am, yeah. I 've been listening to Fred Miller explain why his property dispute with Elgin Farm is a bigger deal than the murder investigation for the last hour and how we're wasting our resources on something that the feds should be dealing with. It was a lovely hour."

"Sounds it. Let me know if you want me to meet you there. I went for a drive. I'm up in Birch Village." Cami started the engine and adjusted her rearview mirror. She pulled up the maps app on her phone to enter Jade's address.

"I think you'll want to meet me there. The 9-1-1 call was placed by Alicia Flynn."

Cami almost dropped the phone. "What? Why is Alicia there?" She tried to remember if Alicia had said where she was going when they were at the apartment earlier. She didn't think so.

"No idea. On my way now."

"Me too. Kelsey, make sure it's just a false alarm and nothing serious, okay?"

Kelsey replied that she would, but Cami felt extremely uneasy. Alicia wasn't the type to call 9-1-1 unless something was really wrong. She looked at her hands clutching the steering wheel and noticed they were both trembling.

CHAPTER TWENTY-EIGHT

Alicia was feeling pretty good on her drive over to Jade's. She felt almost…light. She'd thought for sure that Cami was going to let her have it for keeping the key all that time. Instead, Cami hadn't seemed all that fazed by it.

She didn't *want* to move out of Oakview, but she'd meant what she'd said. At first, Alicia had told herself that if Cami didn't come around to her being back, they would just have to avoid each other and deal with it. But she didn't have the same nonchalance that she'd had when she'd first signed her lease. It was more. Deeper. She'd never stopped loving Cami, but the realization that she was still *in* love with her had been a stark one.

Jade's house was dark when Alicia pulled into the driveway. She had left the right garage bay open for her, so she pulled in next to Jade's SUV. The only spot of light was a warm yellow in what Alicia believed was her bedroom. Why wasn't the place lit up like a Christmas tree? Jade had floodlights attached to the corners of her roof. Alicia knew this from experience. She'd set them off more than once when she'd visited.

She pulled her bag out of the back seat and slung it over her shoulder. She could hear her own footsteps on Jade's paved driveway, and it was freaking her out. The neighborhood was too quiet.

As Alicia approached the front door, it swung open, and Jade stood in the doorway. There were no lights on behind her. "Why are you in the dark?" Alicia asked.

"I prefer it." Jade pulled her cardigan tighter, even though it was still seventy degrees outside. She closed the door but didn't lock it and walked toward the kitchen.

Alicia went behind her and flipped the dead bolt. "You forgot to lock the door."

"I didn't forget anything. I've decided I'm not going to live in fear. I'm ready for him."

"Ready for him?" Alicia felt her heartbeat quicken. "What do you mean?"

Jade switched on a small table lamp that cast a soft glow. She nodded toward the coffee table in the living room.

Alicia followed her eyes and saw a metal baseball bat lying next to a rifle. "You can't be serious. Where did you get that gun? You never told me you were a hunter or a gun enthusiast."

"It's just a BB gun. But at close range, it could do some damage, and I just bought it today, so Evan doesn't know that it's not a real rifle. It might just scare him enough for me to get the upper hand."

"Jade, this is crazy. If Evan is the killer, and if he is trying to kill you, you know that he's doing it with a handgun, right? A real one with real bullets. A BB gun and a bat aren't going to offer much protection. We should lock all the doors and windows and be vigilant. The police are sending a patrol car by every few hours, so we'll be safe inside." Alicia was seriously concerned about Jade's mental state. The woman she knew was not haphazard or uncontrolled.

"Fine. Lock the front door. But I'm still going to keep these with me just in case." Jade picked up the bat and draped the BB gun over her shoulder.

"That's okay," Alicia said. "Whatever puts you at ease. Did you eat? Do you want to watch a movie or play a game or something?"

"I'm not very hungry. But, yes, we can watch something if you'd like. Do you mind coming up to my room? We can relax in the sitting area. It's the only television I actually know how to use. Not much time for TV."

Alicia thought about saying that she was pretty sure she could figure out the downstairs TV, but Jade seemed to want to go upstairs. She was already halfway to the staircase before Alicia could answer. "Sure. Where should I put my bag?"

Jade pointed upstairs. "You can take the guest room next to mine. It's on the smaller side, but the bed is by far the most comfortable."

"Works for me."

She followed Jade up the stairs, the soft glimmer of the table lamp fading with every step. The light was on in Jade's room at the end of the hallway, but everything leading up to it was in darkness. Jade opened the door to the room next to hers. Alicia felt along the wall for a light switch. An overhead light turned on, but it wasn't as bright as she'd hoped.

"Do you think we should turn some lights on? Make the place look alive?" Alicia set her bag down on the fluffy brown bedspread. The "small" room was at least double the size of the bedroom in her apartment.

"You can leave this light on if it'll make you feel better. I'll go get us set up next door."

The room was welcoming and well accessorized with everything she could possibly need. Alicia closed the door and threw on her flannel pants and T-shirt. She turned and caught her reflection in the giant mirror over the dresser. All the shadows that the dim light cast behind her gave her the creeps. *Stop it. You're here to be the voice of reason, not feed into Jade's suspicions.*

Jade was sitting on the chaise lounge in front of the large bay window. She was flipping the remote control over and over in her hand while looking outside. "Maybe he'll go back to that shady rental place and get a car I won't recognize. That would be just like him."

"Have you tried, um, talking to him at all? I know you said he showed up the other day. Maybe you could hash it out over the phone, even. Just kind of see where his head's at." Alicia sat on the floor next to the chaise and stretched out her legs.

Jade didn't look away from the window. "Ugh, are you victim blaming? Saying *I* should make the first move toward a resolution when I've done nothing wrong?"

"No! Not at all, I just meant that maybe it would put your mind to rest if you knew he was just being a dick about money and not actively trying to kill you. I certainly didn't mean to imply that you're obligated to do anything." *Jeez.*

"No, I'm sure you didn't. What do you want to watch? Should we put on *Friday the 13th* or something like it to fit the mood?"

"I was thinking maybe something a little lighter. We don't want to scare ourselves silly."

Jade shrugged but seemed to agree. She scrolled through the guide and settled on a Hallmark-type romance about a big-city girl coming to rescue the family farm. Where her ex-fiancé worked, of course. Not Alicia's typical movie fare, but it was better than *Friday the 13th*.

Jade handed her a box of Cheez-Its. It was clear that while Jade was used to entertaining at a dinner party or cocktail hour setting, sleepovers weren't her comfort zone. Alicia leaned back against the chaise and crossed her legs at the ankles.

About an hour into the movie, Alicia's eyes were closing of their own volition. She sat up straighter and tried to focus. Just before the big reunion kiss, she could feel her lids get heavier and heavier.

"What was that?" Jade asked, sitting up.

Alicia sat forward. "I didn't hear anything."

"Must have been my imagination." Jade leaned back against the lounge, but she didn't look relaxed at all.

Scrape.

"Okay, that time I heard it," Alicia whispered. "Something outside?"

Jade stood. "I don't know. Sounded like it could have been the patio slider."

"Was it locked?"

"I think so. I don't know. I might have left it open when I was formulating my brilliant plan to shoot Evan with a BB gun."

"Really? Great. So we're sitting ducks." Alicia strained to hear any noises coming from downstairs. All she could hear was the sweeping music coming from the television, signifying that the boy had, in fact, gotten the girl. She pointed frantically to the TV so Jade would turn it down.

With the TV off, the house was completely silent. It was probably just something outside. A million things make a scraping noise on concrete.

A soft patter. Followed by a sharp but quick squeak.

"Someone's in the house," Jade whispered loudly. She grabbed the baseball bat off the floor and charged the door.

"Jade, no! We don't know who it is or what they have. If they see you coming at them with a baseball bat, they could shoot you."

"Wasn't it you who told me that the killer's MO was shooting people at an outside location where there weren't any witnesses? I told you it was Evan. He's come to finish me off." Jade had that wild-eyed look again. She raised the bat over her shoulder with both hands as if a fastball was whipping toward her.

"Call the police. We'll just lock the door and stay put. Stay quiet." Alicia's heart was racing, and her mouth was a desert. Her face was hot, and her arms were covered in goose bumps. She'd never felt this kind of fear before. *Am I having a heart attack?* Her chest didn't hurt, but she was sure that a heart wasn't meant to beat that violently.

"You call the police. I'm going to call Evan's phone to see if he was stupid enough to leave his ringer on."

With shaking hands, Alicia grabbed her phone and brought up the dial pad. 9-1-2. Backspace. 9-1-2. *Dammit!* Backspace. 9-1-1.

"Yes, I need to report an intruder. I am at 742 Deer Path Lane. Please hurry, it might be the Small-Town Slayer." Alicia's voice sounded as if it were coming from someone else. A mile away.

"We're sending help. Are you alone in the house?"

"No, it's me and Jade Conley, the owner of the house."

"Your name please?"

"Alicia Flynn."

"We have a unit on the way, Alicia. Where in the house are you?"

Jade pressed her ear to the door. "I don't hear his phone ringing. But someone's coming. I can hear footsteps on the stairs."

Alicia stifled the whimper that rose in her throat. "He's coming up the stairs," she shout-whispered into the phone. "They have to hurry."

Jade whipped around and put a finger to her lips. Alicia nodded, but her heart was beating so loudly in her ears that she wasn't sure if she'd stopped talking or not. All she could hear was the frantic drumming rhythm.

The drumbeat was interrupted by a startling *bang* against the door.

That time, a whimper did escape. Alicia clapped a hand over her mouth. Jade silently shushed her again. Alicia tiptoed over to where the BB gun was lying on the floor. She picked it up and rested it on her shoulder like a soldier. She figured she'd probably be better off using it as a bludgeon than as a gun. She took a deep breath.

Bang on the door again.

Jade jumped and the baseball bat clanged against the wall. "Evan! I'm not going to let you scare me. You want to fight? Let's fight." She threw the bat to the floor and took the gun from Alicia. She cocked it, and the lever made a loud click as it dropped into place.

"Jade, no," Alicia yelled as Jade went for the doorknob. She startled her enough for Jade to retract her hand as if the doorknob was burning.

After a beat, they heard footsteps running from the door.

"He probably wasn't expecting two of us. We can't let him get away with this." Jade opened the door and took off down the hall.

"No," Alicia wailed. She ran after Jade, nearly falling down the stairs as she took them two at a time. She could finally make out the sound of a siren in the distance. *Thank you thank you thank you.*

Jade was screaming incoherently as she ran through the house. Glass shattered. Alicia flattened herself against a wall and prayed that she'd see the sunrise tomorrow.

"He's gone," Jade yelled. "The slider door is wide open. He must have run out when he heard us coming. I'm going to kill that son of a bitch."

A police cruiser squelched to a stop in front of Jade's house. She sprinted out to the front lawn, the gun still clutched in her hand. Alicia realized she was still holding the bat she'd picked up when Jade was running down the hall. She dropped it on the floor and rushed out after Jade.

Two officers were trying to get the story from Jade, who was officially in hysterics. She'd been reckless and rash, but Alicia admired her bravery. She was obviously sick of feeling like a victim and ready to take matters into her own hands.

Alicia had never been so happy to see Kelsey in her life as she watched her pull up behind the police car. She craned her neck to see if Cami was in the passenger seat. She wasn't.

"Alicia, what's going on?" Kelsey asked as she exited. "Was Evan Conley here tonight?"

"I don't know. Jade was so afraid that someone was going to come for her, and I basically told her she was paranoid, but she clearly wasn't," Alicia said. The words just spilled out and wouldn't stop spilling. "We were watching a movie, and then we heard something, but I thought it was just somebody outside, but whoever it was came in the house. And then they were banging, and I don't know what they wanted. To kill us? Does Evan really want Jade dead?"

"Okay, okay. It's possible that this is unrelated," Kelsey said. "Not likely, I'll grant you. But we don't want to jump into the Small-Town Slayer nonsense feet first. I know it's all anyone can think about, but we have to be objective."

"Does Cami know? Should I call her?" Alicia had been wanting to call her since she was stuck inside Jade's bedroom. Not that she'd been thinking of it then, but now that the panic had subsided, everything was weird, and boundaries were sort of blurred.

"She knows," Kelsey said. "She's on her way."

"Oh thank God," Alicia sighed. The relief of being outside in the open with law enforcement officials all around her had built to a tipping point. She wanted to just break down and sob.

"The officers are going to want a statement from you as well. You didn't see anything? Hear anything that might be helpful?" Kelsey asked.

Alicia shook her head. "Nothing. We heard the slider door and footsteps and banging on the door. It was like a phantom. By the time we left the room and went downstairs, there was nothing. Just an open door. Fingerprints, maybe?"

"We'll check. But if it *is* the same person, they've been very careful about leaving prints. We haven't found so much as a smudge. You're okay? Why don't you go talk to Officer Michaels and Officer Graham? I'm going to go inside and take a look around. See what I can find."

"I'm okay. Go ahead, I hope you find something."

Alicia rubbed her arms up and down to warm them even though it was still in the seventies. A few neighbors had gathered on the sidewalk to watch the spectacle. Jade was speaking to an older woman who appeared enraptured by her story. Alicia could hear her recounting the details of the banging, though she seemed to be embellishing certain details. The banging on the door *was* terrifying, but Alicia didn't recall the hinges exploding inward.

Officers Michaels and Graham approached Alicia with their notebooks and concerned smiles. She tried to give them as many details as possible while still keeping an eye toward the top of the street for an anticipated pair of headlights.

CHAPTER TWENTY-NINE

There were approximately five hundred places Cami could have gotten a bagel and cream cheese between Oakview and Birch Village. Why tonight, of all nights, couldn't she have just grabbed one at one of those restaurants? She drove down 202 faster than she should have, grateful that traffic wasn't an issue. The sedan might have had a lot of complicated buttons, but the smooth ride it kept at such a brisk pace was reluctantly impressive.

She wanted to call Alicia to make sure she was okay, but if there *was* an intruder at Jade's house, the last thing Cami wanted to do was give their location away. She looked at the speedometer again and flashed back to earlier in the day when she'd been T-boned in the town center. It felt like seven days ago, not seven hours.

After what felt like hours later, Cami pulled up behind Kelsey's car in front of Jade's house. The fact that the emergency lights were still flashing and there was a small crowd gathered in Jade's driveway lent credence to the idea that it probably wasn't a false alarm. Cami scanned the area for a familiar head of brown hair. Her eyes finally settled on Officer Michaels, who was standing in front of Jade's garage, nodding. Cami craned her neck and saw Alicia looking concerned, her arms crossed.

She jumped out of the rental car and made a beeline for the garage. Alicia caught sight of her and interrupted Michaels. "Cami, I'm so glad you're here. Someone broke in."

Michaels stepped to the side. Cami didn't know how much he knew about their past, but he didn't seem surprised by Alicia's reaction.

"Kelsey told me you called about an intruder. I was hoping it was a misunderstanding or someone Jade wasn't expecting that freaked you both out. I take it that wasn't the case?" Cami turned to Michaels. "Are you all set with her?"

"Just about. We can finish later if you'd prefer."

"I just want to do a quick walk-through. Have you taken Jade Conley's statement?" Cami asked.

Michaels nodded. "Yes. She's inside now with Detective Chandler."

Cami took Alicia's elbow and led her up the stairs into Jade's foyer. It was empty. Kelsey and Jade must have been up in the bedroom. She could hear Jade loudly recounting what had happened.

"You okay?" Cami asked once they were in the living room.

"Scared. But okay."

Alicia grabbed Cami's forearm and pulled her in for a hug. She closed her eyes and wrapped her arms around Alicia's waist. Alicia trembled slightly. *God, she feels good. No. Stop it. Focus.*

"I honestly can't tell you how happy I am to see you. I really thought I was going to die. Thank you for coming," Alicia whispered.

Cami held her even tighter as Alicia's warm breath tickled her ear. She realized her hand was slowly making its way up the length of Alicia's back before she broke away.

"Of course I came. As soon as Kelsey called me, I was on my way. I'm sorry it took me so long. What happened? Why were you here?"

As Alicia filled her in on how the evening had played out, Cami couldn't help but wonder if it actually was Evan Conley behind the break-in. Was he trying to scare Jade into submission so she'd back off the divorce demands? Seemed a little excessive. Was *Jade* the one coordinating a false attack so she could get Evan behind bars and not have to worry about a countersuit? Seemed a little too out there.

Cami had Alicia walk her through step-by-step. Every room and every noise. There didn't seem to be any physical evidence left in the house; that would have been a godsend. Not that Cami expected anything after the crime scenes she'd been through. There had to be something. Either linking it to a domestic dispute between husband and wife or the more sinister possibility of the Small-Town Slayer.

"Anything, Kels?" Cami asked as they entered Jade's room. Jade and Kelsey were looking through her security camera footage.

"We had a few motion trips but nothing of consequence. Jade doesn't have the back of her house set up where they presumably entered."

"I thought you'd said you were having more cameras added the day we went through your garden," Cami said.

Jade was clearly annoyed. "That's the plan, but it's not like I've been twiddling my thumbs these last few weeks. And you can't victim blame. My house and my space were just violated."

"I was just asking, Jade. We want to find out who did this just as badly as you want us to. Do any of your neighbors have any cameras that angle into your side yard?" Cami was getting tired of Jade flipping out every time anyone asked her a question.

"I doubt it. We have rows of arborvitae lining the property for a reason. Privacy."

"We'll check anyway. I'll authorize a patrol vehicle to stay on alert for your house and street to be on the safe side. Are you comfortable staying here, Jade?"

She nodded. "I can't imagine he'd come back tonight. Not after all of this spectacle. Alicia, you don't have to stay. Thank you for being here."

Alicia pursed her lips. "Are you sure? We just had quite the scare. I don't mind staying."

"I'm sure. I'm really just tired, and I know that Deborah and Rachel are keeping an eye on the place as well," Jade said, pointing to the houses on either side. "He wouldn't be stupid enough to come back tonight. He's obviously crazy, but he's not stupid."

Cami wondered if Alicia felt safe sleeping in *her* own place after the terrifying ordeal they'd been through. Maybe Violet could put her up in their spare room for the night.

A glint of metal on the ground near Kelsey's car caught Cami's eye. She switched on her flashlight and walked over to take a look. Alicia hurried behind her.

A nondescript tin container and an unopened bag of Veggie Straws were lying against the curb in front of Jade's house.

"Can you ask Kelsey to grab me a pair of gloves, please?" A quarter, a dime, and what looked like a receipt also lay abandoned on the asphalt. While Alicia ran to get the gloves, Cami dropped to her knees to check the area underneath Kelsey's car. The sharp twinge in her back served as a reminder that she really should have been taking it easy.

The pavement toward the front of the car was clear. Cami shone her light on the rear tires. There appeared to be something next to the right back tire, but it could have just been a chunk of asphalt. She got a little closer to inspect.

"Oh shit."

"What is it?" Kelsey asked, handing Cami a pair of latex gloves.

Cami didn't answer, just snapped them on as quickly as possible. She ignored the screaming in her shoulder as she reached around the tire and snatched the offending object.

A wooden block with the letter "A" emblazoned in sky blue paint.

"Holy shit," Kelsey echoed loudly. "Michaels, bring the evidence kit over here."

Cami held it between her fingers and turned it over and over. She looked up and saw Alicia waver on her feet. Kelsey grabbed her arm and steadied her. Cami jumped up. "Are you okay?"

"Yeah, sorry," Alicia replied quietly. "I'm just kind of in disbelief. The killer was really here. Jade wasn't being paranoid. A goddamn serial killer was in the house after us. I'm not sure if I want to burst into tears or throw up."

"Don't do either of those things," Cami took Alicia's hand and squeezed it. "You're safe now. No one is going to hurt you, I promise."

Alicia nodded, but Cami could tell she wasn't one hundred percent convinced. The thought of this sick fuck stalking Alicia made Cami's skin crawl. If Evan Conley was behind this, Cami vowed to personally ensure that he never saw the light of day again.

"Looks like I picked the wrong time to return home to Oakview. Maybe it's a sign that I really should go. Something doesn't want me here. I should go get my bag and head home." Alicia turned toward the house, her heightened anxiety evident.

"You don't have to go home, Alicia. Maybe you shouldn't be alone. Do you want me to call Violet? She'd love to have you at her house for the night." Cami pulled out her phone.

Alicia shook her head. "No, honestly, I'd rather just go back to my place. I need a good cry and maybe a shower. I'll flip the dead bolt and make sure the windows are all locked."

"I'll walk in with you. I want to get a few more photos anyway," Kelsey said.

Michaels brought over the evidence kit, and Cami bagged and tagged everything she'd found on the ground. The tin was plain metal, without any identifying markings. The crumpled receipt was from March for a bottled water at a gas station outside of town. The block was…the block. An A. Was that really what the killer was spelling? Tact? Was it some sort of Hannibal Lecter-type killing where the murderer was offended by something crass? Cami's head was swimming.

Kelsey returned with a large padded envelope for Cami to slide the evidence bags into. As she bent to make sure she hadn't missed so much as a ball of lint, a shock of pain in her ribs caused her to hiss in anguish.

"Okay, that's enough, Cami. Go home, please. I'll get all of this to the station, and forensics will do their thing. There's not much more you can do tonight. I'll follow up, I promise. Michaels and Graham are both here so I have help. You need to rest, seriously."

Cami tried not to wince as Kelsey helped her straighten. "Did Alicia leave?"

"Yeah. She just wanted to get home and go to bed. Definitely in a little bit of shock. Jade is upstairs on the phone with one of her neighbors. We'll be here for a while longer. I'll get permission from Brandt to send a patrol car to Alicia's building as well so you don't have to worry about that," Kelsey said. She gave Cami the eye.

Cami wasn't sure exactly what it meant, but she was too sore to try to decode it. "Fine. Fine, but I'll be there first thing in the morning. Call me immediately if anything comes up or if they find any DNA, or you figure something out with the block letters." It killed Cami to give in and leave, but she really needed to sit down. Standing up and moving around wasn't much of an option anymore.

"DNA testing at ten o'clock at night? You're funny," Kelsey said with a sarcastic grin.

Cami chuckled dryly. "I know, I just don't want to miss anything. We have to figure this out, like, right now. He's escalating by entering a house."

"Unless it's Conley."

"Right."

Cami gingerly got into her rental car and turned on the heated seat. It wasn't cold out, but she figured the heat might help with the muscle pain. She checked her phone and saw a text from Alicia.

Thank you. And I'm sorry. For everything.

She clicked on the message to reply and then changed her mind. She frowned. Why was Alicia apologizing? For making Cami go to Jade's after a car accident? For the tension between them? For what happened in the past? She pulled out onto the street and gave Kelsey a final wave before heading toward home.

Maybe this was the big break they needed. Cami hoped that at least one of the items the killer had presumably left behind would mean something. Maybe one of them would provide DNA, an identifier, a location they could stake out, *something* they could work with. Anything.

Cami was hopeful for probably the first time since Beverly Lawson's body had been found in the woods near Copper Lake. She couldn't keep her brain from going down the rabbit hole she'd successfully avoided earlier in the night: what if Jade or Alicia hadn't heard him come in? What if the killer had been able to break down the bedroom door and put a bullet in one of them? Or both? Cami shuddered at the thought.

What had Alicia said before she'd left? *I picked the wrong time to return to Oakview. Maybe it's a sign that I should go.* Something along those lines. Is that why she'd texted a broad apology? Was she planning to leave?

Cami took a hard right into the empty Walgreens parking lot. She looked at her phone one more time before peeling out of the parking lot and reversing direction.

CHAPTER THIRTY

Door locked. Check. Chain secured. Check. Windows closed and locked. Check. Closets and shower empty. Check. At least one night-light in every room. Check.

Alicia let out a huge sigh and flopped onto her couch. She thought about going to spend the night at her parents' house but quickly concluded that reliving the whole ordeal was just too much. She'd go see them the following day and tell them what had happened. Her mom would probably be pissed, but her relief would outweigh it.

She took the fastest shower of her life. She knew that she'd secured her apartment like it was Fort Knox, but she was acutely aware of every little hum and clang the old building emitted. Standing behind a shower curtain in a steamy bathroom made her feel like a sitting duck.

Alicia quickly threw on a pair of shorts and a T-shirt and ran into the living room to check the locks again. Chain still across the doorjamb. She exhaled. It was late, but if she didn't blow-dry her hair, it would be a giant mass of snarls in the morning. She just made sure to leave the bathroom door open and the front door in plain sight.

Jade sent her a text asking if she was okay. She replied that she was and asked her the same. Jade sent back a thumbs-up emoji and a heart. Jade seemed to be taking their brush with death quite well.

She flipped the television on and then turned it off. She couldn't really focus, so she picked up a magazine lying on the end table. Old news. She wanted to go to bed, but she didn't want to lie there staring at the ceiling. She wanted to be *really* tired before she subjected herself to nothing but her own thoughts.

A sitcom had to be on somewhere. She picked up the remote again, but before she could press power, there was a light rapping on her door. Alicia dropped the remote. Her heart started pounding the same way it had earlier at Jade's. She swallowed hard and tiptoed over, trying to be as silent as possible. She held her breath and got just close enough to the peephole to see if someone was knocking.

Cami. Cami was standing in the hallway, her back to the door. Alicia closed her eyes as relief spread throughout her body.

She hurriedly slid the chain lock over and flipped the dead bolt. She flung the door open just as Cami was turning around. "Hey."

Cami took a step forward. "I don't want you to go."

"What? Go where?"

"You said that you picked the wrong time to come home and that maybe you really should go. I don't want you to go."

Alicia's heart was still beating rapidly but for a wholly different reason this time. Cami just stood in front of her, her eyes boring into Alicia's. She had such an intensity about her that Alicia's stomach fluttered in anticipation. Her breathing quickened involuntarily.

Fuck it.

She leapt forward and buried a hand in Cami's thick hair, pulling her mouth to hers. She pushed Cami's lips apart and let their natural rhythm take over. Cami didn't resist or pull back. She found Alicia's hips with both hands and gripped them firmly, as though *Alicia* might decide this was all wrong and break away. Never.

The air in Alicia's lungs felt thick and heavy. Her head was spinning with a heady mix of excitement and desire and disbelief. They melted into each other, fitting together as perfectly as they had all those years ago. Cami's tongue slid over Alicia's lips like a raindrop on a windowpane, and Alicia felt a clenching jolt deep inside. She wanted her *so fucking much*.

Alicia pulled back just enough to look at Cami, to confirm she was real and in the moment, and it wasn't some delusional cosmic joke. Cami smiled softly, her eyes dark and teary and full of want. A moan escaped Alicia's lips against her will.

Cami smiled again. She brought her finger up to Alicia's bottom lip and traced it from right to left, watching Alicia's mouth with unbridled marvel. She leaned in again and kissed her harder. She pushed Alicia up against the living room wall and moved from her lips to the spot beneath her ear and down the length of her neck. What had started out sweet was quickly turning ruthless. Alicia fought the urge to roll her hips forward. She didn't want to scare Cami off with too much too soon.

That didn't seem to be a concern of Cami's. She made her way back up to Alicia's mouth and held her tightly with one hand on her waist and the other around the back of her neck. Alicia was dizzy. She flattened one hand against the wall behind her to keep from losing her balance.

Cami pushed her body even closer, a feat Alicia didn't think possible. She was pressed against her in all the right ways. Cami groaned quietly and Alicia could almost feel the hunger emanating from inside her. Alicia toyed with the hem of Cami's shirt and felt her shiver when she ran a hand along Cami's stomach. Alicia's breathing was so heavy, and her throat was so thick, she didn't know if she'd survive. At least she'd die happy.

She pushed Cami away slightly, moving away from the wall but not breaking the kiss. Cami's chest heaved, and Alicia thought it might have been from the way she moved them without warning. But, no, a stifled sob contradicted that theory.

"Are you okay? I'm so sorry," Alicia said hurriedly, not knowing exactly what she was apologizing for but wanting to make sure she hadn't overstepped. She was terrified that their connection would break like a fragile eggshell, and she didn't want to have any part in cracking it.

"No, no, don't apologize." Cami used the palm of her hand to wipe her cheeks. She took Alicia's hand. "I don't know why I'm such a crybaby all of a sudden. Jeez. I guess it just sort of hit me. I always assumed I'd spend my whole life getting over you. But here you are. I don't know what any of this means, and I'm probably setting myself up for a world of hurt, but I can't walk away from you. God knows I've tried to keep my distance and pretend that you're not here, but I can't. You're all I think about, all I want. No matter how many times I tell myself that my life would be so much better if you had never come back, I know it isn't true. I haven't felt as hopeful or as happy or as *alive* as I've felt since the morning I first saw you at the diner. I obviously had a different take on all of this *that* day," Cami finished with a light chuckle. She swiped at her eyes that had repeatedly filled as she spoke. She looked expectantly at Alicia. "I'm still in love with you. I've never *not* been in love with you. I had to make myself forget."

Every brick, every plank, every rock that Alicia had used to surround herself with over the last few years came crashing down, deafening and maddening, in a split second. She didn't trust herself not to melt into a puddle on the floor. She leaned forward and kissed Cami again, softly and quickly. That Cami reciprocated and tightened her grip on Alicia's hand confirmed that she was not delusional.

"I'm in love with you, too, Cami. You are the greatest love of my life, and if I could take back what I did three and a half years ago, I would do anything, *anything*, to make that happen. The number of sleepless nights and uneasy days I've spent since then have left me broken. I've missed you every second of every day since then, and no matter what I did or where I went, it was you, just you, always you. I promise you—*promise you*—if you give me another chance to love you, I will never, ever hurt you like that again. I adore you, Camilla, and you are the only thing in this world that I need."

Cami didn't answer. She brought Alicia's hand to her mouth and gently kissed her knuckles. Alicia closed her eyes and dissolved into the moment. She'd been waiting so long for something she didn't really believe could ever possibly happen again. It was a dream. A fantasy. A wish. But there they were.

Alicia slow-walked them to the couch, keeping their hands entangled. She couldn't just keep standing there feeling as though her knees would give out any second. It was an oxymoron; she felt light as a feather and heavy as a boulder. The lightness was her heart, and the heaviness was her lust.

The couch was low and firm, not exactly the most comfortable thing in the world, but Alicia doubted it would matter. Cami turned and sat first, pulling Alicia down on top of her. Alicia gasped at the frantic, fluid motion with which she found herself in Cami's lap. She didn't have time to feel ridiculous before Cami's lips were back on her own.

The earlier tentativeness between them seemed to have evaporated. Cami's hands were on Alicia's thighs, kneading and gripping, trying to pull her closer, even though they were as close as two people could possibly get. Alicia ran her hand up the length of Cami's arm and over her shoulder, every curve and muscle familiar but new. Alicia sucked in a breath as Cami pulled up the hem of her shirt and held it up with her fist, exposing Alicia's entire midsection. Her fingers danced along the elastic waistband of Alicia's shorts. Alicia couldn't decide what was more alarming: how turned on she was or how surreal the entire world seemed at that moment. It was everything. Everything she'd wanted for so long.

Cami kissed her again, languid and slow. She pushed Alicia's shirt up even farther before pulling back just a little. She made pointed eye contact, Alicia's heart dropping at the honest but cautious hunger reflected back at her. Cami's eyes had a slight sheen.

"Promise?" Cami whispered.

Alicia knew. "I promise."

She'd never meant anything more in her life.

Chapter Thirty-one

A distant train whistle startled Cami out of a sound sleep. She opened her eyes and looked around the room, trying to get her bearings. It all came flooding back in an instant when a lock of chestnut hair tickled the contour of her chin. Alicia was nestled comfortably in the crook of Cami's underarm, her hand draped lazily over Cami's bare stomach.

As the events of the previous evening replayed in her head, Cami felt her body disintegrating. The sensation started in her chest and wiggled its way down to the tips of her toes, eliciting a slight shiver. She knew that the analyzing and scrutinizing and uncertainty would most likely worm its way in sooner rather than later, so just enjoying the moment seemed to be the smartest thing to do. Appreciating how full she felt, how complete, how at *peace* she was amid everything else seeming like a dumpster fire. Cami allowed herself to be happy, for just a few minutes if that was all she could afford. The realization had hit her like a freight train when she'd said it the night before, only because it was the first time she'd let herself acknowledge it. She'd never stopped loving Alicia. She pulled her closer and squeezed her shoulder.

"Mmm," Alicia mumbled. "Hi."

"Hi," Cami whispered back. Goose bumps broke out all over when Alicia starting placing featherlight kisses along her collarbone. She was fully awake at that point and slid down lower on her pillow to allow Alicia to climb on top.

The opening bars of "I Fought the Law" by The Clash shattered the relative silence, and both of them jumped.

"Dammit, Kelsey." Cami stretched her neck and stared at the ceiling while Alicia rolled back onto her side of the bed.

"I assume you need to get that?" she asked while wrapping a strand of Cami's hair around her index finger. Her flirtatious smirk made Cami want to throw the phone out the window.

"Ugh, I do. She doesn't call unless she needs something. Kelsey's a text only kind of girl unless absolutely necessary." Cami reluctantly answered the call and grumbled a hello.

"Hey. Are you feeling up to coming in this morning? I figured once your bones had time to rest, the pain from your accident would really kick in. Brandt wants a briefing on what went down at Jade's and the new evidence we have from last night. I can do it if you still feel like shit, but I wanted to ask you first."

"Yeah." Cami rubbed her eyes. "I'll be there. Give me twenty minutes. Appreciate it, Kels." Cami groaned and sat up, covering herself with a portion of the sheet.

Alicia lightly ran her fingers up and down Cami's spine, eliciting a shiver.

"Did we rush into this?" Cami turned slightly, grabbed Alicia's hand, and wove their fingers together. She didn't want to give her the wrong idea; she wasn't saying they had made a mistake, but she needed to make sure they were on the same page. Lack of communication was what had triggered all that heartbreak a few years earlier.

Alicia smiled and drew circles on the top of Cami's hand. "Definitely. I mean, *I* didn't rush into anything because I've been waiting for this, for you, since I fucked everything up. So to me, it feels like forever. But last night? Yeah, I suppose we did. You okay?"

"Yeah." Cami leaned in and kissed Alicia tenderly on the lips. "I hope you don't think I was pushy. It must have been that brush with death that kind of propelled me forward. I knew what I wanted, and I didn't want to wait another second."

"Pushy? My God, no." Alicia laughed. She brushed Cami's hair away from her forehead. "If anything, what took you so long? I had a brush with death, too."

Cami chuckled softly. "You did. We had a hell of a day yesterday. I woke up wondering if I should tell you that I was…considering things, and I wanted to find out what you were feeling. And now look at us." Cami motioned to the crumpled sheet between them.

"I'll tell you exactly how I'm feeling." Alicia took Cami's hand again and squeezed it tightly. "I've told you that I love you a thousand times. We said it freely. Usually before we left each other or before we went to bed. But I have a new appreciation for those words. I didn't think I'd ever get to say them to you again. So now, after all the distance and time that's passed between us, I'm privileged enough to be able to tell you, unequivocally, that I love you. I've always loved you. I always will. Whatever time you need, whatever feelings you want to work through, I'll be patient, and I'll help you however I can. I am so fucking grateful that you've given me the opportunity to right the most destructive wrong in my life." She slid over toward Cami and wrapped her arms around her neck, holding on as though she were a life raft. Their bodies still fit together like perfectly shaped puzzle pieces.

Cami found herself speechless. There was just too much emotion swirling inside her to process. The telltale lump in her throat made its presence known, so she exhaled slowly. Not now. She had to go, even though the thought of peeling herself away from Alicia physically pained her. That ugly voice deep down inside threatened that if she let go now, she might lose her again, forever. She tightened her grip around Alicia's waist and closed her eyes.

"As much as I don't want you to go, you have to." Alicia sighed heavily and broke away, still holding the sheet against her chest. Her hair was disheveled and draped messily over one shoulder.

"You are so beautiful," Cami whispered. The voice she heard was deeper than normal and cracking. It sounded like it had come from someone else, far away. She kissed Alicia one more time before finally getting out of bed. "But you're right, I have a killer to catch. And now, it's personal."

Elated. That was the only word Cami could come up with to describe it. She was trying to keep it in check, trying to be rational about it. They had a long road ahead of them, especially where trust was concerned. Cami was cognizant enough to know that once the euphoria of being with Alicia faded into contented normalcy, as it inevitably would, the years spent in heartache and anger wouldn't just disappear. But for now, elation was winning out.

"Let yourself be happy," Cami murmured. She winced at the twinge in her back. She was pretty sure the previous night's activities hadn't helped the aching in her bones. Oh well. Totally worth it.

Captain Brandt, Kelsey, and Officers Michaels and Graham were seated around the conference table in the meeting room. Graham was giving Brandt the blow-by-blow of the 9-1-1 call and the team's response. Brandt nodded at Cami as she tentatively slid into a seat. She should have loaded up on ibuprofen before trying to tackle the workday.

"Good morning," she said quietly as she smiled brightly at Kelsey.

Kelsey quirked an eyebrow. "Why are you in such a good mood? I figured you'd be in pain and pissed off that your Jeep was out of commission," she whispered.

"Am I? I don't know, just ready to finally catch this son of a bitch, I guess. The case has been injected with new life after last night. We're close, I can feel it."

"Okay." Kelsey narrowed her eyes and smirked. Clearly, she was skeptical.

Brandt cleared his throat and clicked a button on his laptop. His screen projected onto the whiteboard hanging on the opposite wall. The four blocks were arranged in the order they'd been found. TCTA. Various shapes, sizes, and colors, but all wooden and all plainly marked. The tin, the receipt, the change.

"Aside from forensic evidence, which is unlikely, the receipt isn't of much use. We contacted the gas station where the bottle of water was purchased, and they confirmed that they delete their security footage weekly. The manager checked the employee roster for that day and found that he was the one working that shift. He doesn't remember who came in and bought a Poland Springs twenty-ounce water nearly four months ago, which isn't a surprise. Not exactly a unique purchase.

"The tin box is only slightly more interesting, as it comes from a manufacturer in Shenzhen, China. They sell bulk tins to numerous companies in the United States. We've contacted their administrative department and asked if they have a client in this area. They've been very cooperative and assured us they would get us that information as time permits. Unfortunately, the tin could have been purchased online or in another state, so we're not holding out a lot of hope that this will turn up anything."

The wind was rapidly floating out of Cami's sails. She knew tracing any of the items they'd found back to a particular person was a long shot, but at least it was *a* shot.

"Let's talk about the blocks," Brandt said. "TCTA. Cami had the letters run through a few of our programs to see if anything of significance came of it. Tact is the only four-letter word. Act and cat came up as well, but that doesn't account for the fourth letter. We also don't know how many additional letters are supposed to be included in the message."

Cami looked over the briefing that she'd requested. "From a letters-to-numbers perspective, on a basic conversion, we have 20-3-20-1. Could be 23/21. 44. A Caesar cipher gives us RoT0. Which again, doesn't mean a whole lot without any context."

"What about acronyms?" Kelsey asked.

Cami nodded. "There aren't too many that make sense in the order they were found. We have the Texas Classroom Teachers Association, Tennessee Cable and Telecommunications Association, Tidewater Center for Technology Access, and more like that. TACT has a bunch as well, but again, without any specific direction, we're throwing spaghetti against the wall."

"Right," Brandt agreed. "We also looked at words that begin with those letters in the morbid possibility that there are more to come. We have tactics, tactile, tactless, and the list goes on and on."

Kelsey sighed loudly. "All hope isn't lost yet. We still have forensics that might turn something up. Did they get back to you on their current turn time?"

"Yes," Cami said, flipping a page over. "At least a week. And that's a generous estimate by all accounts."

"How's the tip line going?" Brandt asked. "Are we still getting calls?"

"Some," Kelsey said. "They've slowed down a lot since we found McCallum. Unfortunately, nothing has really come of the tips so far. Some people are honestly trying to help, and others are airing grievances about neighbors or family members they think are a little shady."

As the meeting wrapped, Cami stood and cricked her neck back and forth. Maybe looking into a chiropractor was a good idea. "Chester Bluffs is going to continue to send some of their guys to help patrol Oakview once the sun goes down. We had an offer from the Great Liddington PD as well. If we want to take them up on it, we just need to make a call."

"Good. We'll see where we're at tonight and go from there."

Brandt closed his laptop and exited the briefing room with Graham and Michaels in tow. Kelsey took one of the file folders that Brandt had left on the table for herself and handed one to Cami.

"Nothing new in here, but at least it doesn't have our handwritten notes on everything. So are you going to tell me or what?" Kelsey asked.

"Tell you what?" Cami refused to make eye contact as she zipped up her portfolio with all of the case material.

"Did you solidify things with Maya or something last night? You seem…different. Lighter or something. I know that sounds stupid, but it's the only word that comes to mind."

Cami tried to remain straight-faced but failed. The corners of her lips wouldn't stay in place no matter how much she commanded them to. "No. Maya broke up with me a while ago."

Kelsey rested a hand on her hip. "You don't seem too upset about it. You didn't even tell me."

"Everything has been crazy. I'm sorry, I didn't mean to keep you out of the loop. I'm not upset about the breakup with Maya. Because I'm actually kind of in love with someone else."

Her eyebrows crunched together in confusion, and then her eyes widened. "Oh no. Really?"

"Really."

"I should have freaking known. You never did get over her, did you? It was a flashing neon sign that you wouldn't even allow her name to be mentioned, never mind having a conversation about it. How did this happen?" Kelsey smiled and shook her head.

Cami exhaled with a grin. "How much time you got?"

CHAPTER THIRTY-TWO

The next police briefing was scheduled for Tuesday, Alicia noted on her calendar. She smiled to herself as she wondered if they would conduct the interview in the diner, like usual, or on Cami's balcony over a glass of wine, preferably while holding hands. There seemed to be the *teeniest* possibility that a conflict of interest was, in fact, at the center of the case for transparency, but Alicia promised herself that once the Small-Town Slayer was caught, she'd hand off the monthly task to the new guy, Jared. Or maybe it was something that Sam would like to take over, since she'd shown interest in moving beyond human-interest stories. Either way, Alicia would reluctantly hand the reins to someone else.

Jade waved her into her office. She must have thought along the same wavelength. After the ordeal, it would be better to be in a public place around people than alone at home. Safety in numbers.

"Listen," Jade began as Alicia took the seat across from her. "I'm filling out these forms to file a restraining order against Evan. That way, if the cops even see his car near my house, they can arrest his ass."

Alicia wasn't quite sure it worked that way, but she wasn't going to be the one to derail Jade's plans.

"I don't know every nuance of this, but if they need someone to testify on my behalf, you'll do it, right? No better person to confirm he tried to kill me than a firsthand witness." Jade continued to dot her i's and cross her t's while barely looking up.

But Alicia wasn't exactly comfortable with the idea of confirming Evan Conley to be a murderer. There was no proof that he was the one at the house that night, and he roundly denied that he had any involvement in the break-in. He'd even offered to pay for the new camera installation so that if it happened again, it would prove he had nothing to do with it. Once again, Evan had been alone in his new apartment, so there was no one to corroborate his alibi. He'd vowed to get a roommate just so he could guarantee a defense against Jade's accusations. Alicia had known the divorce would be ugly, but this was next level.

"I'm definitely not arguing the need for a restraining order, but we still don't know for sure that it was Evan who broke in. You even said yourself that the slider probably wasn't locked."

Jade snapped her head up. "And you think that someone randomly picked me out of a town full of people to choose from and happened to check my slider to see if it was unlocked and then terrorized us for fun? Doesn't that seem the slightest bit unlikely?"

Condescending but not entirely wrong. "It does. But if Evan was the one who broke into your house and then dropped…items that probably belonged to the Small-Town Slayer, that would mean Evan is the Slayer. But the PD ruled him out."

"So? He's copycatting as a way to get me out of the picture. It's rather brilliant if you think about it. Crazed killer on the loose, entitled wife looking for her fair share, what better way to take me out of the equation? The PD will chalk it up to another victim of the killer, and Evan is home free."

"And you truly believe Evan has it in him? To kill his wife of thirty years over a potentially messy divorce?" Alicia was walking a fine line between asking questions and pissing Jade off. Lately, her fuse had been pretty short.

"That apostle who said money is the root of all evil knew his shit. Not only that, he'd get the house back, everyone would feel sorry for him, he'd get a new lease on life. Not on my watch," Jade said with a sneer.

Alicia gave her a tight-lipped smile and went back to her desk. There wasn't much else she could say. It was clear Jade's mind was made up, and she was on a mission. Alicia just wanted to stay on the sidelines of that mission for as long as possible, or at least until there was something more concrete than Jade's hunch.

There weren't many calls or reports to sift through. What had landed on her desk were mostly run-of-the-mill reports. Sock theft from a local shop, a drunk and disorderly food fight at Birdie's, domestic disturbance that ended in a tearful reunion, and trespassing on private property. At least it had been a fairly quiet week in Oakview aside from the run-in that she and Jade had faced.

While typing up the police blotter, Alicia's phone vibrated in her pocket. She saw Cami's name pop up, and her heart leapt a little. She smiled in spite of herself and marveled that the teenage-crush rushes of adrenaline could still produce those kinds of physical reactions. She clicked on the text message, praying that Cami wasn't expressing her heartfelt regret at their evening together.

Grabbing a quick dinner with the girls at the Book Cabin tonight. Wanna come? She included a smiling emoji.

Wow. Alicia had just assumed that any stolen moments between them would need to remain a secret, at least for a while. Cami had been so afraid that Alicia would play her for a fool again that she'd sworn off all contact and mention of her for a very long time. That Cami was willing to invite her somewhere where all her friends would be was a feat. Alicia's insides warmed at the though.

Of course. Send me the time, and I'll be there. Can't wait to see you. She sent back a heart and just stared at the text message, grinning broadly. She didn't even realize she was doing it until Sam showed up.

"Good news?" Sam put a steaming cup of hot chocolate on the desk.

"What good news?" Alicia asked, slipping her phone back into her pocket. "Thank you." She took a sip of the hot cocoa, and it coursed through her body like a hot spring. That it would be in the eighties later in the day didn't matter much when it came to hot chocolate.

"I just assumed. You look pretty happy." Sam leaned on Alicia's desk. "Anything you want to share?"

Alicia hesitated. It wasn't that she and Sam had some great love affair where Sam would be jealous, but they didn't have the kind of relationship where Alicia felt comfortable talking about her love life. "I was able to reconcile with someone from my past. Someone I didn't think I'd ever get to talk to again, never mind have a relationship with. So, yeah, I'm pretty happy."

"That is good news. I hope it all works out." Sam toyed with the collar of her T-shirt. "It's crazy that we still haven't gone out for that dinner we talked about. Are you free Friday night? I have a seminar at six-thirty—*The Dark Truth*, which is amazing by the way, really cool insight into why people do the things they do—but it should be over by eight. We could do drinks and appetizers?"

"*The Dark Truth*?"

"Yeah, remember that sage I was telling you about? He's the one running it."

If she was being honest, Alicia had forgotten about it completely. "Oh, right. I do remember that. Friday might be tough. But we'll definitely do it soon. Maybe next week?"

Sam nodded. "Sure, that'll work. Are you okay? After what happened at Jade's house?"

Alicia looked up. "Jade told you?"

"Yes." Sam asked, her discomfort evident. "Should she not have?"

"No, it's fine. I didn't know if it was common knowledge yet or if we were trying to keep it low-key until the police work their magic with the evidence they found."

Sam was obviously surprised by the revelation. "What evidence did they find? Is it enough to lead them to the killer?"

Dammit. Jade hadn't told her the *whole* story, so maybe that part of it was supposed to remain under wraps. "I doubt it. Just a few random items left behind. Nothing of significance, as far as I know."

Sam did a visual sweep of the room as though she suspected they were being bugged. "I heard that Jade's husband was behind it all. Again."

"I don't know. The police are still connecting the dots, but I don't think there's any hard evidence that points to him. At least, not yet."

Sam shook her head. "And I always thought he was so handsome and sophisticated. Seemed like one of those fairy-tale husbands you read about in *Modern Bride* or whatever those magazines are called."

"He put on a good show, that's for sure." Alicia looked over at Jade's office, where she was still locked into her forms. "I'll get back to you about a time for next week?"

Sam took the hint. She stood and brushed imaginary dust from her pants. "Definitely. Maybe we can knock around a few ideas for a new column I'm thinking of creating. Kind of a true crime meets *Unsolved Mysteries* type of thing."

"From a human-interest perspective?"

"I guess so. I'm sure there's an angle I haven't thought of."

"Sure, we can get the creative juices flowing next week. I have to work on this food fight incident that happened at Birdie's. Can't believe that's a real thing, and yet." Alicia smiled and hovered her mouse over the cursor. "Fighting the Good Food Fight" was typed into the center of the page in large black font. She was still wrestling with the title.

"Hard-hitting journalism," Sam joked. She went back to her desk and buried her face in her phone.

Alicia checked her watch and forced herself to focus on the articles she had to write. She refused to be late to her first date with Cami in over a thousand days.

Alicia was nervous. She hadn't expected to be, but facing the old friend group after she'd spent the night with Cami was a little more daunting than anticipated. How would they act? Were they supposed to pretend that it hadn't happened? Or would they go full throttle and kiss each other hello? Alicia decided she would just follow Cami's lead and try not to overthink it.

She was failing.

The Book Cabin was more inviting than ever with the falling sun positioned perfectly behind it, casting a shadowy walkway leading up to the entrance. Alicia took a deep breath and smoothed out any wrinkles in the front of her jeans. She adjusted the bottom of her shirt and gave her hair a toss. Quick application of lip gloss. Okay, she was as ready as she was going to be.

There were a few people in line waiting to pay who blocked her view of the dining area, but she did catch a glimpse of a light brown bob that she was pretty sure belonged to Violet. Alicia exhaled one more time before heading in their direction.

"Hey," Cami greeted her happily. She smiled widely and motioned to the chair next to her.

Violet, Katie, and Taryn all stared at her with awkward grins. Katie's was more of a grimace. Obviously, Cami had told them all *something.*

"Hey, guys." Alicia draped her purse over the back of her chair and slid into the seat Cami had brought over for her. She was kind of squished between Cami and Taryn, so her seat had clearly been shoehorned to fit. "What's going on?"

"Not much." Violet still just stared at Alicia, glancing at Cami here and there. Her head was cocked, and she was all starry-eyed. Alicia wanted to melt into the floor.

Cami cleared her throat. "Okay, this doesn't have to be awkward. As I said earlier, to you, Violet, and you, Katie, a good amount of time has passed since the last time we were all together like this. I know that I've said a lot of things, and at the time, I meant them, but seeing Alicia again and talking to her, hashing things out, made me face what I guess I've always known. I never got over her, I'm still in love with her, and if we don't at least try again, I'll regret it for the rest of my life. Who wants to split fries?"

The four of them, Alicia included, looked at Cami with frozen expressions. Taryn broke the silence first. "I do. Alicia, so glad you're back. Don't do anything stupid this time."

It was all so surreal. It felt as if she had been transported to five years ago when they were eating dinner and planning Violet's kids' birthday parties, no hint of what was to come. Alicia couldn't help but laugh. Taryn was nothing if not blunt.

At her laughter, the rest of the table seemed to relax. Katie wasn't exactly embracing her, but she wasn't actively giving her dirty looks either. Baby steps.

"Does this mean you two are back together?" Violet stuffed a handful of popcorn in her mouth and raised her eyebrows expectantly.

"Shit, Violet. Really?" Katie asked from behind her menu.

"What?"

"It's fine," Cami said. "I figured you would have questions." She looked at Alicia and took her hand, just as Alicia had visualized. Her stomach jumped. "We're taking it slow."

It hadn't felt slow the night before, but who was she to criticize? Alicia smiled and nodded. She brought their linked hands up to her face and gently kissed the back of Cami's fingers. Words couldn't seem to navigate their way out of her throat.

"Aw," Taryn said. "I don't believe you, but it's a sweet sentiment."

Alicia threw a kernel of popcorn at her. Taryn ducked and deflected it off her menu at Katie. Katie looked at Taryn, then at Alicia, and then back to her menu. She was going to be tough.

"Word around town is that Evan Conley is the prime suspect again? Beverly Lawson's mom told Jack that Evan went after Jade Conley with a machete. The only reason he didn't kill her was because a cop was driving by just as he chased her out onto the lawn. Blinded Evan with his high beams, and then Evan took off into the woods behind their house." Violet punctuated the tale with a swirl of her bright blue margarita.

"Where did Mrs. Lawson hear that?" Alicia asked, dumbfounded. "I can promise you, that's *not* what happened. Like, at all."

"Violet, why do you believe these things?" Katie shook her head.

"Why would Mrs. Lawson lie about it?"

"I'm not saying she is, but her source has a very active imagination. I was there when it happened. There was definitely no machete."

They all turned to her.

"You were there?"

So Cami hadn't told them about it. At least not that part.

"Jade was anxious about staying home alone. She felt like she was being followed and watched, and all kinds of creepy things. So I stayed with her just in case, although I assumed she was just being paranoid. She wasn't. But I'm not positive it was Evan. We didn't see anyone, just heard them. It was terrifying."

The server came over and took their orders, but Alicia could see they were champing at the bit for more details. She didn't have much more to offer without mentioning the items the suspect had left behind. Thankfully, she was able to placate them with the particulars of the bat, the BB gun, the banging, and the unlocked patio door.

"And then, my hero showed up." Alicia finished. She popped an onion ring into her mouth while Cami winked at her.

"You were, like, ten feet away from a serial killer." Taryn had leaned forward, and her salad was nearly untouched. "You don't think it was Evan?"

Alicia shrugged. "I honestly don't know. I mean, he makes the most sense, since the way it played out was very different than the other murders. Those were outside and quick, random, it seems. This one was targeted."

"We're looking into every possibility," Cami said. "The incidents could be unrelated. That's an unpleasant fact that might be the case."

"Who do you think it is?" Violet asked. "Do you have a whole list of suspects, and you're crossing them off one by one?"

Alicia knew Cami *wished* that was the situation.

"You know I can't talk about that, Vi. But we do have some very promising leads, so hopefully, we'll be able to make an arrest sooner than later."

"Ladies?" Shelly, the bookstore owner, was passing out slips for trivia night again. She pulled a paper and pencil out of her apron pouch and handed them to Violet.

"Ugh, not again," Violet groaned.

"I'll have to take a rain check." Cami balled up her napkin and tossed it onto her empty plate. "I need to get back to the station. But you guys play. We kicked ass last time."

Alicia panicked for a second. Should she stay? Were the others assuming she would go because Cami was leaving? Maybe they'd all pass on trivia and walk out together. She still felt as though she were treading water with them, even though some of it might have been self-inflicted.

"I'm not writing," Violet said, holding out the pencil and paper. "Alicia, you do it. I'll just sit here quietly knowing I'm being used for my knowledge of science and kid-related questions."

Taryn stood. "I have to hit the ladies' room. Order me another drink when the waiter comes around."

They were staying. And they expected that she would, too. Alicia had almost forgotten how good it felt to be accepted. To be with her friends.

She glanced up at Cami, who was putting her wallet back into her bag. She reached over and squeezed the back of Cami's thigh.

Cami smiled warmly at her and gave her a quick nod. She must have noticed, too.

"Okay, have fun. Don't get too competitive, I don't have time to come back here to break up a fight." Cami leaned down and kissed Alicia squarely on the lips. "I'll call you later."

Alicia just nodded. She swallowed hard. Katie and Violet were watching, seemingly as taken off guard as she was.

Cami gave a last wave and walked out. She called a hurried good-bye to Taryn, who passed her on her way back to the table.

"What'd I miss?" she asked.

Violet spoke up. "Cami and Alicia basically just made out at the table."

Alicia gasped. "We did not. It was a half-a-second peck on the lips!"

"It was more than a half second. I thought she was going to straddle you right in the middle of trivia night," Katie said, smirking. It was the first time she'd said much of anything since Alicia had arrived.

"I always miss the good shit." Taryn shook her head and sat. "Okay, let's whip these other tables into submission."

Alicia laughed as Katie cracked her knuckles and rolled her neck back and forth. It was good to be home.

CHAPTER THIRTY-THREE

Everyone was working late. Brandt was in the conference room, Kelsey was leafing through reports, Graham and Michaels were fielding phone calls. Cami motioned to Kelsey that she wanted her in the conference room for a meeting.

Brandt looked up when they entered. "What's up?" he asked, crossing his arms.

"I think we need to look at Jade Conley," Cami said.

He raised his eyebrows and pursed his lips. "That's interesting. She was in the room with Alicia Flynn the night someone broke in, right? Didn't Alicia corroborate her story?"

Cami nodded. "She did. It's possible that Jade hired someone to break into her house. Alicia noted that Jade made mention of leaving the doors purposely unlocked more than once. And even after Alicia insisted that she lock the place up, Jade conveniently forgot to lock the slider door. She's told anyone who'll listen that Evan Conley is the killer, even though we've confirmed his alibi on more than one occasion. Then, we have the whole buried gun debacle. The only thing I can't come up with is a motive. Framing Evan makes sense in the context of the other night, but that's about it."

"The block found at the scene. How would she know about that? You've kept it under wraps, correct?"

"Yes. But you know as well as I do that these things have a way of leaking out. There were first responders from all over the night we found McCallum. Jade's well-connected in this area."

Kelsey crossed and uncrossed her arms as she leaned against the credenza. "Laurie Garrett has a connection to Evan Conley, as tenuous as it is. She got in his car that night. But I can't see a tie to Beverly Lawson or Patrick McCallum. You think she has a secret mushroom addiction?"

Cami shrugged. "It sounds far-fetched, but who knows? The killer isn't a skilled marksman or someone who wants to get up close and personal with their victims. Each murder has been conducted in, for lack of a better word, a cowardly way, except the attempted one at Jade's house. She could have had Alicia there as a witness solely to eliminate suspicion."

"Okay. What are you thinking?" Brandt asked.

"I'd like to get a warrant to search her house again and this time, her office. She spends more time there than at home, from what I hear. I want to sort through her communications to see if there was a setup and more specifically, find that gun."

"Do it."

By the time she got home after putting together her probable cause statement, Cami was officially exhausted. She really wanted to go to Alicia's, but her instincts told her to take a beat. They'd already slept together, but there was no rule they couldn't take it slow from there. Cami didn't want to; every time she thought about Alicia next to her, skin against skin, she was nearly knocked off her feet by the thunder in her stomach. But she wanted to do things right. Trust Alicia again fully. The last thing she wanted was to get a few months into a relationship with her and then blow it up because she hadn't dealt with the innate insecurity that being with Alicia brought up. They still had a lot to talk about and a lot to figure out if this was really going to work.

Cami pulled the covers around her like a burrito and positioned her phone on the pillow next to her. She texted Alicia: *Finally home. How was trivia night?*

After a few minutes, the typing bubble appeared: *Had a blast. We lost, but it was because none of us knew which continent is in all four hemispheres.*

Cami smiled. *It's Africa. All those late nights watching* Jeopardy *finally paid off.*

lol I know that now. Missed you.

Missed you too.

Can't tell you how hard it is not to get in my car and drive over there.

You don't have to. Same here.

Cami wondered if they were being stupid. Abiding by rules that were made up on the fly, with no one to enforce them and no one to say if they were even worth following. But, no. It was important to her that she show some restraint. There was too much pain and anger—and too much love—to treat it as anything resembling casual. Cami mustered her willpower and texted Alicia a kissy face emoji and a simple good night. Alicia responded in kind.

"Dammit," Cami muttered petulantly as she pulled the blankets over her head.

Jade was *pissed*. Cami knew she would be, but she didn't anticipate just how furious the warrant would make her.

"So you're going to search my place of business and my house? Are your cronies at my house right now?" Jade stood in the doorway of the *Knox County Sun* office entrance, her arm straight across the door to block Cami from entering.

Cami ignored the crony comment. "No, we're trying to be as respectful as possible—"

"Ha!"

She ignored that, too. "We can all go to the house together so that you can be on the premises. We specifically came here at this time of the morning because I knew that you'd most likely be alone for another couple of hours." Cami checked her watch. Six twenty-three.

"Well, *thank you* for that, Detective. So kind of you. Maybe you'll even cuff me in the front instead of the back at the end of this witch hunt. Show me the warrant."

Cami had been thankful that Judge Scott was the magistrate on duty at the time. Her turnaround time for warrants and motions was by far the fastest. She turned to Officer Graham and held her hand out for the warrant. He extracted it from a manila folder and placed it in her palm.

"Here you go."

Jade made a show of reading it aloud. "'Proof by affidavit which is hereby incorporated by reference has been made this day, and the finding is that there is probable cause to believe that property and-or persons found at the location described below may contain evidence of'—oh you have a few boxes check marked here—'evidence of a crime; contrabands, or other items illegally possessed; property designed for use, intended for use, or used in committing a crime.' You forgot to check off 'person who is unlawfully restrained.' I mean, with everything else on this, I assume you suspect me of kidnapping, too? Embezzling? How about elder abuse, you sure you don't want to slap that on to this thing?"

"Mrs. Conley, move your arm, please," Cami said. She'd had enough of Jade's theatrics. Jade was probably just scared and felt violated, again, but she was the editor of a newspaper, for God's sake. She knew how these things worked.

"Are you going to take my computer?" Jade didn't lower her arm.

Cami sighed. "No need. The tech guy can clone what he needs from your hard drive. Is your firearm located in your office?"

"I already told you, I don't have it. It's not here. Evan took it."

"Well, he denied having it, and he allowed the team to search his house. Voluntarily. If we could locate the weapon and rule out its involvement in the murders, we could feasibly cross your name off the list of persons of interest." Cami knew it would take more than that, but it would be a good start.

"Talk to Evan."

"Please remove your arm from the doorway."

Jade dropped her arm slowly and deliberately. Cami brushed past her, Graham following close behind. Kelsey and the others trickled in after them. The intelligence agent Cami had requested from Chester Bluffs went to work on the laptop while Jade stood in the entrance of her office.

"This is a violation of my first amendment rights. Have you never heard of the Privacy Protection Act? The lawsuits will be grand."

"No one is interested in your sources or other documentary materials. This isn't about you as a journalist, which you obviously know. PPA doesn't apply to criminal suspects when the seized material relates to the crime." Cami had gone through the bullet points of the PPA while she was constructing her warrant request. Good thing she'd done that; Jade was armed and ready to fire.

To his credit, the agent working on her computer seemed able to ignore her completely. She kept prattling on about privileged documents and how she'd never have to work again once her lawyers got through with all of them. The judge too; she was going down along with the rest of the police force.

Cami joined Kelsey and Michaels in the bullpen of the office. They had to be specific in their search methods so they didn't step outside the parameters of the warrant. Anyone's personal workspace other than Jade's and their electronic devices was off-limits. Cami put on latex gloves out of an abundance of caution and opened the drawers of the file cabinet outside Jade's office. Reams of paper, staples, regular office equipment. The bottom drawer didn't have much in it. An old rolodex with a few cards filled out, otherwise blanks, and a collection of well-worn mouse pads. Riveting stuff.

The exposed brick wall behind the cabinet had a few notices taped to it. Most of them were boilerplate. New Hampshire Employment Security's unemployment notice. Minimum wage law. Employment discrimination laws. One crooked sheet of paper was stuck up there with a jagged piece of silver duct tape. Cami took it down to read the fine print at the bottom. It was an advertisement for some type of symposium that had taken place in May. She tried to post it back up on the wall—maybe there was a number or something that was still useful—but the tape was too curled to stick any longer. She placed it on top of the filing cabinet and noticed a crack in the mortar where the sheet had been hanging.

It wasn't a huge crack, but it seemed to creep down the wall in the shape of a staircase. One of the bricks in that section had a tiny gap around all four sides. Cami tugged on it, but it only shifted side to side.

"Do you have a nail file or something like that on you?" Cami asked Kelsey, who was inventorying a maintenance closet.

Kelsey paused and pursed her lips. "Here," she said, brightening. "Letter opener."

"Perfect."

The mini sword was exactly what she needed. She noticed Jade watching from her office, her focus no longer on the intelligence agent but on Cami.

Cami paid her no attention and slid the letter opener above the brick and then below it. It was loose enough to come out with very little effort, so they either needed a mason in there ASAP, or someone was using the small opening as a hiding spot.

The hole was rough and dusty. Cami ran her hand slowly along the bottom and each side until she found what she was looking for.

"Bingo." Adrenaline shot up her spine.

She pulled out a mini flash drive and examined it in the palm of her gloved hand. It was no longer than a half inch. All it said on the outside was *Elite 32GB*.

"Kelsey?" Cami called, waving her over. She pointed to the opening the missing brick left and held the drive up for her to see.

"You found that in there?" Kelsey asked. She let out a low whistle.

Jade came plowing out of her office, nearly knocking Graham over. "What exactly did you find?"

Cami showed her.

"It's not mine. I have my thumb drives locked in my office. Whatever you think you've found won't incriminate me." She was haughty but noticeably rattled.

"Good. Contrary to what you believe, I don't want to find anything that incriminates you. We need to rule out anyone close to the murders, and that's what we're doing."

"So I assume that Alicia is next on your list to investigate? She was with me that night. Have you considered the possibility that Alicia is behind all this? Didn't she show up right after the Lawson woman was found dead? Interesting coincidence, wouldn't you say?"

Cami scoffed. "Is this really what you want to do, Jade? Finger Alicia for something you know she had nothing to do with just to take the heat off you? If you're innocent, and you say you are, then I'm sure we'll come to that conclusion without you accusing other people unnecessarily."

"Just saying," Jade said, shrugging. "She showed up after Lawson, the McCallum murder happened right outside of her apartment, and she was in my house when someone tried to kill me. Sounds a lot like a common denominator to my untrained ears."

There was a modicum of truth in what Jade was saying. Alicia did have—very loose—ties to the murders, but she had zero motive to kill three people and attempt a fourth.

"There's plenty of motive if that's what you're lacking."

Creepy. Cami didn't need Jade poking around in her head. "Just stop it. We're finishing up here and then going over to your house. You can come with us, or you can stay here. Your choice."

"You. You're the motive. She wanted you back, obviously, and what better way to do that than to distract you from what happened between the two of you all those years ago? You're exhausted, beaten down, examining your life choices, seeing how it can all end in a fraction of a second. She shows up in town, and how lucky, she's there to pick up the pieces. Once you two are back together, it'll all miraculously end, and everything will go back to normal. No more murders. The Small-Town Slayer will retire, and it'll just be another cold case rotting away in someone's desk drawer. Or maybe she has a taste for it now, and she'll try to up the ante a little bit."

"Enough," Cami yelled louder than she'd meant to.

Kelsey stepped forward and held a bag open for Cami to slip the drive into. "Let's bag it and tag it and head over to the house. Jade, I don't know what you're getting at with all this, but it isn't helping. If we find something that points us in Alicia's direction, we'll investigate her, too. No one is off-limits."

Jade made eyes at Cami before turning back to her office. She was taking this as a personal attack, as though Cami had orchestrated the whole thing.

"Sorry about that," Cami muttered once Jade was out of earshot. "I shouldn't have let her get to me that way."

"I get it. It's harder when it's subjective, but you know she's just lashing out. You're the easiest target because she knows a little bit about you personally. Trying to hit you where it hurts."

Cami nodded. "I do know that. I just need a minute to get my game face back on. I'll meet you over there in a few minutes. Thanks, Kels."

Kelsey ushered Jade out of the building. She was still going on about the unfairness of it all in a man's world. If it were otherwise, Evan would be in jail by now. Cami exhaled softly. She dreaded what lay ahead at Jade's house.

CHAPTER THIRTY-FOUR

I think, maybe, we're getting back together."

Alicia's mother turned from the window where she was hanging the new curtains she'd bought. Alicia was fine with just blinds, but her mom thought it made the apartment cold and barren. Unlived in. So she'd brought over some tan sheers to make the place a little homier.

"What did I miss? Last I knew, she agreed to be civil. You've had a busy few months, I guess. Forgot about your old mother."

Alicia rolled her eyes. "Oh, stop. I still call you every week, and I know I haven't been over as much as I'd like to, but it really has been busy. I'll be better about coming over, I promise."

"Mm-hmm."

"We just kind of had a moment one night at Birdie's. We saw each other out, and she invited me to play pool, and we did and then… it just sort of happened. No one is more shocked than me, believe me."

"Are you happy?" her mom asked, straightening the blinds on each window to make sure they were all raised to the same height. Messy windows had always made her crazy.

"So happy, Mom. I honestly thought she'd never even *look* at me again, never mind give me a second chance. It's weird. It's like I still haven't really allowed myself to feel anything. Because I'm so afraid to have the rug ripped out from underneath me. Like this is all some fever dream that I'll wake up from, and it will go back to the way things were six months ago where we weren't in each other's orbit at all, and I never thought we would be again."

"She was always a good one, that Cami. I'm not too surprised that she forgave you. She was very much in love with you, it was evident to all of us. Your dad used to tell me how surprised he was that the two of you never got married. I suppose in hindsight, it was probably for the best, but at the time, we were just waiting for the big engagement announcement."

Alicia blanched at the hindsight comment, but she knew her mom didn't mean anything by it. She was probably right, much as it hurt. "We talked about it a million times, but we procrastinated. I think we were waiting for the 'perfect time,' but you know as well as I do that isn't even a real thing."

"Nope. If you wait for the perfect time on just about anything, it'll never happen. There are good times and bad times but no perfect times. Look at your brother. Sean and Marie wanted to wait for the perfect time to have kids, but Marie got pregnant while Sean was out of work, and their house was on the market during the housing crash of '08. The exact opposite of perfect. They panicked and cried and wrung their hands, but look what came of it. Perfection. Little Sydney was born, and one look at her told them that it *had* been the perfect time after all." She leaned back and pushed into her hip with her hand. Her sciatica must have been acting up again.

"You're right. Lesson learned," Alicia said. "No more waiting for the stars to align for what I want. I get it."

"The way it should be. Never let perfect be the enemy of good. Make sure you tell her exactly what you want if you haven't already. I have to get going anyway. If I don't force Dad to get to his follow-up appointment, he'll blow it off and tell me he forgot."

"With the oncologist?" Alicia's heart sank.

"No, no. With the podiatrist. His gout's been acting up again."

"Jeez, don't do that to me. Okay, make sure Dad sees his foot doctor. Thanks, Mom. The new curtains look great. I love you." Alicia kissed her mother on the cheek and hugged her tightly.

"Love you, too, Lee-see. Make sure you show up at Sean's pool party in a few weeks. Bring Cami if you can. We'd all love to see her."

Alicia smiled and promised she would. She was so thankful for her family, even though she didn't see them as much as she had thought she would when she'd moved back to Oakview. She swore to herself that she'd make more of an effort.

The curtains did look good, she wasn't lying about that. She pushed an end table to the other side of the room so she could use the color of the curtains to bring out the earth tones in her lamp. Her cell phone chimed with a new text message.

It was the new guy, Jared. How did he even get her phone number?

Hi Alicia, it's Jared from work. Are you coming to the office today? I'm here, but the fob I have isn't working. Jade didn't answer her phone.

She hadn't planned on going into the office. Especially now that her workspace was all new and fresh. *Are you able to work from home?*

I left my laptop on my desk. Planned on working from office.

Ugh. Who left their laptop at the office these days? Alicia chalked it up to Jared being new, even though he'd been around long enough that she wasn't sure he qualified as new anymore. Whatever. *Yeah, I'll come in. Give me like twenty minutes.*

He sent her a thumbs-up.

"Where the hell is he?" Alicia mumbled as she fished her fob out of her pocket. There were only a few cars in the parking lot, and she was fairly certain Jared drove a truck of some sort. Lightning flashed in the distance. Summer was officially underway.

The office was vacant, so the shutting door echoed loudly in the empty space. She set the code to disarm the alarm so Jared could enter without his fob. Alicia was surprised Jade wasn't there. She'd been in the office more often than not lately. Maybe she felt safer from Evan there than she did at home.

Her text chimed again. Jared. *Ran out to get lunch instead of waiting. Be back in an hour or so.*

"So glad I rushed in," Alicia said out loud. She tossed her phone on her desk and connected her laptop to the docking station. She yawned and stretched her arms over her head. "Coffee."

The break room door was shut, which wasn't unusual, but it was also locked. She checked the wall above the copier where a corkboard hung with all the keys to the various locks in the office dangling from thumbtacks. Very secure.

Of course, the kitchen key was missing. Alicia checked the floor to make sure it hadn't been knocked off and left for dead, but the floor was clean. Everything was pretty organized. Again, not unusual, but things had definitely been moved around and stacked differently. Jade must have gone on a cleaning frenzy.

After checking most of the surfaces around the office, Alicia decided to give up her search. She sat at her desk and scanned her last article. *Coffee. Cream. Sugar. Mmm.*

"Dammit."

She picked up her phone again and scrolled through the contacts. She dialed Sam and pursed her lips.

"Hello?"

"Sam, it's Alicia. Sorry to bother you, but do you know where the break room key is? I checked the usual spots, and it's not there. I hope it isn't in Jade's office because her door is shut and locked. The little red light is on the fob thingy."

"It might be on my desk? I was the last one out the other night, so I probably brought it with me and forgot to hang it back up. Sorry."

"No problem, I'll check. Are you coming in today? It's a ghost town in here."

"I wasn't planning on it, but maybe. How long are you hanging around?"

"Just a few hours, I think." A crack of thunder made her jump. "It's just starting to pour, so I'm not leaving anytime soon."

"Okay, sounds good. I might see you later on. Let me know if you can't find the key."

Alicia's other line beeped, so she thanked Sam and clicked over. It was the Copper Bluffs police department's social media contact. Their Twitter account had been on fire recently, so Alicia wanted the scoop on the new poster. Turned out, it was the twenty-something daughter of the police captain. No surprise there.

Sam's desk was neat for the most part, except for a few papers and some snacks that she'd left out. Pushed off to the side was a dusty, extra-large wine bottle with Christmas ribbon still dangling from the neck. Alicia scanned for the key, lifted the keyboard and mouse pad, and shuffled the printed articles Sam had on her desk. Nothing. She checked the cubicle walls that had all kinds of notices and contacts hanging from those cubicle hooks that caused immense bleeding when one of them pricked the cube dweller's finger. No key.

She felt kind of weird doing it, but she opened Sam's top drawer. There were pencils and pens and paper clips, most of which looked to be collecting dust. Her second drawer had glossy pamphlets and a half-full container of lotion. A silver tin of black pepper saltwater taffy was tucked against the side. Alicia lifted the pamphlets, wondering if the key had slipped down the side. No key. She accidentally slid her thumb against the side of the larger pamphlet and cursed at the slice that it left.

"Ouch," she said, hissing in disgust. She went to put the pamphlets back in the drawer but turned it over in her hand. Looked like the stuff from that guru Sam had been talking about. *Free To Be Yourself. Improve and Prepare. Take Advantage, Take Control. Get It, Keep It, Live It.* Alicia looked closely at the third one, which someone, presumably Sam, had circled in blue marker. *Take Advantage, Take Control.* That one must have really resonated with her. Alicia was about to put them all back in the drawer when she dropped them all in a pile onto the floor.

No, that's stupid. It's a coincidence, nothing more. Alicia stacked the pamphlets neatly and placed them back in the drawer next to the nondescript silver tin.

The silver tin. How many of those had Alicia received from the interview with Aunt Ginny's company? She looked at the words on the face up brochure one more time. Take Advantage, Take Control. TATC, or, out of order, TCTA.

Alicia exhaled shakily and stuck the pamphlet in her back pocket. She lifted the tin again to see if there was any type of identifying marker on it. A barcode, a sticker, a stamp, anything. But, no, there was nothing, just like the one they'd found outside of Jade's house. Alicia's eyes were drawn to the floor where a silver glimmer twinkled faintly. The break room key.

Coffee was no longer at the forefront of her mind, but Alicia needed to go pour herself a cup so it wouldn't look like she'd been combing through Sam's things. It was almost certainly a coincidence anyway.

Alicia turned and almost fell backward into the metal desk.

"Did you find it?" Sam asked.

"Find what?" Alicia's mouth was bone-dry.

"They key to the break room?"

Alicia nodded quickly. "Yes, yes, I did. Thank you. I've been dying for a coffee. Little cup o' joe to get the motor running." She cringed. *What the hell am I saying?*

"Good. What's that?" Sam asked, pointing to the tin of taffy on her desk. "Was the key in the drawer?"

"No. Actually, it was on the floor. Must have fallen off when you shut the drawers or something. I saw the saltwater taffy and couldn't resist, sorry about that."

"What did you think?"

"About what?"

"The black pepper taffy."

Sam was cool and relaxed, which made Alicia even more nervous. Was she going to pull out a gun and shoot her? Or was Alicia really making something out of nothing? It was just a brochure and a container of candy. Not exactly damning evidence. Besides, Sam was always friendly and helpful, so why would Alicia even go there?

"Oh, you came in right before I could try it." Alicia smiled, setting herself at ease with a rational explanation. Her heart rate was starting to slow to a normal rhythm. "I'll go get that coffee now. Want a cup?"

"I'm all set. But I think you may have forgotten to put something back in the drawer," Sam said.

Alicia looked at the tin. "Oh, sorry, I'll put it away."

"Not that. You seem to have something in your back pocket."

Fuck. The pamphlet. Alicia pulled it out and handed it to Sam. "You're right, I forgot all about that."

Sam looked at the brochure and then back up at Alicia. "Was there a reason you were taking it with you?"

"Yes. I thought it looked really interesting. I was going to make a photocopy and then put it back. You'd invited me to one of those seminars in the past, so I thought this one would be a good introductory one to attend."

Sam pointed to the date in flashy red letters at the top. "It was in March."

"Oh!" Alicia laughed. It sounded shrill to her ears. "I didn't even notice that. Duh."

"I'm sure there will be another one soon." Sam smiled broadly. "I think I will take that coffee. Cinnamon crunch, please."

"You got it." Alicia smiled back and chided herself for being so silly. Small-Town Slayer panic had finally gotten to her.

She slid past Sam toward the kitchen, the small key pressed between her fingers. She'd make sure to hang it on the corkboard when she was finished so there wouldn't be any more break room key mishaps. "I think Jade was in here earlier—"

A blinding smash to the back of her skull caused Alicia to stumble and fall to the ground in a haze of blackness.

Chapter Thirty-five

"Why did you lie about the gun, Jade?" Cami asked. She was furious that Jade had led them on a wild-goose chase when the gun had been in her possession the whole time.

"I didn't. I'm telling you, Detective, I had no idea the gun was up there. How often do you think I traipse around in my attic?"

"First, the gun was never mentioned. Then, the gun was buried. Then, the gun was stolen. Then, Evan had the gun. Then, the gun disappeared. Now the gun is mysteriously sitting in a jewelry box in your attic. Tell me the truth. Are the ballistics tests going to show this is the same gun that murdered three people? You'll be a lot better off if you come clean now." Cami stood in the doorway of Jade's room while Officer Graham held the open jewelry box. Nestled underneath the pullout trays of earrings and bracelets was a black and gray handgun.

"Run the tests. If they come back as a positive match, it's not going to change the truth. I didn't do it. You want to put me away for crimes I didn't commit, then go ahead. You'll be sorry, I promise you."

Cami ignored the threats. The gun mentioned in the reports was a Smith and Wesson, and the one in Jade's jewelry box was a Ruger. But the lies and misdirects gave Cami enough suspicion to grill Jade as though they were a match. If she had lied about the gun's whereabouts, who was to say there wasn't another one floating around somewhere?

The pocket of Cami's cargo pants continued to vibrate. She lifted her phone out, annoyed, and looked at the screen. Captain Brandt had been blowing up her phone.

"Sorry, Captain, bit of a situation at the Conley house. We found a gun in the attic."

Brandt grunted. "Is it a match with what forensics returned?"

Cami lowered her voice. "It's not. But who knows what else she's hiding?"

"Let Chandler handle things over there. I need you back here now."

Cami was about to ask why, but Brandt had disconnected the call. She waved Kelsey over and let her know she'd be taking point. Kelsey was just as confused as Cami.

The little rental car made it to the station in record time, thanks to Cami's lead foot. Her curiosity was beyond piqued. The Jeep was supposed to be ready in a few days. Couldn't come soon enough.

"What's going on?" Cami asked, breezing into Brandt's office. He was hunched over his laptop with the intelligence guy from Copper Bluffs.

"Agent Franklin here was able to get into the USB drive you found behind the brick. It was password protected. But it was fairly basic," Brandt told her.

"Right," Franklin said. He pushed his glasses up on his head. "The passwords were auto-generated, but there was nothing sophisticated about the encryption. Just a regular password protect on the drive and then on the word processing docs contained inside. Didn't take us too long to access the documents."

"Take a look," Brandt said, spinning the laptop in Cami's direction.

Cami leaned in. It looked like an article setup with a headline, subtitle, and date; only the byline was missing.

The first article, entitled "Unprecedented Homicide in Oakview" outlined the details of Beverly Lawson's murder. Cami double-clicked on the next one, still unsure exactly what she was looking at. The files were all nameless, some combination of Doc1, Document2, those kinds of descriptions. The second article opened to "Community in Crisis: A Second Murder Rocks Oakview." Laurie Garrett's death was described, including apparent interviews with family members and unnamed sources.

"What is this? Someone trying to capitalize on the murders to become a journalist? Do we know who the drive belongs to yet?" Cami asked.

"Open the next one."

The third article containing the information about Patrick McCallum seemed to have a different intent: blaming the police for putting the town in harm's way. "Police Stumped by Small-Town Slayer." There was a smaller article beneath it that appeared to call for vigilantism. "Where is Oakview's Batman? Police in Need of a Fearless Crusader to Protect Town."

"Again," Cami said, "I don't see how this points to a killer. Definitely someone misguided, but I don't understand the significance."

Brandt smiled, tight-lipped and without humor. "The article about McCallum was written a week before he was killed."

Cami whipped her head up. "McCallum was targeted? This is a manifesto?"

"Not necessarily," Franklin explained. "If you'll notice, all references to his name are in red and were added after the draft of the article was prepared. The author didn't disable change tracking, so we're able to see when the edits took place. This doesn't appear to be a complex cybercriminal, by any means. They likely thought that password protecting multiple locations would keep third parties out."

"Open the last one, Lyons."

Cami looked up at Brandt, whose expression set her on edge. He was serious. Concerned.

The fourth document opened to another screaming headline. "Local Journalist Killed by Crazed Killer, Slayer Continues to Evade Law Enforcement." Cami swallowed. Had there been a fourth killing they hadn't found yet? She braced herself.

Oakview, New Hampshire, once a beacon of safety and comfort, has seen safety and public order deteriorate at a rapid pace over the last few months. The latest in a string of killings, local crime reporter Alicia Flynn was found with a telltale gunshot wound on [insert date here] by local

"What the fuck is this?" Cami asked, jumping back from the laptop as though she'd been burned.

"My reaction exactly," Brandt said. "Our killer set their sights on Alicia. Michaels is on his way over to her apartment now to make sure everything is okay."

"Who wrote the articles?" Cami's head was swimming. She'd never been confident in Jade—or Evan Conley, for that matter—as the suspect, but nearly all signs pointed to them. And the lies they'd continually spun didn't help their case, either.

"Franklin?"

"Well, the trial software appears to be registered to a bunch of nonsense letters. The first part of the name was NQHQSZDQ," Franklin said, reading from a notecard in front of him. He adjusted his glasses. "Second part was CFULN. Again, the criminal we're dealing with isn't as advanced as I think they thought they were."

"Okay." Cami didn't want to rush him along, but she actually did at the same time. She needed to see Alicia, to make sure she really was okay. A text, a call, *something*.

"Anyway. I recognized it as a cryptogram, so I input it into a decoder, and the results spit out pretty quickly. The trial is registered to Samantha Lewis."

"Do you know who that is?" Brandt asked.

Cami searched her brain, knowing she was acquainted with that name. The name Samantha wasn't sparking anything. Samantha. Sam. Watermelon champagne. Gavin. Lawn chairs.

"I know who she is," Cami said. That woman Alicia had gone to Violet's barbecue with. A reporter or something from the *Knox County Sun*. Really? *She* was the one behind all of this? "Works at the *Sun* downtown. Same office as Jade and Alicia."

Brandt's radio crackled. "Go ahead, Michaels."

"Alicia Flynn doesn't appear to be home. The Prius you described isn't in the parking lot, and there was no answer at her door."

Cami whipped her phone out of her pocket and dialed Alicia's number. She was probably at the office. Cami prayed that Sam wasn't there with her. "Pick up, pick up, pick up."

Brandt gave her a look, seemingly curious about the freneticism Cami descended into with each passing second. No answer. Cami texted her. Her fingers weren't moving as fast as her brain, and at that moment, she was thankful for autocorrect:

Where are you? I need you to respond to me right now.

She stared at the phone for about a minute before she stuck it back in her pocket. "I'll see if she's at her office."

"Michaels is on his way there now."

"I'll meet him there." Cami didn't give Brandt a chance to contradict her. There was no way she was going to sit idly by while Alicia might be in danger. She hoped that Sam's article was just hyperbole, a plugged-in name of someone she knew as a placeholder, nothing more. She only wished she believed it.

❖

How Cami beat Michaels to the office from Alicia's apartment was a mystery, but she breathed a huge sigh of relief at the sight of Alicia's Prius tucked into a small spot near the newspaper's entrance. She wanted to yell at her for not answering her phone, even if there was a perfectly good reason. Cami couldn't remember the last time she'd been so scared. She allowed herself a half a second to calm down before she opened the glass door into the small lobby. The entrance door to the office was propped open with a wooden wedge.

"Hello?" Cami called out. She didn't see anyone at first glance.

"Hello."

The voice was coming from the other side of the office, near the cubicles. She still didn't see anyone. "Detective Lyons of the Oakview PD," Cami announced.

"Can I help you?" A man Cami didn't recognize stood, a dustpan in his hand.

"Are you here alone?"

He shrugged. "As far as I know. Someone had an accident, so I'm on cleanup duty, I guess." He motioned to the floor in front of him.

"And you are?" Cami asked.

"Jared Fowler. Sports and weather." He paused. "New guy."

"Oh, right," Cami said. She remembered Alicia mentioning a new guy. "Is Alicia here? Her car is parked out front."

"Maybe she went out for a walk or something. I texted her earlier to unlock the door for me since my fob wasn't working. She said she would. I grabbed lunch, and when I got back, the door was open. It would have been awesome if she could have cleaned this up before leaving."

Cami's pulse began to quicken again. Where was she? "What is it?"

"Wine bottle. Maybe champagne. I don't know. You can't smell it?"

After taking a pointed whiff, Cami did smell it. She'd been so focused on locating Alicia that she hadn't even noticed it when she walked in. "Spilled?" she asked.

"Broken. Must have dropped it." Jared held up the dustpan that contained a few large shards of greenish glass and a bunch of small ones.

Cami walked over and inspected the glass. Most of the wine droplets had been replaced by wet clumps of dust from sweeping it off the rug. "Do me a favor. Don't throw that in the trash. Just leave it on the desk over there. Have you seen anyone else in here today? Sam Lewis?" Cami got down on all fours to see if anything else was dropped in the vicinity of the wine bottle. Nothing she could see with a naked eye.

"No. Jade Conley is usually here early, but she isn't in today. I haven't seen Sam, but that doesn't mean she wasn't here. I think she walks to work sometimes because she lives so close."

Cami knew where Jade was: at her house with Kelsey and the other police officers dealing with the gun issue. Sam was the real problem.

Her adrenaline rushing, Cami picked up the pace and opened the door to the kitchen. Empty. She opened both bathroom doors, single stalls. No one. The only other office with a door was Jade's, and the glass walls let her see inside. Vacant.

"Alicia?" she called out as she went desk by desk, checking underneath each one on the side of caution.

"Is something wrong?" Jared looked uneasy for the first time since Cami had arrived.

"I hope not." Cami pulled out her phone and dialed Alicia's number again, hoping against hope that it was all just a misunderstanding, and Alicia was down the street at Dunkin's eating a jelly doughnut that she'd complain about having to burn off later. She wasn't much of a walker, but the storm had cleared up, so maybe she just needed some fresh air. *Please.*

By the second ring, Cami wasn't too optimistic. She paced back and forth until she heard a muffled version of "Für Elise" coming from somewhere in the office. Her blood ran cold.

She followed the sound until it got louder. Not much but enough to follow its direction. In one of the drawers in the cubicles in the center of the office—the one Alicia was sitting at the day Cami went in to talk to Jade about the wretched article—Alicia's phone sang out the final chords to Beethoven's masterpiece. The notification panel showed that she'd missed seven calls and four text messages. Behind the phone, her purse and set of keys were pushed to the back of the drawer. Cami moved the mouse that sat on top of the desk to wake the connected laptop. Alicia's log-in page appeared.

Officer Michaels pushed open the door to the office as Cami was running by him to get a better signal on her radio. "What's going on?"

"Alicia Flynn is missing and in danger. We need a BOLO issued for Alicia and Samantha Lewis immediately. I'm calling Brandt now."

"He had me stop by Lewis's house on my way here since you were coming to find Alicia Flynn. No sign of her at the house, but her car is in the driveway."

Cami nodded. "That might be a good thing. If her car is at her house, and Alicia's car is here, they couldn't have gotten too far unless Lewis has another vehicle we don't know about it. Start canvassing the entire area, and see if the Copper Bluffs team is nearby."

She gulped the fresh air, muggy and thick as it was. Cami breathed deeply twice and radioed Brandt. No time to think or feel, not now. "Captain, it looks like the plan has been set in motion. We need to act fast, no idea how much time we have. We have to find her before it's too late."

Cami tilted her head and prayed to the swirling gray sky as she awaited Brandt's response.

[illegible] continually [illegible] and placed back [illegible] Chris, a county [illegible]

[illegible] from [illegible] protocol.

[illegible]

[illegible] Behind [illegible]

[illegible]

[illegible] boss [illegible]

[illegible] the [illegible]

[illegible] rest of the [illegible]

[illegible] swiftly [illegible]

CHAPTER THIRTY-SIX

Alicia opened her eyes slowly and painstakingly. Her eyelids felt as though someone had attached tiny weights to them. She was in the dark, or at least, she thought she was. Everything was blurry, and there was an internal spin or two as she slammed her eyes shut again to orient herself with her surroundings. She was dizzy and lightheaded and felt a wave of panic as she realized she had no idea where she was.

She tried to call out a loud "hello", but she wasn't sure if any sound had come out. She heard it in her mind, but she didn't remember her lips moving. She attempted to speak again, but the same thing happened. Her mouth wasn't moving in sync with her brain.

What the hell happened to me? Alicia tried to recall how she'd ended up on whatever uncomfortable surface she seemed to be lying on. She was watching a distorted movie in slow motion; hard to make anything out or decipher what was happening.

A new wave of anxiety washed over her when she realized she might be paralyzed. Her extremities weren't moving, even though she was directing them to. Move, she yelled, if only in her head.

Nothing moved. There was pain in her back, in one of her legs, and in her head, which she supposed was a good sign. From her limited knowledge of paralysis, she was pretty sure that there was no pain, or any feeling at all, in the areas that were paralyzed.

Alicia wanted to cry, but that, too, was not an option. The tingling in her sinuses signaled a readiness to release the waterworks, but her body wasn't cooperating. She closed and opened her eyes again, hoping for a better picture of where she was. It was still dark. Blurry. She was claustrophobic in her own skin.

Breathe in. Breathe out. Focus. Nothing happened. She tried to move her arms, her hands, her feet. She felt the tiniest twitches in each of them, but the movement she craved evaded her.

Panic started to creep in again. Alicia refocused her breathing to avoid the ragged wheeze coming from her throat. With a final exhale and some internal motivation and chastising, Alicia grunted and pushed forward with every ounce of strength she could muster.

She sat up.

She gasped for air and wiggled her fingers. She raised her arms over her head and tried to stand. She promptly fell backward onto whatever bench or table or whatever it was she'd been lying on. Standing was a feat too far, at least for now. She leaned back against the wall and closed her eyes to stave off the dizziness.

Now that her hands were working again, she frantically patted her pockets to see if she had her phone. Of course not. She checked her wrist to see if she'd had the foresight to wear the Apple watch her parents had given her for Christmas the previous year. She'd worn it a total of about six days since then, and this day was not one of those days.

"Why is it so dark in here?" she wondered aloud. The sound of her own voice startled her but was quite welcome.

"Hello?" she tried yelling. It came out as more of a broken croak than a yell, but it was a start. "Is anyone there?"

She heard something. Footsteps maybe. A creaking of some sort. A faint swishing sound. Bright light shone directly in her face. She covered her eyes instinctively at the invasion.

"Oh fuck. You're awake."

Alicia opened her eyes and saw Sam standing there, a flashlight pointed at the floor. Sam pushed on something attached to the wall, and a round LED light came to life. Not very bright but it lit up the tiny space they were in.

"Where am I? What is this place?" Alicia's old friend panic was making its way down the path. "How did I get here?"

The room couldn't have been any bigger than an eight-by-eight shed. The light illuminated a built-in bench with a carpet covering it and a few shelves on the walls. Canned food, bottled water, and paper goods lined them. The door seemed to be made of steel with a long black handle as its only means of egress.

Sam sighed heavily and leaned against the wall next to the door. "I was really hoping you weren't going to wake up. That would have made things so much easier."

It took a minute for the words to filter properly through Alicia's foggy brain. "Wait…you wanted me to die?"

Flashes of what had happened before she'd ended up in the tiny room began to infiltrate. Slowly at first, and then it came back to her for the most part. *Take Advantage, Take Control*. Aunt Ginny's new taffy recipe. A blinding headache. Alicia reached up to feel her head and hissed in pain when she touched it. She brought her hand to her face and saw smears of blood on her fingertips.

"Did you hit me in the head?" Alicia nearly yelled, incredulous.

"Stop." Sam held a hand up. "This is uncharted territory for me. Why did you have to go through my desk? This was not the plan."

Alicia's head was swimming. She was trying to decipher what Sam was saying. "So…you *are* the Small-Town Slayer? *You?*"

"What's that supposed to mean? Because I'm a woman, I'm not capable enough to be the killer?"

"What? No. I just don't understand it. I know you. You're a lousy pool player, and you love coffee, and you played softball, and you write articles about lottery winners and climate heroes." Alicia rubbed her temples. Maybe the whole thing was a grand hallucination.

Or not. "Exactly. Lottery winners and climate heroes. Do you have any idea how long I've been standing on this nonexistent ladder, trying to climb out of a sea of lottery winners and climate heroes? You took my shot, Alicia. Jade was going to let me take over the crime desk on a trial basis until I proved myself. Which I knew wouldn't be a problem once I had the chance to show what I can do. But then, she calls me into her office, and oops! The old feature writer that she *adored* and nearly wept over when she up and left was back in town and looking for a job, and really, the crime writer was a better position for her. I was doing so great with human interest. I made my displeasure with it very apparent, but it didn't matter. She told me that a different position would open up eventually, and of course, I'd be considered for it. When I tried to push back, she made it clear that the conversation was over, and if I was unhappy, I was welcome to look elsewhere. So I did."

Alicia swallowed. "Why didn't you just tell me you wanted the crime desk? I'll leave. I can quit, I'm sure there are plenty of freelance openings I can jump on. We don't even have to mention anything about this to anyone."

"Nice try." Sam rolled her eyes. "Like it's that easy. I applied for a bunch of positions. Every response was basically the same. Good effort, nice portfolio, come back when you have more experience, blah blah blah. How am I supposed to get experience if they won't take a chance on me?"

Alicia nodded weakly. She didn't want to be the one to tell Sam that the form responses she'd been receiving were probably based on her writing skills and not a grand conspiracy to keep her down. She remembered the article Sam had had her read all those months ago. It had been filled with inanity and unproven theories. Jade was probably giving her a gift by letting her fill the human-interest quotas. "Like I said, you can have my job. I think at this point, I'd rather go live on a farm and snuggle with baby goats all day."

Sam ignored her. "I had no choice. The only way I was going to get any recognition was to take matters into my own hands. That's what Basil was telling us in all those retreats. If we want something, we have to make it happen. Control is a choice. So I made my choice. I didn't want to do it, I *had* to do it. I have all these great articles to submit about crimes that happened right in my town. A first person, ear to the ground perspective. People eat that shit up. I still had no takers, but that's because your stories are the ones getting read. I realized there's only one thing that will guarantee a blockbuster breakout. You. What better end to this story than a crime reporter being eaten by her own monster?"

"How is this *my* monster? Okay, forget it. Where are we? What's the plan here?" Alicia was attempting to plot out a way to keep Sam talking and to keep herself alive. She kept pushing the dread and anxiety down so she could focus. It wasn't an easy achievement with her would-be killer standing less than three feet away.

"Storm shelter. There was a freak nor'easter sometime in the 1920s, I think, and the owner of this building had a daughter who lost a leg when a beam from their house collapsed on her. He had a small reinforced shelter installed in this basement for his family to hide in if another storm like that one happened. Can't imagine it got much use, but someone over the years updated it. Maybe they used to bootleg moonshine down here. Who knows? Anyway, they boarded it up during one of the renovations, so there aren't too many people who know this space even exists."

"How did you know?" Alicia could feel the small sparks of hope she'd been hanging on to fading quickly.

Sam smirked. "Jade had me do a piece on architecture and infrastructure in Oakview. One of the many, *many* slow news periods. I focused on places I knew. I came down to the basement, and sure enough, a few two-by-six removals later, I found this room. I had planned on telling Jade all about it, but something kept me from doing that. I stashed all the records I got from the town in an old chest in the attic I share with my upstairs neighbor. I kept the whole thing to myself on the off chance it would come in handy. Lo and behold, it did."

Alicia was speechless. This was a calculated and plotted crime spree. There was no passion here; there was no reasoning; there was no spontaneity for Alicia to break through. In a word, she was fucked.

"I guess I can see why you want *me* as one of your victims, but why Beverly Lawson? Why Laurie Garrett? What do they have to do with anything?"

Shrugging, Sam propped her leg against the door. A glint of black metal flashed from her pocket as her shirt shifted. Alicia broke out in a cold sweat.

"They weren't handpicked or anything as grim as that. It was opportunity, nothing more. I have to admit, Beverly Lawson really ate away at me. I waited for someone—anyone—else to show up, but no one did. Taking out a little old lady was never the plan, believe me. It's not like I'm a murderer, Alicia. I don't get any enjoyment out of it or want to keep a memento or anything sick like that. She was walking in front of me. I aimed, closed my eyes, and pulled the trigger."

"You shot them all in the back. So you didn't have to look at them?"

"Right. I didn't want to see the life leave their bodies. I told you, I'm not a deranged lunatic. I had to make my own future, and this was the only way. Doesn't that make sense?" Sam squinted as though she genuinely sought Alicia's opinion.

"Did you plan on killing me?"

Sam sighed. "Eventually. I was actually hoping there was a way to pin it on you, but that plan fizzled quickly. That McCallum guy was outside your apartment so that was perfect. Wrong time, wrong place for that guy. But I quickly learned that framing isn't my strong suit."

Oddly enough, Sam seemed to *want* to talk about it. Alicia had no other choice but to capitalize on her confessional mood. "You still can. Pin it on me, I mean. Put my fingerprints on the gun and take off. They'll think I killed you to save my own ass." Pathetic attempt, but it was all Alicia had.

Sam rolled her eyes again. "Really? I admire your determination, but come on. I'm still not sure how the Evan Conley thing blew up. He never has any airtight alibis, but he keeps getting away scot-free. Our police department sucks."

"Was it you that night at Jade's house? Did you break in?"

"I'd hardly call it a break-in. I tried a few doors. The slider was wide open. If I'd known Jade had a gun, I would have rethought that whole escapade. I almost got my head blown off by trying to throw shade at Evan."

The fucking BB gun. Alicia was thankful Jade had armed herself with it, especially since Alicia had initially thought the whole idea of the rifle was ridiculous. A Daisy Red Ryder, basically a middle school toy, might have saved their lives that night.

"You dropped a few things at Jade's house. I assume you know that?"

"I don't wear panic well. I brought my, um, supplies, just in case there was an opportunity. I didn't relish the thought of hurting either of you but talk about superstardom. The editor *and* the crime reporter? Pure gold. When I was getting the hell out of there, my bag fell and wasn't zipped all the way. I picked up a couple of things, but the police were, like, seconds away. No choice but to leave it."

"Were you there that night to kill us?"

Sam pursed her lips. "I didn't know what was going to happen, honestly. I didn't know if I'd be able to do it, especially since I know the two of you. I psyched myself up beforehand. You know, Jade stole my dream from me, you were the one who took it, that kind of thing. But the whole point of me showing up was for Jade to continue on her 'Evan is the devil' path. Seems to have worked."

"How are you going to kill me now? You know me. We're friends. We've gone out a couple of times, we work together, we even had a kind of…thing. It was just bad timing on my part." Alicia desperately hoped that rehumanizing herself to Sam might point her in a different direction. Put a bag over her head and drive her out to the middle of nowhere. Something. Anything but the trajectory Alicia believed them to be on.

"I know." Sam sounded almost wistful. "I'm sure if we had continued seeing each other, things would have turned out differently. I really liked you. I hated you before I met you, since you were stealing my job and all, but then when I saw you…yeah. Everything changed. I was so pissed at myself for deviating from the plan. But, man, you made my heart stop. I assume it was because of the cop, right? The detective?"

Alicia shook her head. "It wasn't that. I just wasn't in the right frame of mind for a relationship. I had so much going on, and moving back here was a lot harder than I'd anticipated. I never said never. I just said not right now. There's always tomorrow."

"Alicia." Sam smiled condescendingly. "I definitely didn't get that vibe from you. I saw you that night at your friend's cookout. You were like a nervous little schoolgirl as soon as she showed up. And please, don't insult my intelligence. This isn't one of those procedural episodes where the victim charms the kidnapper into thinking they'll ride off into the sunset together. I'm fully aware that ship has sailed."

"I know, Sam." Alicia sighed. "I'm scared. I don't want to die."

"I get that. I do. But I don't think we have a choice anymore. You know everything, and you can say as many times as you want that you'll keep it all to yourself and just disappear, but I know that isn't true. You have family. And I'm sure you wouldn't be able to stay away from the good detective for very long. We're at an impasse. Unless…you want to do it?"

"Do what?" Alicia shifted uncomfortably on the bench, and her head screamed in protest. She shut her eyes tightly to make it go away.

"Go out on your own terms."

Was Sam really suggesting handing the gun over? "That probably would be better," Alicia said. *Please let her be serious.*

"I have a full bottle of sleeping pills on that shelf. Sort of a plan B, I guess. In case things went south."

Ugh. Alicia deflated.

"You didn't think I'd give you my gun, did you? Come on, you'd shoot me so fast, I wouldn't see it coming."

Alicia stifled a sob. How was she going to get out of this? She was in an area of the basement that very few people knew existed, and apparently, Sam had hidden the plans so no one else could find them. Maybe this really was it. This was how her story ended. In a tiny room with a narcissistic cult follower. She tried to send Cami a telepathic message. *I love you. I've always loved you. Thank you for giving me back the only thing I've ever truly wanted.* She didn't necessarily believe in that type of thing, but no harm in trying. Alicia wiped her eyes and took a deep breath.

"Give me the bottle."

Chapter Thirty-seven

The only thing the search at Sam's house turned up was another container of that damn saltwater taffy and a laptop. She might not have been the most technically savvy criminal, but she covered her physical bases well. Sam shared the basement and attic with the elderly woman who lived upstairs from her in the turn of the century, two-family home. The boiler was original, still covered with asbestos to provide insulation. It would probably outlive them all.

The neighbor wasn't keen on letting Kelsey and the Copper Bluffs detectives search her property. She demanded a warrant, so they were at a standstill until it came through.

Cami stayed close to Alicia's office in the slimmest of hopes that she was just out for a walk. Without her phone. For what could be hours. Cami shook her head vigorously and tried to get her head in the game. She couldn't focus on the what-ifs. She had to set her sights on finding Alicia, and that was all.

"Anything?" Cami asked into her radio.

Her radio squelched. Michaels was going door-to-door to the few other businesses that occupied the building. "Nothing yet. The offices on this side of the building are open floor plans, so there aren't too many places to hide."

"Attic? Basement?"

"The attic is just plank and beam with a giant air-conditioning unit it. The door is here in the manager's office of this insurance agency, so they definitely would have seen someone come through. I took a look around, but I wouldn't want to walk on that floor without something underneath it to catch me. Just a few old newspapers, a lot of dust, and the AC unit."

Cami sighed and rubbed her forehead. "Basement?"

"Nothing down there, either. Old storage area basically. Some furniture, Christmas decorations, a few ancient desks and chairs. Musty and it smells like mildew."

"Thanks. Let me know if you find anything." Cami reattached the radio to her pocket. She couldn't just stand around and do nothing, even though she knew the team was working diligently to find Alicia. There had to be something they missed. A clue, a location, something.

Alicia's workspace was clean and organized. Cami knew it wasn't specifically her desk, just one that she shared with whoever else decided to go into the office on any particular day. Her phone had a passcode to get into it, and her bag just had a few essentials. The new guy Jared was sitting in the small conference room on his phone. Cami brought the bag to her face and inhaled, the light scent of Alicia's perfume stinging her nostrils like a flowery ice pick. She swallowed the lump in her throat and chastised herself for being so negative. Kidnapping wasn't the Small-Town Slayer's MO. Maybe she had different plans for Alicia. As long as those plans kept her alive until Cami could find her, they could deal with the ramifications together.

Brandt's voice came through the radio. "Warrant came through. Lyons, any sign of Lewis or Flynn where you're at?"

"Nothing, Captain. I'm going to do another sweep of the office and surrounding areas to make sure I didn't miss anything. No hits from the BOLO?"

"False alarm for Lewis. That's the only thing at this point. We've got eyes everywhere. The city K-9 unit is on their way, too."

Cami couldn't shake the foreboding that time was working against them. She knew Sam had liked Alicia at one point, so there was the slightest possibility that she wouldn't be able to carry out her plan. Or maybe that would propel her forward since Alicia had rejected her advances. She just needed to fucking find her.

The hallway leading toward one of the exits had a few doors among the exposed brick. The first one was a broom closet. Cami pulled the string, and a light bulb crackled on. Cleaning supplies, a broom, a mop, light bulbs, and trash bags. Lots of cobwebs. Nothing else.

The second door was locked, but it was a back entrance to the newspaper office. Cami had opened the second means of egress from the inside when she was searching the office the first time.

The third door was the basement door. It was unusual to have a basement in an office building, but this had most likely been a stately home when it was first built and had been turned into offices by a contractor before real estate flipping was even popular.

Cami looked down the basement stairs. The railing was just a long piece of wood held up by a few wooden balusters. One good trip and the whole thing would crumble like pie. Every stair creaked, and Cami could almost see the dust cloud pop up from every step she took. Michaels had done a good job in his description. The space was mostly unfilled except for a few crowded corners and some furniture strewn around. The smell of moisture and dirt was unpleasant, to say the least.

There weren't too many places to hide except for a small cutout that looked like it was at one time a canning room or a root cellar. Wooden shelves lined the walls. Cami bent and looked underneath the shelves to see if there was a crawl space or something else that they'd missed the first time around. Nothing.

She sighed and headed back toward the stairs. The basement door was cracked open so a sliver of light poked through the darkness. The stairs creaked just as much on the way back up. Cami ran her hand along the makeshift railing and stopped abruptly when a sliver lodged itself into her thumb.

"Shit," she muttered, squinting to see if it was sticking out enough to grab with bare fingers. It wasn't. But she did see something on the top stair, tucked against the knotted riser. Cami lifted it and switched on her flashlight. The dim glow of the fluorescent tube lights that hung throughout the basement didn't provide any detail.

It was a sterling silver infinity bracelet. The small round identifier by the broken clasp, that looked as though it had been torn off a wrist, read *Tiffany & Co.* Cami nearly dropped it. She was here.

Cami ran back down the stairs, nearly tripping and killing herself over a splintered piece of wood near the bottom.

She fought the urge to call out, to scream Alicia's name into the dark room. If she was there with Sam, and Cami had just missed them on her multiple sweeps, she didn't want Sam to suspect anything different. Frustration continued to build as Cami checked and rechecked every inch of the basement she'd already gone through. There were no new hiding spots. The furniture had been overturned, the boxes moved, the decorations shifted. There was no sign of them except the broken bracelet. Maybe Sam had tried to drag Alicia down into the basement, but Alicia had fought her off, and then Sam had rethought the plan. Maybe she'd hit her. Maybe she…

"What the *fuck*?" Cami shout-whispered. She pounded on the wall with the side of her fist. And then she took a step back.

Huh. Felt almost hollow.

She pushed on the wood with her fingertips. It gave. Not much but a little. She ran her hand along the wall, knocking lightly. There was either something behind the wall, or a long-ago repair job had been pretty shoddy.

An old canvas painting of a lone tree standing in a river was propped up against the wall. Cami looked at the ground and noticed a disruption in the dust. It had been slid back and forth, seemingly numerous times. She could feel her adrenaline kick up a notch.

Sure enough, the canvas glided easily to the right and revealed a large plank of wood that could be pushed back and forth, allowing enough space for a relatively small person to squeeze through. Plenty of room for both Sam and Alicia.

Cami unbuckled the flap of her holster and pulled it clear of her firearm. She knew she should call for backup, but she didn't want to lose the element of surprise if she even had it in the first place. She was terrified that a loud noise, the squelch of a radio, or any sort of tip-off would push Sam to the point of no return.

Her breath caught in her throat. A steel door to a capsule of some kind sat in front of her. There was a limited amount of space all around it, as though it had been boarded up for a reason. She had visions of a torture chamber or a cannibal's lair race through her brain. She chased them out with the necessity of focusing. This was it. Make or break. Life or death.

Cami closed her eyes and prayed that Alicia was in that room. And that she was safe. She wouldn't allow herself to think anything different.

In one hand, she held her pistol. She reached for the long black handle, knowing she had one shot to open it quickly. If she fumbled at all, it could very well be over.

The handle was cold. On a silent count to three, Cami summoned all her strength, pushed the heavy handle down, and pulled the door open with one fluid motion. Her now free hand flew to her gun, and she pointed it directly into the open doorway.

Sam whipped her head around, her eyes wide and full of surprise. She pointed her own gun at Alicia's head. Alicia. She was in there, her back against the wall, bloody streaks across her face, and she held a container of something. But she was alive.

Relief mixed with fury flowed through Cami's veins like a raging stream.

Alicia drew in a shaky breath and exhaled with a sob. Cami steadied her gun. "Drop it, Sam."

"I can't do that, Detective. As soon as I lower my hand, you'll either shoot me or arrest me. This doesn't end that way." Her hand was trembling. From the way she had taken out the victims, she probably wasn't too keen on face-to-face confrontations.

Cami needed to use that to her advantage. "I won't shoot you if you place the gun at your feet and kick it away. That's the only way this doesn't end in bloodshed. Do it, Sam."

Sam shook her head. She took a phantom of a step toward Alicia so that the gun was just inches from her head.

Cami took a step forward. "I'm not going to let you hurt her. One more move like that and they'll have to clean you off the wall with a squeegee. Put the gun down and surrender peacefully. That'll help with any leniency they might be willing to give you." Cami knew that leniency was not in Sam's future, but she needed her to drop the weapon. Alicia's face was an alarming shade of gray.

Sam scoffed. "What am I supposed to do? Drop to my knees and beg forgiveness? Show that I've come to my senses, and now I'm remorseful? Well, surprise. I'm not. I'm sorry that a few people had to lose their lives for the greater good, but we wouldn't be in this predicament if I hadn't needed to create my own destiny." She tightened her grip around the gun.

Cami just had to keep her talking until an opportunity opened up. If Sam decided there was no way out and tried to go out in a blaze of glory, it would be a matter of who had the quicker trigger finger. With Sam's proximity to Alicia, Cami didn't hold out much hope that she'd win that battle.

"We found your flash drive, Sam. We know this was all part of the plan."

"How did you…" Sam trailed off and shook her head.

"How did we what? Find the drive? Get into the docs? Figure out who was behind the mock articles?" The tension in Cami's aiming arm was starting to ache.

"So I've been on your hit list the whole time?" Alicia asked. She reached for her head as though speaking set off a sharp pain.

"Not the whole time. But does it really matter? Listen. I need to get out of here before the rest of her people show up. Time is ticking. Detective, just let me walk away, and I'll disappear for good. You and Alicia can ride off into the sunset or whatever the fuck you two have going on. Otherwise, I guess today will be the day we both meet Jesus." Sam glanced at Alicia before adjusting her grip on the gun again and turning to Cami. "Which is it?"

Sweat had broken out on Sam's forehead. She was swallowing rapidly. Cami could see it playing out on her face. Sam knew she was running out of time and was quickly approaching her boiling point. "Okay. You win."

A calculated risk, but it was her only option. She couldn't take the chance that Sam was bluffing.

"Put your gun down."

Cami bent slowly and placed her gun at her feet. She used the tip of her shoe to slide it a few feet away. She raised both hands in the air.

Sam didn't seem to know how to react. Clearly, she hadn't anticipated Cami's cooperation. "Good. Alicia, stand up."

"Why?" Cami asked, her hands still raised.

"If I don't take her with me, you'll pick up your gun and shoot me in the back."

"That wasn't the deal, Sam. Just leave."

"I'll let her go when I get outside. If I walk up those stairs into an ambush of police, we're both going down."

As far as Cami knew, the only police officer on the premises was Michaels. But she also knew it wouldn't be long before someone figured out Sam's hidden lair. She just hoped they'd take a little bit longer. Sam was too volatile, and Alicia appeared too weak to fight back. The blood on her face and the broken wine bottle were good indicators she hadn't come to the basement willingly.

Alicia stood slowly. Sam dug the gun into her back and pushed her forward. Alicia winced. She didn't seem to fully trust Sam's intent. She walked slowly past Cami and mouthed the words, *I love you.* She had tears in her glazed eyes.

Cami took a step toward them, but Sam stopped abruptly.

"Stay right there." She continued to hold the gun to Alicia's back while they walked backward slowly toward the basement stairs. There was still no commotion aboveground, to Cami's relief.

"You can let her go now. I'm not going to jeopardize her safety, so you're free to walk out of here. Just let her go."

"You don't think there should be one final exclamation point on this story? Something to kind of tie it all together?"

Cami's heartbeat quickened. "What do you mean, Sam? What kind of 'exclamation point'? The exclamation point is you getting away with it all, isn't it?"

"Every newsworthy crime spree ends with a bang, not a whimper. Why should mine be any different?"

Cami looked at the floor, calculating the amount of time she'd need to reach her weapon and cock it. Sam didn't just want a way out; she wanted fireworks. "You don't want to do this, Sam. This is your shot to walk out of here in one piece, a free woman. Don't blow it. Let her walk away."

Sam laughed. "No, I'm aiming higher. We only regret the chances we didn't take, right, Detective?"

Cami dove for her gun as Sam took a step forward and fired at her. The acrid smell of charcoal smoke and sulfur infiltrated her senses as she reached for her weapon. Cami leaned up and cocked her gun as Sam was taking another step closer, this time guaranteed to hit her target.

Before Sam could pull the trigger a second time, she was thrust forward with such force that she gasped before hitting the floor. Cami was up in a flash and crushed her heel into the back of Sam's hand before she could grasp the gun that she'd dropped as she hit the cement floor. Cami kicked the gun forcefully and watched it glide to the other side of the basement.

Alicia sat on the ground behind her, carefully rubbing the shoulder she'd just plowed into Sam's back.

"Should have gone out on *your own terms*, huh, Sam?" Alicia hissed.

Cami didn't get the reference, but Sam certainly seemed to. "Well played, fancy crime reporter. I turned out to be the unicorn you were chasing, didn't I?"

"Unicorn? Don't delude yourself. You're a piece of shit, nothing more." Alicia groaned as she stood.

Cami pressed her shoe between Sam's shoulder blades, eliciting a grunt. She reached for her radio as the basement door opened, and a swath of light illuminated the dust motes dancing in the air.

"We're down here," Alicia yelled.

Officer Graham, Officer Michaels, and Kelsey came flying down the stairs, their weapons drawn. Cami slowly removed her foot from Sam's back as Graham cuffed her.

"Looks like I'll be trading in my journalistic credentials for a book deal. I'll appeal this all the way to the Supreme Court. Just you watch," Sam said as Michaels lifted her by her underarm.

"I'm sure you'll be the most feared supervillain at Knox Correctional. Just remember that most of the inmates there have no problem looking their victims in the eye." Cami stared directly at Sam as Michaels walked her by. Even then, Sam dropped her eyes first. Coward.

"We found her little design plans tucked away in the neighbor's chest. Sorry it took us so long. Let's get Alicia to the hospital." Kelsey looked at the back of Alicia's shirt and grimaced. "Good amount of blood here. You okay?"

Cami nodded. "I'm fine. We'll be right behind you. Just need a quick minute."

Kelsey looked from Cami to Alicia and then toward the stairs where Sam was being led up by Michaels and Graham. "Quick one. Captain Brandt is going to want a whole lot of answers."

"Copy that." Cami smiled faintly as Kelsey walked back upstairs. Alicia was leaning against the rickety railing of the basement stairs. "Hey." Cami stepped toward her gingerly, the not-yet-healed aches and pains from her car accident screaming from her lunge to the ground.

"Hey." Alicia smiled and wiped a smear of blood from her cheek. She whispered, "You saved me."

"*You* saved *me*."

Alicia nearly fell forward into Cami's arms. She held her as tightly as she could, savoring every second as if it was the last. She really thought she'd lost her again. This time for good.

"So you're saying we saved each other?" Alicia clasped her hands behind Cami's waist and didn't let go, even when she pulled back.

"I think that's the perfect way to describe it." Cami smiled again and kissed Alicia lightly on the lips.

"My head really fucking hurts," Alicia said with a derisive laugh. She grabbed Cami's hand and pulled her toward the stairs.

Cami stopped and squeezed Alicia's hand. "Alicia?"

"Yeah?"

"I love you, too."

CHAPTER THIRTY-EIGHT

The constant beeping should have been her first clue, but Alicia had to blink a few times to get her bearings. Her head was throbbing, but the ache was dull and not nearly as bad as it had been earlier. She lifted her hand to see an IV attached to it. She sucked in a breath as the events that led her to the hospital room flashed before her. It hadn't just been a nightmare.

She sat up as much as she could and looked around the room. Next to her bed, in a beige vinyl recliner, Cami slouched over the arm, apparently asleep. Alicia touched her thigh lightly.

Cami jumped awake. "I'm here. Are you okay? Do you need the nurse?"

"No, I'm okay. I'm fine. Are you okay? I'm a little fuzzy on what happened. Is Sam in jail?" Alicia raised the back of the bed so she was sitting rather than lying. "What time is it?"

Yawning, Cami checked her watch. "It's only eight. God, I thought it was midnight. I'm good. Sore, but that's the accident more than what happened earlier. Did you see my little dive and roll move?"

Alicia laughed, then grimaced and put a hand to her head. "Of course I did. That was some serious *Mission Impossible*, *Tomb Raider*, James Bond shit right there. I've never wanted you more."

"Right?" Cami laughed along with her. "Yes, Sam is in custody. She's meeting with her lawyers and going through those motions now. She clammed right up once we got her to the station. I have to head over there soon to meet with Brandt and Kelsey to go over the game plan. You should see the circus. Word about a serial killer, even though it doesn't technically meet the criteria, is out, so we have media from Manchester, Concord, Boston. CNN even sent someone. You're going to be famous, you fancy crime reporter, you."

Alicia's smile faded. She played with Cami's fingers, laced them through her own. "It's surreal. I felt so close to death. I wish I could explain it. It's, like, the whole thing about life flashing before your eyes is true but only sort of. I went through a few big regrets, present company included, and wishing I had spent more time with my family, wondering how they were going to deal with the news that I'd been killed. And then, you. I was so *angry* at her for depriving us of our second chance. I thought my heart might explode at the thought of never being able to see you again, never kissing or holding you again, never being able to right the wrongs that destroyed the best part of me."

Tears pooled in Alicia's eyes, but Cami brushed them away with her thumb.

"It's over," Cami whispered. "As much as she tried, she took nothing from us. I'm not saying there won't be times when I struggle or times when I get pissed at you all over again for what happened and act irrationally. But I have never been surer of anything in my entire life, Alicia. I know we said we'd take things slowly, but I don't even think that's an option for me. I'm still hopelessly in love with you, and I want to spend the rest of my life with you."

Cami took something from her pocket and slid it over Alicia's wrist. It was her infinity bracelet, but instead of the normal clasp, the chain was knotted together.

"You do?" Alicia asked. Her voice was full and thick with emotion. She swallowed hard, the pain in her head momentarily forgotten.

"I do."

Cami leaned in and kissed her gently. Alicia threw both arms around her neck, nearly knocking over the IV pole. "Ouch," she said through teary laughter.

"I found the party," Taryn yelled, coming through the door with an armful of flowers. A nurse outside the room asked her to keep it down.

Katie, Violet, and Jack followed. Alicia covered her heart with her hand in gratitude as Cami stood to hug all of them. Maybe they were still her friends after all.

Violet scooted past the herd and made her way toward Alicia. She took her hand and squeezed it. "So thankful you're okay. When Kelsey called Katie with the news, we were shocked and freaking out. I am so sorry I invited that nutcase to the barbecue. I didn't know."

Alicia shook her head. "Don't be sorry. Of course you didn't know. I'm the one who introduced you and Jack to her that night at Birdie's. Aren't there supposed to be signs if someone is an all-out psychopath? If she was giving any off, I'm the least observant person on the face of the earth, which doesn't bode well for my career choice."

"I heard she was in a cult?" Taryn said, sidling up next to Violet. She leaned in and gave Alicia as much of a hug as she could without ripping her wires and tubes off.

"Is it a cult?" Alicia asked incredulously. Good thing she hadn't gone to one of the "seminars" Sam had offered.

Katie spoke up. "I don't think it's a cult, just a self-help group that had cultish tendencies. Focused on making your life what you want it to be at all costs. Sam obviously took that and ran with it in the wrong direction. I heard Captain Brandt briefing the chief, and I guess they're going to interview the sage or guru or whatever he calls himself."

"Feels like we're in a movie," Alicia said. Her head was starting to pound a little.

Jack made his way over to the bed and gave her a quick kiss on the forehead. "Still can't imagine what you must have gone through. Maybe someday, if you're up to it, you can tell us about it. All of those lives lost and others ruined for a *job*? Make it make sense."

"I wish I could."

"I heard you were the ass-kicker who took her down in the end. Doesn't surprise me at all. Glad you're okay, honey."

Alicia smiled and squeezed Jack's arm. She was surprised to see Katie coming her way. When the group had gathered at the window talking about the logistics of the room in the basement, Alicia had assumed that was as far as she'd go.

"Do you feel like a queen holding court?" Katie smirked and looked at everyone listening to Cami. Alicia couldn't imagine her saying anything other than pleasantries, but Katie wasn't normally one to keep her feelings to herself.

"More like a pope. I'd offer you my ring to kiss, but I seem to have left it at home."

"Listen, when I heard that you were missing, I was really upset. Not only that you were missing and might be hurt but with myself for the way I've treated you these past few months. I just…I need to look out for her. That's all. I'm sorry." Katie stared straight ahead, but Alicia still appreciated the sentiment. She knew that Katie's insides must be folding in on themselves under her admission of wrongdoing. Certainly not something Katie was comfortable with.

"I understand. I brought it on myself. It's not like I'm the innocent party in all of this. No hard feelings."

"Good." Katie gave Alicia a tight smile. She looked back at Cami, who was still in deep conversation with the others. "Never again?"

Alicia nodded. "Never again. Honest."

Katie exhaled. "I'm glad you survived, you pain in the ass. Always making it about you, even with serial killers. When you break out of here, we'll all do dinner, okay?"

"Definitely."

Katie nodded and turned toward the door as the nurse came in. She nicely but sternly kicked everyone out except Cami. Alicia angled the bed down again and realized how exhausted she was. At least her heart was full.

Cami sat next to her on the recliner and took both her hands again. She kissed Alicia's knuckles softly. "I hate to leave you, but I have to go meet with Kelsey and the captain. You wouldn't believe the amount of paperwork this kind of thing creates." Cami checked her watch. "And we're giving a press conference in an hour."

"Who's going to cover it from the *Sun*?" Alicia asked.

"I'm guessing Jade? She's so pissed at me. But if she hadn't been so shady or lied to us, we never would have suspected her in the first place. She isn't completely absolved of everything that's happened, either. There will be an investigation, as toothless as it might be."

"Maybe she'll send the new guy, Jared. Go. I'm tired anyway. I'll be out before you leave the room." Alicia hesitated, unsure how much of Cami's feelings were tied to their circumstances. "I love you."

Cami wasted no time leaning in and kissing Alicia again, softly and carefully. She brushed the hair out of her face and ran the back of her index finger down Alicia's cheek. Alicia's stomach flip-flopped even as she lay in the sterile hospital bed.

"I love you," Cami responded. She looked back one last time before she exited to the hallway. "Never stopped."

❖

Alicia seemed to have finally reached a place where she could sleep without immediately seeing Sam's face close to hers, the smell of blood and wine pungent in the air. She had been terrified to close her eyes, and the lack of sleep was taking a toll. She didn't think she'd been dreaming of Sam, but she still woke up startled. She sat upright and felt a twinge in the back of her head. How much of it was physical pain versus psychosomatic pain, she wasn't sure.

Cami jolted up next to her and gently rubbed circles on her back. She yawned and used the back of her hand to rub the sleepiness away from her eyes.

"I'm okay, you can go back to sleep." Alicia leaned into her and rested her head on Cami's shoulder for a second. She'd never felt so on edge and so safe at the same time. The slight hint of coconut calmed her.

"I'm good," Cami said, stifling another yawn. "I'm right here, whatever you need. If you want to get up and go in the other room or you want to put on the TV, we can do that."

Alicia pulled her down with her and wrapped Cami's arm around her waist. She felt Cami place a light kiss on the back of her head before her breathing started to get heavy again. Alicia snuggled deeper into Cami's body and matched her breathing. A few minutes later, it worked. She could feel her eyes closing of their own accord.

After the first night home from the hospital, when Alicia had woken up screaming in her bed, Cami had insisted that she stay at her place instead. Cami had slept at Alicia's apartment that first night, so cautious and tender that Alicia had felt like a porcelain doll. It was almost comical. But when the nightmares had started, she'd appreciated it on a whole different level.

It had been a rough week. Alicia's mom had gone to her apartment to water her plants and had taken over feeding Beverly Lawson's pigeons while Alicia was recovering. She was physically better at this point; it was the emotional trauma she was struggling with. There was no quick fix, but the therapist she'd met with had assured her that she'd come through the other side feeling whole again if she was willing to put the work in.

There was nothing Alicia wanted more.

Cami was amazing through the chaos. In between her court appearances and press conferences and meetings with the mayor, she'd been Alicia's personal nursemaid. No matter how many times Alicia told her that she was physically okay, just sore, Cami insisted on waiting on her hand and foot. She cooked or brought home takeout, she would jump up to bring Alicia her phone or laptop if it was located anywhere other than directly in front of her, and she accompanied her to every appointment. Alicia marveled at how quickly Cami made the adjustment from exasperated ex-girlfriend to doting wife. If she was being honest, she kind of loved it.

Now, it was cool for an August night. September's inevitable thievery of summer was making an early threat. An involuntary shiver snaked its way down Alicia's back.

"Here, take the blanket." Cami turned from the paperwork she was filling out and grabbed an old blanket from the back of the couch and handed it to Alicia. "We'll be apple picking before you know it."

Alicia smiled. That was a happy thought. "You know, I really do feel better. My head is basically healed. I know they have to watch some for some long-term effects, but I'm okay. You've been phenomenal, and I love you with all of my heart for how perfect you've been. I don't want to overstay my welcome and have you think I'm taking advantage. I'm sure I can go back to my place now."

Cami looked up at her, incredulous. "You can't be serious. Overstay your welcome? Really? You're welcome here forever. You should just move in."

The statement hung in the air for a second. Alicia tensed, waiting to see if Cami was going to freak out and walk back what she said. She didn't. She stared calmly at Alicia with a wisp of a smile. A challenge.

"Fine. I'll move in. We'll live together again. I'll be all up in your shit twenty-four seven." Alicia looked away as though she was making a concession. Happiness bubbled into her throat like a wayward science experiment. At that moment, Samantha Lewis no longer existed.

A full grin broke out on Cami's face. "Don't threaten me with a good time." She pushed Alicia's legs off her lap and leaned in to kiss her.

Alicia pulled Cami by the back of the neck to deepen the kiss. Cami's hands started roaming, lightly at first, then with fervor. Alicia moaned in appreciation, but Cami withdrew them quickly.

"We can wait if you're not ready. I know the therapist said that sometimes—"

Alicia shut her up by kissing her again, forcefully and feverish. She pushed Cami down on the couch and climbed on top of her to show her just how ready she was.

"Does it look like I'm not ready?" Alicia cocked an eyebrow and ran her tongue over Cami's lips.

Cami's eyes were half-lidded, and her breathing was erratic. Alicia had her right where she wanted her. "You win. You're ready. Come on." Cami flipped Alicia over like she was a ragdoll and pulled her to her feet. "Let's go to our bedroom."

Alicia followed close, still holding Cami's hand. *Our* bedroom. As she glanced quickly around the house, some things the same, some very different, Alicia realized that for once in a very, *very* long time, she wasn't yearning for the past. A new wick had been ignited, and seeing a flicker of the future filled her with love and hope. She smiled as Cami turned to her, eyes and body full of happiness and desire. She had taken advantage. She had taken control.

EPILOGUE

One Year Later

Cami shook her head and sighed heavily. This wasn't going at all the way she'd planned. Her clipboard had almost no checkmark completions. If this was the future of the Oakview Police Department, the town was in serious trouble.

"Piper! You climb *up* the rope ladder, not swing from it. If you're chasing a mugger through downtown and he hops a fence, do you think you're going to catch him by twirling through the pickets?"

Alicia came up behind her and slid an arm around her waist. "You look stressed. What's the matter?"

Cami blew her whistle as Piper got caught up in the ropes again. Alicia tugged on her earlobe to regain hearing in the ear next to Cami. "Oh, sorry. They say they want to learn and condition themselves, but they don't even look like they're trying. What the hell is Piper even doing? Is she *eating* something?"

"Honey, she's four."

"I know she's four, but your brother told you they wanted to practice the police academy obstacle course so they could be just like their Aunt Cami. Charlie was the one who said he's really serious about this. He joined the Junior Police Academy in Manchester. They're not going to let them just screw around." Cami scanned the playground to find Charlie. That kid could disappear better than a mob boss. "Where is Charlie?"

Alicia pointed to a tree across the park. "On his phone. He's thirteen, what did you expect?"

"I had high expectations. I thought they'd see me as a warm, tender drill sergeant. You know, loveable but also someone that commands respect. I even brought my whistle," Cami said, lifting the whistle off her chest as though Alicia hadn't watched her get dressed before they'd left the apartment.

"I know, baby," Alicia said.

Cami knew she was patronizing her, but she didn't care. She appreciated the sympathy, as phony as it was.

"When we get home later, I'll give you *all* the respect you deserve. Will that make it better?" She tried to keep a straight face but failed.

Cami tilted her head and smirked. "Probably," she whispered. She regained her composure as Piper walked over to them with something in her hand.

"I found a lollipop on the swing set. It isn't open. Can I eat it?"

"Definitely not. Throw it in the trash over there. I don't even want you touching it," Cami told her.

Piper lowered her eyes and wiped the hair off her forehead. Her ponytail was a complete mess from dancing in and out of the rope ladder. "Can we get ice cream?" she asked, brightening a little.

Alicia held up her hands in a shrug.

It was Cami's decision. After the abhorrent behavior on the obstacle course, the only logical answer was absolutely no. "Dairy Queen or Richardson's?"

"Dairy Queen," Piper yelled. She dropped the lollipop into the trash as she skipped to the big metal slide that had been there since Cami was a kid. Many legs had been burned on that contraption.

Alicia laughed. "If that kind of hard-assed discipline doesn't command respect, then nothing will."

"Oh, shut up. She was all sad and dejected about the lollipop. I'm only human. She's going to be such a sucky cop. He won't be much better." Cami nodded to Charlie, who was smiling at his phone with earbuds lodged in both ears.

"He'll just need a tough captain to whip him into shape. Or maybe he'll decide to go to college and become an engineer like his dad." Alicia pointed. Piper was digging for something in the sand underneath a bench. "She's so curious, she'll work at the *Sun* with me and get *all* the scoop."

Cami smiled at the thought. She checked her watch. "We should probably get going if we're stopping for ice cream on our way to bring them home."

"Ten more minutes," Piper shouted from her spot by the bench. She was forming the sand into little piles.

"How does that kid hear everything?" Alicia asked. "Come sit with me."

Cami followed her to a small metal bench underneath a massive oak. The waning days of summer lent the slightest chill to an otherwise warm afternoon. She took Alicia's hand and laced their fingers together. It still seemed surreal sometimes. Everything they'd been through, ending up together stronger than Cami had thought possible. She was still hit with waves of mistrust or hesitancy, but they faded as soon as they came on. Alicia's promises were real. Cami believed her, and that belief satisfied her.

As though Alicia knew Cami was waxing philosophical, she squeezed her hand. "Now that we've cemented ourselves as soulmates and that we'll be together forever and ever, we should probably lay out some ground rules."

"Ground rules?" Cami turned to Alicia quizzically.

"Yeah. Forever is a long time, you know. So, for example, as much as I love our nightly couch sessions in front of *Law & Order*, we should have a date night at least once a month. Like a real, get dressed up, and go somewhere new kind of date."

Cami smiled. "Okay, I can agree to that. Although nights with new episodes are off the table. What else?"

"Your turn."

Charlie walked by them toward the swings. A young girl about his age waved shyly at him. He awkwardly sat next to her, trying to play it cool. "No wonder his head wasn't in the game today," Cami said. An idea hit her. "Okay, I have one. Vacations. I know we both get so caught up in work and the day-to-day minutiae that we treat our vacation time as a way to wind down and just do nothing. And we should still do that. But at least once a year, we should get away from town and go somewhere completely unfamiliar to us. Maybe this winter we can go skiing in Utah."

"Neither of us ski."

"Irrelevant."

"Okay, that's a good one. I can definitely agree to that." Alicia nodded. "I want you to be honest with me when I'm not at my best. I know I can fold inward sometimes when something is bothering me, or I feel out of sorts. If I'm doing something that feels off or if I'm acting distant, tell me. I can promise you, it has nothing to do with you. Ever."

Cami looked off into the distance at Charlie and the young girl swinging together. So innocent. "I can do that. Same goes for me, too. I know I'm pretty vocal about that sort of thing, but if you feel any sort of distance between us, it's only because of external bullshit. Never because of us." The conversation had taken on a more serious tone, but Cami was okay with it. "My turn. No lies, no secrets, and no shutting down. We have to talk about things no matter what. If you're feeling stifled or distracted, if I'm insecure or afraid, we need to talk through it. Always."

"Yes, one hundred percent. I will talk to you if I'm even the slightest bit unsure of anything, which I am confident I won't be. But you never have to worry about me keeping things inside. Never again."

Cami leaned in and kissed Alicia softly. "I know. I love you."

Alicia slid closer and stroked the back of Cami's hand with her thumb. "I love you, too. I'll never take you for granted. Just like you'll never eat the last Oreo in the package."

Cami laughed. "I didn't agree to that. We're discussing *realistic* things here, not—"

Piper's sudden dash over to them interrupted Cami's train of thought. She had a handful of goodies she'd dug up from underneath the bench.

"Look, I found a comb, a lipstick, a plastic frog, headphones, sunglasses, and a block. Look!" she said again and laid her items out next to Alicia.

Cami's eyes widened, and she heard Alicia swallow. The block was much too familiar. Wooden, scratched up, with a faded but still red P on its side.

"Where did you get this, honey?" Cami picked the block up with the tips of her thumb and index finger. She stood and followed Piper, who was happily pointing to a spot next to the seesaw.

"This is where I found the sunglasses and the block. Can we take this stuff home?"

Alicia appeared behind them. "Um, you can keep the frog if you wash it. Everything else has to go." Piper pouted but went back to the bench to get the frog. "What the fuck?" Alicia whispered.

Cami shook her head. "I don't know. It looks like it's been here for a while. Sam's spending the remainder of her long life behind bars, so she didn't just drop it here for us to find."

"I don't like it," Alicia said.

"Me either. I'm sure it's just a creepy coincidence."

Charlie and his friend approached them slowly. "This is Olivia from school. Can we go to Richardson's Ice Cream? Olivia likes Aunt Ginny's Black Pepper ice cream, and they have it there."

Cami clapped her hands. "We're actually going to Dairy Queen. Aunt Ginny's is off the menu, but they have a mean soft serve. And no ties to Oakview. Who's in?"

About the Author

Nicole Stiling lives in New England with her wife, two children, and their pets. When she's not working at her day job or procrastinating on her next book, she enjoys video games, horror comics, clearing out the DVR, and traveling to someplace warm. Nicole is a strict vegetarian who does not like vegetables, and a staunch advocate for anything with four legs.

Books Available from Bold Strokes Books

Blood Rage by Illeandra Young. A stolen artifact, a family in the dark, an entire city on edge. Can SPEAR agent Danika Karson juggle all three over a weekend with the "in-laws," while an unknown, malevolent entity lies in wait upon her very skin? (978-1-63679-539-3)

Ghost Town by R.E. Ward. Blair Wyndon and Leif Henderson are set to prove ghosts exist when the mystery suddenly turns deadly. Someone or something else is in Masonville, and if they don't find a way to escape, they might never leave. (978-1-63679-523-2)

Good Christian Girls by Elizabeth Bradshaw. In this heartfelt coming of age lesbian romance, Lacey and Jo help each other untangle who they are from who everyone says they're supposed to be. (978-1-63679-555-3)

Guide Us Home by CF Frizzell and Jesse J. Thoma. When acquisition of an abandoned lighthouse pits ambitious competitors Nancy and Sam against each other, it takes a WWII tale of two brave women to make them see the light. (978-1-63679-533-1)

Lost Harbor by Kimberly Cooper Griffin. For Alice and Bridget's love to survive, they must find a way to reconcile the most important passions in their lives—devotion to the church and each other. (978-1-63679-463-1)

Never a Bridesmaid by Spencer Greene. As her sister's wedding gets closer, Jessica finds that her hatred for the maid of honor is a bit more complicated than she thought. Could it be something more than hatred? (978-1-63679-559-1)

The Rewind by Nicole Stiling. For police detective Cami Lyons and crime reporter Alicia Flynn, some choices break hearts. Others leave a body count. (978-1-63679-572-0)

Turning Point by Cathy Dunnell. When Asha and her former high school bully Jody struggle to deny their growing attraction, can they move forward without going back? (978-1-63679-549-2)

When Tomorrow Comes by D. Jackson Leigh. Teague Maxwell, convinced she will die before she turns 41, hires animal rescue owner Baye Cobb to rehome her extensive menagerie. (978-1-63679-557-7)

You Had Me at Merlot by Melissa Brayden. Leighton and Jamie have all the ingredients to turn their attraction into love, but it's a recipe for disaster. (978-1-63679-543-0)

All Things Beautiful by Alaina Erdell. Casey Norford only planned to learn to paint like her mentor, Leighton Vaughn, not sleep with her. (978-1-63679-479-2)

Appalachian Awakening by Nance Sparks. The more Amber's and Leslie's paths cross, the more this hike of a lifetime begins to look like a love of a lifetime. (978-1-63679-527-0)

Dreamer by Kris Bryant. When life seems to be too good to be true and love is within reach, Sawyer and Macey discover the truth about the town of Ladybug Junction, and the cold light of reality tests the hearts of these dreamers. (978-1-63679-378-8)

Eyes on Her by Eden Darry. When increasingly violent acts of sabotage threaten to derail the opening of her glamping business, Callie Pope is sure her ex, Jules, has something to do with it. But Jules is dead…isn't she? (978-1-63679-214-9)

Head Over Heelflip by Sander Santiago. To secure the biggest prizes at the Colorado Amateur Street Sports Tour, Thomas Jefferson will do almost anything, even marrying his best friend and crush—Arturo "Uno" Ortiz. (978-1-63679-489-1)

Letters from Sarah by Joy Argento. A simple mistake brought them together, but Sarah must release past love to create a future with Lindsey she never dreamed possible. (978-1-63679-509-6)

Lost in the Wild by Kadyan. When their plane crash-lands, Allison and Mike face hunger, cold, a terrifying encounter with a bear, and feelings for each other neither expects. (978-1-63679-545-4)

Not Just Friends by Jordan Meadows. A tragedy leaves Jen struggling to figure out who she is and what is important to her. (978-1-63679-517-1)

Of Auras and Shadows by Jennifer Karter. Eryn and Rina's unexpected love may be exactly what the Community needs to heal the rot that comes not from the fetid Dark Lands that surround the Community but from within. (978-1-63679-541-6)

The Secret Duchess by Jane Walsh. A determined widow defies a duke and falls in love with a fashionable spinster in a fight for her rightful home. (978-1-63679-519-5)

Winter's Spell by Ursula Klein. When former college roommates reunite at a wedding in Provincetown, sparks fly, but can they find true love when evil sirens and trickster mermaids get in the way? (978-1-63679-503-4)

Coasting and Crashing by Ana Hartnett Reichardt. Life comes easy to Emma Wilson until Lake Palmer shows up at Alder University and derails her every plan. (978-1-63679-511-9)

Every Beat of Her Heart by KC Richardson. Piper and Gillian have their own fears about falling in love, but will they be able to overcome those feelings once they learn each other's secrets? (978-1-63679-515-7)

Grave Consequences by Sandra Barret. A decade after necromancy became licensed and legalized, can Tamar and Maddy overcome the lingering prejudice against their kind and their growing attraction to each other to uncover a plot that threatens both their lives? (978-1-63679-467-9)

Haunted by Myth by Barbara Ann Wright. When ghost-hunter Chloe seeks an answer to the current spectral epidemic, all clues point to one very famous face: Helen of Troy, whose motives are more complicated than history suggests and whose charms few can resist. (978-1-63679-461-7)

Invisible by Anna Larner. When medical school dropout Phoebe Frink falls for the shy costume shop assistant Violet Unwin, everything about their love feels certain, but can the same be said about their future? (978-1-63679-469-3)

Like They Do in the Movies by Nan Campbell. Celebrity gossip writer Fran Underhill becomes Chelsea Cartwright's personal assistant with the aim of taking the popular actress down, but neither of them anticipates the clash of their attraction. (978-1-63679-525-6)

Limelight by Gun Brooke. Liberty Bell and Palmer Elliston loathe each other. They clash every week on the hottest new TV show, until Liberty starts to sing and the impossible happens. (978-1-63679-192-0)

Playing with Matches by Georgia Beers. To help save Cori's store and help Liz survive her ex's wedding they strike a deal: a fake relationship, but just for one week. There's no way this will turn into the real deal. (978-1-63679-507-2)

The Memories of Marlie Rose by Morgan Lee Miller. Broadway legend Marlie Rose undergoes a procedure to erase all of her unwanted memories, but as she starts regretting her decision, she discovers that the only person who could help is the love she's trying to forget. (978-1-63679-347-4)

The Murders at Sugar Mill Farm by Ronica Black. A serial killer is on the loose in southern Louisiana and it's up to three women to solve the case while carefully dancing around feelings for each other. (978-1-63679-455-6)

Fire in the Sky by Radclyffe and Julie Cannon. Two women from different worlds have nothing in common and every reason to wish they'd never met—except for the attraction neither can deny. (978-1-63679-573-7)

A Talent Ignited by Suzanne Lenoir. When Evelyne is abducted and Annika believes she has been abandoned, they must risk everything to find each other again. (978-1-63679-483-9)

An Atlas to Forever by Krystina Rivers. Can Atlas, a difficult dog Ellie inherits after the death of her best friend, help the busy hopeless romantic find forever love with commitment-phobic animal behaviorist Hayden Brandt? (978-1-63679-451-8)

Bait and Witch by Clifford Mae Henderson. When Zeddi gets an unexpected inheritance from her client Mags, she discovers that Mags served as high priestess to a dwindling coven of old witches—who are positive that Mags was murdered. Zeddi owes it to her to uncover the truth. (978-1-63679-535-5)

Buried Secrets by Sheri Lewis Wohl. Tuesday and Addie, along with Tuesday's dog, Tripper, struggle to solve a twenty-five-year-old mystery while searching for love and redemption along the way. (978-1-63679-396-2)

Come Find Me in the Midnight Sun by Bailey Bridgewater. In Alaska, disappearing is the easy part. When two men go missing, state trooper Louisa Linebach must solve the case, and when she thinks she's coming close, she's wrong. (978-1-63679-566-9)

Death on the Water by CJ Birch. The Ocean Summit's authorities have ruled a death on board its inaugural cruise as a suicide, but Claire suspects murder and with the help of Assistant Cruise Director Moira, Claire conducts her own investigation. (978-1-63679-497-6)

Living For You by Jenny Frame. Can Sera Debrek face real and personal demons to help save the world from darkness and open her heart to love? (978-1-63679-491-4)

Mississippi River Mischief by Greg Herren. When a politician turns up dead and Scotty's client is the most obvious suspect, Scotty and his friends set out to prove his client's innocence. (978-1-63679-353-5)

Ride with Me by Jenna Jarvis. When Lucy's vacation to find herself becomes Emma's chance to remember herself, they realize that everything they're looking for might already be sitting right next to them—if they're willing to reach for it. (978-1-63679-499-0)

Whiskey and Wine by Kelly and Tana Fireside. Winemaker Tessa Williams and sex toy shop owner Lace Reynolds are both used to taking risks, but will they be willing to put their friendship on the line if it gives them a shot at finding forever love? (978-1-63679-531-7)